Previous novels by D. M. Samson

Silent Violence
Nails
Bottle
Deutschisch
...and the man who loved cats

About the author

David M. Samson, born in Wallasey (near Liverpool) in 1957, lives with his wife and two daughters in Germany.

A   D E R
U   N
S L Ä N D
    L   E
A U S   R

First published in 2013 by David M. Samson, 20 Arundel Road, Bath, Avon BA1 6EF.

Printed and bound by Lulu.com.
Lulu Enterprises Inc.
860 Aviation Parkway
Suite 300
Morrisville, NC 27560
United States of America

ISBN 978-0-9556796-5-0

British Library Cataloguing in Publication Data.
A catalogue record for this book is available from the British Library.

Cover design by David M. Samson.

www.davidmsamson.com

This book is the result of a quarter of a century pregnancy and six major rewrites.
I'm relieved it's over.
Let's dedicate it to doggedness and poor driven souls like Dannaks.
(D.M. Samson, March 2013)

The word *Ausländer* can be translated in English as non-resident, non-citizen, foreign person, foreign national, foreigner, alien, stranger and outlander. This last and most literal definition means: "from outside this land."

List of principal characters (listed in importance within each group)

The Police:
Dannaks	Oberkommissar (Narcotics/REX)
Reinhart Keller	Kommissar (REX)
Uwe Albrecht	Kommissar (Narcotics)
Frank Neumann	Hauptkommissar (REX)
Detlef Borchardt	Kriminalrat (Narcotics)
Rolf Schuppenhauer	Kommissar (REX)
Olaf Reupke	Kommissar (Homicide)
Lampe "Pretty Boy"	Kommissar (Narcotics)
Wilhelm (Willy) Fischer	Polizeidirektor
Rüdiger Krohn	Polizeioberrat
Weske	Kriminalrat (LKA 7)
Wulff	Kommissar (REX)

The British:
Craig St. James	Freelance journalist
Robert Norton	Craig's friend and journalist

The Turks:
Cenk	Gang member
Suleyman	Faruk's father
Hasan	Gang leader
Murat "Basha"	Gang leader
Nazim	Gang member
"Ponytail"	Gang member
Cemal	Head of the Community
Faruk	Schoolboy
Ahmed	Faruk's friend

The Right-wingers:
Karsten Krohn	Gang leader
Stefan "S-Bahn" Ahrens	Unemployed youth
Volker Herbst	Right-wing politician
Jutta	Karsten's girlfriend

The German civilians:

Carina Kowalski	Craig's girlfriend
Petra	Robert's girlfriend
"Freddy"	Uwe's Informant
Jürgen Dannaks	Dannaks's brother
Diana Sohn	Editor of Hamburger *Tagespost*

The Left-wingers:

Klaus	Left-wing group leader

Glossary of commonly used words and phrases

Ausländer raus (foreigners out)
Der Meister (the Master)
Die ruhenden Handschuhe (the resting gloves)
Einsatzleiter (co-ordinating officer)
Gastarbeiter (guest-workers)
Hamburger Tagespost (Daily post)
Henker (Hangman/executioner)
Kriminalpolizei/Kripo (detectives)
Länder (states)
Lan (man/comrade)
Landeskriminalamt/LKA 7 Staatschutz (Criminal office for State Security)
Lutscher (sucker)
Mobiles Einsatzkommando/MEK (mobile task force)
Narzisst's Eck (Narcissist's corner)
Organisierte Kriminalität/O.K. (Organised crime)
Peterwagen/Peter (Hamburg police patrol cars)
Polizeipräsidium/Polizeistern (police presidium)
Rathaus (City Hall)
Schutzpolizei/Schupo (uniformed police)
Schwarzer Freitag (Black Friday)
Sonderkommission/Soko (special unit)
Universitätsklinikum Eppendorf/UKE (University Clinic Eppendorf)
Verfassungsschutz/VfS (Counter-intelligence: equivalent to GB's MI5)

The shorter woman, Silke, thought she saw him first. But when she gasped and her pace faltered her companion didn't question her.

After a few steps both joggers stopped.

Of course they had immediately seen the ravens after rounding the deserted restaurant building and entering the expansive play area. The birds were as at home in Hamburg's city park as those of the Tower of London. Only they didn't need their wings clipped to keep them there. Then again, neither of the women had seen so many congregated in one place. Too many to count. Fifty? A hundred? Intimidating in number.

Silke pulled down the scarf that covered her mouth, but kept her hand there. "My God."

"He can't be alive," said Kathrin.

Their words were visualised as ashen plumes that almost instantly vanished in the vastness about them.

"We–" the cold and the shock stole her voice "–we, er, should go closer."

"Around the edge."

The girls skirted the sandy recess that encompassed the dry concrete basin. The basin was a large shallow pool in the summer. Now it was littered with leaves that hugged its edges. The drop to the sandy margin, some twenty metres wide, was about a metre and a half and hinted at a larger pool in the past. Embedded in this margin were children's swings, slides, climbing frames and other apparatus.

The bleakness dispelled all traces of summer and any memory of children's voices. Indeed they appeared to be the only ones in the entire park, except for the man they had seen from afar at the start of their run. He had been walking his dog.

In the high summer the park teemed with 100,000 people picnicking, barbecuing, playing football, Frisbee or simply strolling or lounging. Parking too was nigh on impossible. Today, at this time and time of year, they had chosen a prime spot from which to start their jog on Hindenburgstrasse, the road that split the park.

The sky was clear, the sun ornamental. The path, normally clay, was hard like marble. At a walk the crisp air was bearably cold, but when they were jogging or the wind gusted it stung and cut tears from their eyes. The cold was that of a deep November day. Only winter's darkness was missing. Brown and golden leaves lining the verge of the path were sodden or crisp and twitched and tumbled with the occasional gust.

They continued to walk the boundary, getting closer in a roundabout way.

A bird gave a sharp metallic tock. There were guttural croaks too. The ones on the ground in iridescent purple and blue-black moved like proud-chested undertakers in tails. They seemed ruffled by the presence of the women. One flew a short hop.

The body gently swayed in the wind. Gently, because of its bulk. For a moment the unseeing wide eyes followed the girls' progress. It looked like a sack or bloated punch bag hanging under the slide. Green-brown camouflage fatigues clad the limp figure. A long black boot, a paratrooper's boot with white laces, touched the sock upon the other foot. The other boot lay on the ground a few metres away. Too far to have slipped off. Perhaps kicked off during his death throes?

They were coming to a point where the body no longer faced them. Kathrin stopped to scrutinise his face. His bullet head was a shocking white. He was a big man. Fat. Round. A lug. Something orange filled his mouth, splitting it into a grimace: a silent scream. White face, heavy-lidded eyes, orange mouth: stark clown-like colours.

"What's in his mouth?" asked Kathrin. She didn't wait for an answer. "A gum-shield?"

There was a piece of crumpled cloth on the ground. Other than this there was very little litter. No discarded cans or cups. But scrutiny showed cigarette butts to have merged with the sand. Silke couldn't identify the woolly dark blue or black clump.

A bird was edging its way sideways up the slide towards the man's head.

"Hey," Kathrin suddenly yelled waving her hands. Silke jumped.

"What are you doing?"

"Trying to frighten it away. It's going to peck his eyes." She turned and searched the ground. "I'll get a stick."

The wind twisted the body a mite.

"Wait," said Silke. His arms were not hanging at his side but were pinned back. A strand of white waved in a sudden breeze.

8

Distant leaves scuttled for attention. She looked to the boot on the sand. It was open; the leather tongue askew. She looked back at the man. "He didn't kill himself."

"Wh–"

"Look. His hands," said Silke unnecessarily, for Kathrin could see that his arms were pulled behind his back and his podgy thumbs were bound together with the missing shoelace.

A short piece of wood or plastic hung near his neck. A similar piece was attached to the end of the rope that was tied to top of the handrail of the slide. A single bird stood above the body, its head in profile, a black bead of an eye watching the women and Silke, an English literature student, heard the word *Nevermore* in her head. And the word took on a new meaning as she stared at the dead boy. For despite his repulsive nature he was dead and would never do anything any more. She shuddered.

As in most large city parks, the distant trees about them were a mixture of the seasonal and firs and other evergreens. So that when the breeze rose again with surprising force, as if some rosy-cheeked, golden-locked God of Wind blew periodically, the forest was united in a rushing wall of sound. It was as if far greater forces were at work. As if Nature was suddenly unnatural: dwarfing and alienating the two joggers.

The girls didn't look at each other or the dead boy. They fearfully scanned the woods and bushes, the smaller children's play area in the distance, the shuttered buildings, the play of light, the shadows and corners.

Kathrin dug under her tracksuit top into a small pocket of her tight jogging trousers. Eventually she retrieved her handy and Silke watched her fumble tapping in the numbers 110.

"Stop crying," Silke said impatiently. She wanted to suggest that she make the call. Instead she closed her eyes and the terrible image of the hung youth branded in her mind was fixed with Poe's concluding words:

And my soul from out that shadow that lies floating on the floor
Shall be lifted — nevermore!

When she snapped her eyes open, she too couldn't focus. "Now look, you've started me off."

Dannaks saw Uwe snatch up the handset in the middle of the second ring. His colleague's expression was enough to stop him emptying his desk drawer.

He surveyed the open plan office. More than half the desks were unoccupied. One of the men got up, opened his desk drawer and clipped his holster containing his Heckler and Koch P 2000 to his waist-belt before slinging on his jacket and leaving the room. That left only three others. One was on the phone; the other two were staring into computer monitors. Nobody appeared to have noticed them.

Even as he scrawled something on a piece of scrap paper Uwe's expression did not ease. He suddenly jerked the receiver from his ear and stared at it as if he could see the person at the other end of the line. Dannaks's questioning look met blankness. His colleague tentatively returned handset to his ear.

Dannaks could see that he was still puzzling as he replaced the handset.

After a moment he acknowledged him, but his expression remained emotionless. Dannaks left his desk but before he reached him, Uwe's phone rang again.

"University Clinic Eppendorf. Radiography... Hallo... Hallo..." Uwe replaced the handset and looked up. "Redial," he said.

Dannaks remained standing and Uwe waited too. But the phone did not ring again. Uwe pocketed the piece of paper. Dannaks nodded and then left the room.

Uwe didn't need to be told where he had gone. He followed a minute later.

"We're alone," said Dannaks, standing at the urinals.

Uwe closed the toilet door and started to wash his hands. "That was Freddy," he said. "The location's changed. It's an abandoned farmhouse in Duvenstedt."

Dannaks zipped up and came to the bowl next to Uwe. He knew there was more.

"Does the name Nobby Kabel mean anything to you?" said Uwe, shaking his hands over the bowl.

Dannaks shook his head, Uwe catching the gesture in the mirror before going to the blow-drier. The sound of the machine curtailed further conversation.

11

"What about him?" said Dannaks when the sound died.

"Freddy asked me whether I remembered him."

"Remember him?" Some twisted code of honour prevented Freddy from grassing directly.

Uwe nodded and Dannaks punched the blow-drier.

Uwe returned to the mirror and combed his hair. He still looked worried.

The blow-drier stopped. "What else?" said Dannaks.

"He hung up mid-sentence."

"What was he about to say?"

"He didn't. When he asked me about Kabel I said he knew I didn't like puzzles. He was about to answer, but then just hung up."

"And then there was the redial?"

"Yeah." Announcing that he was University Clinic Eppendorf had at most gained them some time.

"You think they're on to him?"

Uwe shrugged. "We'd better go to Detlef," he said resignedly.

"Let's look up Kabel first."

The two detectives returned to the office. At his desk Dannaks shoved a box to get to his keyboard. He made a cursory check of the room. Nobody appeared to be paying them any attention.

A search brought only one hit that fit perfectly.

Norbert Kabel had been a corrupt Hamburg detective. He had been on the take. Before he could be arrested he shot himself with his service weapon. There was more, but Dannaks didn't read any further. He marked the entire text and sent it to the printer.

"It's enough for me," said Dannaks.

Uwe spoke quietly too. "What do you think of the change?"

"It's crap, of course. Before it, we were already at the edge of the abyss. Now we're just one step further. If they're on to him then it is disinformation."

On the way to Detlef's office Dannaks grabbed the printout.

10:49

Kriminalrat Detlef Borchardt's office door was open but Uwe knocked.

Detlef was a small man. His grey hair was greased down to the contours of his skull. He had started to spread and this made his head seem proportionally small compared to his body. Wrinkles crumpled his face with worry and some nicknamed him: poison dwarf. He favoured sleeveless jumpers and patterned shirts. His manner was that of a model train enthusiast or stamp collector: hunched and self-absorbed. But nothing so dignified seemed to occupy him. He collected the toys from chocolate eggs. Every available surface was littered with them. When they came in he leaned forward, greeted them and flicked a balancing man carrying a ball in each arm in a rocking motion.

Dannaks believed that Detlef was living proof that everyone got promoted to their own level of incompetence. He'd ascended the career ladder to a rung upon which he was decidedly wobbly.

"Nibble stuff?" the dwarf held up a small plate of assorted biscuits. Dannaks believed he thought he could win the respect of his team by plying them with biscuits and cakes?

They both declined. "More for me."

"I just had a call—" Uwe began.

"Is it to do with tonight's operation?"

"Yes."

Detlef raised a finger to halt further talk. He got up and closed his door.

When he was seated Uwe related the call from his informant, emphasising the abrupt ending.

"How do you know it was a redial?"

"I saw the number on the display." Freddy always used phone-boxes. He didn't trust mobile phones. They could get into the wrong hands. But he had also said that he thought they microwaved the brains.

Detlef thought for a moment, staring absently at the address Uwe had scribbled on the piece of paper. Then he got up and walked to the map on an adjacent wall. Dannaks and Uwe also got up. Detlef traced a finger on the map stopping at the location. "It's here in Duvenstedt. Where's the Rahlstedt location?" He knew, but he wanted someone else's finger on the map. Uwe obliged. "It's not quite the other end of the city, but it's quite a distance. And this is legit?"

"Yes," said Uwe. That meant Freddy had opened with the key phrase he'd agreed with Uwe.

Deep in thought, Detlef returned to his desk. Dannaks and Uwe felt compelled to return to their seats.

"Gentlemen," began Detlef after a moment's pause. Dannaks shrank from his patronising address. "We're not the only ones involved in this." This was a joint operation with the O.K. (*Organisierte Kriminalität* – Organised crime). Dannaks dulled his eyes. It was a wasted sentence: a politician's padding. And Detlef knew it. He realigned his approach. "The change in location is certainly news." The rocking toy man was slowing. "We'll have to cover the original location." He glanced at Dannaks, who avoided looking at Uwe. Detlef suddenly leaned forward to emphasise the importance of what he was about to say. "Your nark has always come through." The word nark jarred. He was trying to be hip and sounded the opposite. "I don't think he'll let us down now."

Dannaks snapped. "Maybe my colleague didn't impress upon you the nature of the call. He was cut off and then there was the redial–"

"I think I got the picture, thank–"

"If they were on to him then he would have been fed crap. Maybe he'd been fed crap for some time: good crap that brought results, results with Raul's competition. And now maybe he's run out of use. He–"

"That's enough." Detlef barked.

Dannaks noticed that the toy man had stopped.

Detlef let the silence settle. When he spoke his voice was thick with reason. "You both know that these operations sometimes yield the unexpected. And you know as well as I that the time is right to wrap up Luisa."

"Not like this."

"What was that, *Kommissar*?"

"I said not like this, sir. Catching them with the junk could clinch it. If we don't, we might not have enough to nail Raul." Raul was Hamburg's kingpin: Germany's Colombian connection. He ran such a tight-knit team that they'd been unable to penetrate it. No chance of an undercover agent. Now they wanted to turn this very closeness against him. The hand-over was the weak link. A week ago customs officials had discovered the secret compartment on the South American freighter. But it had been empty. Emptied at sea? Yet another instance of Raul being one step ahead? Another gang controlled western distribution. A hand-over was necessary. Catching members of Raul's gang with the merchandise could be the hook to unravel the network. That was what the state prosecutor had insisted upon: a red-handed catch to clinch the case. "And if we get him, he could get off on a technicality."

"We've got all we're going to get."

"It's not enough... Sir." He knew the dwarf could handle men like Uwe, but not mavericks like him. Dannaks didn't fit the mould. He was not climbing the ladder the right way, taking it a rung at a time. He wasn't even on the ladder, but fashioning his own structure, scaling the service in an unorthodox way. A way so unorthodox that it was debatable whether he was climbing at all. This made him unpredictable.

"That decision is not your concern. I've got a briefing at one. I'll bring this up then."

The stillness was terrible.

"Gentlemen," he began calmly, his voice treacly with reason. "I can only act on the information I've been given." His smile turned Dannaks's stomach. "How your nark chooses to hang up is irrelevant. I think the operation will go ahead. I'll suggest covering both locations."

The detectives had nothing to say.

"Anything else?"

Dannaks wanted blood. "Yes, sir. I believe that this operation is no longer secure."

Detlef sighed. "Meaning?"

"Meaning: we have circumstantial evidence of a leak."

"Don't you have any other tunes?"

"No."

"What?"

"No, sir."

"Have you anything other than your nark's reference to Norbert Kabel?" The printout lay in front of him.

"No, sir."

Detlef suddenly turned to Uwe. "Do you have anything to add?"

Uwe had assumed the role of spectator and wasn't ready to be written into the play. "Er, no. No, sir."

"Then will you leave us alone, please?"

Uwe hesitated as if he had to decode the instruction. Then he got up and left the room.

His absence precipitated a vacuum.

"What I'm going to say doesn't leave these four walls," he began when they were alone.

Dannaks immediately felt uncomfortable but nodded.

"I know you don't think much of me and in all honesty you may be justified." Dannaks suppressed his shock. "You see I'm being set up. They're going to move me to a cushy, harmless back room job. It'll be billed as a side-step, but it's a demotion."

"It's an expensive way of going about it," said Dannaks, alluding to the operation.

"Justification. Luisa needs to be closed and the team reorganised."

"So our ineffectiveness has gone official?"

"I'm not saying that," he returned irritably.

"Why are you telling me this?"

Detlef paused, debating whether to proceed. "You don't give an inch, do you?" Dannaks was silent. "It may surprise you because although we don't see eye to eye I respect you. You're an odd ball Dannaks, but a good man." They stared at one another for a moment. "There's an outside chance we may see some results tonight. In the end it's all the same for me. And in some respects for you too."

By subjugating himself and taking Dannaks into his confidence, Detlef had temporarily pre-empted criticism. They both knew no love would be lost. After all, the man was one of the reasons for Dannaks's departure. He had even insisted on Dannaks having his leaving celebration now, rather than after the stakeout in a combined celebration to mark the end of Luisa. Then again, perhaps he was taking into the account there would be little to celebrate with the winding up of Luisa. Success could only be measured in the amount of damage they could inflict on Raul's organisation. And Dannaks thought in terms of flesh wounds.

He wanted to leave but sensed that Detlef had more to say. Was he going to get morose in front of him?

"I don't know how to approach this so I'll just come out with it." He took a deep breath before the plunge. "We've spoken about a leak before. About six months ago, if I remember correctly." He stopped. "I don't want to get embroiled in a discussion of that affair with you." Klaxons went off in Dannaks's head. Why couldn't he be more specific? "That was thoroughly investigated. But perhaps the focus of attention was too small."

Dannaks was stunned. "That's almost a contradiction."

"Almost," he admitted, relaxing as if a hurdle had been overcome. "Somebody thinks there's more dirt to be dug out."

"Who?"

"Not me."

"And you're not going to tell me who?"

Silence.

"Well, good for them," said Dannaks.

"Only they can't investigate."

"Why not?"

"Because they've no room to manoeuvre. And it has to be independent."

"Then it should go to DIE." The *Dezernat Interne Ermittlungen* was similar to the Complaints investigation Bureau of London's Metropolitan Police or Internal Affairs in various US States. DIE investigated not only complaints against the police, but all other authorities in the state of Hamburg.

"Unfortunately not. They're inundated with work. And they've covered this territory already—"

"Wait, wait. Are you saying the Krohn affair has something to do with our lack of success?"

"I don't know." Detlef seemed flustered. "There's no evidence to say so."

"Okay. What's this got to do with me?"

"You're a resourceful man. If anyone could dig it out, you can."

Dannaks grew angry. There was more going on than Detlef cared to tell. The resourceful man comment seemed out of character, as if he'd heard it from someone else. "I've had my baptism of fire. Why should I go through it again?"

"Nobody's asking you to."

"Well, that's great then." He stood up. "Good luck to them."

Detlef was uncharacteristically calm. "It's just a suggestion." Calm was the wrong word. He was relieved.

Dannaks was rigid but at the same time rooted to the spot. He wanted to sit down again.

"I'm the worst person to chose."

"No. You're the best. You've proven you're incorruptible."

Dannaks sighed and fell back into the chair. "This is

unofficial?"

Detlef nodded.

"On my own time?"

Silence.

He didn't want to admit he was hooked. "Assuming I do it, who do I contact with my results?"

"When you've something concrete, DIE, of course. They'll take over."

Dannaks gave him a sceptical look. "What support do I have?"

"Anyone you can trust."

"Who else knows? I mean, who can I trust?"

"I'd say no one. Me, perhaps? I've nothing to gain or lose. Uwe? I don't know."

"What about the interested party? The instigator?"

"No. He's too close. He wants to be left out." He. Well that was something.

"If I knew who he was I could rule him out. I could mark him as one of the good guys."

"No. You have to start with a blank page."

"So, if I need help I come to you?"

"You can. But I don't think I can do much."

"I haven't said yes. I'll think about it."

He got up and flicked the rocking man into action. He rocked furiously to and fro, but he was going nowhere.

12:13

At his desk Dannaks picked up the telephone without looking over at Uwe. Only after he had replaced the handset, having been told that the person he wanted was at lunch, did he wink at Uwe. His colleague gave a lopsided smile.

"Manna?" called Uwe.

Dannaks looked down at the state of his packing and nodded. It was a good time to eat.

Narcotics was situated in the sixth, seventh and eighth wings of the second floor. The Hamburg police headquarters, completed at the end of 1999, was situated in Alsterdorf and was known as the *Polizeistern* because it resembled a star. The five-storey building was circular in structure with ten spokes or wings radiating from it. The canteen was on the ground floor in the space between the eighth and ninth wings. They took the stairs.

"You're not going to tell me what Detlef said," said Uwe, when they'd settled themselves at a table with their trays of food.

"You won't like it."

"I'm tough."

"You won't believe."

"At this rate I won't hear it."

"He said he thought I was a good man."

"I don't believe it."

Uwe waited before pressing further. "Come on, he didn't wax lyrical for a full quarter of an hour."

"He expressed his doubts about tonight, but didn't want to de-motivate the others."

"I can believe that." Uwe shook his head. "It's typical of him." He picked up a forkful of mashed potato. "You need a straw for this." He demonstratively let it drip back onto the plate. "You're right. If he was straight with us instead of trying to play politics we'd have more respect for him." He shovelled his desert spoon into his mash. "And there's another first: you two in agreement." But he hadn't given up. "So it was all politics and budget, then?"

Dannaks didn't answer. He needed time to mull over what he'd been told. He trusted Uwe and would tell him at some point. But now he needed to think. He needed to make a decision without outside influences. "I'll tell you later. I have to think."

20:47

For a junkie Luisa's death was not unusual. The inner fervour drove all fluids to the surface leaving her in a pathetic slumber of sweat, tears, saliva and urine: an all too typical picture in the toilets of Hamburg's main station. Most of the papers carried the same photograph of a covered wheeled stretcher at the open doors of an ambulance; inset a posed portrait of a smiling eight year old schoolgirl. There was nothing extraordinary in the fact that she had choked on her vomit. The unusual aspect was her youth. Of the 136 Narcotics-related deaths that year, at thirteen she was the youngest.

Bad stuff had killed her, they said. There was no consolation in the fact that she had chosen to remain one step ahead of the social workers and police. She had been little more than a child, eking out an existence between the floorboards of society.

The two-year investigation by a section of the Narcotics Squad had been named after her and tonight was the climax of

19

Operation Luisa.

At eight a major briefing had taken place in the ground floor auditorium of the *Polizeipräsidium* (police presidium) in Alsterdorf. *Polizeidirektor* Wilhelm "Willy" Fischer, being tailored to take over from the retiring police president, had addressed them. He was a shooting star, having cleaned up a number of notoriously bad areas, earning him the nickname "der Meister" (the Master) itself originating from the detergent, Meister Proper.

Kriminalrat Detlef Borchardt's team was now assembled in the large open plan office on the second floor. He'd just finished his speech and with obvious trepidation handed control to *Kommissar* Dannaks.

Dannaks had shrivelled during Detlef's speech. He'd opened with strained praise of Dannaks before mercifully dropping into a rehearsed let's-make-it-a-good-one pep up. Everyone's expression said it was not going to be a good one. And there was certainly no pep in sight.

Detlef stepped to the side to lean against one of the desks, away from the small conference table laden with sandwiches and three flasks of coffee and one of tea. Dannaks took up his position to address the group.

"*Ausländer raus* (foreigners out)," Lampe chided, before he could begin.

A spike of anger impaled Dannaks, but he smiled awkwardly as a ripple of chuckles went through the team of twenty or so.

On Monday he would join a *Sonderkommission* (special unit), abbreviated *Soko. Sokos* were temporary task forces that were born with demand. When the workload sufficiently diminished or the case closed, as with the apprehension of a serial killer for example, the task force was disbanded. Some *Sokos* existed for years, others a matter of weeks.

The hanging of Kai Doermer in the city park and similarity to the more recent murder of Markus Jensen, had led to the merging of *Soko* Doermer and *Soko* Jensen into *Soko Henker* (Hangman). The obvious right-wing background to these murders had drawn resources from *LKA* 7 *Staatschutz* (*Landeskriminalamt* Hamburg's criminal office for State Security), the criminal division that dealt with politically motivated trouble.

Although considered transitory, these manpower problems had necessitated the creation of *Soko* REX (Racism and extremism) as departmental extension.

Dannaks would be promoted to *Oberkommissar* and join *Soko* REX.

"I'll keep it short," Dannaks said. There were murmurs of approval. "I'll say thanks for the gifts, now." Space had been made on the table for a plastic bag. "After I open them I may not be so thankful." He pressed on before anyone could comment. "What I'm going to say now is going to sound negative–" Detlef shifted and Dannaks made an effort not to look his way.

"What's new?" said one of the team.

Murmurs and nods concurred.

"I know that I'm not the most popular person in the team." The silence was awesome. "So I can't wax lyrical about how much of a pleasure it's been working with you. I like to think that with those I have worked closely I have at least gained their respect if not friendship." No one was looking at him. Most were looking at the floor. "Suffice to say it has been an interesting two years. I have learnt a lot." He paused. "It's a shame it has to end like this." He felt Detlef stiffen. No-one appeared to be breathing. "Yes, it's a shame for all the man-hours we put in." He ignored Detlef clearing his throat. "But I think it more of a shame for the little girl–"

"Dannaks," Detlef snapped.

"– whose name this operation carries."

"That's enough." He'd pushed himself off the desk.

"We all know tonight is going to be a farce. I–"

"I said that's enough," he shouted, walking round the desk to stand directly in front of Dannaks. "My office," he seethed. "Now." He strode away, leaving Dannaks to face the team.

"I declare the buffet open," he said, adding as he went after Detlef: "I've been told the pepperonis are mean."

When Dannaks entered, his superior was already sitting behind his desk. "Close the door," he said unnecessarily.

Dannaks seated himself and waited the silence out. He knew Detlef's silences and knew not to become uncomfortable. So he scanned the toys, as always his eyes coming to rest upon the chrome balancing man carrying a ball in each arm.

"Was that really necessary?" Detlef began. It was a rhetorical question. "What did you hope to gain?" His demeanour said that he was not expecting any answers. "Damaging the team's morale as you did just now, shows me that you're not team material. And that'll go in your personal file. How you're going to fare as *Oberkommissar*, I don't know. Have you anything to say?" He had played his trump-card early: a mark in his file.

"No," he said, waiting a tick before adding: "sir."

Detlef huffed. "I was afraid you'd say something stupid."

"I'm glad I didn't disappoint."

"Don't be obnoxious, *Kommissar*."

In the ensuing silence the stiffness left Detlef.

"Didn't it occur to you that other forces are at work?"

Dannaks waited for him to elaborate. What other forces could there be other than tipping off Raul as to how close they were?

"Not everything is that black and white."

Apparently he was not going to say any more. In fact he seemed at a loss as to how to proceed.

"May I say something?" Dannaks asked.

His question was met with raised eyebrows and a cautionary pursing of the lips.

"I really thought the operation would be called off." There was a thinly veiled accusation that Detlef had failed to convince his peers and superiors that there was cause to suspect that tonight's bust had been compromised.

"You're not that naive, are you?" The silence returned. "If it had been cancelled there would only have been three of us at your leaving do: Uwe, you and me. And I'm not sure about me."

The small man kept his thoughts to himself. Whatever they were put a wry tired smile on his face.

He came out of his reverie with a questioning look.

There was nothing more to say.

21:27

"*Guten appetit.*"

Petra, Carina, Robert and Craig were sitting at the dining table in the inside corner of the room. The walls were lined with shelves of books and resembled a library. The lounge was an extension of their workroom. He would later see their bedroom and realise that all the rooms were workroom extensions. The kitchen had a good selection of cookbooks and the toilet-bathroom had a shelf of books next to the toilet. The portable television on a chest of drawers was lost to them.

They ate quietly for a while, Carina and Craig praising the food.

"So, let me get this straight," Robert began, "you've got yourself a commission to write about neo-Nazis in Germany."

Craig felt suddenly tired after his London/Hamburg flight. The flight itself was just over an hour's hop, but security and customs turned it into over three hours. Robert was of course making conversation but Craig would have preferred more idle talk in front of Carina. He was still trying to find a balance between avoiding her hazel eyes and staring. She was intoxicating.

"Yes and no," he said, looking at Robert, glancing at Carina and, to compensate, smiling at Petra. Her pageboy cut dark hair could not have contrasted Carina's loose classic blonde more. "I have a commission, but it's more about extremes in Germany. You know, Right and Left."

"How long are you going to be working on it?" asked Petra.

"You mean how long am I staying here?" he laughed. He had been given the box room.

"That's not what I meant and you know it."

"He's staying two weeks," said Robert.

Craig was aware that Carina knew he was only over for a short time. Nonetheless, he didn't like the idea. Voicing the fact damaged his romantic aspirations.

"Yes, yes, but the article is in three parts. The features editor has seen a draft of the first part. On the strength of it he's given me a commission and a slot in next Sunday's edition. I just have to get the final draft to him by Thursday."

"I don't understand," said Carina. Craig's heart skipped a beat and he lunged at the opportunity to look at her. Her small earrings were no-nonsense and her expression severe. He didn't remember her being an uptight schoolmarm. Then he noticed her fingers. They were long, with wickedly manicured nails. Her clothing was plain: a blouse and skirt, nothing striking. But to him she was the kind of woman who'd look good in rags. Like a model in a man's suit her radiance could not be suppressed or disguised. "If you've already written it, why are you here?"

Somewhat crushed he valiantly bounced back. "The bare bones are written. But I need to put it in perspective, to anchor it. What I've written is too dry, too factual. I need a human element to anchor it. An incident or two to underscore what I'm saying." He had heard from a contact at *Der Spiegel* (The Mirror) that a right wing extremist called Mad Max would be ideal for his article. "The meat's really tender."

"And if you don't deliver?" Petra asked. "Or they don't like it?"

"Then I'm up shit creek without a paddle."

Petra smiled, but Carina gave him a quizzical look and he explained the term.

"I mentioned you to my editor," said Robert, when he'd finished explaining, "and she said that she'd be interested in a page or half-page filler from you. I must have been dizzy or something because I said you were good."

"Thanks, mate." Robert worked for the *Hamburger Tagespost* (Daily post).

"It's not a nice subject," said Carina.

"That's the way of the world," he knee-jerked glibly.

Then he noticed the tautness of her skin and the thinness of her lips. Humour was absent in her hard eyes.

"There has been too much attention to racism in Germany," said Petra. A front appeared to be building: the Germans against the Brits. And Craig was alone, because Robert was sitting smugly on the fence.

Was his friend enjoying his discomfort? It was bad enough he had not been forewarned of Carina's presence. Petra and Robert knew he fancied her.

"Has there?" He put his knife and fork down, leant back and took a sip of wine. "I believe the authorities have looked Left for too long. It's understandable. The country was the East-West front line for a long time. It's a legacy of the numerous attacks against the aggressive capitalist policies of the country in the seventies. Baader-Meinhof, the Palestinians... And then along came 9/11 and its Hamburg connection and with it the so-called Islamic threat. All this has led to a neglect of the right wing threat."

"Thanks for the Germany for Dummies," said Robert.

"Well, you'll at least agree with me when I say, reporting is fashion."

"For the British and Americans reporting on neo-Nazis in Germany is always in vogue," said Carina. When she spoke her animation dispelled the severity. Her straw-blonde hair was lank, not bouncy or voluptuous, but when she moved it waved and he wanted to touch it, to feel whether it was wispy or coarse.

"Maybe. But it's what the public want to read."

"We will always be the nasty, arrogant Germans."

Alarm signals caused him to fall silent. Being English he was at once exotic and hampered. He knew the Germans well enough to know that they had a different cultural signal box. But he didn't know them well enough to decode all their signals.

Carina too was silent and he felt compelled to say something. He thought of saying, "don't be silly" but decided that this would be unwise. He glanced at Petra who raised her eyebrows. Robert had his head down.

Craig thought of the decrepit copy of *Pride and Prejudice* he'd seen balanced on the edge of the bath. Petra said she had lost count of how many times she had read it. He thought of the stiff politeness of Austin's time. In modern England such respect for the elders and other inhibiting social manners was laughable. But then the Germans were bemused by the English politeness of today. Whereas German communication was based on directness, English entailed more indirect speech: conversing using inference, innuendo and allusion. At worst the Germans interpreted this quirky speech as impotence. Conversely, many English people perceived German frankness as coarse and blunt.

"Okay," Robert began, as if he were a referee. "Being a Brit and having lived here for a few years I see things from both sides. Germany isn't an island like Britain. Organised crime has another meaning here. There are Polish car thieves stealing to order; selling further east or back to the Germans. They get more money here and don't have to transport them too far. The Serbs deal in prostitution and illegal gambling. Rumanians sell babies and children for adoption or prostitution. The Russian Mafia deals in almost anything: from weaponry to art treasures, you know, religious icons." He took a breath. "And I haven't mentioned the extortion of the Chinese Triads and the Italian Mafia. On top of all that, Hamburg is a harbour city, the gateway to Germany and beyond. And that means a big drug problem. So, you can understand the mild prejudice, if not racism. I don't condone it. I'm just explaining."

"Listen," Craig said, leaning forward and picking up his utensils. "I want to show that the likelihood of a Fourth Reich is greater in, say France, than Germany. Think of Algeria, the Vichy and the Dreyfuss affair. But I think the main reason it can't happen here is because it already has. But the Germans must become more diligent. And that's why it's three articles. The first to paint a dark picture: a warning to the German people."

"You think we need warning?" said Petra, challenging him with her eyes.

Before he could answer Carina spoke. "When I was an Au Pair in London I was called a Nazi and given the salute. They thought it was hilarious–"

"That's silly. You should have ignored them." He found himself with a piece of gristle in his mouth.

"I did. But it still hurt."

"It's just ignorance. They were just having a bit of fun." He chewed the gristle.

"At my expense."

"Don't take it so seriously."

"Not having a sense of humour was another thing."

A discussion on British and German humour was not the place to go. "Look, the war was a long time ago. You and I weren't even born. I don't think you're a Nazi. Give me some credit."

"Yes," said Carina, "I can give *you* some credit. But not everybody is like you."

He made a concerted effort to bite down the gristle, but it was like rubber and too big to swallow.   "Articles like yours keep the ignorance alive," said Petra.

"Why don't you write about racism in England?" Carina suggested.

"I could. But it's more interesting here."

"Why?"

"Because Germany dominates the European Community. And historically..."

"The nasty Germans."

He picked up his paper serviette. It was white. He waved it at them. "All right, all right. I surrender."

"Why don't you spit that piece of gristle out?" asked Petra.

He smiled sickly and dropped it into the serviette.

21.49

Uwe turned the unmarked car left onto Kirchenallee in front of Hamburg's main station. Despite the hour there was a lot of activity. A line of taxis edged forward to take people away, others arrived, their drivers helping their passengers with their luggage. Private cars continually manoeuvred in the pay and display parking area. Pairs of uniformed police strolled the station, talking to loiterers

26

and tourists, moving buskers and beggars along. And then there was the mass of hasty people trying to maintain B-lines but having to give up to the congestion the further they went into the station.

Uwe slowed and somebody behind him hooted. He flicked on his hazard-warning lights and stopped. He jumped out and flashed his ID at the driver. The effect was immediate. The man grew crimson and anxiously looked over his shoulder to pull into the outer lane.

Dannaks and Uwe pulled boxes off the back seat and went into the building.

The station reception area was typically barren; the hard-wearing linoleum smelling of cheap disinfectant. Opposite the main entrance was a single door that would be locked. Except for a wooden bench opposite the counter on their right it was standing room only. A clear Perspex partition at the counter screened off the police area. A wire rack fixed to a wall was virtually empty, its offering of a handful of limp leaflets a gesture.

The duty officer who got up from a desk further behind the counter showed no signs of recognition when Dannaks showed his ID. Behind the officer were two wooden desks laden with paper, files and forms. Closed cupboards lined the walls. Above these were framed posters. The usual crime prevention ones were on display. Dannaks noticed an old one from an advertising campaign by the *Morgenpost*. It was a picture of a crazed looking youth pointing a revolver at the onlooker. In red block lettering was the question: Do you know somebody who will take the revolver from him for 100 DM a day? The currency betrayed its age, but didn't diminish its truth.

"You want some help?"

"Sure. We're double-parked." The man buzzed him through.

With the help of two uniforms, the shifting of Dannaks's belongings was over within ten minutes. By way of a thank you he gave them some sandwiches to share. He had too many left over and had intended to distribute them when tonight's bust was over.

Back in the car Uwe passed comment.

"Back to the roots then." He was referring to the old style of the police station.

"Okay the decor and furniture are not up to much. But they've got telephones I can use."

"Yeah. At least you're out of the fiasco." Uwe changed down a gear. "You've got yourself a lifeboat."

"Women and children, first."

"You're no child, so is there something you haven't told me?"

"The ship hasn't gone down yet."

"Yet."

Dannaks smiled resignedly. "The Devil's advocate is not one of my better roles."

"I didn't know you had any roles other than the down-trodden detective." Uwe's stomach gurgled and he wound down the window and the sound of traffic invaded their isolation. "I can think of better ways of wasting a Friday evening."

The journey to the farmhouse area was staggered. A convoy was the last thing anyone wanted. Dannaks had taken the opportunity to move his gear into his new office.

They drove on in a silence that neither of them wanted.

"Still," Uwe began, "I'm not so sure you're making a good move." Dannaks waited. "Yeah, it's a promotion." If it wasn't for his promotion to *Oberkommissar* the move would truly be sideways if not backward. "But you'll be the first to admit that you're no leader of men." Uwe smiled. "I'm not even convinced of your team ability." His words echoed Detlef's: "...you're not team material." His colleague pressed on. "You know they'll catch him sooner or later and then you'll be buried there." Dannaks couldn't deny that he was joining the team hoping to become involved with the serial killer investigation.

He knew Uwe was annoyed with himself. His last comment had been unnecessarily harsh. Perhaps he'd wanted to shake Dannaks into responding. Or perhaps his apprehension about the success of the bust and Freddy's unsettling call were taking their toll. Uwe alone had spent the last few months grooming Freddy for this big swoop and persuading him to join the witness protection programme. Although Freddy sat on the fringes of Raul's organisation, he was close enough to glean quality information.

Uwe had spent the afternoon checking prearranged safe numbers and contact places for messages or Freddy himself. There had been nothing.

"My belly's feeling delicate." Dannaks took the statement as an excuse for his irritability and caustic attitude. "Where did you get those sandwiches?" The pepperonis had cleared sinuses and checked the working order of many a tear-duct. "Seriously, does your stomach feel funny?"

The name Luisa meant "glorious battle" and the men of the *MEK* (*Mobiles Einsatzkommando* – mobile task force), with their machine pistols and matt-black body armour over green fatigues, were the warriors of today. Anonymous soldiers behind thin black balaclavas under transceiver-carrying visored helmets. But the glorious battle was heavily outweighed by the waiting. A waiting that was never meditative; a waiting that was taut and grew tauter with the passing of time.

These commandos were to add punch to the presence of the regular police officers.

They were in the countryside north-east of the airport, in the Hamburg district of Duvenstedt.

The *Polizeiobermeister* took a last pull on his cigarette. He flicked the remaining stub over the top of the partly rolled-down window. It hit the cold ground were it glowed mutely with the death-throes of a fish out of water.

The lingering smoke and the constricting bulletproof vest prickled Dannaks's skin. He shifted uncomfortably. Rather than becoming shiny with sweat he became oily, as if his sweat glands melted a film of oil upon his skin that in turn clogged his pores. He hated the feeling.

His bowels felt funny too. Gases were gurgling in his stomach. Was that what Patel meant about watching the pepperonis? He suddenly tightened his bowels to quell the sound. The subsequent hiss was a relief in more ways than one.

It was too cold to wind down his window and he hoped his companion would not notice.

Dannaks regarded the travelling blanket covering his knees. Although he felt clammy, his legs felt cold. Bad circulation, his father said. He ignored his clamminess and his companion and brooded. The more he thought about the operation the worse he felt. It was too big, too planned and susceptible to failure. Such a waste of time, money and effort.

"You can make these operations secret, but as soon as you want bodies there are bound to be leaks," Uwe had once said. Dannaks had lamented that they couldn't use fresh uncorrupted officers. "You can't recruit inexperienced cadets. That's the stuff of movies. There are too many laws and rules to be observed. You'd be fried alive if something went wrong."

The cigarette butt gave a last weak flare against an eddy and then died.

Dannaks and the *Polizeiobermeister* were just one unit in the stakeout. There were five unmarked cars, two police vans and a communications van positioned at strategic points about the burnt-out farm. A "Libelle" helicopter was on standby. Not a single marked police car was within five kilometres of the area.

Nevertheless, the man beside Dannaks was in uniform. He was from the *Schutzpolizei (Schupo)*. Dannaks was a detective, a member of the *Kriminalpolizei*, known colloquially as the *Kripo*. As always there existed a certain rivalry between the *Schupo* and the *Kripo*: the uniforms and detectives.

Dannaks had got off on the wrong foot with the *Polizeiobermeister* from the start. He knew he had not given the man a chance.

"I assume we're in for a long wait," the man began as he had driven them from the rendezvous. Uwe had been teamed up with another local officer. The *Polizeiobermeister*, assuming the German familiar form of speech, introduced himself, offering his first name and family name. Dannaks had promptly forgotten both.

"Dannaks," he returned, surprised by the man's openness. Most strangers retracted. He put it down to his attire. He favoured sweatshirts, because they didn't need ironing. But he had to admit many of them had become washed out.

"No first name?"

"No." Dannaks did not want to be uncivil and mustered the energy to acknowledge the man's offer of first-name terms by saying that he had nothing against using the German familiar form.

"You've landed yourself with the right man here," the *Polizeiobermeister* had boasted.

Dannaks was not one for small talk and he wasn't renowned for his tact. And tonight he didn't want conversation at all. Finally he was too weary to guard his words with a *Schupoman*.

"I grew up here. Know this area better than my vest-pocket."

This was one of the reasons for the Narcotics team splitting. Another was to be on hand should on-the-spot decisions arise. Naturally, the real decisions would come from the operations van in which Detlef, and a Polizeirat from local district unit, sat. But out here the area expert had to be coupled with the case expert.

"Remember the code word?"

Dannaks nodded.

"It's always good to check. Some hear it and forget. And your life could depend on it." He paused. "I knew a man..." Dannaks listened wearily to the man's story. "And those *MEK* boys can get nervous. I'm not saying trigger-happy, but mistakes have been made. Don't get me wrong; we're in good hands with those boys. I wanted to join them myself, but I failed the physical. I like my beer too much."

Dannaks said nothing. His stomach rumbled.

"There's talk of a hundred kilos changing hands. What would be the street value of that much stuff?"

Of all the men to be teamed with, this man was probably the worst.

"A damned good lottery win," Dannaks muttered. His bowels ballooned and he tensed himself. He knew he'd have to put a stop to the conversation, but wanted to soften the blow by using the man's first name. But what was it?

"Yes, but how much?" the man persisted.

"About eighteen million."

"Eighteen big ones." He whistled, the sound stabbing Dannaks's miserable demeanour. "What Rainer would do with that. Phew. You know I love sailing. But it's damned expensive. I–"

"Look," he began. "Rainer, I'm sorry. I really don't care for conversation at the moment."

"You mean you really don't care for conversation with me."

Dannaks stonewalled. He knew the *Polizeiobermeister* thought he was a stuck-up detective looking down on a uniformed man, but he could not be bothered to explain. Instead he passed air, but not through his mouth. And they both rolled down the windows.

23:59

The abandoned farm and surrounding area were still and as dark as pitch. Somewhere out there were forty officers, but to Dannaks it was as if Rainer and he were the only people who existed. His companion had taken advantage of the lack of conversation and the necessary radio silence to do some catnapping. Dannaks felt weary but Rainer's posture – his head tipped back, mouth agape – dispelled the urge to sleep.

He stared into the darkness but he could not make out the derelict buildings.

Ironically, the old farm had been earmarked as a home for

asylum-seekers. At the time the authorities had vainly tried to keep it out of the local public eye. Their efforts failed and the place was burnt to the ground. Rumours abounded, but the culprits were never caught.

His stomach gurgled, but he had it under control. He had decided that the cheese spread was off. He would have to talk to Patel. Hopefully he hadn't poisoned the entire team as a parting gift.

The radio crackled into life. An innocuous message that conveyed that a vehicle had turned onto the track that led to the farm was relayed. Everyone was to go on alert.

Dannaks looked at his watch as his companion sat up. Perhaps the bust would be a success after all.

After taking everything to the kitchen, they had relocated. Petra and Carina had taken the sofa. Craig and Robert sat in the easy chairs. Conversation had left Craig's investigation at the dining table. They had moved on to talking about the organic nature of the English language. To do so they had dropped speaking in German. They spoke of semantic drift: how the meaning of words change, be it through fashion or carelessness. Stretching the continental drift analogy and seismic changes on the Richter scale, they referred to a rigor scale.

Although the girls didn't work directly with English – Carina was a travel agent and Petra worked in a bank – they both had a healthy interest in the language.

Craig was exuberant, surfing on alcohol and Carina's approval. He wasn't sure of her sincerity and knew he was gushing, but either she accepted him for what he was or be damned.

"His German was still in the let's translate English stage." He was relating an early faux pas by an acquaintance and fellow countryman. "He was quite keen on this girl who happened to be in the bar with her mother. This didn't stop him. He was crazy like that." The girls were smiling knowingly. "It's not me, really. I don't know where he is now. Munich, I think. We lost contact–"

"Get on with it," said Robert wearily.

Craig sipped his wine. He knew he should stop or at least slow down. "He wanted to show the mother that he was a perfect gentleman, but also compliment the daughter."

"Oh, oh," said Petra warily.

"Because he found her conversation witty, he said: 'you're sharp, this evening'. You know: '*Du bist scharf, heute Abend.*'" Craig looked from one to the other. Their English was better than that of the outraged girl and her mother. The speaker had translated sharp into the German word *scharf,* which colloquially meant horny. "I don't think he ever saw her again."

They laughed and in the pause Carina left to go to the bathroom.

Carina returned and said she was leaving. Her imminent departure sobered Craig. Petra, Robert and he watched her put her shoes on at the door. Craig felt appallingly distant and desperate. He wanted to see her again, but couldn't think of what to say without being obvious. But then, perhaps he'd been obvious all evening. Her shoes elevated her and left him feeling foolish in socks: stumped physically and mentally. He fluttered at the sight of her smooth calves. And stood by impotently as Robert helped her into her jacket. She shouldered her handbag and smiled. What a delicious smile. Petra and Robert were saying their goodbyes with continental pecks on the cheeks. Then it was his turn. Alcohol doused his inhibitions and holding her a little too firmly, he kissed her cheeks too. He wasn't satisfied with the customary three and surprised her with a fourth as she was pulling away. He just missed her lips.

"I wanted to be fair to both cheeks." He couldn't read her smile and when she left he looked to Robert for help, but he said nothing. Had he blown it?

With her departure Craig felt like a third wheel, but before returning to the lounge Petra announced that she was going to bed.

"So what's your plan?" said Robert, when they had resumed their seats and topped up their glasses.

"Well, I'm going Harburg tomorrow. I need to get some gear."

"Carina is teaching in the centre tomorrow. You could have arranged to meet her."

"You don't think I blew it just now?"

"No. I don't know. Phone her tomorrow morning. What have you got to lose?"

Craig nodded distractedly.

"What's in Harburg?"

"I need to get some gear. There's a place there called the Bunker."

"I've heard of it. Go on."

"There's a rightwing concert on Sunday. Somewhere north of Hamburg."

"And you're going?"

Craig nodded.

"So you're buying rightwing gear."

Craig nodded again.

Robert shook his head. "You're not going to try to pass yourself off as one of them."

"Yes. But I'm not going undercover. My German's not good enough. I'll be an overseas visitor."

"They'll see through you."

"It's just this one time. Like I said I'm not going undercover."

"You didn't say this earlier."

"I couldn't really." He sipped his wine. "Talk about hostile."

"It's a blow on a bruise, mate. And it's something that happened more than half a century ago."

"The Jews are burdened with the crucifixion and the Germans are blighted by the holocaust, a crucifixion of humanity."

"Jeez, Craig. That's heavy. And radical. And I don't know that it's true. I mean, we could talk about the atrocities made in the name of the British Empire."

"Let's not go there."

"I still think you're being extreme."

"I'm drunk."

He yawned.

"You know that next Saturday the Cohen Holocaust exhibition opens in the centre, at the *Deichtorhallen* near the main station. A rightwing demonstration has been approved."

Craig tried to focus on his glass. "I don't believe it."

"Democracy, mate. It's all perfectly legal. The right to protest and all that." Pause. "What I wanted to say is that you'd be safer going there."

"Next week is too late."

"Yeah, well, maybe it wouldn't be that safe. The Left applied to stage a counter-demo, but permission was denied. They'll probably turn up. They always do."

"That makes it more interesting. It could certainly beef-up a follow-up."

"Craig, you do know why I was talking about safety, don't you?" Receiving no answer Robert continued. "There is a serial killer bumping off right-wingers."

Craig sat up, struggling to focus. "Uh?"

"He's killed two so far. They call him the *Henker.*"

"Executioner?" he croaked, then shook his head.

"In this case hangman would be a better translation. Although what he does is execute, I suppose. He killed one in October last year. And then one in February. He strings them up and puts a fruit in their mouth."

"Fruit?"

"Yeah, the police kept a lid on that until the second murder. When it came out, well, you can imagine, we all had a field day."

"What does it mean?"

35

"I don't know, mate. I do know that I am getting tired."

"Tell me tomorrow. I can't concentrate any more, either."

01:09

After hearing about the car turning towards the farm they heard nothing for twenty minutes.

If it was the hand-over it was early.

Also Dannaks had been wrong and there could be a perfectly innocent reason for Freddy's abrupt hanging up. What had Detlef said? "Your nark has always come through." But why hadn't he phoned back? Dannaks remained sceptical but a successful end to Luisa would be more than welcome.

Dannaks sensed Rainer's growing impatience. The man didn't speak but he wasn't comfortable in his seat. Dannaks wanted to ask him whether he wanted to relieve himself, but such a quip would fall into the chasm between them. So he remained silent too.

The radio again crackled into life. False alarm. But remain alert. They were still in the time window. And that was it. Silence.

Rainer blew air and slumped.

Dannaks sighed. He put his head in his hands and massaged his eyebrows and forehead. He wanted to talk, but didn't have the energy for explanations. He again chose silence.

Rainer closed his eyes.

Dannaks looked at the haggard reflection in the window that stared back at him. Did he always look this tired?

He heard the hoot of an owl. Listened for it to reoccur and was satisfied when it did. He waited for a third call and was disappointed to the point of willing it to happen. He wished he'd had an afternoon sleep. Of course had he tried he wouldn't have slept; he had too much on his mind.

They jolted when the radio gave them the alert. Another vehicle had turned onto the track. Rainer confirmed their readiness.

"Hopefully this is it," muttered Rainer gruffly.

Dannaks only nodded. He studied the darkness as if he could see beyond the black trees and bushes, hear past the rustle of leaves, gusts of breeze and see the vehicle.

They were within the time frame, almost smack in the middle. It felt right.

He heard no shots. No shouts. Just Nature's silence.

Ten minutes later they heard that the rest of the operation had been given the go-ahead. Numerous flats, a discotheque and brothel would be raided. Raul and everyone associated with him would be taken in.

Rainer reached for the ignition key in the steering column. They were to proceed to the rendezvous. "That wasn't too strenuous."

"No," was all Dannaks could think of saying. Luisa was a success. He'd been wrong. That meant there was no leak. There would be a reasonable explanation why Freddy had hung up so abruptly.

01:36

The first brick went through the window of the pub, hit the far edge of the table nearest the window, bounced on the edge of another which sent it askew and went skating across the parquet floor coming to a stop near the opposite wall.

Glass exploded across the room.

Wolfgang jumped up in bed and his wife started.

Good Lord, what was that?" she exclaimed. He had closed up half an hour before and they had only just turned out the lights.

Wolfgang ignored her and went to the window.

"Don't switch on the light," he ordered, carefully separating the curtains.

Although it was dark at the paved parking area near the building, the street lamp at the roadside gave off sufficient light for him to see the figures.

"Call the police," he said.

He was not sure what to do and remained at the window.

Brigitte's bedroom light suddenly hazed the darkness at her window.

"What is it?" his wife asked, dialling the 110 from their bedside telephone.

"Brigitte," he called loudly, "stay away from the window and switch your light off."

The landlord looked down and was horrified to see the faces turned to the light at his daughter's bedroom. He hoped she had not shown herself.

"What is it?" his wife asked. Before he could answer she was forced to speak to the person answering her call.

He turned back to the window. There was movement nearer the building and he heard the sound of more glass breaking.

With her hand covering the mouthpiece his wife whispered a plea. "I have to tell them something."

37

His eyes hardened and his lips thinned.

"Stay here and lock the door," he said, crossing the bedroom.

"Wolfgang, what shall I tell them?" She was terrified. The light from the slightly parted curtains illuminated part of her face and he could see the whites of her eyes.

"Skinheads. About fifty of them." He unhooked his night-gown from the back of the bedroom door.

She urgently repeated what he had told her into the telephone.

"I think they want to smash up the place," he said.

"Don't go down," she called after him, but he was already out of the room. Nonetheless she called after him in a restrained voice that hissed with imperative. "The police said it'd take them ten minutes to—"

Wolfgang was a formidable man of local renown. His face alone bespoke character: a head crowned with a bush of wispy, ash-grey hair and mouth straddled by a large handlebar moustache. The rings under his droopy-lidded eyes and his spreading jowls betrayed his true age of fifty-eight. There was a jolliness and sternness in his face. In his youth he had been a great womaniser and drinker and brawler. Only last year he had single-handedly overpowered two youths who had tried to get away without paying. He held them until the police arrived. He was a big-boned man: not fat. Despite having lost some height he was still well over six-foot. He still believed he could kill a man at six paces with his shout.

He opened his daughter's bedroom door, which he had to pass to reach the stairs. She swung round and gasped, her hand coming up to cover herself as if she were naked. She was wearing her oversized American football shirt. Under normal circumstances he would have knocked. She was at the window. The curtains were closed.

"Lock your door," he said, as the sound of the breaking of furniture shattered the relative stillness. "And stay away from that window."

Wolfgang made for the top of the stairs. He heard them mumbling and could see irregular shadows of movement at the open doorway to the lounge.

He heard his daughter lock her door, but rather than feel reassured he felt isolated. Shut out. The feeling was a shock. Age was creeping up on him. He wondered whether he should fetch something to protect himself, but dismissed this on the grounds that it could provoke them. He would go down empty handed.

There was the crash of another piece of furniture followed by slobbering laughter. The hydra in the lounge was not a monster at all, but a bunch of stupid kids. Although he did not entirely believe this, it steeled him to what he had to do.

He took a deep breath and stormed down the stairs loudly as if he had only just heard them. When he neared the bottom he boomed: "What the Devil's going on here?"

He froze at the doorway. The anger that had rashly spurred him on was momentarily flicked to fear. He suppressed the feeling under his will to be angry: his face reddening with the effort.

"Get the hell out of here!"

They did not answer but seemed unsure of themselves.

Everything had a surreal feel to it. The majority were skinheads and their close-cropped hair unified them in caricature. Their appearance also alienated them. They looked aggressive and incongruously passive.

Wolfgang's mind was hyperactive. It was too dull to distinguish any one of them. Nonetheless he scanned them, searching for a leader, someone with whom he could possibly talk or overpower and threaten to "snap his neck like a twig."

The broken window was full of skinheads and with sick irony they reminded him of beefed-up concentration camp victims. The ones in the room, standing between the up-turned benches and tables stared back at him. Their numbers appalled him and the thinness of his gown and his bare feet upon the stone floor made him feel vulnerable.

He knew he could not show hesitation. He had to shout them down.

"You heard me, get out." For added effect he hit the light switch. Everyone squinted as if recoiling from a disagreeable sight.

But they did not move.

01:43

Dannaks and Uwe were tearing the Velcro tabs from their bulletproof vests when Lampe came over. He ignored Dannaks and spoke to Uwe saying that Detlef wanted to speak to everyone. Dannaks gave his vest to Uwe who returned them to the *Schupoman* with whom he had shared a vehicle. The vests were personal property.

That they were not supplied was one of the many long-standing gripes of the police union.

He saw Rainer talking to other uniforms. No doubt he was moaning about spending his time with a stuck-up, shabby detective, who couldn't stop farting.

Detlef was about to speak to the gathering when he was called back to the control van.

"Those bloody pepperonis have set my bum on fire, Dannaks," said one of the men.

"My guts are in a state," said another. "I think it was the cheese."

"It was all freshly made," said Dannaks. Despite feeling windy his own stomach was like a goat's, hardened by years of bachelor fare. Others were apparently not so hardy. He had been desperately trying to estimate how many cheese sandwiches he'd left at the station.

"I'm okay," said Lampe triumphantly. Dannaks wasn't sure, but he thought Lampe hadn't touched a thing. "But Gunnar's got the shits. Detlef sent him home."

Lampe then started talking about the false alarms. The first car had been somebody pulling over to make a call. The second car that had entered the track just after midnight was more interesting. "I don't know who was more shocked. Those *MEK* boys who moved in or the occupants." The car had pulled off the track onto a grassy verge before reaching the farm. All units were ordered to wait. A full half hour went by before the order was given to move in. "The two in the car were caught in an *extremely comprising* position. Handprints on steamed-up windows. I'll let you use your imaginations. I've just heard that it was a married man stopping for some extra-marital nuptials before taking the baby-sitter home."

"*Babysitterin*," someone corrected.

"You heard me correctly," Lampe smiled. "The boy sat tight, but the man tried to clamber into the driver's seat to make a getaway. Luckily the *MEK* boys kept their cool. Some of them have real itchy fingers."

To Dannaks Lampe was a spiteful little shit. By playing the sonny boy he kept in with the team.

Detlef returned. His expression said that something was wrong.

"Listen up," he said. Detlef had a knack of rising to the occasion. Maybe that was how he got so far? In the office he might as well be a manager of a department store. He oversaw their cases, but his direction rarely extended beyond the political. Out here he was a director of operations with a sharpness in his voice that could be mistaken for decisiveness. "We've got a new problem. The arrests have been made. They're not going anywhere. We've got a job before the interrogations or–" he found Dannaks "– going home."

Dannaks knew that he would not be involved in the night's interviewing. But he was pleased to be on the operation. Detlef had surprised him by not giving him the original hand-over location.

"A large gang has besieged a pub not far from here. Because of the numbers we've been asked to assist."

01:44

Switching on the light may not have been the wisest of things to do. It propped up Wolfgang's fragile bravado but it also exposed the twenty or so youths in the room.

The first person to move was a skinhead near the bar. He reached over and picked up a wooden baseball bat. Wolfgang then noticed the weapons. There was a piece of rubber hosing and another baseball bat on the bar. Those at the window carried various forms of bludgeons from thick pieces of wood to the popular baseball bat. These were the visible weapons. Undoubtedly the vicious flick-knife was concealed in many a pocket and some would carry a heftier knife in the top of a boot.

Wolfgang remained steady and shouted at them once again, hoping that the youth at the bar was retrieving his weapon to leave. He was wrong.

01:46

Wolfgang's wife complemented her husband in formidability. Physically she was shorter than him, but she was tall for a woman. Her large girth, however, made her appear dumpy.

Disobeying him she got out of bed and looked out of the window. On seeing the number of youths she decided that it was too much for him to handle. She had no thought of tackling the youths. She knew that her husband would not be intimidated. His aggression could provoke them. She hoped to avoid this through reason. It would not be the first time she had defused an explosive situation.

She pulled on her dressing gown and went out onto the landing. Through the locked door she whispered to her daughter to stay in her room.

At the top of the stairs she realised that there was some kind of struggle taking place and without thinking of her own safety she grabbed one of the crossed cutlasses that ornamented the wall.

With the sword held behind the back of her leg she proceeded down the stairs that tried to betray her with their creaking. But she sensed that she had not been heard.

A rectangle of light extending from the lounge gave the stairs and hallway dullness. This meagre light fluctuated in intensity with the movement within. The grunts filled her with trepidation and like her husband minutes before she steeled herself.

All thought fled when she heard her husband grunt and she descended the stairs hastily. The noise of her descent alerted them and the fluctuations of light stopped.

Unfortunately, her haste made her reckless and just as she reached the entrance, shocked by the sight before her; a hand gripped her wrist from behind. The assailant twisted her wrist until the pain caused her to give up the cutlass.

02:07

"*Scheißbullen*! (shit-bulls)" shouted a skinhead at the large broken window. He was warning those inside the building. German police were not called the pigs, but bulls.

The headlights of the police vehicles suddenly illuminated the pub. They hazed the area and the flashing blue strobed the surrounding buildings and scattering figures pouring from the gaping window like ants.

The call to remain still was ignored.

With a cursory glance to check that others were with him, Dannaks charged towards the dispersing mass. He hated this kind of action. Completely bereft of intelligence, it forced him to draw upon primitive parts of himself.

The reaction of the youths should have been predictable. Even though the pub was effectively surrounded, the local area police chief had not been able to finish his command on the loud hailer before they tried to escape.

Everything moved with cat-like swiftness and human clumsiness. Darkness encroached the headlights and stillness accentuated the clamour that jarred the night: scuffling footsteps, boots scraping concrete, sharp noises and shouts.

Dannaks chose his man and went directly for him. Movement to his left distracted him momentarily: the smashed window of the

42

pub through which skinheads were hastily climbing, those at the frame mindful of the snarl of jagged shards. His colleagues were converging on them and he continued his pursuit.

A litany of "this is not what I want" began a few strides into the chase. Dannaks used it to bolster his determination, to give him a false aggression and a sense of control.

He could only see the back of the skinhead he was pursuing: a youth of fifteen or a man of thirty-five. He wore black paratrooper boots with white laces, camouflage trousers and a black denim jacket over a light T-shirt. The sleeves of the jacket had been hacked off, exposing impressive biceps and forearms, adorned with gothic smoky-blue tattoos. He was carrying a baseball bat. A more archetypical skinhead Dannaks could not imagine.

Dannaks knew that two or three figures had entered the alley ahead of his man, but he had no time to think; they were fleeing and he was chasing.

When he turned the corner, some five steps behind the skinhead he saw the forms at the brickwork at the end of the alley. Items flew into the air and he needed a moment to realise that their weapons were being hurled over the two-metre wall. Light played on the faces of the three pulling themselves up the wall, their features rendered harsh by a spotlight on the corner of one of the buildings. At the top one of them turned and said something. Instead of dropping over the other side they paused. Perched, ready to drop down.

Time slowed to an excruciating level. Dannaks felt the portent of the moment, like prescient moments before an accident: a sickening inevitability. And his father came to him. "Get a good breakfast inside yourself, son. We're like steam engines. Your stomach's the engine room and you've got to get a good fire up to keep you going till midday." Nowadays he rarely ate before leaving the flat, preferring to catch a roll at a bakery on the way to work. He usually slung back a hot coffee: something to stoke up the ashes of the previous night. Now he was slowing like the man in front of him. It was a painful screeching of a locomotive at full speed: brakes on, wheels suddenly rigid, the momentum of the machine carrying it forward, sparks flying, and of course the ear-splitting shriek.

Dannaks faltered. His lungs were afire. The skinhead stopped. He looked at his three mates on the wall, then over his shoulder. His eyes became slits. A smile thinned his lips to nothingness: the insentient smirk of a lizard at an unwitting prey. He was about five steps away from Dannaks, his friends upon the wall a further ten.

Dannaks was also still, struggling to control his breathing. Shining in the half-light. He stole a glance over his shoulder and saw the empty entrance. He was alone. He could tackle the skinhead before him, but should they begin to grapple the others merely had to drop down and he would be finished.

During the chase he had been carried along. "This is not what I want." Now he was at a loss as to what to do. Alleyway fights did not fit in his world of detection. At best this was the beat policing he had left behind.

The idea of drawing his service weapon was abhorrent. He was appallingly close to the man. Should he use his gun, he could find himself on thin ice with respect to the law. Nonetheless his hand began to edge its way towards the holster just behind his right hip.

The man before him did not turn round: such was his confidence. He seemed to relish the moment and playing to his audience he began to smack the bat in his hand.

Both men were panting. Huffing like anxious locomotives, their pale breaths visible in the chilled air. Neither spoke, as if awaiting a steam-scolded whistle to scream action.

Dannaks made a show of unhooking the safety clip of his holster. The law required him to give a warning, but he knew words were useless. He knew that there was no reasoning.

The skinhead still had the side of his face towards him when Dannaks registered movement behind him. He had not heard anything, but a subtle change in the light, the stiffening in the skinheads on the wall and the hate flaring the whites of the eyes of the skinhead in front of him, told him that help had arrived.

"Stop," shouted someone behind him.

Dannaks had expected the man to make a dash for the wall and had been poised to lunge forward. This readiness to propel himself helped him avoid the baseball bat, for the skinhead swung round, the bat extended in his right hand. The man swung clockwise with a backhand motion, covering the shortest distance, aiming for the side of Dannaks's head.

The bat did not make contact, but only by a hair's breadth and to the onlooker it appeared as if it struck home. Dannaks rode the wind of the blow. He moved swiftly, making use of the skinhead's lack of balance, shoving the outstretched weapon-wielding arm onward and pulling the free arm. The skinhead's upper body was twisted further than his lower half and it was a relatively simple matter for Dannaks to use the man's momentum. He yanked the free arm round so that the skinhead virtually had his back to him again and then drove him forward. With his hips swivelled and legs twisted the skinhead grunted as he fell heavily to the ground.

He pressed a knee between the skinhead's shoulder blades. Then he forced his arm until his wrist was pinned into the small of the back. A colleague kicked the bat away.

"Are you okay?"

"Help me slap an eight on him," said Dannaks feeling for his handcuffs.

In the half-light, as he cuffed him, he could make out the smoky-blue tattoo of a letter on each of the captive's fingers. Together they made up the word *Hass* (hate). Naturally the last two letters were drawn with the familiar sharp-SS.

Dannaks looked up. The skinheads on the wall had disappeared. An officer having hoisted himself up was dropping back down.

02:21

Dannaks felt exhilarated and wretched as he returned to the pub. There were a number of scuffles going on outside the building, but everything was under control. About nine groups of two or three policemen grappled with skinheads who were being uncooperative to varying degrees.

Intriguingly the name of the pub painted in large letters on a board above the arch of the doors was *Die ruhenden Handschuhe* (the resting gloves). At the end of the words there appeared to be a clump of potatoes.

Uwe was in front of the smashed window talking to a young woman in a dressing gown. Their superior Detlef appeared from the entrance at the side of the building escorting a man Dannaks took to be the proprietor. A woman he assumed to be the man's wife was also with them. She was crying and trying to comfort her husband. She looked ruffled but was more concerned about him. He was dazed and she was struggling to get him to put a coat on. But he was head and shoulders above her. He looked strange in an oversized shinny, blue housecoat. It was theatrically brash with a hood, something a stage magician might wear. As he turned to put an arm into a sleeve Dannaks saw what looked like a tilted black hammer in a black circle

45

on the back of the housecoat. His physical wounds were superficial. But there was something in his expression, made all the more appalling by the blood and oddly clipped whiskers. One droopy length of his moustache was longer than the other. Despite his bulk he looked broken.

The girl left Uwe. Dannaks took her to be their daughter. Her parents were numbed with shock, but she was angry to the point of hysteria. Whilst trying to comfort her parents she attacked the police with venomous comments. She vented her anger with shouts of incompetence. Why had they taken so long? Apparently it had taken them half an hour to come. Had someone tried to tell her that it had taken time to assemble and mobilise a large enough group, she would not have listened. She wanted to know why she paid taxes. Then she repeated the incompetence bit.

One comment in the tirade directed at a senior officer struck a chord in Dannaks.

"It's monstrous that such large gangs can roam about at will."

As the proprietor was helped into the fluorescent orange ambulance the interior light exposed his face. He seemed totally overwhelmed by what had happened. But it was not his expression that stopped Dannaks in his tracks. Streaks of blood lined his face. The wounds were not large, but they looked painful. Safety pins and needles punctured his face. A safety pin had been driven through his nose, another through his bottom lip. There was a nail or large needle in an ear lobe. Another oversized safety pin went into his cheek.

03:51

He lay on the roof of the building, biding his time. The window was locked and the drainpipe was now his only way down. But the bulls were still hovering around in the building and on the street. Didn't they have beds to go to? Should they look up they could have seen the tips of his boots peeking over the edge of the gutter. But then it was too dark.

10:03

The sound of the curtains on the rail jarred. Light exploded in the room and Craig cringed. The muffled sound of cheerful birds made him pray the window was not about to be opened. He peeked between gritty eyelids. Light silhouetted the figure at the window. "Morning old man," said Robert.

"Uh? What?" He was aware of a crick in his neck.

"I brought you a coffee."

46

"Thanks," he croaked.

"Don't get used to it. You feel as bad as you look?"

"Worse." His left shoulder felt dislocated.

"Good."

"What time is it?"

"Just gone ten. Breakfast is in the kitchen."

Robert was about to leave.

"Wait. You were talking about a serial killer last night."

"We don't know whether he's a serial killer. The police say he is not a serial killer, but he has killed twice. Two neo-Nazis have been hung."

"Hanging is unusual... Sensational."

"Yes and he puts fruit in their mouths."

"Fruit? Wow. That's weird. I suppose the police have pulled in every left-winger and foreigner in the city."

"They've looked right too."

"Maybe I could use it."

"You could. But what if the killings have nothing to do with them being right-wingers?" Robert waited a moment. "Anyway, breakfast. And er, let's make it taboo whilst we eat, eh?"

Robert left.

Craig stretched and sat up. He sipped his coffee, but knew he couldn't lie in for too long. His thoughts conjured up last night. It seemed full of unfinished conversations. He wanted to know more about the *Henker*. Could he use it? For the serious tone he wanted to capture using a serial killer could be too sensational. And where did he stand with Carina?

He got up and fetched some clothes from his trolley case on the floor. He pulled on some boxer-shorts and grabbing the bath towel, Petra had left out for him, he went to the bathroom.

"It lives," called Robert from the kitchen.

Craig grunted.

The shower did him good. He was still a wreck, but a clean wreck.

"You still look like crap, mate," said Robert, when Craig entered the kitchen.

They were at the small breakfast-laden circular table, at the end of the kitchen, in front of the window. The radio was fighting a losing battle with the sound of traffic.

47

"Thanks," he returned. "But at least with me it's a temporary state."

"Ouch," said Robert.

Petra's confusion and perhaps disgust broadened the lads' smiles further. Despite living with Robert for a few years, Petra hadn't got used to the lads rapport. Greetings of shit-head and fart-face were a mystery. Perhaps it was a peculiarly British trait? Craig had noticed that Mainland Europe had no equivalent. Other than the British he'd not met a European who was at ease with such abusive banter.

"I've got some good news for you," Robert said.

"My lottery ticket came up?" He cut a bread roll in half on his plate and reached for the butter.

"Maybe. I've got two things of interest for you. There was an item on the radio this morning. A pub, somewhere north of here, was attacked by a gang of skinheads early this morning. What was its name?"

"*Die ruhenden Handschuhe*," said Petra.

"Funny name for a pub: the quiet gloves," said Craig. He took a slice of ham and laid it on the buttered half. He attached the idea to his article. Like the *Henker* it didn't possess the right tone. He wanted the subtle, latent stuff.

"It could be the resting gloves."

They ate in silence.

"And the second thing?"

"I phoned in work and they told me a Turkish schoolboy was attacked by skinheads last night."

"It's all happening," he said, noticing Petra's jaw tighten. Craig glowed, but he took the excitement out of his voice. "What happened?"

"I don't know the details. It was around ten o'clock. He was with a friend, walking back from a pool hall or something when a group of skinheads attacked them. His friend got away but he was beaten to the ground."

"So it was unprovoked."

"He's a schoolboy. I don't think he would have taken on a gang."

"Was he badly hurt?"

"He went to hospital, I think. Last I heard he was back at home. So it couldn't have been that bad. One of our guys is going to see him. I really don't know much more."

He could see that Robert's paper would sideline it. But Craig knew that such an event was the key to one side of his article. "Perhaps I could interview him?"

"I thought you wanted to meet Carina?"

"I– I do." He glanced at Petra, hoping for encouragement or something, but she said nothing.

"You can't chase her and research your article."

"We'll see."

"If you are going to call her, you will have to do it now. I think she teaches at half past ten and then she'll have her handy off."

He looked at his watch, using the pause to scour his mind for the right words.

Robert could apparently read him. "Tell her you heard she was in town and invite her to lunch."

"Her number's in the black book next to the phone," said Petra.

Craig looked at each of them for further advice or comment. When none was forthcoming he abruptly stood and theatrically braced himself before marching off to the phone in the hall.

She picked up on the second ring.

"Hi, it's Craig."

"Oh, hallo."

"I– er, I'm going to be in town this morning." He certainly wasn't going to tell her why he was going into the centre. "I thought maybe I could take you to lunch."

12:00

The alarm woke Dannaks with a start. Daylight frayed the edges of the curtains. They did not quite meet and a brilliant stalactite pierced the ceiling. He could hear the traffic three storeys below. The small room was dull. His flat was too compact to look cluttered. Clutter was a luxury of space and his flat had a total area of only twenty-five square metres. The entrance corridor, the length of three adjacent telephone boxes, separated a door-less kitchen no bigger than a walk-in cupboard and a bathroom, containing toilet, sink and shower all housed in an area the same size as the corridor. Every wall of the one room in which Dannaks lived was occupied, compromising the floor-space further; the two alcoves were filled and the area above the door shelved. His portable TV was on a shelf in the double-door wardrobe. His bed was of necessity a sofa bed. During the working week it often remained open, although it took up too much space and he didn't like coming home to it. At the weekend he made the effort to turn the room into a living room for a few hours.

"Dannaks, are we in Tokyo or Hamburg?" Uwe had asked his wife when they had first visited. "This is no bigger than those sleeping capsules. Do you get attacks of agoraphobia at work?"

Dannaks returned from the kitchen with the casserole. His two guests had left the sofa and were sitting on the floor around the small coffee table.

"How do you put up with him?" asked Annelore.

"Sorry, did he say something? I'm deaf to his facetious comments."

"It's room enough for one," said Annelore. "And the view's to die for." True. His small flat overlooked the outer Alster: the large lake in the heart of the city. But his flat had no balcony, just full-length windows. When they were open the four lanes of traffic below polluted the room with noise.

Dannaks had slept well. Exercise and the country air, he mused. Then, as if he had to bring himself up to date, his thoughts inexorably went over the night's events.

There was something bothering him and he couldn't put his finger on it.

The farmhouse stakeout had been uneventful, unless one considered nabbing a man and his male baby-sitter. When they were packing up, Detlef had told them of a request to assist in the apprehension of a large gang of right-wingers. Due to the size of the gang they were to congregate half a kilometre from their destination and wait for other units.

When everything was under control at the pub, Detlef called his team together for an impromptu debriefing. He spoke about the pub first. The whole thing appeared to be an act of gang warfare. According to one of the local area officers punks and left-wingers frequented the pub and there was an ongoing war between them and the skinheads. The previous weekend a skinhead hangout had been attacked.

They were congregated underneath a large billboard currently advertising Bacardi: a beach scene of carefree, beautiful people, bronze and happy. It was a scene about as far as could be from this one of scrappy darkness, scuffles, harsh light and broken glass.

Detlef paused before launching into the night's main operation. "I've not had the final word from the others." He was referring to the controllers of the raids across the city. "So it's too early to talk of successes or failures." The darkness made it easier for him to avoid eye contact.

"Have we got Raul?" asked Dannaks.

"We nabbed some middle-men; secured some crack and pills, but I haven't any news on the big boys. The night's not over, though." Almost, thought Dannaks. "We've got some interrogating to do. And I want it done whilst the trail's still hot."

Dannaks nodded into the darkness. "Is that horse vomit over there?"

Detlef stared in disbelief before glaring at him. "I never did care for your humour." He teetered on losing his temper. "You realise you're the reason some of the men are ill. There'll be repercussions. Gunnar was sent home and three others have complained." Dannaks made to speak but Detlef held up his hand. "You might as well go home." Then more for the benefit of the others than Dannaks: "Nothing personal. There's no point in debriefing you, unless you have something?" Dannaks looked at him blankly. He was fed up and ready to accept the dismissal. "Get your report to me on Monday. You've got your move tomorrow – sorry, today." His last remark was an appalling attempt at levity. "No one else is going home, are they?" He should know. "Then we'll debrief before the interrogations."

Dannaks walked away.

He overheard Lampe ask one of the others what he had meant by horse vomit. "Horses can't vomit."

"Yeah, so?"

"It's like the Brits saying pigs might fly."

"Eh?"

Ten minutes later he was with Uwe in the car. He spoke of the skinheads in the alley.

"Not the kind of policing you enjoy," Uwe said. Dannaks smiled at his own litany: "This is not what I want."

"These are the people you're going to have more contact with," said Uwe.

"It can't be any worse than chasing the likes of Raul." The conversation was becoming caustic. "We're both tired."

Uwe didn't say anything for a while. "You know who that was back there?" Dannaks had no idea who he meant. "That was 'the Hammer'. You know, Wolfgang 'the hammer' Hänisch."

"Never heard of him."

"Neither had I. One of the *Schupo* mentioned it. He was a hopeful who stopped because of eyesight problems."

"That explains the name of the pub."

A short time later Uwe had dropped him off outside his flat.

Dannaks climbed out of bed. He almost knocked over the carrier bag and card on the coffee table. The Merlot, Bordeaux and Cabernet Sauvignon were in his six-bottle wine rack in the kitchen. The carrier bag was empty except for the clear plastic packet of white powder – no doubt flour – with a short straw taped to it. They hadn't bothered supplying a mirror and razor-blade.

None of this was what was bothering him. Was it Detlef's talk? The offer of support? He now knew why Detlef had not given him the old location. He had wanted to talk to him. But only if the operation failed?

Detlef had given him a rag with a whiff of corruption and he, Dannaks, the stupid bloodhound, dripping saliva had bitten.

Luisa was over. It had probably been a failure. In some ways it didn't matter. He was out. Had Raul been nabbed? Without Raul the operation was a failure. He would have liked to call Uwe, but he would have worked through the night on interrogations.

Then words surfaced from the depths. "It's monstrous that such large gangs can roam about at will." Yes it was. But so what? Why did the girl's words haunt him?

In the bathroom he returned the stare of the pasty face in the mirror.

12:37

Hasan and Nazim were already on the corner when Cenk arrived. Cenk thought they made an odd couple. Yet they were related: cousins. Hasan was chubby going on plump, his shirt like a tube, beige trousers covering his legs like sausage skins. He had a rounded face with cheeks that did not have the fullness associated with laughter; they tended to flatten his features. His eyes were intelligent and he carried a Clark Gable pencil-thin moustache. In all he looked more Egyptian than Turkish. He was eating an apple. Nazim was skinny; were he taller he'd be lanky, instead he barely filled out his jeans and his T-shirt yearned for shoulder-pads. Hasan had an intelligent look about him and Nazim rather startled as if life was continually surprising him. Hasan was in his mid-twenties and looking it, Nazim looking like a schoolboy, a reversed baseball cap on his

52

head, although he was almost twenty like Cenk. He had a droopy nose and an open fresh face that went with his eager manner.

"You're late," said Nazim.

Cenk ignored him and greeted the older man. He turned to Nazim. "Morning."

"Thought you'd lost your arse," said Nazim.

A thousand volts of anger shot through Cenk. Strange that he was Nazim's friend since school. He didn't know Hasan very well. They'd met on two occasions and both times Cenk had been struck by his warmth and intelligence.

They began walking. Hasan finished his apple and tossed the core in a bin at the bus stop.

"If I wasn't going to come I would have said so." He didn't want to lose his temper and tried to elevate himself above Nazim. "Nazim only told me a little about—"

"I told you all I knew," he said truculently.

Cenk braced himself. Hasan came to his rescue.

"What do you want to know?"

"How do you know Murat, for instance?"

"You mean someone like Murat?" Hasan smiled but didn't wait for an answer. "A couple of years ago I took up karate. Don't ask me why. I know I'm not the right build. Maybe all of us go through this phase? You know, wanting to back up that youthful sense of invincibility with something solid. I couldn't get any of my friends to come so I went alone. It didn't last long. About eight months, I think. Murat was also a relative newcomer. He'd been there a few weeks. So the teacher often paired us off." They stopped to cross a road. "I don't think I lost interest, I think the commitment increased beyond my limits. We were expected to train out of class. I barely found the time."

"You've got to make the time," said Nazim. "When the shop's empty—" he worked in his father's grocery "— I exercise. And carrying all those crates—"

"That's how you met," interrupted Cenk. "Whose idea was the gang?"

But Hasan chose to answer Nazim first. "I could have continued if I'd shelved my lute. But my playing brings extra cash." Then he turned to Cenk. "I wouldn't call it a gang. In fact I don't like the word. I'd say organisation."

"Organisation," repeated Nazim disparagingly.

"Murat was my opposite. He excelled. To me he became fanatical. But I don't want to take anything away from him. He just got better and rocketed through the belts. We didn't hit it off socially either. So when I stopped going to the club I didn't see him for a long time." He paused. "Do you remember that attack on the grocery? About a week after it I bumped into Murat. He asked me whether I was thinking of starting again, after what had happened. I said that I didn't have his dedication. But with the way things were going it was good he hadn't given up. Let's hope you'll never have to use it, I said. He was shocked. I agreed that if things got worse we'd have to do something. He said that if I thought anything more about doing something I should call him. That was it, a chance meeting in the street."

"We'll have to train more often," said Nazim excitedly.

Cenk did not answer. He'd heard the doubt in Hasan's words. And what had motivated him to form the ga– organisation? Was it simply the attack on Faruk? There had been worse in the past. Why now? He knew that Hasan was to marry later that year. It was an arranged marriage. So was this his last fling, a last scream before succumbing to humdrum?

"I can make it Mondays, Tuesdays, Wednesday," Nazim went on enthusiastically, "Thursdays are possible... What about you?"

"I don't know," said Cenk, unable to contain his exasperation. "I can barely make it twice a week as it is. We've tables on the street now. That means more work." Cenk worked in a restaurant.

"We're here," Hasan announced stopping at the open doorway of a four-storey house.

12:42

When they entered Murat's bed-sit flat that he insisted on calling a studio, eleven other men were already present and the gathering resembled a meeting of the community leaders. In a corner of the living room sat Faruk's school friend Ahmed.

Standard welcomes of "*Salaam Alacum*" met by replies of "*Alacum salaam*" were made by acquaintances and strangers. Longer greetings with kisses, the duration of which reflected the depth of friendship, were made between friends and relatives. The majority of Murat's karate club friends were unknown to Cenk, although he recognised a couple of the faces. Two of Hasan's friends were present. They looked out of place.

Nazim was the first to approach the lean stranger with his hair tied back in a ponytail. "You don't want to know my name. I'm here to hear what this is all about." He then ignored Nazim and dug his fingers into a small plastic bag of sunflower seeds on his lap. He munched a handful before looking at Nazim with dead eyes. Cenk and Hasan remained emotionless and Nazim nodded and smiled as he backed away.

Murat's room was a blaze of colour. There were small wall hangings and numerous posters. The latter being of curvy scantily clad women, martial arts tournaments, kick-boxing competitions in Hamburg and, of course, his one-man-army movie heroes.

At the end of his bed stood an angled workout bench and numerous weights.

After everyone was seated, accepting or declining the offer of coffee, Hasan spoke. He chose to speak in Turkish.

"I think you know why we're here." He was speaking to everyone but addressing Murat in particular, who was sitting on the table.

Murat nodded slowly. He looked bored. The seating was such that he appeared to be sitting before a congregation and the table upon which he sat gave him elevation. In addition to this position of power he stood out in the gathering because of his all-black attire. He liked clothes, especially suits that he tended to reserve for the night-clubs, and he prided himself on a yakuza-like taste for a sharp and fitting cut. He sported a black silk shirt and black trousers. His feet were bare.

He was rivalled only by the impressively detached stranger with the pony tail.

Hasan went on. "A couple of months ago Murat and I spoke of getting a group together. That is, of setting up an organisation to protect ourselves. I believe that that time has come." He glanced at Nazim, who had the juvenile habit of shaking his right leg, and then turned to Ahmed, the youngest in the room. "But first, I think we ought to hear what Ahmed has to say about last night."

The boy went pale. When he spoke, he spoke in German. "We, er, were attacked."

Hasan also switched to German. "There's no need to be nervous. You're amongst your own. Here, take these." He handed him some worry beads. But Ahmed didn't seem to know what to do with them.

"Farrie– er, Faruk, we, er–"

"He's called Monkey, isn't he?" said Nazim, clearly wanting to show his connection.

"Yes," said Ahmed uncertainly.

"Monkey?" said Murat.

"Yes, Farrie. It's, er, his nickname." Ahmed looked around, embarrassed by the digression. "His dad caught him swinging from the light-bulb of his bedroom."

"Playing Tarzan?" said Hasan.

"Yes," Ahmed smiled and relaxed. "He'd seen him on television." Then he grew serious. "He got a belting for it, though."

"It's a wonder he didn't bring the ceiling down," said Hasan, "or get electrocuted."

"He probably wanted to be nicknamed Tarzan," said Nazim.

"Yes, very good," said Murat. "Farrie's called monkey. Shift it. You were jumped, who by?"

"Skinheads."

"Where was this?" asked Hasan.

Ahmed told them.

"That's practically on our doorstep," exclaimed Nazim, his brashness turning him scarlet.

"The nerve," said another.

"You got away?" said Hasan.

Ahmed cast his eyes to the floor. "Yeah. I can run faster than Farrie."

"How many of them were there?"

"Five or six."

"And just the two of you?"

He nodded.

"It seems reasonable that you ran away. Farrie tried to run too." Hasan checked the concern of the others. "What happened to your hand?"

Ahmed regarded the reddened knuckles of his right hand.

"One–" he cleared his throat "– one of them got me by the shoulder and I, er, swung round and hit him."

"Good for you."

This comment seemed to instil the boy with a trace of confidence and he piped up. "Look I, er, don't think this is right. What you want to do, I mean. I just think we'll, er, make things worse."

Hasan nodded. "I understand your concern. But we can't sit by and get pushed around."

"Exactly," agreed Murat. "Check out the Jews."

There were nods of agreement from Murat's karate colleagues.

Ahmed was unconvinced. "We don't want things to escalate."

"They already escalate," said Murat.

"But if we s— strike back, then we'll be doing wrong. The public always looks at us as if we're the trouble makers."

Murat smiled. "You're shitting but—"

"Don't worry," assured Hasan. "We're not going to strike back."

"I'm not couching, waiting to be beat," said one of Murat's karate-club friends. "I'm going to beat first—"

"And beat hard," finished Murat, miffed by Hasan's earlier interruption.

"We'll strike when we have to," Hasan said.

Nazim had either not caught on or had chosen to side with Murat. "The Germans will respect us if we hit back. They don't like weakness."

Hasan was irked. "We won't be weak. But we won't be foolish either." Without allowing time for further comment he turned to Ahmed. "I don't know what you told your parents, but I think you'd better get back home."

"I'm almost sixteen, you know," he protested.

"I know. But maybe it's best if you don't know what goes on from now on. For your own safety."

Ahmed was perplexed but did not protest. To save face he spoke as he rose. "Huh. My parents say I have to stay at home when it gets dark. So, I, c—can't join your gang."

"We know," smiled Hasan.

When he was gone, Murat mumbled: "*Korkak.*"

"He's not a coward," scolded Hasan.

"He talked fossil. We'll beat back, and we'll beat back hard." He swelled as he spoke.

"We'll be sensible," insisted Hasan.

"You came here. You came to me." Murat looked at his karate friends. "We've got our shit parcelled."

"Okay, Murat, but we've got to stick within certain boundaries."

"Which?"

"We've got to be seen to be doing right."

"Wake up, *Lan* (man/comrade). The Germans are behind those who did Fa– Monkey."

"That kind of thinking doesn't help us."

There was an awkward silence.

"I don't know what the boundaries are," Hasan admitted. "I see us as a group like the Guardian Angels of New York."

"Guardian Angels," Murat scoffed. "Wearing poncy berets and stuff?"

"We can be called whatever you like. But our purpose is protection. If it's not going to be that, then we'll be as bad as them."

"It's about respect, *Lan*."

"And what of our self-respect?"

"That's fossil-talk: pensioner-talk. They wanted self-respect and still do. An' we've no more respect than they had decades ago. Don't talk respect."

"Things are getting better."

"I agree," interjected Cenk. "The Germans are being forced to face the foreigner problem head-on. If we go over-the-top now we'll be alienated forever."

"You really swallow that? Bloody omega. They're laughing. Can't you spot it? Why you here? Here, now, with us? We have reason to beat back."

"What do you propose we do?" said Hasan, wearily.

Murat smiled. With his eyes trained on Hasan he reached into the bowl beside him and held up two walnuts. He let them roll into the palm of his hand, his smile growing manic as he curled his fingers into a fist.

Crack.

13:40

Craig arrived ten minutes late. He checked inside before returning outside. Spitalerstrasse was an open pedestrian area in the city centre. The restaurant spilled out in tables and chairs. People at a table in front of him suddenly rose and he claimed a chair as they picked up their shopping. Although he was famished he vowed to wait for Carina and ordered a cappuccino. At least she wouldn't know that he had been late. He enjoyed his drink and watched the ever-changing flow of shoppers. The cluster of tables was an archipelago in a river.

He had read the papers on the underground journey. Robert's paper, the Hamburger *Tagespost*, had nothing on the pub and a single paragraph on the attacked schoolboy. Of course it was a sign of the times, but Craig was disgusted that the article appeared little more than a filler. He noted that Ahmed, Faruk's companion, who had got away, refused to be interviewed.

He peeked into his shopping bag but refrained from digging out his purchases. He even thought of hiding the bag under his chair or covering its contents with his jacket. In the end he did neither. If she asked he would tell her.

The Bunker had been an unimpressive dilapidated shop in a rundown part of Harburg, south of the river Elbe. Even the walk from the station had been depressing.

He had not expected a loud shop, but the general state of disrepair had surprised him: flaking paint, grimy windows. Predictably there was little in the window display. A few boots and harmless jackets, some knives were pinned to a hardboard wall that prevented one looking into the shop. Behind the door was a heavy curtain, similar to those found in the sex shops of the Reeperbahn.

A bell announced Craig's entrance. As he parted the curtain a large, longhaired man in leathers, a man resembling an ageing Hell's Angel, emerged from the depths of the shop to stand behind the counter. His head was a grey brown bush. His legs were clad in black leather; a matching waistcoat covered a taut T-shirt with a faded motif. His size demanded respect.

There were no other customers.

Craig smiled and glanced around. The shop was no bigger than Petra and Robert's lounge. Instead of books, rails of heavy woollen jackets, flak jackets, leather jackets, camouflage jackets and a matching selection of trousers lined the walls. There were trench coats and leather coats too. The room, already diminished by the clothing that stretched to the ceiling and could only be reached by the harpoon against the wall behind the counter, was choked with oil drums containing hats, gloves, balaclavas and socks.

All the standard labels were represented amongst the clothes: Consdaple (with its inherent NSDAP reference), Lonsdale, Hatecrime, Thor Steinar, Doberman, Patriot, Pitbull, Troublemaker. A stack of shoe boxes containing New Balance sport shoes (the stitched N of which was adopted to mean Nationalist or

Nationalsocialist) leant into a corner. Another corner was filled with a similar pillar, but of boxes of white-laced Doc Martens.

The man nodded but did not smile.

"I'm looking for a jacket and trousers."

The man gestured at the racks of clothes.

Craig wanted to laugh, but the man's humourless expression restrained him. He went to the racks and began parting the clothing for a better look.

"Your size is up here," said the man in a gravelly voice. Craig then noticed the tiny bits of paper with hand-written sizes taped to the rails. He moved closer to the glass counter and was distracted by all manner of military paraphernalia it contained.

He tore himself away and went through the jackets.

"Is this double-sided?" he asked.

The man nodded.

"Can I try it?"

Without coming round the counter the man deftly unhooked the jacket with the harpoon.

Craig lay his own jacket on the counter and put on the new jacket. There was a full-length mirror standing near the counter. The sleeves were a little long and the camouflage reminded him of pyjamas. He took it off and turned it inside out. Now he was in a nondescript black cotton jacket. Perfect. He checked the price tag and asked whether matching trousers were available.

The man came round the counter, sized Craig up, bent down and rifled through the rows of trousers. He pulled a pair out and handed them to Craig.

"I'd better try them on."

"You'd better," agreed the man, returning to the counter. Evidently there was no changing room.

Craig felt awkward taking off his jeans in the middle of the shop, but the man thawed and asked him whether he wanted to look at belts. He pointed to the strips of leather hanging from a carousel.

"Buckles are here," he said nodding into the counter.

The excuse to look at the treasure-trove was irresistible. The buckles were skulls and flags and medals. Craig chose one and a strip of leather. The man turned to a machine and clamped them together. Craig used the time to view the rest of the artefacts. There were plenty of badges and buttons and medals, but also embroidered patches old and new: hammer and sword, black sun, *Landser*, *Werwolf*, Vikings,

White Power, Wolfs Angel (Gibor Rune), Sig-Rune (the double Sig used by the SS) sleeve eagles, Death's head collar tabs and shoulder boards. There were swastikas too. Surprising in that it was a banned symbol in Germany. He was tempted by the SS dagger with its blade inscription: "*Meine Ehre heißt Treue*" (My honour is loyalty). The man noted his interest in the weapon and said he had more stuff. Craig checked his watch. He didn't have time. But he was intrigued and vowed to return. Had the man a stash of illegal things too? The swastika was a banned symbol and Craig had not seen one, not even on a belt buckle. "We do piercing in the back," he said, as Craig was about to leave. "And tattoos, anything you want."

The thinly veiled desperation smacked of an uncomfortable familiarity and Craig paid up and left.

He checked his cappuccino, forgetting he'd finished it moments ago. Where was Carina? Could she be sitting elsewhere? He leant over and asked a nearby couple whether there was another restaurant with the same name in the centre. They weren't sure, but thought not.

He didn't have her number. Did she carry a handy? He should have at least given her his number. Petra's voice on the answer-phone in their flat greeted him. Without leaving a message he cut the connection and scanned his contacts. He didn't have handy numbers for either of them. He turned to the couple again and placing his bag on his chair, he asked them to save his place. Would they think the bag contained a bomb? He didn't want to get the clothes out. So he lifted it breezily and said it was full of clothes.

He made a circuit of the restaurant within two minutes. Had he been stood up? It didn't seem possible. He grew annoyed. What a waste. He could have used the time to try to interview the landlord of the pub and if not him then their neighbours. Then he went over what they had arranged. Had they spoken German or English? He couldn't remember. Then he remembered what he had said in English. "We'll meet at half one," he had said. The sinking feeling in his stomach came before the thought that she could have thought in German. *Halb eins* was twelve thirty. Had she been here over an hour ago?

He thought of rushing back to Petra and Robert's and searching for her number. He'd skip lunch as evidence of his penitence. He was being silly. He picked up the menu and ordered a submarine sandwich and a cola.

A uniform buzzed him through the utilitarian reception area after he presented his identification. "You leave those sandwiches?" Dannaks nodded. "A couple of the guys are down with Rameses Revenge. You'll probably be hearing from the chief." Dannaks could only apologise.

On the way Dannaks had dropped into Patel's. Taking him to one side he told him to expect a surprise visit from the health authorities. Patel thanked him, but assured him that he had nothing to hide. His kitchen was clean.

He climbed the stairs to the deserted offices on the third floor. Unlike the *Schupo*, the *Kripo* rarely worked shifts. There were two offices each with a pair of desks facing one another. A third office on the opposite side of the corridor belonged to the boss. On that same side was a utility room with sink, kettle, filter coffee machine and small refrigerator. Finally there was a room with a PC, photocopier and fax machine. This was their floor. The rest of the building belonged to the *Schupo*. Space had decreed housing REX in a standard police station. He was disappointed that they had no interview room. That meant contact with the *Schupo*, something Dannaks always tried to keep to a minimum.

He entered the first of the two offices.

The room reminded him of a school classroom: high ceilings, mustard-coloured walls, old single-glazed sash windows. The space above meant cold in the winter and the two windows meant airless in the summer. The only advantage over the *Polizeistern* was the thickness of the walls. It made the rooms virtually soundproof. The Polizeistern was a typical modern building of glass and steel and lacked this feature.

For the first time he had doubts whether moving to REX was a step in the right direction.

The word REX could be taken to be a play on the German word *rechts* which meant right and referred to everything that was politically right; for example right-wing radicals or extremists. However, the work entailed not only attacks on *Ausländers* or left-wingers or sympathisers, but conversely attacks by Ausländer-groups or left-wing extremists upon right-wingers. REX stood for Racism and Extremism.

Dannaks picked up the small pile of papers and files that had been placed squarely on his desk. A list of important telephone numbers. A list of REX's duties. A file of statistics and propaganda, including a graph of right-wing disturbances.

He stared at the graph until he realised that he was drifting. He could take these papers home. Looking at his boxes to be emptied he sighed. His colleague's desk was clear. This could only mean one of two things. Either it was a good policy, hinting at efficiency or it was the opposite. Either the man was terribly organised or he had so little to do he was on top of his work.

Dannaks opened one of his cardboard boxes. He placed his plastic holder, containing pens, pencils, highlighters, stapler, scissors and a roll of Sellotape on his desk. He tore off the heavily doodled top sheet of his blotter – a new job, a new sheet. He was deciding whether to take a break from unpacking to write up his report when the telephone rang.

"How did you get this number?" Dannaks asked.

"Elementary, my dear boy," Uwe answered, in heavily accented English. "How are you settling in?"

"Slowly. The sandwiches didn't help."

"Nobody died." The line crackled. "I thought you'd like an update before *I* went to bed."

"Thanks."

"You missed the fireworks. The men they nabbed at the stakeout weren't Raul's."

"What?"

"OK said they were from a rival gang. They might have enough to break them up."

"And Raul?"

"He's gone."

"What do you mean?"

"Packed up and gone."

"Fled?"

"Looks like it. It's too early to tell. We got some of his gang. And we may be able to peg some minor offences on them. OK think he hit the other gang as a favour to the new gang boss. They won't let on who. But somebody's got to fill the vacuum." At the very least his departure would precipitate turf wars. "Whatever, Raul's in the wind."

"Who gave the command to go? I mean somebody should have checked they were not Raul's men."

"It was a botched job." So that was it. Luisa was a failure. The early morning breast-beating had been premature. He had never expected a fanfare, but last night had given cause for at least a few trumpet blasts. He bit back saying that his gut feeling had been right. Detlef's head was now squarely on the chopping block.

"So Raul had been planning to pull the plug for a while," said Dannaks.

"Yeah. It's too neat. There're no loose ends."

"Including Freddy." Uwe didn't answer. "He'd probably been given disinformation for a while."

"Maybe."

Talk of Freddie was a no-no and Dannaks sought something positive to say. When he did, he couldn't quite dispel the despondency from his voice. "I suppose you could say we scared Raul enough to send him home."

"Who knows? He may not be out of the picture. He could be running things from wherever he is." Uwe again fell silent before perking up. "We heard about the pub too. The proprietor said he couldn't remember any of his attackers. He said they all looked alike. And the skinheads we nabbed said they were innocent bystanders. Coming to see what the commotion was." Dannaks knew that they would get off lightly: cautioned or fined. Those that could be tied to the attack would claim drunkenness and also get off lightly.

"I think you're right about Freddy," Uwe said. "The location was false information. Not only to mislead us, but also to trap Freddy." He was thinking aloud. "Last night's operation confirmed their suspicions."

"And probably signed Freddy's death warrant." Dannaks regretted the suggestion. Uwe and Freddy went back a long way.

"Perhaps."

"You don't think Freddy could have been bought off?" he asked, backtracking.

"No." They both knew he had turned down lucrative opportunities in the past. His reason for turning informant could not be purchased.

Uwe was silent for a moment.

"I think I'll go round to his flat. If he's not there, his neighbours or landlady might know something. Then I might try his local this evening. He was – is – a keen *Doppelkopf* (card game) player. Or do you think it's too soon? We could be endangering him?"

"Snooping around can't do any harm," said Dannaks. "You

know how these things are. Being sought by us can give him some street cred."

"Do you fancy coming along?"

"I'll come to his local for an hour or so, but I'll pass on the trip to his flat. What's the pub called?"

"*Der Windjammer.*"

19:20

"Where are they?" asked Cenk.

"They'll come," said Hasan.

"I thought one of us could carry a camcorder," said Nazim.

"That's not a bad idea," said Hasan.

"The police do it."

"Suggest it."

They were silent for a moment, Nazim glowing with his idea.

"What time is it?" he asked.

"You only asked five minutes ago," said Cenk.

"So, what time is it?"

"Five minutes later."

"What did you tell me last time?"

"It's seven twenty," said Hasan, making no attempt to hide his exasperation. They had arrived ten minutes to seven at the appointed rendezvous: the place where Faruk had been attacked. Three others from that morning had also turned up at the agreed time of seven o'clock.

"Basha's always late," said the man who had introduced himself as Bilal. Cenk struggled to remember the names of the other two. "He likes to make an entrance."

"Basha? Why do they call him that?" asked Nazim. The three of them knew that this was Murat's tag.

"I don't know," said Bilal.

"I know," announced another. "He got it from a cousin who'd worked in London. He was over for a couple of weeks and came to the club. He told us of a film, whose main character was a comical Turkish officer: a Bimbashi. He was always trying to be cool and make it with women, but always blew it. He said he was a spitting image of Murat: same wedge moustache, same joined eyebrows. And Bimbashi became Basha. He said that in English to bash is to beat. So it stuck."

"Basha," Nazim chuckled.

The roar of motorbikes cut him down. The riders drove straight towards them and for a moment Cenk thought they were under attack.

The foremost rider removed his helmet. Murat smiled at them. There were six of them, all dressed in black, weathered jeans, leather trousers or tracksuits. The shirts or T-shirts were black as were the bomber-jackets. Only their socks were in some cases contrastingly light. Murat and another were wearing weight-lifter's finger-less leather gloves.

"What's this?" asked Hasan.

"Mobility, *Lan*," said Murat. They had dismissed the idea of using cars to patrol because they couldn't agree on sharing petrol costs. Four at the morning meeting were unemployed and most didn't want to spend money.

"*Hammer*," exclaimed Nazim, using the German word for strong or powerful.

"You're late," said Hasan. Arriving together made it obvious they'd met elsewhere.

Murat ignored him and Hasan continued. "I had hoped we could have split into two balanced groups. Some of your karate friends could have helped us." Murat smirked. "You should have said something."

"Stay loose. With wheels we can get about and –" he reached into the pannier behind the saddle and pulled out two handies "– with these we get to you in minutes." He gave Hasan one.

"Why can't I use my own?"

Murat raised his eyebrows and looked at those about him with incredulity. "These are throwaways. Their numbers are under favourites."

Hasan wanted to ask why they needed throwaway handies, but Nazim who had been itching to speak got in first. Cenk thought he was afraid someone would steal his idea and reap the glory from the group. "I er," Nazim said, "thought we could carry a camcorder."

Basha snorted. "So you play Steven Spielberg, you *Lutscher* (sucker)? We do the beating and you hide behind the lens."

"I thought it was a good idea," said Hasan.

"You want film, use a handy."

"Why can't we just exchange handy numbers?" asked Cenk. "We've all got one."

"Use your *Birne* (literally pear/bulb/nut – here brain). You want us linked?" said Murat. "I expected so an idea from him," he nodded to Nazim. "Anyway, it'd take too long." This had not been discussed that morning. Murat had brought up other ideas for the gang. He wanted an initiation for new members. There was even talk of a death circle. (Gang members would surround and beat a new member.) Hasan had successfully argued against him. "Now, have you thought of a name?" He was referring to a name for their group, the topic that had concluded their morning meeting. In case there was publicity and for everyone to understand their cause, Murat had suggested that they choose a German name. The ideas had started off seriously, but had quickly degenerated into jokes, bringing the meeting to an inconclusive end.

"Because we're a kind of citizens' militia, we could be," Hasan hesitated, "the *Altona Schutzengeln* (Altona protecting angels)."

"What?" Murat exclaimed. "We need something more alpha than that. It sounds like a bunch of fairies."

"Have you an idea?" Hasan knew the answer but he had to ask.

"*Schwarzer Freitag* (Black Friday)."

"That's no good. It sounds like a terrorist organisation. We want something that represents what we're about."

"That is what we're about. It refers to our Farrie."

Cenk wondered whether Murat knew Faruk to call him Farrie.

"It's not. It hints at revenge. We're here to protect."

"We're defenders not attackers," Cenk added.

"Well," began Murat, "until we come up with better, we'll stick it. Vote it. All those in favour?"

All the riders raised their hands, as did Nazim – probably in the hope of redeeming himself in Murat's eyes – and one of the other walkers.

"Looks like you're outnumbered," said Murat.

Cenk realised that there was no use protesting that the vote had been undemocratic because it had been cast only against Murat's choice. However, he had not given up. "The name's too aggressive. What about Farrie's *Friedenskorps* (Peace Corps)? Or *Friedenstruppen* (Peace troops)? Or–"

"We've voted," snapped Murat.

"But–"

Hasan hushed him with a gesture of his hand.

From that moment on Cenk decided to call Murat Basha. Not to his face, but to himself. He saw now how he strove to be cool and ended up being un-cool. The cracking of the walnut that morning was just such an example. Had he positioned the bowl before they arrived? After their morning meeting Hasan had pointed out that it was May and the nuts would have been old and brittle. But now he was assuming leadership. Yet, without Hasan he had no legitimacy. The community, especially the community leaders would not accept him. He was little more that a street gangster, marginally above skinning school kids: relieving them of their handies and MP3 players. Cenk knew that Hasan thought he could harness Basha and his followers. He wondered whether he now had doubts.

"We shouldn't be loafing around here arguing," Basha said. "We should be hunting."

19:24

Dannaks looked out across the dark harbour to the multitude of cranes that bristled the hushed panorama. Lights winked. An occasional echoing clang punctured the lulling sound of the water. It was too dark to see the workers, but the slow movement of containers and the long swing of cranes attested to their presence.

He turned at the sound of a car's tyres upon the cobbles. Uwe's car passed him in the search for a parking place. They acknowledged one another with nods.

Two minutes later he was at his side.

"Good morning," said Dannaks.

"I've been up since four," Uwe returned.

They both leant upon the stone parapet and viewed the scene before them.

"All settled in?" Uwe asked.

"More or less. I've inherited the department's worst chair, the keys to one side of the desk are missing and I've no cupboard space."

"As good as home, then."

"You mean hour null." Yes, out of the modern *Polizeistern* and into ancient police station.

They were quiet for a moment. "We could have done with you on the interrogations. Schmidt and Pescalles went down during the night. And my stomach is still a little dickey. Anyone could think you poisoned the team on purpose."

"We've had our moments but I wouldn't have poisoned you. And Lampe was fine. Did he eat anything?"

"I don't know."

"And I wouldn't have poisoned the *Schupo* at my new place of work, would I?"

"Hey, you don't have to prove anything to me. I'm just saying what it looks like."

Uwe was five years older than Dannaks and the more cynical of the two. His ambitious keen edge had long been dulled by disillusion. Looking for Freddy in his free time was an exception. He had been working with the informer for the last six years.

"There was a mountain of paper on my desk," Dannaks began. "I think I'll be spending my first month reading."

"I wouldn't believe that."

"No." Dannaks smiled. "Not if a graph of right-wing activity is anything to go by."

The one-way street was relatively dark. The worn cobbles shone as if wet and complemented the dappled light upon the water. Apart from *Der Windjammer* the street was made up of tall houses. At one time they could have been used for storage. Now they were flats for a motley of people, from prostitutes, pimps and petty criminals to law-abiding people who worked in the harbour or on the Reeperbahn.

"I saw Freddy's landlady," said Uwe despondently. "She hasn't seen him. And a neighbour said Freddy had promised to return a film last night."

Dannaks didn't speak.

"Did you hear what I said?"

"Yes."

"Sorry," said Uwe, irritated by his colleague's silence. "I didn't want to interrupt."

"I need to tell you something." Dannaks continued to stare at the harbour activity. Then, as if talking to the scene before him, he told Uwe of Detlef's proposal. When he finished it was Uwe's turn to be silent. "That's it," he said, in case he thought there was more.

"Let me get this straight. Detlef says someone in authority thinks there's more dirt to clean up. But this someone can't have anything to do with cleaning up. Detlef wants little to do with it too. And they want you to unofficially investigate. If whoever it is has suspicions, why can't they set up a proper investigation? It doesn't make sense. What are you going to do?"

"I don't know."

"And why now?"

"Because I'm out of the department. Independent, I suppose."

"Keep me out of it."

"Okay."

"You're going to do it, aren't you?"

"I don't know."

"I do." Uwe shook his head. "You're a mug."

The two men started to walk towards the pub.

"I'll lead," said Uwe.

"It's your show. I'll get the drinks."

"Sounds good."

The heavy door opened onto partially parted brown curtains as thick as blankets. They pushed them aside to enter a small L-shaped lounge. Everywhere was dark oak and brass fittings. The heavy curtains suited the place, but there was nothing seafaring about it. The brass fittings could well have been oversized belt buckles, tack from horses and coaches. Even the barometer behind the bar was modern. Fair weather. Tall stools stood at the bar; otherwise curved backed wooden chairs surrounded rectangular tables. At either end of the 'L' were polished oak partitions topped by a window of coloured glass squares. These private areas were special places for the regulars. Indeed, although the place was relatively empty, Dannaks had the feeling that most of the seats had names carved upon them. Two old men and a woman sat at a corner table next to a partition and another old man sat alone reading a paper in one of the cubicles. The barman was the only other person present. He looked up from his paper.

"Good evening," greeted Uwe.

The man nodded.

Uwe introduced himself and flashed his brass *Kripo* tab. "We're looking for Hermann Witzeling." Freddy was his informer's code name.

The barman's face remained expressionless. "I don't see him."

"When did you last see him?"

"I have no idea."

"A Pils and a dry white wine," said Dannaks.

Their order did not please the man but he complied nonetheless. Dannaks did not think it was because he had ordered wine in a drinking men's pub.

Craig was struck by the vibrancy the moment he left the S-Bahn station, Altona.

Although the buildings resembled those of the up-market area of Eppendorf with their strange mixture of Art Nouveau and Victorian styles: box windows, balconies with bulging black wrought-iron work, even some mock pillars. Crowning it all were ornate undulating gables extending beyond the roofs, reminding Craig of the headboards of beds, the graffiti betrayed a different culture.

The whirlwind of kids weaving between the parked cars that choked the street and the clumps of languid dull-eyed youths further testified to the change in culture. A German neighbourhood would be deserted.

As he neared his destination he was aware of being watched. But he felt more wary than endangered.

At the front door he adjusted his shoulder bag containing his notepad, pens, dictation machine, spare batteries and camera.

He scanned the intercom for the family's name. The door was wide open – another cultural marker – but he wanted to announce himself. He stated his surname when a male voice crackled an almost unrecognisable: "Hallo?" At the unnecessary buzz Craig glanced about the street. Some forms were at the windows of the nearby houses. The kids too, latching on to the curiosity of the youths, had paused to look in his direction.

Ascending the stairs he noted the seediness of the inside of the building. Carina's place was similar. The hallway always seemed dull. Although the tenants paid for the cleaning of this common passageway the carpets were always of the hardwearing, drab type. The paintwork or wallpaper was similar. It was an area that was cleaned but rarely renovated.

The true yardstick, of course, was how people individualised their flats.

A man stood in the open doorway to one of the two apartments on the third floor. He wore a herringbone jacket that despite its essential Englishness only served to highlight his foreignness. It was a phenomenon that had always puzzled Craig. He had seen it many times with English flat caps on Greeks and Italians, for instance. Under the jacket the man wore a wine coloured jumper which Craig thought was sleeveless. This covered a tired shirt that he had buttoned up to the neck. It had a faded pattern and weak collars.

On one shoulder, at the edge of the neck of the jumper he could see part of one of his braces that evidently held up his charcoal grey trousers. The man's wiry hair was dark with flecks of grey. He sported a full moustache that had started to thin. His bluish stubble bespoke of a man who really needed to shave more than once a day. His nose was long and thin and his skin was dark, almost olive green. Despite the severe look in his eyes, his features were neither lean nor hungry. His eyes alone had a predatory look, but his furrowed brow and creased face, a face etched out of wood rather than granite, softened him. Craig had the feeling that the man had been through a lot and had maintained his dignity. He was no taller than Craig, yet perhaps because of his experience he appeared so.

The day had been warm, but nothing had penetrated this windowless area. Every second floor of the stairwell had a window covered in a film of grime. Thus the man's jacket, jumper and shirt were not excessive.

Craig became unnerved when his smile was greeted with suspicion. They shook hands and Craig repeated his name.

"Thanks for letting me see your son."

The man remained gruff, "Yes. We have enough of reporters. But you English. Correct? Yes. Maybe you different."

"What do you mean?"

"Not so useless, like Germans. International publicity maybe makes people notice."

Craig merely nodded and was glad of the respectful hush as if entering the intensive care unit of a hospital.

There was a horribly awkward moment of silence as he tried to remove his shoes. The entire family's footwear was just inside the flat door. The man, who wore slippers, used the moment to slip off his jacket and hang it up. He was indeed wearing a sleeveless jumper.

Craig rapidly surveyed his surroundings as he padded into the family's lounge. He didn't want to immediately whip out his notebook. Therefore his mind worked furiously, trying to take in all the details of the flat to get a feel for the people.

The furniture was durable and functional and reminded him of what he had seen in former Eastern Bloc countries. What the family considered important – whether it be a sofa, dining table, chairs or shelving – or what they had inherited was usually the most expensive item. Generally it stuck out like a sore thumb. The luxury of style in such homes always gave way to practicality and cost.

On one wall was a six by three rug. It had a simple pattern with a base colour of burgundy. He had seen a map of Turkey in the hallway and in here hung the sickle-moon and star flag of Turkey. A framed extract from the Koran shared a wall with some shelving. The piece was an elegant, and as far as Craig was concerned, indecipherable mass of Cyrillic squiggles. However, he recognised it to mean: "There is no god but God and Mohammed is his envoy."

The large television was imposing and perhaps demanded the tower of machinery: a video recorder, BluRay player and satellite receiver.

The front door behind him opened. "Aloha," called a woman's voice. The girl on the sofa scowled and the toddler sitting next to her beamed.

Behind him their mother was removing her shoes. Craig was intrigued by the Hawaiian greeting, but the father's expression was severe and the mother's one of embarrassment bordering on shame.

Eventually the family were assembled in the room. The large television was glowing in a corner, but the volume had been turned down to the threshold of audibility.

Craig realised that he was not going to be introduced and took the opportunity to take out his notebook.

"Could I take down your names?" he asked.

"My wife, Zeynep," said Suleyman gesturing the moon-faced woman, who was now at the dining table sewing something.

Craig hesitated and smiled weakly. The man saw nothing funny in Craig's floundering but immediately spelt his wife's name for him.

Craig reddened with the embarrassment. The man was doing nothing to make him feel welcome. He was directed to the daughter and son. They were sitting on the three-seat sofa.

"My daughter, Leila. L-E-I-L-A." Craig thought he could have spelt her name but he allowed the man his fun. "And son, Ali. A-"

This time Craig went on the offensive. "I think I'll be all right with that one." He caught the boy's eye and the latter looked away with a naughty smile on his face.

He kept up the offensive. "And could I have your first name?" In making this request he made it sound as formal as was believable. He did not want the man to suspect that he was in any way attempting to build a bridge of intimacy. The positions had been laid down and they were to be respected.

Out of the entire family the youngest child seemed the most animated. The daughter was either sulky or bored, the mother seemed indifferent and the father was virtually antagonistic.

"Faruk in the bedroom," said Suleyman. Then he hesitated. "You are reporter from England. Which newspaper? The Times?"

"I'm freelance." Craig pulled out his card. "I'm researching an article on racism in Germany. I can give you some London numbers if you want references. I haven't got them with me but I can be reached at this number."

Suleyman took the card and Craig felt him noticeably soften.

Craig declined the offer of tea.

"Well, you want see my eldest son, so let us see him."

The two men left the rest of the family in the living room and after a soft knock on a closed door they entered Faruk's bedroom.

19:49

The boy was sitting up in bed, apparently waiting for them to enter.

There were two beds in the room. The walls were covered with posters of pop groups, magazine cuttings of sports cars, war planes and ships, football teams and film stars. On the wall nearest the second bed were similar cuttings with the addition of space heroes, monsters and cartoon characters. Craig surmised that this was where Ali slept.

"Na, Monkey?" said Suleyman.

"Papa," protested the boy.

Suleyman smiled and glanced at the light fitting. "I call him Monkey because I caught him swinging from that." Craig looked at the central rosette that elaborated on the plasterwork pattern that bordered the ceiling. A thick twined cord emerged to suspend a shaded light bulb.

He was ushered to one of two dining table chairs that had been brought in for the occasion. Suleyman seated himself upon the other, placed nearer to the head of the bed.

Faruk's arms rested limply at his sides. He was naked from the chest upwards. High up on his right cheek was a purplish swelling; his nose looked sore about the nostrils and his bottom lip was split. His brown eyes were sparkling with a mixture of defiance and fear. Craig was perplexed by the fear.

The boy had the intense stare of his father.

"Hallo, Faruk. My name's Craig." Pause. "You know I'm a reporter and I know that you've seen some reporters already, but I'm from England. Like you, I'm an *Ausländer*. I want to ask you some questions. I promise I won't keep you too long."

The boy nodded solemnly and licked his broken, swollen lips. Craig noticed an exchange of glances between father and son. It was obvious who the boss was in this house.

"Don't be intimidated but I'd like to record what you say." Craig retrieved his dictation machine from his bag and held the small microphone towards the boy. He ignored Suleyman in case he protested. "It's just so I write everything straight."

He would have preferred interviewing the boy alone, but the father seemed unapproachable.

"I've read what came out in the German papers, but I wanted to hear it first hand." Then he smiled and as an afterthought added: "Perhaps, we'll discover something you didn't feel like telling the German reporters?" This was a wicked statement, but he was versed in using everything at his disposal to create empathy.

Craig began by asking obvious and superficial questions. Which school did Faruk attend? How did he travel there? What were the lessons, pupils and teachers like?

The boy's German was noticeably better than his father's.

When Craig asked him whether there were racial problems at school, he answered first with a shake of his head and then after a moment's reflection with a flood of insignificant incidents. Put together they amounted to nothing other than the cruelty and tormenting of school children. Craig related them to his own school experiences: fatty, four-eyes, wog, and curry-muncher. Nevertheless, he noted the venom with which the boy spoke of the heckling and pranks. From the sound of things, however, the Turkish boys gave as good as they got. Faruk admitted to having German friends.

There was an interruption when Ali appeared at the door. He asked meekly whether he could come in and Suleyman said only as long as he sat quietly. He charged in, jumped up onto his bed, turned and sat watching them intently.

After this pause Craig launched into the incident itself, again mixing the trivial with the noteworthy.

What had they been doing? Where had they been and where were they going? Had there been anybody other than Ahmed with him?

Faruk's answers were a mixture of vivid detail and sparse recollection. Of the attack itself, as he had told the police and reporters, he remembered little. It had happened too fast.

For the majority of the time Faruk chose to cast his eyes downwards. Whenever he looked up Craig tried to connect with him, but his efforts were thwarted by Suleyman's presence. The boy continually glanced at his father as if to verify what he was saying.

Ahmed and he had been alone that evening. After eating with their families they met up at around seven. They shot some pool until around nine then they went to a snack bar, setting off for home about an hour later. When they were under-way they were attacked. Turning a corner they found themselves face to face with about half a dozen skinheads. There was nothing for them to do but flee. Ahmed was nearly caught – he hit one of the assailants – and Faruk almost got away. A hand tried to grasp his shoulder, nicked him instead and he stumbled. He regained his balance and seeing his escape blocked by another skinhead, made a sideways dash for an alleyway. This was his mistake. They caught him at the mouth of the alley, dragged him into it and began to punch and kick him. He was not sure how long they beat him. He fell to the ground, curled up and tried to protect his face as best he could. The blows rained down on him. Suddenly they stopped. He peaked out and saw them running down the alleyway. Chasing them were about eight youths, two stopped to offer him assistance, but he was too frightened and despite his injuries and their protests he jumped up and fled.

Craig looked up from his notebook and glanced at the others in the room. Ali was wide-eyed with fear, although he had no doubt heard it all before. Suleyman looked enraged.

"Terrible," muttered Craig, shaking his head. Yet, he had the impression that the boy was a bit of a scoundrel. Perhaps the entire incident was the result of gang warfare?

"It's outrageous," snapped Suleyman.

Faruk remained silent, his eyes downcast.

"An unprovoked attack," remarked Craig.

"You surprised," said Suleyman, who despite his harsh tone had been softened by his son's recounting of the attack. "It's nothing new. We're used to it. I see it time and time."

Craig felt uneasy. This was the stuff he wanted, but it bordered on unabashed propaganda.

"It's in the language," he went on. Craig guessed that the man was referring to the little prejudices. For instance, that the cheap, gaudy-coloured, crinkly plastic bags used to carry groceries were called Turkish briefcases. "You have to live here. I have—"

"I think we've kept your son long enough," Craig interrupted.

"Yes," he agreed, although he was surprised and perhaps offended by the interruption.

When the three of them left the bedroom, shutting the door behind them, Suleyman turned to Craig.

"Are you interested reporting our plight? Really interested?"

"Yes." How could he say no? He was not sure Faruk's plight was enough for his article and wanted more, but he was wary because the man appeared to hold blinding convictions. Suleyman stared at him, nodded and then suggested they have some coffee.

20:15

Hasan's group wandered the streets until they grew tired. They took a break, stopping at a snack bar to eat kebabs and gyros. They stayed longer than necessary, but eventually mustered the energy, but not the enthusiasm, to move on. In the beginning suggestions of where they should go in their allotted area had come thick and fast. By the end of the first shift, before they took their break, they had covered three quarters of the allocated ground. An hour into the second shift their feet began to drag. As a group there had been an element of bravado, but the lack of direction, in every sense of the word, caused this to wane.

At eleven o'clock they were spotted by a patrol car that began to shadow them.

"Let's leg it," said one of the group.

Murat had said that should the police stop them they should demand to see a service number. Then they could claim harassment, racial discrimination, verbal abuse and if possible police brutality.

"We're not criminals," said Hasan. "We have nothing to hide."

However, Cenk saw that Hasan too sensed the uneasiness in the group.

Ten minutes later a second patrol car appeared in front of them and he was not surprised when Hasan whispered that they should be ready to run. The patrol car ahead of them stopped and the one behind them picked up speed. In a moment they would be sandwiched between the cars. One of the gang spotted an alleyway next to a restaurant on the other side of the road. The moving car stopped. They were going to be questioned. Hasan gave the signal when he heard the door of the rear patrol car click open. The group charged between the tightly parked cars across the road and into the alleyway. An officer shouted at them. Others gave chase. One of Hasan's group slipped on some shit, but quickly got up. The last one into the alley pulled over some boxes that contained waste from the restaurant. The two policemen who charged after them fell straight into the appalling mess. Without stopping Cenk turned to see the scrambling figures swimming in the garbage.

They made a number of turns, by and large using alleyways rather than streets. When they felt safe they talked excitedly of the chase. But within twenty minutes they were as bored as before the incident. For them it was a night on the town without the fun.

Someone suggested stopping at midnight and piling into a club or discotheque. Perhaps something of their Saturday night could be salvaged? But Hasan said that they should carry on until one o'clock as agreed. Other than the police incident the evening remained uneventful.

At one o'clock they called Murat's group, who'd fared much the same. Naturally they had covered more ground. According to Murat they had seriously patrolled and only stopped to eat. He too sounded bored.

20:15

Craig was trapped. Suleyman had twisted his sympathetic ear. Craig knew a lot of what he was being told, but he didn't want to appear rude and there was an off-chance he might hear something he could use.

In the late sixties and early seventies many Turks were drawn by the offer of employment and the comparatively big money. Before them the majority of the so-called *Gastarbeiter* (guest-workers) had been Portuguese, Yugoslavian or Italian. Germany desperately needed workers to build up the country. The work was mainly manual labour. Office work, management and the like were the preserve of the German people. This deepened a divide: a sense that menial work was the domain of the *Gastarbeiter* and nobler work that of the German people. And the split society became a society with tensions.

The divide was made official by the very word *Gastarbeiter*, chosen to signify a temporary work force. The German government had not foreseen that many would choose to remain.

In the early seventies Suleyman's father had left his wife and five year old son in Turkey. With many other men of similar disposition he had made the gruelling the three-day train journey from Istanbul to Frankfurt. There had been nothing to eat or drink except what they could carry. On arrival some internal company wrangle sent a group of them northward to Hamburg. Work was not a problem: the problem was accommodation. The newcomers could afford neither the deposit nor the rent. Suleyman's father had no choice but to share a cellar. At one time there were seven of them in the cramped room.

An obvious consequence of the relatively high rents was the segregation of the foreign work force into the cheapest parts of the city, creating islands of cultural isolation. Whilst Hamburg had no Little Turkey integration was hampered by the natural bonding within the community.

Many firms were willing to help the Turkish workers find somewhere to live, but few were prepared to help entire families. So Suleyman's father had worked hard to pay the rent, send enough money to his wife, put a set amount aside, leaving him with pittance to survive upon. During this time Suleyman's father – as he later told his son – had not lived; he had survived.

He weathered this hardship until he was able to rent a place just large enough for the three of them. She joined him eight years after his arrival and with Suleyman at school she worked as a cleaner.

The thirteen year old Suleyman had a difficult time settling in at school, not least because of his inadequate German. The culture was alien and the German children suspicious, if not scathing.

He had hated Germany.

With his family's support, that of his peers and the Turkish community he got through school.

And he had stayed.

Although he had lived in Hamburg for over thirty years, he remained a *Gastarbeiter*. His poor command of German didn't help.

He was Turkish in blood, culture and mannerisms. His children were of a new generation growing up in the German environment. They had been born in Germany and their thinking was more German than Turkish. They spoke Turkish, but they were only Turkish by blood. In Germany their appearance set them apart and at tender ages they had felt displaced. The problems of his children were problems with which he could not empathise. He could sympathise, but to him their displacement was inexplicable.

He was embedded in the Turkish community and culture. But he saw ambivalence in today's Turkish youth. They needed the community but were resentful of it.

Suleyman wanted his children to be proud of their heritage. He had told them folk tales when they were younger. They knew of Turkish history, especially of Ataturk and the Ottoman Empire. And of course he had made them study the Koran and follow the Islamic faith.

At the same time he had encouraged them to fit in. He had drilled into his sons, especially his sons, that education was imperative if they wanted a greater chance of acceptance. He was resigned to the fact that he would never be completely accepted. His sons were not *Gastarbeiter* and hopefully, if they were well-educated and could present a challenge to the establishment, they would be better treated and have greater opportunities.

Craig, who jotted notes, occasionally let his attention wander to the things in the room.

Except for items that had been grafted on from German culture the room could have been in Turkey. On the walls was a sepia of ancient photographs: parents, grandparents, great grandparents, uncles and aunts and children. There were some recent photographs too. The immediate family, colourful snaps of brazen life bursting from the mono-solemnity of the past.

He was aware of the familial hierarchy in the silence of the family in the room. And he could imagine the knitting of families making up the community; evident in the religious artefacts, the fringe on the patterned tablecloth, the faded wallpaper, and the proud display of bland crockery. There was an incongruity in the artefacts. As with any quarter in a city, such as a Chinatown or an Italian quarter, a great deal of their culture had been retained, but here and there some of the host country's culture intruded. There was an ornamental stein on a shelf and a model ship inside a bottle. A 1989 ornate plate with a photograph of the *Landungsbrücken* in the centre, commemorating the harbour's 800 year old birthday, stood alongside an exotic candlestick holder that was of Middle Eastern extraction.

All in all Craig associated the feel of the place with the late seventies: Suleyman's arrival.

Suleyman's wife, daughter and youngest son were all great, but exceedingly sluggish, readers.

"The police not interested in attack. They think we all drug dealers. But this *Henker* makes again fashionable to debate the Turkish problem. So Faruk in papers. But no name." Craig knew he meant anonymous. "Normally beating of Turkish boy not news. The reporters do telephone interview. They not really interested. Their papers keeping up trend."

"You're saying there's only mild interest in what happened to your son?"

"Yes. Tomorrow forgotten." Suleyman pondered for a moment. He picked up his glass by the rim and sipped the hot quivering liquid as he spoke. Because of the hour Craig had asked for tea instead of coffee. The beverage had come in a small handless glass with a gold rim and looked more like a generous helping of whisky than tea. Craig looked at Suleyman's gaudy chronometer with its bracelet of silvered-coloured links. He noted the fat dull silver ring with an amber stone that resembled a boiled sweet or something an American college graduate might wear. "The world is harsher place. If my son killed then outrage. But this also short-life."

Craig felt that it was time to assert himself and show the man whose side he was on.

"If you can get the numbers together, why not protest? It's outrageous –" he purposefully used Suleyman's word – "that he should have been beaten. The Germans should not be allowed to accept this kind of behaviour as normal. Such an attack should have been more prominent in the papers." He knew he was exaggerating, but in an ideal world...

"It is too small thing."

Craig became animated. "But it shouldn't be. Don't you see?"

"A protest is be registered."

"I know what the bureaucracy is like. You have to fill out a form to blow your nose. Why don't you take things into your own hands? Action is called for. Even without permission I don't think the authorities would try to stop you."

"No, it must be properly. Registered. Approved. But I don't know. My people maybe not happy."

"Then ask them."

"Maybe not bad idea. But not for beating."

"I don't understand."

"I was at work today. Farrie – Faruk – you not know... gets sick and bad headache."

"I didn't know."

"Monday he must do knock-out tests to stay in school. You understand school system? Faruk is at *Realschule*."

Suleyman was obviously proud of this fact and Craig nodded approvingly. A *Realschule* was the middle level of a three-tiered school system and somewhere between an English secondary modern school and a grammar school.

In the pause Craig had the feeling that he had missed something.

"You see, my son get better chance. With education he beat them. He can be part of system. I've pushed him a little, because he's a little rascal in him. I was at his age. Time iron out rough edges. But he has brains – from his mother." He smiled at his wife. "All children clever." He looked at Ali and then at Leila. "Leila is educated, but she not go further." Pause. "She is woman so not important."

Suleyman seemed to realise that he had digressed. "The tests start Monday. He can not. I call teacher at home. He say with doctor's note maybe. Leila call hospital. First doctor say no internal injuries or complications. Monday okay. Unbelievable. Farrie is hit in face and is sick and headaching and they say is nothing. These people racist. Doctor say superficial. You think hurt superficial?"

Craig could do nothing but shake his head in wonder.

"If German schoolboy attacked by Turkish boys no problem with moving tests. But no. They all together, the doctors, the teachers. The police too. They do nothing. No skinheads arrested. They not interested."

"Can we make this public?"

Suleyman calmed himself and then nodded slowly. "It do no harm. Perhaps school change mind and he do tests later."

"Did the doctor issue a medical note?"

"Yes."

"Why don't we announce the march, stressing that it's to protest against your son's beating and then, as an aside, mention that he's unable to sit these tests?"

Suleyman pondered. "Me make call first."

Craig waited out the telephone conversation in Turkish.

He thought the man would tell him whom he had called. He was wrong. "Okay, telephone. You have connections. Tell them about school, protest and they publish our name. You are right. They cannot stop us on streets."

"To make an impact we'd have to protest in the city centre, at the *Rathaus* (City Hall)."

Suleyman nodded.

Craig called Robert and discovered that authorisation wasn't needed to organise a march. Germany exercised a right of assembly. However, police needed to be furnished with the name of the person in charge, the proposed route, time and an estimated number of marchers. Once registered the police could only contest it if it was likely to be publicly disruptive or lead to violence or clash with another march. Craig related all but the last point to Suleyman.

"As for my article," Craig said afterwards, "it will take me a day or two to put it together. It'll be written in English." He hadn't decided what he was going to put in his filler for Robert. "If you wish, I can have the appropriate parts translated and you can check them before I send them off. I don't want to prejudice your son's chances."

"Parts? Your article not about us?"

"No, it's more general."

"You interview other people?" Pause. "You interview right-wing bastards too?"

Craig hesitated. "I don't know yet."

"Make sure you report right."

Craig nodded. He did not like being told what or how to write.

"It's getting into contact with them that's difficult. Don't forget, I'm an *Ausländer* too." Then as an afterthought he added: "I've been given the name of a chap called *S-Bahn* Stefan. Have you heard of him?"

"Yes." Suleyman considered something for a moment. "I don't think we get bastards who beat my son, but you talk to all racists, yes? You talk to politician Volker Herbst." Craig had already written him off. He could find enough of his diatribes on the net. And at some point writing about these people, no matter in what light, not only gave them a voice, it also gave them publicity. "Better, talk to Krohn. He is racist and he is police chief."

Craig thanked him, taking down Krohn's name.

"One last thing. What about Faruk's friend? I'd like to interview him."

"He not speak to you."

"Why?"

"He speak to no one."

Craig waited.

"No reporters."

"Can I have their number, anyway?"

"Cowardice in family. He still my son's friend. But he never come in my home, again."

Craig nodded. "I'd still like to try."

Suleyman disapproved but got up and went to his son returning with a slip of paper.

Shortly thereafter Craig left.

On the street Craig called the number on the slip of paper. Sure enough, Ahmed's father said they were not taking any interviews.

20:35

By eight-thirty the atmosphere had completely changed. Nearly all of the seats were occupied and there was the constant murmur of voices and occasional laugh. The *Windjammer* was a smokers' pub and heavy smoke had turned the place into an opium den.

Dannaks and Uwe knew that the clientele were aware that they were detectives. The message had gone round.

The majority of people were in their mid-forties, giving the impression that this was primarily a haunt of the old set. But there were two groups of youngsters, lads in their late twenties; a couple were totally out of place in suits with whetted creases. Everyone had the common denominator of appearing to be a character. Although they were not in pirate costume they projected that same brash individuality. There were liberal helpings of tattoos, rings, earrings and even a couple of bandannas; audacious statements lending the scene its *Jamaica Inn* feel.

There were no foreigners.

"You were right about the closed circle," said Dannaks, widening his smarting eyes in a vain effort to relieve them of the cigarette smoke. His skin was beginning to prickle with irritation.

Strangely this comradeship reminded him of his time in the *Schupo*. They too were a clique with their pubs and clubs. An officer's true friends tended to be his colleagues. Dannaks had been shut out of the warmth of this world. True, he was not a social animal and had

84

never been totally at ease in their company. But he had missed the sense of belonging.

"Yes, it may have been a mistake to come here," Uwe admitted. "See the big man with the red face to your left? The one playing cards? He's one of Freddy's friends."

Dannaks was enveloped by the futility of the exercise. Even if someone knew of Freddy's whereabouts, he or she was unlikely to tell them.

"I'm ready when you are," he said, drinking the last of his wine.

The two detectives got up and walked over to the big man. His face was not really red but threaded with tiny blood vessels. He, like the other three men at the table, ignored the newcomers and concentrated on their game.

Uwe placed his identity card on the table long enough for them to see it. Still the men ignored them. "We're looking for Hermann Witzeling."

"He's not here."

"Do you know where he is?"

"You're the detective." There were a couple of smirks at the table.

Uwe and Dannaks remained stationary. As if the action was a tedious effort the man slowly turned his head from his cards and then wearily lifted it.

"New shoes?"

The question seemed to be directed at neither of them in particular, but he looked knowingly at Uwe and then at Dannaks.

"What?" said Uwe.

The man extended his knowing smile. He then noticed Dannaks. "Warm?"

The smoke in the room had sand-papered Dannaks's skin and something like anxiety had unbalanced his metabolism and his sweat glands had gone into overdrive. He shone like a pig and was yearning to get outside.

"You're the one who's red." Dannaks hated primitive confrontation. He wanted to use his brain to detect. This kind of situation took him to the edge of himself. An abrasive edge.

The man recovered quickly. "I see from what you were drinking that you play the female role in the relationship." They'd been observed. "Why don't you go and powder your nose?"

"You're the one wearing rouge," retorted Dannaks.

Eyes flared and there was a moment's silence.

The man gave a dismissive half-smile to hide his contempt.

"Run along girls," said one of the other players.

Words could not span the sudden chasm of silence.

Dannaks ignored the insults and was trying to fathom what the exchange had meant when Uwe said that they would be hearing from them. The threat was weak but it was a way of announcing their departure.

As they left Dannaks glanced at the barman; he was concentrating on wiping a glass. Behind him the barometer registered stormy weather. The message had gone round.

Outside he took a moment to turn around and look at the building.

"Look at the upstairs window," he said. The light was off and the curtains closed. On the windowsill was a pink piggy with red-eyes that blinked. "A bull would have been better. Pigs are easier to come by, I guess." No doubt now that they'd departed the lights would go out and inside it'd be fair weather again.

Sunday
06:10

Heike saw the tramp but looked ahead. She was walking briskly. Near the harbour there was always a biting breeze at this time in the morning. However, she kept the man in the corner of her eye. Initially, she had been watching for movement for he was a man sitting at the mouth of an alley. One could not be too careful. But there was something in the way he was slumped that puzzled her.

She had left the hotel where the rates were charged by the hour and was making her way to one of the 24-hour cafés for breakfast. Being relatively new to the game she still felt abused by her customers. Somehow they could sense the resentment burning within her, misinterpreting it for spirit or defiance. Her fire was not yet ashes and emptiness. One of the older women had said that she had the radiance of a newcomer. It attracted the customers. She should take advantage of it, because it wouldn't last.

These back streets were deserted. From about 5:00 a.m. there had been an exodus from the Reeperbahn St. Pauli to the Fischmarkt. The Reeperbahn itself would now be worse than deserted: it would be desolate. Only incapacitated drunkards would litter the streets. Tourists spilling out of the discotheques bewildered by the fact of a new day; night creatures caught unawares by the passing of night, scurrying off home.

The Reeperbahn had shrunk considerably since a then unknown band called The Beatles had first played there in 1959. Many of the long-standing establishments had closed. For the punter there were still enough sex-shows, transvestite clubs, pubs, restaurants, discotheques and naturally prostitutes: some two thousand of them. Prostitution was not illegal. The main reason for the decline of business was the high cost of berthing in the harbour and the establishments relied more on tourists than sailors.

Behind Heike was an especially bad night. One customer had demanded Caviar, faecal-fetish, and another Natural sparkling wine, urine-fetish. Two fetishes in one night was unusual. But for Heike the adage 'these things come in threes' would be true.

Only when she had passed the alleyway, ears alert for the sound of movement, did she hesitate. She had taken another half a dozen steps before stopping. Tugged one way by curiosity and the other by the warmth of the café and breakfast, a chilly breeze forced a quick decision.

As she came adjacent to the alleyway she moved out towards the road.

The demolished cardboard box covered him almost completely. He was in a half-sitting position with his limp-necked head turned away from her looking into the alley. One leg was outstretched, the foot showing; the other seemed to be tucked awkwardly under him. She realised it was this awkwardness that had caught her eye.

Heike looked about. There was nobody in sight.

She did not speak to him because despite the awkwardness of his position he could be asleep. Instead, continuing to give herself the benefit of the doubt she stepped nearer.

Only when she was opposite him, just inside the alleyway, did she see the blood. Most of it was under the shadow of the cardboard. From where she now stood she could see his face. His eyes were pupil-less and there was something in his mouth.

She peered closer and then jumped back aghast.

Heike ran straight to the public telephone she knew to be nearby. She knew that the nearest police station was *Die Davidwache*, famous for being situated on the Reeperbahn, but she did not know the number. So she dialled 110.

The official who took the call at the *Einsatzzentrale* (operations centre), noted the details, ordered her to wait there and hung-up. He saw that *Peter* 15/7 was in the vicinity. In Germany a police patrol car was known as a *Streifenwagen*, but in Hamburg it was known as a *Peterwagen*. This was because the 1946 occupying British force called them patrol cars. This became P-Cars and because in the radio communication alphabet P is Peter the name *Peterwagen* was born. A call was patched through and *Polizeimeisterin* Stahl acknowledged it.

Stahl's partner *Polizeiobermeister* Vogt took the next turn and headed for the destination.

They were on the early 6:00 a.m. to 1:00 p.m. shift and this was their first assignment.

When they arrived they found a cold Heike stamping her feet to keep warm. Nobody else had come by. They found an even colder man lying under a piece of cardboard.

"No, I haven't touched anything," Heike answered Vogt. Stahl had returned to the car to make calls. "Do you think I might be able to get some breakfast? I'm freezing my tits off out here. I'll tell you where I'll be."

"I'm sorry; we'll all have to wait until someone from Homicide arrives. You can sit in the car, if you like."

An ambulance arrived during Heike's questioning. Seeing that there was nothing to be done the attendants had returned to their vehicle. Another call would send them on their way before the officers of the Homicide arrived.

Stahl returned carrying a roll of tape to seal off the area. Her partner was ashen. He was leaning forward, straight arms supported on bent knees, gaping at the dead man.

"What's wrong?" she asked.

Vogt was startled. "Nothing. Let's run the tape from that lamp post."

"Hey, I'm tough. I can take it. What's wrong?"

He stared at her for a moment, contemplating, and then told her to look at the man's mouth.

10:45

Craig arrived a quarter of an hour earlier than arranged. Carina had buzzed him in and he'd climbed the stairs to her top floor flat. This was a six-storey apartment house in Eppendorf. Built at the turn of the century, it was older than Petra and Robert's house. The façades were art nouveau with laurel and blossom plasterwork.

Carina had not been ready, but ten minutes later he was again on the street. Their initial conversation was awkward. He had apologised enough for yesterday's lunchtime misunderstanding. He talked of his meeting with the Turkish schoolboy, but walking he couldn't look her in the eye and gauge the sincerity of her interest. He spoke warily and hoped the intimacy of the pub would relax them. The walk was mercifully short.

Breakfast was a buffet and Craig followed Carina's lead: taking morsels, eating languidly and returning frequently.

They talked of everything and nothing. At times Craig thought that their conversation bordered on banter. For his part the reason was to deny the sexual undercurrents. He felt them. But he didn't know whether she did too.

She asked him about the schoolboy interview and at the risk of spoiling the magic he felt between them he briefly skipped over it.

"What knock-out tests? You said he is in a *Realschule*."

"End of year exams, I assume."

"*Realschulen* function on a continual assessment basis."

"I can't believe he lied. Although come to think of it, I felt I was missing something. Strange. Well, whatever, it's still discrimination."

"The father of the boy, Suleyman," she began, "sounds as though he really wants to stir things up."

"His son was attacked." His outburst shamed him, but she didn't seem to notice.

"You are sticking your neck out forcing this march," she said. "If it goes ahead not many people will turn up. You may even be marked as an agitator."

Craig smiled.

"You will attract all the wrong people. Leftists. Extremists–"

"Me."

"Me too, I suppose," she added. "But the majority of people will not be bothered. It is not that important."

"It should be."

His suppressed inner turmoil was stirred when they returned to her flat two hours later. It was quashed the moment she said that she had to leave in half an hour to take an aerobics course. She suggested meeting in the evening, but he had to admit that he was attending a right-wing concert. He quickly suggested meeting on Monday. When she said that the first day of the working week was her busiest, they agreed to leave it to calling one another. They parted with pecks on the cheeks.

Back at Petra's and Robert's flat he hid himself away on the pretext of working on his article. In truth he wanted to give them some free time. Nevertheless he did work with his text. Checking over his notes he came across the reference to Krohn.

He went online.

The bulk of the information revolved around a corruption scandal with a racist background. A uniform named Götz D had brought Krohn down and shopped a number of uniforms under Krohn's command. Krohn had then made some ill-advised racist remarks in public. Nonetheless he had apparently kept his job.

Craig knew he was straying from the theme of his article and when Robert asked whether he would care to join them for a walk in the city park – it was too sunny to stay in – he said yes.

"Can you tell me anything about the police officer Krohn?" he asked, as he put on his shoes.

Robert chastised him. "It's Sunday Craig. Even I need a rest. Get to the archive library."

"Go tomorrow," said Petra. "Information will definitely be open then."

11:20

Dannaks regarded his friend.

"We could go for a drink," he suggested. "Lunch?" They were standing at Uwe's car in a parking area of the UKE (*Universitätsklinikum Hamburg-Eppendorf* – University Clinic Eppendorf).

"No. The stakeout has done my weekend enough damage. I want to get back to Annelore... Thanks anyway."

They were silent for a while.

Dannaks felt the need to occupy his friend's thoughts. "They called you pretty quickly."

"I left word with KDD (*Kriminalpolizeilicher Dauerdienst* – 24/7 on-duty Criminal Investigation Services) to contact me should anyone resembling Witzeling's description turn up. They thought I could do a preliminary identification and also interview me. By the time I got here Witzeling's sister had confirmed his identity." Uwe reflected before continuing. "They said he was mutilated, maybe tortured." He fell silent again. "A prostitute found him in an alley at the Reeperbahn."

Uwe was talking to the Homicide detective when Dannaks arrived. Of course he needn't have come. The detective could have interviewed him on the telephone. He could add little or nothing to Uwe's contribution. He had really come to be with Uwe.

"That detective," Uwe began, "had Freddy's worldly goods in a goldfish bag." Dannaks didn't know what to say. "Everything that meant anything to him in a tiny plastic bag. His roll-your-own kit, a couple of rings, some scraps of paper and a wallet – empty."

"Maybe they can pull some prints from that."

"Maybe?" said Uwe. Both knew better.

Silence engulfed them again. Had they been women they would have embraced.

"Do you want a lift to the station?" Uwe said suddenly. He pushed his key into the car door.

"No, thanks." But neither moved. "Uwe," Dannaks began suddenly, "we'll get the bastards."

Uwe nodded unconvincingly.

"What about Detlef's proposal?"

"I guess I really decided just now. Are you with me?"

"Not if it takes up too much time. I've a marriage to look after." Pause. "What do you have in mind?"

Dannaks smiled. "I don't know, yet."

"I'll help. Within limits." Uwe looked hard at him. "I get the feeling you're happy about this. You've forgotten how it was."

"I wouldn't say I was happy."

"No," he conceded. "You've got the go ahead to play maverick and tidy up unfinished business. And you may get your teeth into the Henker investigation. I'd say that was your idea of paradise."

"Maybe." Dannaks felt rotten.

Uwe looked at his own shoes. "I'm sorry. It's not been a good weekend."

Silence.

"I'll phone."

"Not today."

He waited until Uwe left before he started to walk.

Freddy had been Uwe's informant but it was a relationship that had blossomed, not quite into friendship, but the next best thing: mutual respect. Of course Dannaks knew of Freddy, although he had not known him. He had heard his voice and seen him from afar. He had been in his mid-fifties; his character etched in the lines of his face. He had been of the old-school, where the use of firearms was the province of hardened criminals and not those who inhabited his immediate world. To settle a bar-room difference you'd put down your drinks and go outside for fisticuffs, return and carry on drinking. Nowadays an altercation often involved knives. The changing face of crime had set him firmly in the past and he had become a dismal character. His gruffness no longer had its sagacious edge and his gravelly voice had slowly been gutted to a rattle and wheeze: the result of years of roll-your-own cigarettes.

He had been in and out of prison most of his life. The petty nature of his crimes had meant minimal stretches, making him more a nuisance than a criminal. He had always been a party to a crime, either as a fence, buying stolen goods or as a middleman for items such as false passports. When his son overdosed he turned informant. With the fall of the Wall his Hamburg became a playground for foreign drug barons, who used the port to feed not only Germany but also the rest of Europe. As far as he was concerned they had killed his son. The idea of foreigners dirtying the underworld and bringing Germany down with drugs upset him further. Consequently the only information he had ever been willing to sell was drug-related and to do with foreigners. Strange that something positive should come out of xenophobia.

The cruel manner of Freddy's death would have been unthinkable in his heyday. The sad fact was that although horrible it was no longer unthinkable. His death was an indicator of the times: the changing face of an increasingly brutal criminal world. If there was such a thing, he had been a more acceptable criminal.

19:30

Cenk and Nazim and a few others of Hasan's original team had adopted the black uniform. Basha's team were dressed pretty much the same as yesterday: black jeans, trousers, Lycra cycling shorts or jump suits. Without exception they wore black canvas moccasins. What made them look ridiculous in Cenk's eyes was that they all wore headbands which were, of course, black.

The numbers had changed. One had dropped out of Hasan's group, claiming a prior engagement and three new faces had swelled Basha's group. Ponytail was conspicuously absent.

Everyone was on bicycles. This was a minor victory on Hasan's part. As a consequence of their mobility, Basha's protests were overruled and there was a trading of members from each group. Hasan gave up Cenk and Nazim for three lithe-looking, black-clad members of Basha's team. There was a mild altercation over the bikes with Basha claiming a lack of versatility in the ones of his new team members. They had normal bikes whereas his group had robust mountain bikes.

There was talk of Faruk's headaches and sickness. Cenk felt a buzz of collective energy in the air. Yet, why should this evening be any different to yesterday?

"I'm the only one with a handy," Basha announced.

"What?" said Hasan.

"The others forgot theirs."

Hasan sensed a ploy. "Cenk's got one."

Basha hardened. "Good."

The two groups agreed their allotted areas and set off. After a few minutes cycling, Basha, in the lead, veered off to the left. Cenk and Nazim bringing up the rear had no choice but to follow.

Cenk felt impotent on his cumbersome bicycle. He envied Basha's team on their robust mountain-bikes with their characteristic straight handle bars and deep-tread tyres: like tyres covered in small bricks.

Many main road pavements in Hamburg had bicycle lanes. They are roadside and distinguished from the pedestrian area by a white line or by being of a contrasting material such as redbrick tiles. These lanes are barely wide enough for two to ride side by side and the group of eight dominated the entire pavement, sometimes the road.

They stopped at Altona *S-Bahn* station.

"What are we doing here?" Cenk asked.

"Palm me your handy."

Cenk reluctantly gave it to him. Basha switched it off.

"What are you doing?"

He tossed it to a companion who pocketed it.

"Hey?"

"You'll get it, *Lan.* Trust me."

"But–"

Basha had his handy out. He put a finger to his lips.

"Hi, Hasan. There's something wrong with Cenk's handy. Mine's low on battery. Yes. I know. Look I–" He switched off the gadget.

Cenk looked on incredulously. Apart from Nazim and him it was obvious that everyone was in the know.

Basha smiled. "We're making a little excursion. You come or stay."

"Where?"

"Bergedorf."

Basha turned away and walked his bike towards the station entrance; the others followed suit. Nazim and Cenk looked at each other. Nazim, rashness masquerading for decisiveness, followed the black-clad group. Cenk's conflicting thoughts flashed through his mind. There were many reasons not to be led astray by Basha. However, he reasoned that he would have to go to make sure things did not get out of hand. He had promised to report back to Hasan. Finally, he had to keep an eye on Nazim.

19:41

After returning from the UKE he had strolled around the outer Alster. This took a large chunk out of his afternoon. Gulls swung above numerous small one-man boats with single white sails fluttering like unsettled butterflies. The sound of traffic disappeared under the swish of leaves of the trees at the path near the water's edge. There was a continual train of people going in each direction: joggers, couples of all ages, families, bike riders. The open patches of green that separated the road from the path had people playing football or Frisbee or flying kites. Queues formed at a wheelbarrow icebox of an ice-cream vendor and a hot dog stand and hindered progress.

Dannaks queued and bought himself a hot dog. He ate it on the move and felt slightly nauseous by the last mouthful. A sheen of sweat sent him to a space on a bench. He watched the boats and the walkers and took in the breeze.

Naturally the bust and Raul's escape continued to preoccupy him.

During the two years spent identifying the various gangs and verifying the affiliations, tediously sorting out the alliances, recognising the bosses, lieutenants, dogs' bodies and muscle, they had had minor successes. Even here Dannaks had his suspicions. Some successes appeared to have been lucky breaks: breaks that could have feasibly been handed to them on a silver tray. As if Raul was using them to get rid of his opponents. Unwanted gang members were taken care of in other ways. In other words the *Kripo* disposed of the competition. It was an aspect of the investigation he had championed and brought to discussion, but priorities meant that it remained talk and was never acted upon.

What could he do? The more he thought about it, the more he came to realise that the only way forward was to smoke them out.

Dannaks spent the rest of the day collecting his thoughts. He sat in front of the washing machine in the cellar in the late afternoon before *Frau* Schumann disturbed him and brought him up to date with the gossip. She was the well-meaning widow of the house: always on the lookout for the opportunity to exchange a few words. Depending on how you looked at it the exchange rate was a phenomenal, thirty-to-one: thirty of her sentences to one of yours. She genned him up on all manner of trivialities. He heard about little Hartmut, the son of some people in a neighbouring building, having had his bike stolen. She had not realised or accepted that he was no longer with the *Schupo*. All her well-meaning diatribe needed now and then was a grunt of acknowledgement. More was not required; indeed more was encouragement and would be buried under even more from her. She talked him through rinse and second spin, leaving him out to dry in the neighbouring room. That is, he was half way through hanging his clothes up on a line when she left. By then he was completely bewildered. For she had spoken of Fritz being found and he couldn't remember whether Fritz was a boy, dog, cat or budgie...

Washing was normally a form of meditation. He didn't enjoy such chores, but acknowledged their value. Reading the paper took him away from his work. Ironing often set his thoughts in free-fall. But he rarely ironed. His clothes had to be shoehorned into his small flat. That was why he favoured sweatshirts and jumpers. Doing the washing fitted with his current state of mind. He needed to think.

After the washing, he set about cooking his evening meal. During the week he was usually too tired to cook and generally didn't bother. A sandwich or a take-away often sufficed. Or he chucked a frozen pizza in the microwave, a machine he was convinced a bachelor had invented. Before he set to work he opened a bottle of red wine. Good for the heart. One of the few things he felt the medical profession had got right. It was a little early to start, but he let it breathe. He poured a glass and peeled the potatoes, washed them and put them in a pan of water to boil. He picked up his glass and took it through to the window to look over the Alster.

The papers he'd taken from his desk were still spread on the small glass coffee table. He sat on the floor and began to shuffle them together. He came across the graph again. "It's monstrous that such large gangs can roam about at will." The girl's words echoed in his mind as he followed the electric peaks and troughs of the graph. The peaks occurred on anniversaries: the Unification, Hitler's birthday. But there were other peaks too. A member's birthday? Simple gang warfare? Why hadn't they known of the skinhead gathering? Perhaps not Narcotics, but then Hamburg's criminal office for State Security or even REX. Could such movements be predicted?

The *Verfassungsschutz* (VfS – Counter-intelligence: equivalent to Britain's MI5) had produced the graph. They had combined *LKA* 7 data with other sources. Roughly put, the *Schupo* policed, the *Kripo* investigated and the VfS collated. The *Kripo*, notably REX's parent department *LKA* 7, may have enhanced *Schupo* reports with information relevant to the bigger picture.

Dannaks took another sip from his glass of Bordeaux, but continued to stare at the graph. Being single had its advantages. Not many, but some. Time was one of them.

His mind wandered and he looked into his glass. Red.

Freddy's mutilation had occurred after being dumped. The meagre amount of blood at the scene supported this. The mutilation was a warning. Just as the location was a warning. A warning to whom? Other criminals were the most likely explanation. Although a warning to them – the police – was not out of the question. Freddy's body had been found not far from *Der Windjammer*. Other questions surfaced. What had the big red-faced man meant when he referred to their shoes?

He stood at the phone for a few moments before making the call. A woman he took to be Detlef's wife answered.

"Dannaks?" said Detlef.

"Yes, sir. I, er, need your help. You know about Uwe's informant?"

"What about him?"

Dannaks explained, ending with: "I've decided to dig around a little. I'd like you to set up a search of Freddy's apartment after Homicide are done with it."

Detlef was silent for a moment. "Okay. I think I can swing it."

"Good. I want to search–"

"Are you sure you want me to know, detective?"

"No. But I'm going to tell you anyway."

After telling him he hung up and stared at the phone.

After a while he rose and searched the drawers that made up the lower half of the wardrobe. Then he had it. A Christmas present from his brother. Well, not really a present so much as a promotional gift from the health insurance company where he worked. It was a pocket-sized diary Dannaks had never started to use. More a notebook than a diary. He rasped the pages with his thumb; took the small pen from its spine and sat down again. He thought for a minute. Sipped his wine. Then he opened the diary on his knee and wrote out a cryptic entry on one of the days in the first week of January. "See K. at 15:00." He turned the pages at random and documented further appointments with letters of the alphabet.

19:45

The eight youths piled into a carriage. Only four bicycles, two per entrance area, were allowed in each carriage, but their overwhelming presence quelled any protest and encouraged newcomers to use a different coach. They travelled on the S3 northwards and changed to the S21 at the first station, Diebsteich, which would take them across the breadth of Hamburg southeast to Bergedorf.

Because they might be overheard Cenk discreetly pressed them for what they intended to do. Basha and the others larked and answered jokingly. One said they were going to pay a Kurdish family a visit. They then distracted him and Nazim by teaching them their ritual handshake. Nazim was happy to be swept along by the adventure. One of the riders pulled out a map and Cenk eventually discovered that they intended to "visit" a snack bar that was known to be a right-wing hangout. Someone said that a pub was attacked on Saturday and words to the effect that the skins needed to be shown that they couldn't rampage with impunity.

At Bergedorf station, near the steps descending to the exit at ground level, Basha shouldered his bike and dashed down the steps. The others followed suit. At ground-level Basha turned sharply and pedalled away. Cenk and Nazim couldn't keep up and, by the time they reached the bottom, the others were out of sight.

The boys looked about anxiously. Before they could begin to think of what to do the gang appeared at a corner and waved them over.

On the way to their target they passed a building site. Basha signalled for them to halt. Three of the gang collected bricks and handed them out. Everyone accepted them, stuffing them in their shirts or saddlebags.

20:41

"I'll start at the beginning," said Dannaks.

"Always a good place," said Uwe.

"I spoke to Detlef about what I want to do."

"Was that wise?"

"I need his help." Uwe was silent and the hiss of the telephone line came to the fore. "I'm going after Pretty Boy." This was Lampe's nickname. He was a flash lad, easy going, the brash sunny boy and snazzy dresser. Everything Dannaks was not. He had sported a trendy haircut, most of his hair on the left; perfectly suited to his undercover work in the pill-popping scene. *Kommissar* Lampe was their techno-drugs boy. The parties themselves were innocent enough, but fast money drew salubrious operators and violence. When he was caught selling the pills he had confiscated Detlef had merely given him a warning: a verbal slap on the back of the wrist. Everyone knew he used his assignments to pick up women. Yet despite a vindictive tendency, he was popular with the rest of the team. Dannaks was the newcomer. Because he had sent Lampe's cousin down, Lampe was his natural enemy before he joined Narcotics. Dannaks had no evidence against him, just a tingling in his gut.

"What do you mean: going after?"

"I could flounder around for months with this or I could go with my gut feeling." He didn't give his colleague a chance to interrupt. "So I'm going to try and smoke him out."

"Go on."

"Detlef will arrange for us to search Freddy's place after Homicide are finished. We'll be looking for his diary."

"What diary?"

"The one I have in my hand."

"Eh?"

"I'll hide the diary and get Lampe to look where I hide it. You can call me away. Use your handy or call me over to show me something. Whatever, he's got to be in the right corner and alone. We'll give him a couple of minutes. Then carry on.
We'll find nothing and break up. If he says nothing and the diary's gone; we'll know won't we? If he's clean I'll drop him. But it'll be hot and if he takes it we'll see what he does."

"You mean tail him?"

"Yes."

"You haven't got a— I'm the wheels."

"Right."

"It's all a bit iffy. Wouldn't they wonder why Homicide didn't find it?"

"Maybe. But his flat wasn't the scene of the crime."

"It won't take long for whoever he gives it to, to realise it's a fake."

"I know. But that's not the aim of the exercise. I want to see who he takes it to."

"Hold on. When they realise it's a fake, they'll know it's a plant."

Dannaks smiled. "Probably."

"It's not even Freddy's handwriting." Dannaks continued smiling and Uwe became irritated. "And eventually they'll tie it to you."

"Bingo."

"You're putting yourself up as bait?"

Dannaks met his gaze. "I've got to draw them out."

"I don't believe you. After all you've been through. You're crazy."

"What's new?"

"So the great plan is to shake the tree and see what falls out. And what if they don't react?"

"I don't know. It depends who Lampe meets."

"He may sit on it for a couple of days."

"He may." Now Dannaks was irked. "It's a chance I'll have to take."

"And you'll have nothing on Lampe even if he takes it. It's entrapment."

"I know."

Uwe was about to continue but changed his mind. "One day I'll be identifying you in the UKE."

When they hung up Dannaks felt bad. He should have felt the opposite. The search would go ahead and with luck Lampe would give him something. He was the panicky sort and the diary would burn a hole in his pocket. Of course, anything could happen. Lampe's contact could tell him to wait. Dannaks could end up spending the night on some street. Or a couple of nights. Lampe could even throw it away. The whole thing was held together by thread. It wasn't a great plan. It was a crummy plan. More than iffy. What else could he do?

As he sipped the last of his wine he realised what really bothered him. He was at a disadvantage without a vehicle. He needed Uwe. If he had his own car he'd be all right. He couldn't justify getting one from the pool. As long as he needed others he had to justify his actions: lay his crummy plans bare.

20:42

Craig had given up trying to get a drink. The mass of youths at the trestle tables that bounded the alcove of beer-crates was more than ten deep. Four burly men behind the makeshift bar were frantically wrenching tops off beer bottles and throwing money into a box. About five hundred were packed into the place. There was hardly room to turn.

On his way through the town he had noticed a couple of police vehicles. They were conspicuous but withdrawn, parked in side roads. Out here, easily a kilometre from the *S-Bahn* station and from what one might term civilisation there was none to be seen. He stopped and reversed his jacket when he was near the barn.

He recalled Carina's words when he told her how he was going to spend his evening. "I hope you are not going to make a habit of pretending to be a neo-Nazi. You have heard of the *Henker*?"

Craig was searched. "I'm not packing," he said.

"We're not looking for weapons." When he entered the hall he realised they were looking for recording equipment. A speech was in progress.

"... and I tell you to ignore the history books written after forty-five. That's the victor's history talking." The man's red neck strained in his collar and tie. Craig recognised him. Robert had made six hours worth of recordings. He'd seen the documentary profile of Herbst. "They tell you Zyklon-B was used to gas Jews. How could that be?" He extended his palms. "Zyklon-B was used for delousing. You need 26 degrees C for it to become a gas." He paused to scrutinise the faces in the crowd. "And I'll tell you, the so-called gas chambers at Auschwitz were not heated, so how could it become a gas?" One of the younger men behind him, also in suit and tie, began to clap. The crowd erupted. If Craig had been tired of living he could have shouted that the body heat of the tightly packed victims had been enough for the pellets. He too clapped. The man on stage nodded and then raised his hands to silence the throng. "I'll not keep you any longer. I know you want to hear the band." The musicians' equipment stood behind him. "I expect to see you all next Saturday at that shameful exhibition. We want to show Hamburg that the time for hanging our heads in shame is over." He began gesticulating, sometime a finger but more often a fist, all the time looking more and more as if his head would explode. "I want us to show the politicians, that they may hold the seats, but the streets belong to us. The time for holding our heads up is here. The time for saying I am German is here. The time for saying I am proud to be a German is here."

"Sieg Heil!" shouted the same youth behind him, throwing out his arm and extending two fingers and a thumb. The crowd responded with the same. Craig joined in. He was impressed and scared. This continued until the same youth, joined by those on stage in similar attire, began to sing "*Deutschland über alles.*" The crowd followed. The band sauntered on stage and picked up the song.

Apparently they didn't need to tune up. The speaker waved and he and his disciples left.

At the door Craig had made no attempt to pass himself off as a German. His German was good; his accent wasn't. His best bet was to say he was an American member of the Aryan Nation. Maybe it was a blessing that the music rendered conversation impossible. After all, he could find himself having to wax lyrical or, worse, being dragged up on stage as a guest speaker. He tried to appear nonchalant as he pocketed leaflets and flyers.

Mayhem prevailed. The band thrashed at their instruments and yelled lyrics garbled by the racket. The din was reminiscent of heavy punk. A body of youths bounced at the foot of the platform that was also made up of the trusty trestle tables. In unison they yelled the chorus and punched the air.

Craig tried to remain at the back of the barn, furthest from the thudding speakers and near to the entrance. The heat was unbearable and he was sweating. He had felt drained and refreshed by the aerobics. Now he only felt vulnerable. After the sport, he'd taken Carina to lunch and then an ice cream and walk in Planten un Blomen. When they separated their parting cheek kisses were charged. He would have loved to meet her after the concert. An evening could offer the night. Maybe Robert had been right: juggling romance and research was not easy. Hearing Herbst's speech had been worth the trip, but the rest was just head-bashing.

So here they were in all their glory, he mused, proud Germans. They were in complete contrast to the wasters he had met the previous evening. Black was the predominant colour, although there was a lot of combat gear on display. Swastikas, medals, badges and SS-insignia were in abundance. All the paraphernalia of the Third Reich was in evidence. Some T-shirts carried home-made motifs others carried the standard "Hitler's European Tour 1939-1945" print or pictures of burly youths pinning down weak *Ausländers* with their jackboots. The common denominator was blatant propaganda: racism, blind hate and uniting against the enemies of the German people. He did not dare to think what kind of weapons some of them might be carrying. The studded leather gloves he had seen on one of the men queuing to get in had been enough. They exchanged cold glances when Craig spoke, his accented German giving him away. But the man was distracted by his companions and Craig slipped into the crowd.

The gut-vibrating throb of bass and drums and the manic rush of the guitars unnerved him. There was something malevolent in the dark energy. A frightening amount of force was bottled-up and waiting to explode. And explode it did. A scuffle turned into a fight, which grew nasty with broken bottles, knives and knuckle-dusters. About twenty were involved. The fight carved a strange path in the crowd, recklessly pushing and forcing its way through the multitude, gaining and losing members.

In a rare moment of comprehension Craig caught the lead singer's announcement of their next song: "*Fleisch* (Flesh)". The crowd roared and Craig assumed it was a favourite until the music became the wall of sound indistinguishable from all their previous songs and lumps of raw meat began being thrown about as if this was what everyone had been waiting for.

Although it was only eleven fifteen Craig decided it was enough.

On his way to the entrance however, somebody was forced against him. He lost his balance and fell to the floor. Shadow and light distorted features, but the studded gloves gave away the identity of the man on the floor with him. Craig was more concerned about getting up, for knees and shoes threatened him.

Craig smiled as he began to hoist himself up, thinking their shared predicament was camaraderie. The man grimaced and Craig saw the loathing in his eye and before he had the presence of mind to take action one of the studded gloves slammed into the side of his face and he crashed to the ground. Feet stamped about him and he tried to keep his hands close to his head. Somebody fell upon him, then another. Everything went black for a second and he thought he was going to be crushed. The salty taste of blood was in his mouth. That and the music made him dizzy with nausea. He tried to push himself up and grunted with pain as his shin was stepped upon. Others were falling and pushing and grabbing. Then suddenly there was space and only a few of them upon the floor. He got up and squeezed and pushed his way to the entrance. And suddenly found himself outside. Bewildered, his only thought was to get away. The idea of questioning somebody in the relative quiet had dissipated and he ignored the loitering huddles. Then he was alone as if he was the last person in the city. The thought that the movement in the shadows on the opposite side of the road was not a plain clothes man but the *Henker* quickened his pace. Not until he was well on his way to the station, continually looking over his shoulder, did he use his tongue to probe the fleeciness inside his cheek and check his hurt.

20:45

The cover of darkness was too flimsy for him. His heart pounded and he had difficulty gathering saliva in his mouth. He wondered how he had come to be in this situation. The name Cenk meant warrior, but he didn't feel like one.

His original motive for agreeing to join Hasan and the gang was not because of any feeling for justice. This was part of the reason, but there was a deeper level: something he shared with Nazim. Had anyone other than Faruk been attacked he may have hesitated. However, they were not doing this for the beaten boy. They were doing it for his sister, Leila. Both of them held a candle for her. She was unaware of their admiration and they had heard unsubstantiated rumours that she had a German boyfriend. It did not matter. They knew the family well enough. Only another Turk would be a threat. In any case, here Cenk was, doubting, but hoping that word of his chivalry would reach her.

They had congregated on a corner diagonally opposite the snack bar. Cenk could see two huddled forms inside, but nothing that distinguished them as right-wingers. All in all there did not appear to be much activity. According to Basha there would be loads of right-wingers here. He looked disappointed. Was there a back room?

The snack bar was one of a small row of local shops, all of which were shrouded in darkness. It had a large, bright shop-window front rising from waist height. The door was at the far right. There appeared to be an eating surface or bar running round the inside walls, broken by a computer game machine at one wall. In the middle of the room stood high round-topped tables with adjacent tall stools upon single fluting legs one might expect to see in a cocktail bar. Everything was of white moulded plastic.

Nazim voiced Cenk's thoughts. "Is this really it? What if it's the wrong place?"

Cenk cringed at the traces of racy fear in Nazim's voice.

"Hide your baseball cap," he hissed angrily. Nazim was still wearing it back to front. He was shocked, but tore it off and stuffed it in his trousers.

Basha overheard them. "It's a Nazi *Frittenbunker* (Fry-up bunker). If you're going to drop your arse better run home to your mother's now."

The ensuing restrained chuckles were extinguished by the arrival of a dilapidated car. As if some divine power had summoned the necessary proof, two skinheads and a greasy-haired youth in a bomber jacket climbed out.

Basha looked at Nazim with questioning eyebrows. "Proof?" Then to no one in particular: "Allah is with us."

The three newcomers disappeared into the building and the vicinity was once more relatively deserted.

Basha spoke urgently and quietly. "We ride past and we—"

"We'll take out the wheels," recommended the one with the slicked-back hair and ponytail. He was already there when they arrived. The pungent stench of petrol surrounded his motorbike and Cenk wondered whether it was as well tended as it appeared.

"Good idea. A job for the boys." He smiled at Nazim and Cenk. They were probably the youngest of the group, but calling them boys had nothing to do with their age.

"Take out the second one. I'll take the first. You better do it good," said Ponytail, with a sick smile. "We don't want them wheeling after us."

Cenk wondered whether they could see the redness in his face. Dreading catching some of his friend's fear he avoided looking at Nazim. He had enough of his own.

Cenk wanted to say that he was not ready, when Basha gave the signal to attack. Then he wondered whether he would ever have been ready.

To him it seemed to take forever to reach the car, brick in hand upon his bike's handlebars. He was with the group and yet he felt sluggish and, in the open road, acutely vulnerable. He knew what he was doing was wrong, but jolted by the sound of the main window of the snack bar shattering and the ensuing confusion, he found himself hurling the brick with all his might at the front window of the car. Being of laminated glass the impact produced a dent from which a milky web radiated. Further bricks were thrown into the building and either met glass or thudded somewhere in the depths of the room. Nazim's brick hit the driver's side window and bounced off ineffectually.

Basha had paused at the broken window and shouted above the roar of the motorbike: "We're the *Schwarzer Freitag*. And that's for the Turkish schoolboy." He then pushed himself onward.

A sixth sense caused Cenk to look over his shoulder. Nazim

had stopped. Remaining on his bicycle he was stretching down and scrambling for his brick. Cenk saw the skinheads charge out of the building. They had not yet seen Nazim bent over on the other side of the car.

Cenk was caught by the flutter of a flame to his left. Ponytail had lit a rag stuffed in a bottle. He elbowed the rear side window and threw the bottle in. There was a bright flash and he revved his bike and roared away.

Without thinking Cenk turned and headed for his friend, shouting at him in Turkish.

Other members of the gang were disappearing down the road.

Nazim looked up, distracted by the flames and heat. For a split second he seemed not to realise what was happening and continued to try to pick up the brick. One skinhead was almost upon him. Then he had the brick. Cenk snatched it from him and threw it at the approaching skinhead.

"Come on," he yelled, arcing into the centre of the road, for his bike was now facing the wrong way.

Nazim launched himself off and pedalled like mad away from the skinheads. Cenk attempted to make a U-turn but his turning arc was too shallow and he was heading for a parked car. He had to stop and physically pick up his bike to realign it.

He kicked himself forward with a frenzied force and although he moved rapidly away he screamed at his leaden legs and his bike that seemed to have seized-up. He felt the graze of fingers as a skinhead tried to grab his shoulder. At first he did not seem to move; the wind was against him, the world was against him. Nazim was way ahead. Cenk heard the commotion about him, but did not look round. A brick missed him. Only when he had turned the corner and caught up with Nazim did he dare look back.

They had given up the chase.

Basha and the rest were gone. It had been agreed that they break up into small groups and head for the *S-Bahn* station separately or make their own way back, either as a long cycle ride or by entering the rail system at another station. Cenk and Nazim went back to Bergedorf *S-Bahn* station.

They were high on adrenaline when they entered the station. The others were nowhere to be seen. The two were so excited that they just looked at each other and spoke in broken sentences. As they waited for the train, anxious that skinheads or the police could appear, they interrupted their one-sentence comments on the event with talk of cycling home.

Only when they were safely on the train – even then they wondered who would board at each of the many stations – did they argue about whether Nazim had had time to smash the car window with his brick. His leg shook furiously throughout the journey.

"So you're the one who nobbled the E-shift," said the uniformed officer buzzing Dannaks through the reception area. He looked Turkish, one of a few but growing number of non-Nationals in Hamburg's police force. The integration and language advantages of uniformed foreigners were obvious, but it wasn't until a relaxing of the law in 1993 that it became possible to recruit them.

Dannaks muttered an apology as he pocketed his ID.

The officer's outspokenness unsettled him. He had drawn attention to himself. It was only a matter of time before the *Schupo* here tied his name to the Krohn scandal.

That raw feeling he had after a shower had waned before entering the building and, although he was not sweating, he could feel his familiar clamminess rising.

The third floor was a wakening hive of activity in contrast to the stillness of Saturday.

"*Moin, moin,*" greeted the man sitting at the desk opposite Dannaks's place. He was in his late forties and eating a banana. "The early bird catches the worm," he said in English. Dannaks didn't know what he meant. Was he trying to show off his English? Did he mean that he was always early? Or was he inferring that Dannaks was late? "I believe the Tommies have a proverb for every eventuality." Where was this guy from? Nobody used the word Tommies nowadays?

He put the fruit on his desk and wiped his palms on his trousers before shaking hands and introducing himself. Reinhart sat down and resumed his breakfast. The man was undoubtedly wondering why Dannaks had insisted on using his surname, but was quelled by the fact that he had agreed to adopt the familiar form of speech.

"You want me to call you: sir?"

"Dannaks will be fine."

On Saturday Dannaks had noticed the clean-swept desk opposite his own. Fresh flowers now stood in a vase on the desk. A notebook and a single file lay open, but the man appeared to be more interested in his banana.

The flowers intrigued Dannaks. They were an indulgence most officers couldn't afford.

"Bananas make one jolly," he announced. Dannaks sensed that they were not going to get on. He nodded the next statement away. "Lots of potassium, good for high blood pressure."

"A Peanuts fan, eh?" the man went on. Dannaks's Snoopy blotter sat squarely in the middle of his desk. "That's great."

"A present from my niece," he muttered and gave him an awkward smile.

So this was where all the odd balls rolled: into a quiet corner hole. He knew he was an odd ball himself. But this man could be pigeon-holed a "has been".

"What are those?" Reinhart was looking at the open box full of twists of chromed metal.

"Puzzles," he answered. "I find them relaxing."

The man nodded, but he appeared thrown. "The meeting is at eight thirty. I–"

He was interrupted by the telephone.

"*Soko* REX, *Kommissar* Keller speaking. Yes, one moment." Then to Dannaks with an intrigued look: "Homicide for you." Reinhart swung the moveable stand upon which the shared telephone sat.

The case officer introduced himself and said he had more questions about Freddy.

Essentially they had little more than what had appeared in the Press. The papers reported that a man had been found on Sunday morning. He had died as a result of a heroin overdose. Such an occurrence was nothing new. There had been 184 drug overdose victims in Hamburg the previous year. The harbour city offered the cheapest heroin in Germany. The fact that the amount found in Freddy could have killed a horse was not disclosed.

"Without a crime scene we're stuck. Have you any ideas?"

Dannaks thought for a moment. "No."

"Do you know of anyone else we can go to? We've checked his neighbours. His so-called friends went into a rugby scrum. We'll get nothing out of them. If you have any leads we'd like to hear about them."

"Of course." Sensing the conversation almost coming to an end Dannaks said: "I have a question." With Reinhart listening he had been unsure about asking the question. He waited a tick. "Have you seen this kind of mutilation before? I know that the Russian Mafia gouge out the eyes of their victims."

"I'd say the location and the mutilation were meant to convey the message: this is what we do to informants." Although the general public would remain ignorant of the fact that Freddy's penis was found in his mouth, it would be common knowledge in the underworld.

"Well," boomed Reinhart, as Dannaks replaced the receiver, "shit on toast," he exclaimed in English before reverting to German, "you're not five minutes in the office and Homicide is calling you. I can see I'm going to have to watch you."

Dannaks shrivelled.

09:15

Dannaks had been formally introduced at the regular morning meeting in Frank's office. Although his rank put him above the other three, he understood that he would initially be treated as an equal. He made up the second pair of the small team, whose predecessor had retired. Reinhart and his previous partner would have made a great team: one burnt out, the other on the way out.

"I'll pass on the *Einstand*," said Wulff. A newcomer normally bought something to introduce himself to the team, be it breakfast, afternoon coffee and cake or an invitation to buy the drinks. This was called an *Einstand*. Of course, Wulff was obliquely referring to Dannaks's poisoning of the uniforms.

"Then I'll give your HSV season card to someone else." Dannaks had noticed the blue and white flag in their office. He was taking a chance that Wulff, rather than Schuppenhauer, was the football team's fan.

"Alright," said Frank, before the group became too unsettled. "I haven't got much time. So let's get on." He checked he had their attention. "You've all heard about yesterday's Molotov cocktail attack. I won't go into the details. But we could have a terrorist cell on our hands. No one has claimed responsibility. Needless to say Seven–" he was referring to their parent department: *LKA* 7 "–has taken that one. We have a schoolboy who was attacked by skinheads on Friday." Dannaks sensed the unease in the room. They were getting the bagatelle cases. "I'll come back to that." He then spoke about the pub attack.

"It was a big event involving about eighty right-wingers," said Frank, reading his notes. "Thirty were arrested. Four were from Berlin, eight from Itzehoe and five from Rostock. The rest were from Hamburg and its surroundings." The fact that some had come from as far as Berlin, a three hour drive to Hamburg, implied that the event had been planned. "You want to add anything, Dannaks?"

110

"I was surprised by the numbers, but that's about all." He had noted that the papers had said the landlord had been attacked. There was no mention of torture.

"There was a concert yesterday. They could have been there for that."

"I was thinking of the organisation."

Frank nodded, his distraction showing that this was a new aspect.

Coming out of his brief reverie, he continued. "Seven knows of an ongoing battle between the Left and the Right. Maybe the snack bar attack has something to do with it. They've taken that, but they're short-staffed: illness, *Soko* Doermer, the usual." The usual was exacerbated by the fact that the entire service was understaffed: a result of over-enthusiastic purging and other cost-cutting measures. These things came in waves, often with a newly appointed police president, which coincided with a new mayor taking office. The service would bleed until it was almost dry, barely able to handle the daily crime, then there would be a recruitment drive, which would initially burden the overworked with breaking in the newcomers. By the time something akin to equilibrium had been achieved the process would begin again. They were currently in a low-staff period with rumours of a recruitment drive only just beginning. "Anyway, this Molotov thing has tied them up. They want us to take the pub attack. I get the impression it's just a protocol job." He looked at Dannaks. "I want you and Reinhart to take it. I'll get the initial statements to you about eleven. There are some questions that need clearing up. They said the proprietor himself wasn't very helpful." Statements were taken immediately after the attack. Follow-up interviews were routine. The initial statements would have thrown up questions. Anomalies between witness statements would need ironing out. Also things were sometimes forgotten in the initial aftermath of shock. Only much later something insignificant could come to mind. And because of its apparent insignificance the witness wouldn't think to bother the police. It was true that a majority of follow-up interviews were carried out on the telephone, but Frank obviously wanted them to get something from the proprietor.

"On Friday a schoolboy was attacked by skinheads. We've no leads or witnesses. The *Schupo* have received reports of unrest in Turkish quarters and they've put extra manpower in the area. Anyway, the boy needs to be interviewed. It's after five, when his father's home, so I won't bother asking whether anyone wants it." He waited a tick, but no one moved. "So I'll take it."

Frank waited a moment before asking the other three about ongoing work. Reinhart, Schuppenhauer and Wulff outlined their plans for the next few days. Frank made some suggestions and then dismissed them.

Dannaks stayed behind.

A phone call interrupted Frank before he could begin.

His small office couldn't be more unlike Detlef's. Knick-knacks did not clutter the surfaces. In fact the room was sterile. Books and files, a wall-planner, a calendar and that was it. Nothing personal. No family photographs, no clues to hobbies or interests, nothing.

"I intentionally said nothing of your past," he began after replacing the receiver. "That's your business."

"Thank you, Frank."

Frank nodded.

"Before you begin, I have to tell you I have some unfinished business with Narcotics. *Kriminalrad* Detlef Borchardt will no doubt call you." He explained Freddy's murder and, without going into detail, the possibility of making a search of his flat.

"I assume it doesn't end with the search. What time-frame are we talking here?"

"It's hard to say. I'll, er, try to limit it to my free time."

"Impressive." Frank smiled.

Dannaks couldn't gauge the sincerity of the smile. There was a hint of worry in his expression.

"I wanted you to stay behind for a number of reasons. I've got a meeting with the chief downstairs. He wants to talk about those sandwiches."

"There's not a lot I can say."

"Okay. I'll hear what he has to say. He may want to take it further."

Dannaks nodded.

"Good. We'll forget that for now." He paused. "I want you to take on any odd jobs from the rest of the team. This'll familiarise you with how we work. Some of the time though, I want you to support Reinhart. He's probably the least motivated. I'd like you to push him along, if you can."

Dannaks thought that Frank was being generous. Apart from

Reinhart the team was young and appeared keen. Frank himself looked to be in his mid-thirties. Reinhart was over fifty. He was one of those pieces of dead wood that never got promoted and was shunted from department to department. Most startling of all was that he did not seem to care. Dannaks revised his impression. The man was not a "has been", so much as a "never was."

"I'm probably going to say a lot of what you already know, but I don't want any misunderstandings about our work here and your position." Dannaks knew the pause marked the start of Frank's standard spiel.

"I believe in getting things done. I know many departments spend a lot of time at meetings. Well I don't do that. You and the rest of the team will rarely come into contact with other departments or the state prosecutor. I do that. You're freed up to get on with things that matter. This only works if I'm kept up to date. I like the entire team to be up to date. That means working as a team. The downside is that I'm not always here.

"You know the official reason for REX. And looking at your file, I think I know why you joined us. Well, quite frankly, you may be disappointed." Dannaks's brow furrowed. Had he made a terrible mistake? No. He had to get out of Narcotics. Whatever he was going to do here could be no worse. But then there was Reinhart. "REX was formed to ease *LKA* 7 – State Security problems. As you've gathered we abbreviate them to: Seven. I come from the left-wing department myself. Schuppenhauer is from the right-wing department. The other two are new." He began handling a letter-opener. "And, of course, because of its right-wing aspect, we were created to support Homicide with the Kai Doermer investigation. And the Markus Jensen murder. The so-called *Henker* murders. You'll have time to acquaint yourself with these cases. I know that interests you. We have our investigations on file here and copies of some of Homicide's files, but we're probably not up to date." He fingered the tip of letter-opener. "We've done some other work for Homicide: mainly legwork for cold corpses." Dannaks nodded. These were primarily the old unsolved cases where DNA analysis of old evidence looked promising. "The truth is that working with Homicide is an exception. Their cases may have priority, but the majority of our work comes from the criminal departments." He regarded Dannaks, who remained impassive. "We get the overflow – as you heard – the bum jobs." He placed the letter-opener on his desk and leant back in his chair. "Disappointed?"

"It's too early to say." Frank had said that within the team they dispensed with formality. He didn't want to be called sir.

Frank smiled. "Quite right." He leaned forward again. "At the moment there's no talk of us disbanding. You wouldn't have come to us if that were the case. The amount of work we get from the criminal departments almost eclipses these murders. Volker Herbst, the right wing politician, is stirring things up. Whatever they say about him, there's no denying he's a charismatic figure. And he's causing our department a headache. There's a lot of activity. The Asylum problem continues to irritate. And then there's Seven's budget." The bloody budget again. Was REX privy to some of the *LKA's* pie? What about Homicide's purse? And how big was their own? "Whichever way you cut it, I think you'll agree that we're not exactly a *nullachtfünfzehn Soko.*" 08/15 was embedded in the German language as standing for anything run of the mill. It originated from the novel of the same name by Hans Hellmut Kirst, which was about the MG 08 (*Maschinen Gewehr* – machine gun), the most common of which was the 08/15 built in 1915.

"I have a question." Frank nodded for him to continue. "There was a *VfS* graph of right-wing activity on my desk. I'd like to get the details behind it."

"I know the one you mean. We've nothing here. Seven may have something. Why?"

"Nothing. It's just an idea."

"Dannaks, we are a team. I know you're a bit of a maverick. But you've been promoted. I expect you to take on the responsibility of being my second in command. Understand? That means leading the team. There's no room here for lone investigations. Are we clear on this?"

"Yes, Frank."

"Okay. Reinhart can acquaint you with our work and our progress with the Homicide cases. You heard Reinhart. You're busy this afternoon, of course."

"Any chance of looking over the Henker files this morning?"

"I suppose so. An hour or so." Then Frank spoke as if he'd had an afterthought. "I'd like you to understand how we work here. I mean how *I* like us to work."

Dannaks nodded. If this was where all the oddballs ended up, who had Frank upset? He didn't appear to be an oddball.

"I believe in mixing with people," he said, leaning further forward and resting his forearms on his desk. "Showing a high profile," he emphasised. "Take the Turkish community, for instance. Many of them came from the countryside and are relatively simple people. They hold great respect for their community leaders – in particular a *hodja* called Cemal Atasoy. Turkish society is hierarchical. Of course the youth is a different matter. But don't under-estimate the influence of these men. They want to fight crime as much as we do and we liaise with them. There's a meeting at a tearoom this Saturday. It wouldn't hurt to show your face. There's also a right-wing rally planned, but there should be enough people to cover that one. Either way, could you spare a couple of hours?"

"Yes."

"I'd like you to get to know the Turks. You've got to understand their problems and gain their confidence. Learn some Turkish if you can. I encourage the team to work with the Turkish social workers. It all helps."

He turned to the windowsill behind him and picked up a thin book. "Here's an introduction to Islam. It won't hurt to read it. Most Muslims here are Sunni-Muslims. You can split these into the orthodox and a collection of other groups that come under the title of People's Islam. When someone mentions Muslims to us we picture the orthodox group." Pause. "Some of the community leaders are orthodox. They believe that life, the state and Islam are inextricably entwined. You can read about the five pillars of Islam and all the rest, but don't get bogged down. Nearly all the 70,000 or so Muslims in Hamburg are Sunni-Muslims of the People's Islam. They only follow some, if any, of the laws heeded by the orthodox. They drink alcohol, pray when the opportunity arises and not at the specified times, fast during Ramadan if it suits them and thankfully have no problem in separating state from religion. The Turks probably get singled out from the rest of the *Ausländers*, because they're non-Christians."

Dannaks took the book. This was obviously Frank's realm. It sounded like a passion.

Dannaks left the room. Reinhart was slouched at his desk behind an open file, but mumbling or grumbling to his notebook. He pocketed his notebook and sat up. "He gave you that, did he?" he said referring to the book Dannaks was carrying. "I started it. If I were you

I'd shove it in your drawer and forget it for a couple of weeks. He'll ask for it eventually. Don't worry there's no test."

"He wants you to show me around," Dannaks said, sitting and picking up the telephone. "And show me the *Henker* files."

"There's not much here. Didn't Frank tell you that most of our work is from his pals in *LKA* 7?"

"Yes."

Dannaks dialled.

"The truth is that we get the dross from Homicide and the scraps from the Seven."

He listened to the ringing.

"Certainly for Homicide. We didn't get the promising leads from *Soko* Doermer. Oh, we get complete cases from Seven. But they take the cherries."

"Dannaks," he announced down the line. Reinhart sharpened a pencil. "Hallo, Max. Is Uwe there? No. Tell him to call me, please."

"We get the crap, then?" he said, after replacing the receiver.

Reinhart nodded triumphantly. He had a welcome-to-the-pits look.

"You want to show me around?"

They left the room and Reinhart took him to the rooms in their corridor. He'd seen them all on Saturday. Then he took him to the ground floor. Dannaks wasn't really interested. He was introduced to the duty officer and the chief and then a wealth of others whose names were forgotten as soon as they were said. The subject of the sandwiches was conspicuously avoided, but he felt compelled to broach it and meekly apologised, promising to make good. All the time he wanted to get to the Homicide files.

Reinhart then took him past further offices. They peaked into an empty ground floor examination room and an unoccupied cell in the cellar, the walls of which were scratched with graffiti: the usual abuse, attempts at humour, infamy, immortality. Dannaks asked his standard question: "Maybe you've got an answer? I've always found it an enigma. How come, if the prisoners are stripped and searched in the examination room; shoe-laces, ties, belts and all sharp implements removed, they can still scratch the walls?" Reinhart looked at the markings and suggested fingernails or teeth. But even he was unconvinced. The walls and doors looked exceedingly hard-wearing. A trouser fly zip was their best explanation.

They climbed the stairs back to the REX floor.

During the train journey to the centre Craig scanned the papers.

The lead story was the Molotov cocktail attack by a group called *Schwarzer Freitag*. Tacked on the end of it was Saturday's pub attack.

A prostitute had found the body of some old junkie in the back streets of the Reeperbahn. He had overdosed in the small hours of Sunday morning.

There was no mention of the right-wing concert.

He had spoken to Robert about it over breakfast, mentioning Volker Herbst's talk.

"He's Hamburg's very own right-wing shooting star," said Robert. "He's the head of his own party. It's even named after him. The Herbst party—"

"Autumn party?"

"Yeah. And he's getting a lot of mileage out of the Cohen Holocaust exhibition."

"I thought denying the Holocaust was prosecutable."

"He's not that stupid. He's playing the Allies-knew-about-it card. It was in their interests to let it happen."

"That's not all, of course. He doesn't deny it; he denies the extent. It was exaggerated to make the Germans frightened of their own shadow."

"Or the shadow of National Socialism?"

Robert nodded. "In his own words he wants to give the German people their pride back. And he's whipped up a lot of support. Saturday's rally at the exhibition could be big."

"Where is the exhibition?"

"In the city centre."

"Hamburg?"

"You know of another city centre here?"

"Where exactly?"

"Near the main station."

His mind now buzzed with the explosive potential of Faruk's protest march in the city centre and a possible clash with Herbst's right wing rally.

Reinhart took Dannaks to the storeroom, which housed the PC, fax and photocopier. He unlocked the large steel cupboard and pulled down a box. But Dannaks was distracted by the contents of the cupboard. He was reading the etiquettes of the files and boxes. There was a cassette recorder and a box of cassettes, diskettes and CD-ROMs. Reinhart placed the box on the desk next to the PC. Dannaks pulled out one of the two hard-backed thinly-padded chairs.

"Enjoy," said Reinhart.

When he was gone Dannaks sat down and lifted the lid of the box. There was surprisingly little. Three or four paper files. Homicide would have boxes of transcripts, taped interviews, etc.

A photocopy of a leaflet or a pamphlet slipped out of the first file. There were six watches on the sheet. A pair of large asterisks sandwiched a bronze-coloured Seiko automatic.

He took the file containing the crime scene photographs. The first was a panorama shot that covered a large area of the dried out pool and encompassing sandy area with its swings, slides, and climbing frames. The dark shape hanging under the slide like a chrysalis immediately caught his eye. Despite it being bright he could feel the bleakness of October in the grey and sepia. There were more photographs of the area. Attention had been paid to a large metal steamboat that was an all-in-one activity frame. Its hull offered two rooms with portholes and doors cut out. The deck, accessed through thick rope netting, ladders and a wide slope of wood with a thick strand of rope to pull yourself up, sported a helm, rope walkway and chained scoops for hauling up sand. An area on ground level, a below-deck front cabin, had been meticulously photographed. Numbered cards marked important finds. The cards were photographed close up with the piece of evidence, be it a sweet wrapper, cigarette stub, etc. To give scale a graduated strip, or L-shaped card was in the picture. Then there was an all-encompassing photograph to show the relationship of the evidence. Further photographs led the way to the slide. Here again there were close-ups of objects and shoe-prints. The slide itself had been carefully photographed. Then Kai Doermer, from afar, middle distance and finally close-up, especially his face, hands and mouth, the skipping rope and boot lace and knots. His face looked unreal. There were minute haemorrhages under the skin and in the whites of his eyes. His lips and his ears had a bluish hue. A slip of brushed steel showed that some of these close-ups were autopsy photographs. There were bloodstains at the corners of his mouth, his painful grimace showing an ample portion of the wedged tangerine. A further photograph focussed on the hefty bruise just below and behind the ear. The examiner said the blow to his carotid sinus would have knocked him unconscious. Damaged ligaments in the neck and the bruise were consistent with a violent blow from a blunt instrument such as a baseball bat or a boot. He'd been hung with a skipping rope, one handle of which was at his neck. There were tiny flakes of red paint on the back of his head. They were from the top handles of the ladder to the slide.

Dannaks replaced the photographs and turned to the documentation.

He skimmed the victim's background. He'd seen from the boy's bulk that he was a loner who'd probably become a skinhead for social reasons. His right-wing policies probably didn't go beyond breaking heads of non-Nazis.

He and his friends left a party in Billstedt at about two on that Wednesday morning. Five of them piled into a VW Golf. On the way through the city park he got out to take a leak. Instead he was sick on the pavement. As he relieved himself his so-called friends abandoned him. They said he was too drunk and they didn't want him up-chucking in the car. Even amongst them he was stigmatised by his bulk and forever having to prove himself. In a fight he could be the best person at your side, but socially he was an embarrassment.

The trains were no longer running and he couldn't afford a taxi. So Doermer may have decided to walk to his flat in Bramfeld. Whether through drunkenness or exhaustion, he had chosen to run the risk of exposure and sleep in the park. Evidence suggests he lay down in the front cabin of the children's ship. He was found dead by the two joggers at about 6:45 am. The forensic medical expert put the time of death between 5:00 and 6:00 am.

Dannaks scanned the evidence. There was very little to go on. A scuffed print of a training shoe on Doermer's abandoned black scarf was the best they had. The killer had retraced his steps, sweeping away his path but forgotten to check the scarf which had been blown further away. The skipping rope was common as was the knot.

The joggers' statements were straightforward and, other than a man walking his dog, offered no leads. Asked why they had not checked to see whether he was still alive, the girls had no answer. They said they just knew he was dead. Even in death Doermer was imposing.

The man who had walked his dog had been found. His route had not taken him to the play area and he'd seen nobody.

Doermer's friends had been interviewed. As too were his family and relatives. His work colleagues, packers at a warehouse, and all the party guests were questioned. The circle widened to leads in the Right-wing scene and the Left-wing scene, the various Ausländer groups were followed. Uniforms were placed in the park in the early hours of every morning for a month, questioning anybody they met.

Homicide surmised that Doermer had met his killer by chance that morning. The theory went that either he was awake or his killer woke him. An argument ensued escalating into a fight. There was evidence of a scuffle near the ship. Despite his bulk he had been felled. The blow to the neck had brought him down, although his arms and hands showed defensive bruising. All the fingers of his right hand were broken. The assailant had carried and dragged him to the slide. There were double tracks in the sand consistent with someone being dragged. But the tracks were broken. Homicide thought he'd been carried in a fireman's lift rather than dragged. He had been placed on the slide and one end of the skipping rope had been tied about his neck. The killer had probably looped the other end through the top handles of the slide and hauled the unconscious man up the rungs by pulling like a bell-ringer. Once he'd got him to the top, he'd secured the rope to a crossbeam under the slide and pushed him over the side. At some point the killer had tied Doermer's thumbs together. After this he had retraced his steps, kicking out any shoe prints. Carrying Doermer had deepened the indentations made by his shoes.

The motive wasn't clear. But Doermer's watch was missing. It was described as a Seiko automatic with a worn brown leather strap. He didn't have any money on him either. Apparently he didn't possess a wallet and carried his cash in his pockets. Nobody could say whether he had any money with him that night.

By far the most important clue was the partial shoe print on Doermer's scarf. Somebody wearing a size 45 or 46 training shoe had stepped on it. The most likely candidate was the killer. And this said something more than that the killer wore training shoes. It said that he was disturbed or panicked.

Even though the whole thing appeared to be a chance incident, there were a number of contradictions. Supporting the chance theory was the circumstance of the attack. The killer could not have known Doermer would be in the park. Doermer had left the car at about two thirty. He would have taken between ten and twenty minutes to reach the playground. Evidence confirmed that he'd bedded down in the ship and the earliest time of death was put at five a.m. It seemed unreasonable that the killer would have waited around until this time to make his move. The use of a skipping rope also pointed to chance. Everything pointed to a jogger or fitness freak coming into contact with Doermer. Then again, perhaps it was made to look that way? Against this theory was the hanging itself. Why hanging? Once his man was down the killer could have beat him to death or choked him with the rope. A heated exchange usually results in a cluster of blows. Yet, apart from some faint marks – Doermer was well clothed against the cold – the only sign of real violence was the blow to the head. Hanging suggested execution. Removing the shoelaces to tie his thumbs together meant the killer was cold-blooded. Then there was the tangerine in his mouth. If it was used to stop him speaking, why hadn't the killer used his scarf? Doermer's wide eyes said that he had regained consciousness at some time. Finally the killer had the presence of mind to retrace his footprints. Again, these were not the actions of a normal person, but those of a cool mind. And then he'd forgotten the scarf.

Homicide felt it was possible, but unlikely, that more than one man had attacked Doermer. Only one set of prints had been retraced and obscured. Given Doermer's bulk this was surprising. Of course two could have beaten him to the ground with only one taking it further.

Dannaks packed up the files and replaced them on the shelf. He pulled the file of the second murder. Returning to his seat he took a moment to close his eyes and twist his neck. He looked down at the file and pushed back his shoulders, feeling his shoulder blades bunching the flesh of his back.

The contents of the Doermer file had been meagre. Although the Jensen file looked as thick, it contained less substance. There were no photographs but a wad of photocopies listing names and addresses from the database of *Perfekt* Pizzas. Handwritten notes were scrawled against each entry. The poor copies rendered the writing barely legible. The originals would be with *Soko* Doermer. It had obviously been REX's task to check the customers who had their pizzas delivered. But like all such places one could order a pizza over the counter as a takeaway.

"*Mahlzeit.* (Mealtime)"

Dannaks swung round. He hadn't heard Reinhart enter the room. He checked his watch. "I just opened the second murder file."

11:08

"Craig?"

"Yes," he stood to greet the man. They shook hands and seated themselves. "I haven't ordered."

They were in the Alsterpavillon on the inner Alster. Craig had been looking out onto the water, watching the rainbow shimmering in the spray of the single water-jet in the centre of the lake. The sky was bathroom marble: azure with a webbing of thin clouds; the sunshine was like late afternoon, pleasant, but failing to take the chill out of the shade. He had been reflecting how he had once envisaged Hamburg as an industrial harbour city of redbrick and rust. He had been surprised to find a contender for the greenest city in Europe. Truly a city built on water; the Elbe, the inner and outer Alster, and the numerous streams and canals allowed it to boast more bridges than London, Amsterdam and Venice together.

"I'm afraid I haven't got much time," he said. "It's too early for lunch and too late for breakfast."

"I'm paying." Craig's tongue checked the fleeciness of the wall of his mouth.

"Thanks. I'll have a coffee and a B-L-T sandwich."

His name was Manfred Schmidt and he was a friend of a friend and was a freelance photographer who did a lot of work for *Der Spiegel*. Craig had arranged to see him before coming to Germany and wanted to support his articles with a choice of his photographs. He already had a couple of pictures but it was good policy to make as many contacts as possible.

"Okay." After they'd ordered the reporter pulled his tattered briefcase – a piece the Chancellor of the Exchequer would be proud to inherit – onto his lap.

"Here are some photos I managed to dig out. They're unused and my own; so don't complain. You can have them."

"Thanks."

"I'll pull in a favour some time," said Manfred.

"Sure."

Craig looked over the photographs of the *S-Bahn* surfers. Distance or shadow anonymized the figures.

"Have you heard of a surfer called Stefan, *S-Bahn* Stefan?"

"Yeah. Wait a minute." He reached out and took back the

photographs. He perused them and eventually returned them pointing to the one on top. "I think that's him." The picture was the back of a youth hanging outside the door looking upon the rails ahead. He had seen a similar one in the German article that had first attracted him to the youth. The flak jacket with its Ku Klux Klan confederate patch and the boy's earring were helpful, but not enough to identify him, should he have changed either. Nevertheless, the picture gave Craig a better idea of the boy's build and how he dressed.

"Have you any surfers' phone numbers?"

The reporter shook his heard. Craig was deflated. The number he had been given for Stefan was either wrong or old. He got a dead line every time. All he had was the route Stefan favoured and a sliver of hope that the boy would be the anchor he needed. He could only use these photos if he found him.

The reporter pulled out a wad of material held in a thin cardboard file. "You might find something useful in there," he said, handing it over.

Craig opened it upon the table. A lot of it was photocopies of right-wing publications. The quality was appalling and the reporter assured him that the originals had been no better.

"Don't let the amateurish material fool you. It's a long established and evolving culture. Within the last two years its membership has steadily grown. Right-wing meetings, publications, camps, music, the Internet have drawn a lot of disenchanted youth. It's the aspect of belonging, like a youth club, that appeals to the majority of them."

Their food arrived and Craig was obliged to pack the papers onto the vacant seat beside him. Over the short lunch they spoke of their career histories. They mentioned their mutual acquaintance, the person who had brought them in contact, at a magazine for which Craig occasionally wrote.

"You should be careful," warned the reporter, rising from the table. "There are death lists with the names of journalists as well as politicians."

"And then there's the *Henker*," said Craig.

Manfred looked at him peculiarly and Craig realised the ambiguity of his remark. Before he could elaborate Manfred left.

Craig ordered a pastry and another cup of coffee and sifted through the material. The most graphically shocking thing was an advertisement for the Ku Klux Klan: a poorly reproduced picture of

Martin Luther King with the words: "Our dream came true." The most valuable item was Manfred's own compilation of addresses and telephone numbers.

He checked his watch, paid up and headed for the archive library.

12:12

On the way to lunch Reinhart précised his career path and Dannaks did the same. Dannaks had been correct in thinking Reinhart had come straight into the *Kripo* rather than joining the uniformed ranks.

During the time in which Dannaks looked over the murder files Frank had handed Reinhart promised statements. Reinhart had phoned the pub and informed them of their visit.

They walked to the side-street restaurant that was too expensive in the evenings, but offered a good lunchtime menu. It was one of those Asia eateries offering all manner of dishes from India, Thailand, China and Vietnam. The place was small and packed; a few minutes later and they would have had to wait for a table. Before queuing they claimed seats at a table with their jackets.

The food was served directly from brushed steel trays that steamed under the glass counter. Neither of them spoke until they were seated in front of their food. Reinhart began quietly without prompting. "Marcus Jensen was killed by a pizza delivery man. He–"

"I've a few questions about Doermer first," said Dannaks around his mouthful of fish.

"Fire away."

"Were any fingerprints found?"

"Loads. From the ship and slide. But they couldn't dust them in entirety. They got a lot of partials and mainly from children. They went through the bins too." Reinhart took a sip of his apple juice. "But you've got to remember that it was October. Most people were wearing gloves. The killer probably was too."

"Not to tie the boot laces and rope."

Reinhart nodded thoughtfully. "I don't think they got any leads there. If they did, one of their lot followed them up."

"The killer didn't leave much."

"No," he agreed, "but we were thorough. Everything was followed up. And when Jensen was murdered, we double checked everything on Doermer. Homicide pushed us hard. Everything done by yesterday."

"I've worked with them before."

"Oh?"

"We had a spate of courier killings. Black Africans entering the country carrying a stomach full of heroin. They'd end up on some waste ground with their stomachs slit."

"The Jaffa cake killings?"

Dannaks nodded and winced. The reference to the orange-filled chocolate cakes conjured up the image of their brown skin and the glistening wound all too vividly. Yet another entry in Raul's account. He hadn't been directly responsible for their deaths. They had been his people, his drug couriers. He had been trying out a new route. Whether they were carrying at the time of their deaths was irrelevant. The message from the rival gang was clear. A tip-off had broken the gang and the killers had been put away. So again the police paved the way for Raul to operate unhindered.

They ate in silence for a moment.

"Why are you so interested in murder? That's not what we're about."

"I know." Dannaks cut a piece of fish on his plate. "Let's say it's a hobby."

"You'll have to wait for the next time he strikes."

"That's optimistic."

"*Soko* Doermer is almost at a standstill with Jensen's murder."

"Tell me about it. Start at the beginning."

"How's your fish?"

"Good."

"You should try their sweet and sour soup."

"Next time."

Reinhart shook his head. "You're one of those workaholic types, aren't you?"

Dannaks steeled himself from saying "by comparison". He could tell that the hard work with *Soko* Doermer had left its mark on Reinhart. "It gets me through the day."

"That's a funny way of looking at life."

He didn't like the personal turn in the conversation. "When you're busy time passes quicker." Even this wasn't quite what he wanted. "Then you can get on with your own things."

Reinhart perked up. "Like what?"

He was getting fed up with boxing from a corner and ducked the issue. "Let's talk about Jensen."

They ate in silence, each trying to fathom any meaning behind the exchange.

Did Reinhart shake his head before beginning? "Markus Jensen was one of those who vandalised the Jewish gravestones in February. You remember?" Dannaks nodded, seeing again the swastika smeared headstones and the ones they'd been able to topple, lying in broken slabs. An anonymous witness had called the police. "Jensen was said to have stood by and watched." He was found innocent; the others were fined or given short sentences. "He was what, sixteen?" His young face, an impassive passport shot, stared from the front pages. "But he wasn't camera shy and quite outspoken."

"Okay. I know he was hung in his flat. I also know the killer delivered a pizza."

"He didn't leave it. We had only one witness. The witness didn't see his face. He was wearing a full-face helmet. She said he was carrying a pizza box. It was probably empty." Reinhart sipped his drink. "Jensen liked pizzas and ordered regularly from *Perfekt* Pizzas. On the day of his death he didn't make an order with them. But the witness is certain that the box was from *Perfekt* Pizzas."

"What you're saying doesn't make sense. You're saying he hadn't ordered a pizza, but one was delivered."

"It makes sense if it was a complimentary pizza," Reinhart smiled triumphantly.

"That's what Homicide thought?"

"Yes, mainly because the witness said the pizza box was different. She orders from *Perfekt* Pizzas and she remembered the logo being the wrong colour. *Perfekt* Pizzas said they used such boxes for complimentary pizzas for promotions and faithful customers. You know those who bought more than ten in a month. That sort of thing."

"Why did the witness remember him?"

"Because he left when the screaming and commotion started."

"And?"

"And he didn't stop or turn around. He just kept going."

"And nobody in the block ordered a pizza."

"Correct."

"And he left with the box because it was evidence."

"Yes."

"Jensen could have known his killer."

"That was Homicide's first theory. Jensen obviously let him in. A friend wanting to share a pizza. They got nowhere."

"All you've got is a biker carrying a pizza box. Do we know what he or she was he wearing?"

"Unfortunately not. She thought it was a one piece affair."

"In which case he could have been wearing anything underneath."

"I suppose so. What are you getting at?"

"I'm saying he didn't appear at Jensen's door as a pizza delivery man."

"Yes, you're right. You're thinking he could have been in police uniform, for instance. It's an idea. I should think Homicide would have looked into that. Like I said we weren't kept up to date."

"Okay, so Jensen let the pizza man in. What happened then?"

"He was beaten. Not much. Again there was a knockout bruise to the side of the head. The killer stuffed a kiwi down his throat and tied his thumbs together wi–"

"Did the killer bring the kiwi?"

Reinhart was surprised by the interruption. "I don't remember. Wait. Yes, they couldn't say. There were no other kiwis in the flat, but Jensen could have had some. But there were no skins anywhere. You know, in the bin. You can't eat the end bit. But nobody could say for certain."

"He was tied and hung?"

"The killer tied his thumbs together behind his back. He used one of those plastic binding tags, you know, the ones used to bind cables." They used them sometimes as makeshift handcuffs. "He used Jensen's belt to tie his feet. Then he waited until it got dark. Maybe he ate the pizza? Around five thirty he carried Jensen onto the balcony, tightened a noose around his neck and then threw him off. That's it."

"What did he–"

"Wait. There's a detail that didn't make the Press." The dramatic pause irritated Dannaks. "The hanging didn't kill him."

"What do you mean?"

"He choked. Choked on the kiwi some hours before." The press were right in coining him the Henker. At the time they didn't know about the fruit. But it had eventually leaked out, rejuvenating interest, increasing the pressure on Homicide, giving rise to all sorts of speculation and ultimately sensationalising the killer.

"Give me some times. When did the killer arrive?"

"Around twelve thirty, a quarter to one."

"When was the body discovered?"

"Six fifteen or so."

"Time of death?"

"Between one and two. The autopsy found residue of his breakfast in his stomach. No pizza, of course. Digestion takes about four hours, so he had a late breakfast."

"Too early to order a pizza, wouldn't you say? The killer was in the flat from twelve thirty till five thirty. What did he do?"

"Pressed away flecks."

"What?"

"This was interesting. It didn't get us anywhere. But I found it interesting. Jensen died between one and two. There was a line on his back from the edge of a rug in his lounge. He was only in his underpants. Perhaps he had a dressing gown on when he let the killer in."

"At two in the afternoon?"

"The theory was that he'd just finished his shower and was getting dressed. Let's say he died at one. Twenty minutes later his blood would have started to sink. In this case to his back. The skin pales, but red or violet flecks are left behind. The thing about these flecks is that in the first hours of death you can press them away. And Homicide thinks that's what the killer did. There was a patch on Jensen's body where they were absent. Who knows what the killer was doing. Perhaps he touched one accidentally and then he played a little."

"Macabre."

"Yeah."

"What were the theories about why the killer waited around?"

"There's only one. That he was waiting for darkness before taking Jensen to the balcony."

"Could he have left and returned?"

"It's possible, I suppose."

"There's something else I don't understand. Jensen lived in a tower block in Steilshoop. How did the killer know he ordered pizzas? The deliveries would have gone inside. That points to a delivery-man or someone within the building."

Reinhart smiled. "Homicide said Jensen used the recycling bins at the front of the block. The killer could have seen him dumping a pizza box."

Dannaks nodded slowly. "Okay. But there must have been some forensic clues?"

"No fingerprints. There was no blood of course. Fibres were collected, but without something to prove them against they're pretty useless."

"What fibres?"

"Sweatshirt."

"Any hair?"

"Everything discovered was traced to family or friends. Oh, the television was on stand-by. But Jensen could have been watching television when the killer arrived."

"Homicide thinks it's the same killer?"

"The M.O. fits." The modus operandi was strikingly similar. Even the displaying of his handiwork was telling. There had been no reason for the hanging. And certainly no reason to hang him publicly.

"One last thing. Our Jensen file was pretty thin. I didn't see any photographs."

"We don't see everything. We just help. And they don't tell us everything." Reinhart appeared smug. "I didn't see many photographs either. We were given all we needed to know." His expression froze and his gaze drifted as he went into recall. "As an example I didn't see any photos of Jensen's forehead. There's a rumour the killer wrote something. But Homicide is cagey." He forked a last piece of food. "I get the impression they were holding something back." Reinhart looked at their empty plates and then his watch. "We'd better get going."

12:27

After leaving the Alsterpavillon he went to the archive library on *Neuer Jungfernstieg* and with the help of one of the staff looked up the publicity surrounding the police officer Krohn.

"Foreigners are bringing this country down." The police chief's outspokenness led to calls for his resignation and he was asked to explain why he didn't consider his remark racist. "It's a fact that fifty percent of all crime is committed by an *Ausländer* and they make up less than ten percent of the population."

He pondered the statistics. The crime figure of fifty percent was frighteningly high. However, he knew that many foreigners found it impossible to get work or the necessary permits and authority. Therefore, if they worked, they worked illegally and perhaps this crime was part of these statistics. Then again, who were these foreigners to whom Krohn was referring? Were they part of the population? Or was this figure of fifty percent being bolstered by criminals making expeditions into Germany from the East, for instance?

The man had made his comments after his wife had died. Sympathy had helped him keep his job. Craig noted the obscure fact that the man loved fishing.

He handed the material back to the member of staff, who said: "His son's also interesting."

"Oh?"

"Are you researching Krohn for his policing or for his political leanings?"

"Political."

"Then you might want to look up his son. He's a skinhead."

"Give me all you've got," Craig stammered. When the man returned Craig was feeling lucky and asked about *Bahn* surfers. Twenty minutes later he found himself with an article on Stefan. There was no picture. He checked the time. Half the day was gone. Rather than read all the material, he made photocopies and left.

He needed to find Stefan. Krohn and his son could only offer titbits. He'd seen enough to know that Stefan was his centrepiece. Perhaps he had enough material to pretend he interviewed the boy? It was a wicked thought. He could make up a character, a surfer. Don't panic, he said. But it was Monday. By the end of the Thursday the article had to be out.

Outside was another pleasant day, but he'd spend most of it riding trains. He first went to a bank, where getting cash took longer than expected. No time for a sit-down lunch. He bought provisions from a kiosk before descending the steps to begin his search for Stefan.

13:39

The buildings that lined the roads looked familiar and yet drab in the daylight. As if darkness had shrouded them in a collective mystery. Dannaks only glanced at the map once.

They spoke about their immediate assignment, but most of their talk was a continuation of their lunchtime conversation.

Reinhart had told him that his assignment on the Markus Jensen murder had been to go through the backlog of pizza orders. The killer could have picked up an old box, but there was a chance he had made an order. Homicide had not told REX why, but they asked them to report any occurrences of the initials S.F. or words that could be so abbreviated. He knew that others had made database and Internet searches for the letters. They'd been applied as initials to everyone connected to Jensen. And they'd looked into secret societies.

Dannaks had questions that Reinhart had been unable to answer. The first murder was in October and the next in February. What did the lapse in time mean? The first seemed to be a chance or accidental killing, but the February one was planned. The killer at least knew Jensen's eating habits.

A standing sign near the parking area announced that the pub was closed until Wednesday. Reinhart parked near the entrance next to where a tangle of broken chairs stood and a group of black bin liners that propped one another up.

Dannaks saw that in the cold light of day the Bacardi advertisement didn't look so enticing. The colouring had faded and meaningless graffiti littered the depicted beach.

Apart from a woman pushing a pram on the other side of the road it appeared as if the town was deserted.

The window that he'd seen broken on Friday was now just a frame. There was no glass to be seen. Underneath it were four wooden foldable garden chairs around a further barrel with a piece of hardboard on top. On this makeshift table was a used ashtray surrounded by rings of dried liquid.

One of the double doors under the arch was open. In front of the other were four large metal beer barrels. He saw that what he took to be a clump of potatoes at the end of the name of the pub was in fact a pair of hanging boxing gloves.

If outside was barren, inside was a hive of activity.

The pub was one big room, practically a hall.

The first person Dannaks saw was a carpenter prizing a remaining good leg off a broken chair. He was sitting next to a small selection of chairs that could be scavenged or repaired. The tables looked indestructible. They were thick workman-like benches, scarred and uneven, buffed with age. Benches with backrests, a little like church pews, fitted corners and ran along some walls. A few cushions had survived the devastation.

Two men in white overalls were at the walls. One had a spatula and was filling gouges in the plasterwork. The other was using a clear solution to remove obscenities. A repaint was necessary because where he'd worked could be seen as watermarks. Dannaks recognised a swastika.

Two women, one of whom he recognised as the daughter, were at a table assembling torn photographs in broken frames.

"Can't you read? We're closed." It was the proprietor's wife, *Frau* Hänisch. She was behind the bar filling empty shelves with glasses from a box.

The place stank of beer and spirits.

Reinhart whipped out his ID card. "We called earlier."

She came round the bar to them. "I don't know what else we can tell you." Her tone didn't disguise her impatience.

"We can tell them about the statue." They turned to the daughter. Dannaks saw that the large photographs were those of German boxing greats. In their frames they had probably adorned the walls. He recognised some of them: Max Schmeling, Bubi Scholz, Henry Maske, Axel Schulz and Regina Halmich. There was one who looked strangely familiar, but he couldn't put a name to him.

A phone rang. *Frau* Hänisch went to the bar. She listened for a moment. "No. Leave us alone. We're not doing interviews. Please don't call. No. I said no." She slammed it down and stared at it before turning to them. "A bronze statue is missing."

Dannaks got out his notebook.

"Can you describe it?" Reinhart asked. The detectives had agreed that although he was outranked Reinhart would do the talking. Under the guise of getting to know the ropes Dannaks had actually wanted to motivate his colleague. He had agreed to take the next assignment.

"I can give you a photo."

"Even better."

She turned away from them and headed out of the room.

"The thing is," said the daughter, "it disappeared after the skinheads had left."

"Are you sure?"

"Absolutely. My father says he saw it too."

"So only the police were here?"

"Yes. Although they caught a skinhead in the house. He didn't have the statue on him."

Her mother returned.

"You're accusing the police officers, then."

"We're not accusing anybody at the moment," said *Frau* Hänisch. She handed Reinhart the photograph. He looked at it before passing it on to Dannaks. The bronze statute was that of a bare-fisted standing boxer. He stood on a black pedestal, probably heavy plastic. The inscription on the small bronze plate screwed to the pedestal had caught the flash of the camera and was unreadable. "But it was here when we left."

"Did you see it?"

"Er, no."

"We'd like to go over your statements and ask a few questions." Reinhart glanced about. "Could we sit down somewhere?"

"We'll go outside. Do you want something to drink?" They both declined.

"Do you want me also?" asked the daughter.

"Yes, but we'll call you."

The phone began to ring again. "Don't talk to them," said *Frau* Hänisch to her daughter.

"I know," she said.

They went out and sat about the makeshift table. "Bloody reporters. This is the third day, now. You'd think they'd give up." *Frau* Hänisch produced a packet of cigarettes from somewhere and lit up. She didn't offer the detectives one.

"You don't have to repeat your statement. I've got it here." Reinhart held up the file he'd been carrying. "We'll race through it. If you want to add anything, just say. I'll have questions as we go along." They'd closed the pub at one in the morning. They had been in bed. Around one-thirty her husband had heard voices outside and got up to go to the curtains. Before he got there, there was a crash downstairs. He looked out of the window and told her to call the police. The time of the call was recorded at 01:36. He told her that there was a horde of troublemakers outside. Whilst she dialled he pulled on his dressing gown and picked up the baseball bat. She told him not to go, but he didn't listen. He told her to lock the door and she heard him tell their daughter to do the same. She looked out of the window and knew that they were too many for him to handle. She opened her door and listened. She heard her husband shout at them to get out. Then there was a commotion. Then nothing. Between longer silences she heard voices, grunts, chuckles, the scraping of furniture, things smashing and taps running, heavy liquid, which she knew could only be beer slapping the floor. "I was worried sick, that's why I went down."

Frau Hänisch stubbed out her finished cigarette and lit a second.

"You pulled down an ornamental cutlass from the wall," said Reinhart. Her husband had once boxed in Scotland and they had a shield and crossed swords hanging on a wall in the first floor landing.

She had gone down and been so aghast at the sight of her husband that she had easily been tackled from behind. He was bent backwards over a table. A broom that went through the sleeves of his housecoat was held at each end by a youth. One sat side-saddle-style on his thighs. He was pinned down. There were at least a dozen others in the room. She was relieved of the sword and manhandled to the floor. Despite her age she was molested. Her husband struggled but he was powerless. They looked at each other for strength.

Frau Hänisch paused and took a deep drag on her cigarette.

The tall blond youth, the leader, stood next to the table and was speaking to her husband. He was torturing him with pins. She didn't hear what was said. There was too much movement and the some of the skinheads were at the pumps, letting them run and helping themselves to glasses full.

"Then the police arrived?"

"Eventually." She thinned her lips with bitterness. "I heard someone at the window shout: *Scheißbullen.* The leader, the big blond one, said: what the fuck. And then it was chaos. Most of them went out of the window. I don't know what happened. I crawled to W–, my husband."

"The leader said: what the fuck?" said Dannaks, titling the statement in Reinhart's hand so that he could see.

"That's not here," said Reinhart.

"No. I–"

"That can happen. That's why we're here."

Her second cigarette was finished and she stubbed it out. "Is it important?"

"I doubt it." Dannaks disagreed but remained silent. "Well, thank you very much *Frau* Hänisch. If you think of anything else, no matter how trivial, please don't hesitate to contact us." Reinhart gave her his visiting card. "We'd like to speak to your daughter now. And after that your husband."

"You won't get anything more from him."

"We'd still like to speak to him."

"He's resting."

"Then we'll have to come back again."

Frau Hänisch got up.

"Do you think I could have a glass of water?" said Reinhart.

She nodded and looked at Dannaks. "Two?"

"Please."

They heard her talk to her daughter. "Britta you're on. But wait. Take these waters for them."

Britta's story was brief. She had stayed in her room until she saw the police catching the skinheads outside. She'd waited until all was quiet before going downstairs. Even then her parents had chastised her. She should have waited until the police had properly searched the building. She was with her parents comforting them and assessing the devastation. She remembered checking the rooms and seeing her father's prized possession, the statue he'd won, still standing high up on a shelf above his bed. When she returned from the hospital with her parents at five in the morning, two uniforms were sitting in their patrol car in front of the building. When they'd left there'd been dozens milling about. She knew more had been ordered to tidy up. The glass had been swept into a heap and as far as her mother was concerned they'd mopped up in such a way as to spread the pool of beer behind the bar over the entire floor. But it was the missing statue that irked most of all.

"We'd like to see your father now."

She left them. A minute later *Frau* Hänisch came out and taking their empty water glasses said that her husband would see them, but he wasn't getting up. She led the way through the building, telling the workmen on the way that they could take their break now. They went upstairs.

On the way up the stairs Dannaks stopped. "What about this?" he asked, nodding to the shoe-print on a windowsill.

"One of them was caught in here," said *Frau* Hänisch.

Dannaks nodded contemplatively.

Reinhart leaned forward to check their height from the ground. "Maybe he thought he could escape. But a jump like that would have broken his legs." He glanced at Dannaks before turning to follow *Frau* Hänisch.

Dannaks leaned forward and noticed the drainpipe.

He turned his head to look up. He leaned out and pulled on the guttering. It appeared firm.

"What are you doing?" It was Reinhart.

"Hold me by the belt."

"What are you doing?" Reinhart repeated.

"I want to look at the gutter."

Dannaks carefully stood on the window sill and backed out when Reinhart was holding him by his trousers' belt. He peeked over the edge of the gutter.

"I don't like this," said Reinhart.

In the gutter Dannaks saw cigarette stubs. They didn't look weathered.

He climbed back in.

"And?"

"Somebody was up there recently." Then looking at *Frau* Hänisch who was watching them from further up the stairs: "You haven't had any roof-work done recently, have you?"

"No."

Dannaks brushed himself down and Reinhart closed the window. Then they continued up the stairs.

Pillows propped him up in bed. Wolfgang was in a faded buttoned pyjama shirt. Greying hair like wire peeked above the top button. His beard was trimmed. The picture of his wife and him on the bedside cabinet showed him sporting a magnificent handlebar moustache. He was a larger than life character: a big man. Now he looked neat and tidy and ordinary. And Dannaks realised that the photograph of the clean-shaven boxer he had recognised but could not name was a younger version of this man: Wolfgang when he was "the Hammer".

Reinhart looked about.

"You won't need chairs," said Wolfgang.

"Okay. It's good to stand," Reinhart said. "We've been sitting for a while." He glanced at Dannaks for agreement. He merely brought his notebook to the ready. "I'd like to begin by asking you about the motive. What–"

"I've said all this. Shouldn't you be out there getting on with?"

Dannaks spoke before Reinhart could react. "The sooner we get through this, the sooner we'll be back out there."

They glared at one another until Reinhart began. "What do you think the motive was?"

Wolfgang sighed. "It's no secret I don't like the brown shit. A few months ago I kicked two of them out of here."

"Why did they come?"

"Maybe they lost their way. I'd never seen them before."

"How did you, er, kick them out?"

"I grabbed them and threw them onto the street."

"You didn't report this."

"What was there to report? It was early. There weren't many guests. I don't have leftist and punk conventions here, but they come. So there was no escalation. I just think they didn't know."

"So this attack was a revenge act?"

He thought for a moment. "Maybe. Or maybe it's an ongoing thing with the punks." He wearied. "Is that it?"

"I'd like to go over your statement." Wolfgang's face hardened. "Briefly. You may have forgotten something."

"I'll go over it. You know the times. A window was smashed and I told my wife to phone you lot before going down to confront them." Dannaks realised that his angry expression was a mask. "I grabbed a baseball bat and went down." Dannaks saw it as a flicker in his expression, revealing itself in his repetition. "I switched the light on down there and saw them." Here was a man who'd reached his limits: a man who'd seen fear. "There were too many of them. And they all looked the same." His face softened. "Funny, like beefed up holocaust victims. I saw those black and white pictures of the liberation at concentration camps." He snapped back. "I didn't recognise any of them. They all looked the same–"

"Even the leader, the one who spoke to–"

"Yes, even him."

"But they we're all skinheads, were they?"

"Maybe. But I still didn't – and wouldn't – recognise any of them."

"You switched the light on."

"Yeah. And then they were on me. They put a broom-handle through the sleeves of my gown and pinned me down. There were too many of them."

"And then the leader stuck you with needles. What did he

137

say?"

"I don't remember. The usual brown propaganda and that I should know better. I was a traitor." He stopped.

"What propaganda?"

"Oh, come on. Do I have to spell it out? That I was a lover of leftist scum, lily-livered greens, Punks, the filth of society that dirtied the proud German race."

"Are you sure you can't describe the leader or the others?"

"You didn't get him, eh?" He smiled cynically.

"What about clothing? Anything distinctive?"

"No."

"Swastikas?"

Wolfgang shook his head. His face was setting again.

"The baseball bats, metal or wood?"

"I don't remember."

"Tattoos?"

His eyes darkened and he clenched his jaw and shook his head again.

The three of them were silent for a moment. They knew that the interview was at an end.

Since discovering the cigarette butts in the gutter Dannaks had toyed with the idea of bagging them for DNA tests. He now knew that there was no point. With no charges he wouldn't be able to clear the expense of the analysis.

"One final thing," said Reinhart. "There's talk of a missing statue. A boxing prize. When did you last see it?"

"When I went downstairs. It was on the window sill."

"The one on the stairs?" said Dannaks.

He nodded.

16:10

In the office Dannaks found a see-me note from Frank on his desk.

"I'll start the first draft," said Reinhart, referring to the report of their visit.

Frank's door was open.

"You wanted to see me?"

Frank glanced up at him. After taking another look at the paperwork on his desk he sat back and invited Dannaks to sit.

"*Kriminalrat* Borchardt called earlier. He's set up a search for tomorrow at three. He wants you to call him back." Dannaks could sense there was more. Frank took a deep breath. "I have to admit I'm not happy that this is during REX time." Pause. "So I'd like to suggest a trade-off." Dannaks braced himself. "Do you remember me talking about interviewing this beaten schoolboy this morning?" Dannaks nodded. "Nobody volunteered and I said I'd go. Well, it turns out that it is inconvenient for me." He fell silent.

Dannaks cleared his throat. "I, erm, I've got nothing on. I suppose I could do it."

"Good man." Frank was visibly pleased and Dannaks wondered whether he'd landed himself another Detlef. "There are some snippets on the attack in here, if you haven't read them." He tapped the three daily newspapers on the edge of his desk. "I know it's not what you expected, but it is good PR. If it helps I can give you a lift."

"It'll help. I haven't got a car." Frank raised his eyebrows questioningly. "I live in St. Georg." He didn't need to elaborate. Not only did he live walking distance away, he lived centrally where parking was horrendous.

"We'll leave at five-thirty."

At his desk Dannaks called Detlef, who hastily came to the point.

"Somebody from Homicide will meet you there. He or she'll let you in and if you find anything, they want you to hand it over. Okay?"

"Yes."

"He'll seal up after you." Detlef paused as if expecting Dannaks to protest. "Who do you want with you?"

"Uwe and Lampe. Anyone else."

"I still don't believe he's your leak. He's small fry."

"He's all I've got."

17:40

Craig broke off his search for Stefan at five. He felt as if he had been riding the trains all day and the thought of doing it all again tomorrow depressed him. Wednesday was his last chance to find him, although at a push he could use Thursday morning. By Thursday afternoon his first article had to be complete.

During his travels he dialled some of the numbers but even when he got through to somebody an impregnable wall of suspicion and occasionally outright hostility confronted him. He did not have

139

the time to infiltrate the structure, making the search for Stefan all the more important.

His tongue searched out the fleeciness in his mouth. He was despondent. So far all his efforts had been in vain. He would just have to try harder.

He'd written off the idea of going undercover. Aside from the risk, the concert had given him a taste of the futility of getting anything of worth in such a limited time frame. The bonus was that he would have more time with Carina.

18:00

Frank drove slowly down the street. He was wary of the playing children and aware of the youths standing about watching him with curiosity.

Frank stopped in the middle of the road in front of the boy's house. To get to this road he had negotiated a disorientating labyrinth of one-way streets. Dannaks climbed out and Frank drove away.

The Altona Alt-Stadt buildings resembled those of the up-market area of Eppendorf. They too had that strange mixture of Art Nouveau and Victorian styles: box windows, balconies with bulging black wrought-iron work, even some mock pillars. Crowning it all were ornate undulating gables extending beyond the roofs, reminding Dannaks of the headboards of beds.

As he walked up to the house he was aware of being watched. He scanned the intercom for the family's name. The door was already open but he wanted to announce himself. He stated his surname when a male voice crackled an almost unrecognisable: "Hallo?" At the unnecessary buzz Dannaks glanced about the street. Some forms were at the windows of the nearby houses. The kids too, latching on to the curiosity of the youths, had paused to look in his direction.

Ascending the stairs he listened for an opening of a flat door. Hearing none he had to check the nameplates on the flat doors of each floor.

On the third floor he rang the bell.

The door opened on its chain.

"Yes," said a small woman.

"Who is it?" called a boy's from deeper in the flat.

Dannaks held up his ID card. "*Kripo*. Hamburg. Dannaks."

"We've already spoken to the police," said a boy, forcing himself in front of his mother.

"I know. You spoke to my uniformed colleagues. I'm a

140

detective."

"My father's not here."

"I'd like to speak to you. You are Faruk, aren't you?"

"How do you know?"

"The bruise kind of gives you away."

The boy regarded him cockily. "Maybe you are a detective."

"Can I come in? I won't keep you long."

His mother said something in Turkish and the boy replied.

The door was opened and Dannaks thanked them as he removed his shoes.

"My father should be home soon," said Faruk leading Dannaks to the sofa.

They passed the kitchen and Dannaks saw an older girl with the mother.

Faruk sat in a large easy chair and a smaller boy sat on the arm of it.

"This is Ali, my brother."

Dannaks smiled taking out his notepad.

"Can you tell me what happened on Friday? From the top."

Faruk groaned.

"Please."

Faruk then told him of being chased, caught and beaten after playing pool with his friend, Ahmed. Dannaks asked questions to fill in the details he thought the uniforms had left out. But he didn't learn anything not already reported.

During this the older girl was introduced as Leila when she asked Dannaks whether he would like some refreshment. Faruk scolded her, perhaps because he felt it his duty as man in the house to offer refreshments. A few minutes later the mother came in and defiantly placed a tray of glasses with a jug of what looked like apple juice. Faruk fumed but said nothing. He merely waited to continue his story. Dannaks caught the mother's eye and conveyed his thanks. She nodded almost imperceptibly. The boy resumed his story the moment she left.

Faruk had almost finished when the flat door opened.

Dannaks felt a change in the air.

"You said you wouldn't recognise your attackers," Dannaks said hastily. "What about your rescuers?" The boy hesitated. "Would you recognise them?" He then shook his head.

Faruk and Ali stood when their father entered the room.

Dannaks rose too and introduced himself.

The man ignored Dannaks, instead talked severely to his eldest son. "You should in bed?"

"Yes," said Faruk meekly. He turned to leave.

"Wait," said Dannaks. "I haven't finished."

"We have spoken to police already."

"Yes. But I'm from a different department."

"You not speak together?"

"Yes. But I have more questions."

Suleyman walked over to a larger easy chair and said something in Turkish. Faruk sat. Ali rushed over to sit on the floor at his father's feet. Dannaks reseated himself and looked at his notepad. "So you wouldn't recognise your rescuers?"

Faruk glanced at his father before answering. "No. When they came I got up and ran."

Dannaks nodded appreciatively. "I only have one more question." They waited. "My, er, colleagues canvassed the area for witnesses," he said. "They said no one came forward."

Faruk was about to speak but his father intervened with a hand gesture. "Are you surprised? This is climate of fear." It sounded like a phrase he had picked up.

Dannaks nodded. They all waited. Then he closed his notepad. "Okay. Thank you for your time." He rose. They remained seated.

"You not waste much of mine," said Suleyman.

Dannaks didn't know what to say. The man had no faith in the police and Dannaks wasn't going to change his mind in the next few minutes. "My involvement means we are taking this attack seriously."

His statement harvested no reaction and he knew it was useless leaving his card. Nevertheless he got it out. "If you think of anything else that might help us catch your attackers, Faruk, then—"

"Keep it," said Suleyman.

Dannaks looked at Faruk.

"Yes, keep it."

Dannaks raised his eyebrows wearily and walked to the flat door wondering whether to place it on the next flat surface.

Passing the kitchen entrance he again caught the mother's eye.

He was about to put on his shoes when she came out to open the door for him. Without speaking he gave her the card.

Embarrassed she hid it under her apron.

18:22

Cenk was leaning against the wall next to Murat. His arms were folded, one foot pushed against the wall. Nazim was telling a joke. He seemed at pains to be the entertainer and Cenk wondered why he couldn't give it a rest. The group was losing patience.

The early evening often found them on the street. This was their custom. Home was for the women and the old. As youths they were often banished when other females visited. Many of the young men had their patches. Younger children were inside now. Most women too. Murat told them that Hasan said they should show presence near Faruk's place.

Cenk had never been comfortable on the street, but he had grown used to hanging around. He knew that the streets were definitely not Hasan's thing. Hasan lived alone – his parents lived in Hanover – so he had no reason to loiter. Although he was Murat's age he acted older. Hasan's own youth could be measured in weeks. He was comfortable playing his lute in a tearoom. But Cenk was never at home there. Tearooms were for old men. Here, on the streets you could at least ogle the occasional woman.

Murat also lived alone. But he was another beast altogether. He was at home on the streets. When he was younger he had skinned many a schoolchild. But Cenk doubted Hasan knew of Murat's past, especially skinning: relieving school kids of their valuables.

On Saturday they agreed that on Fridays, Saturdays and Sundays they should be out in force. During the week one group would suffice. They'd do alternate evenings. Tomorrow Hasan would be out.

Cenk had worked. His restaurant shift was from ten to six during the week and then on every other Saturday evening. His youthful looks worked against him. The proprietor wasn't ready to let him do evenings and for the moment Cenk didn't mind.

Bilal and two others were with them.

Standing around often contained periods of numbness. But they all agreed that sitting at home watching the box with their parents was even duller. Some evenings the dullness was startled by fire-cracking conversation. When that happened they felt good.

And tonight the theme that devoured their time was indeed the Molotov cocktail attack. Most were excited by it. Some allowed their shock a little room. Cenk had been the first to express his concern. Hasan feared someone would claim responsibility and had told him to distance them from the terrorist. He said he had called Murat with the same advice, but he wanted Cenk to emphasise his position. The current discussion had grown heated. Murat had extinguished it. "We know we're not terrorists. What's really important is we're not sheep. Or Jews." That silenced them. They slumped into themselves and Murat told a joke to pull them back. Then Nazim had started his tirade.

Nazim was searching for another joke when Bilal spotted Ponytail at the end of the road. He came towards them and Cenk sensed the awe in the group. He had never seen him before Saturday and didn't think he lived in the area.

Greetings were exchanged.

Nobody spoke and Cenk hoped Nazim wasn't going to continue with his playground jokes. Thankfully, his visible fascination held his tongue.

Murat was the only one who seemed at ease with Ponytail. Were they close friends?

20:25

Dannaks opened the wardrobe and switched on the portable colour television that sat on one half of a shelf. A folded pile of sweatshirts took up the other half. He took the remote control and flicked through the channels. Finding nothing, he scoured the evening's offerings in the television guide. He checked the time and tossed the guide on the coffee table. He then chose the channel that would bring the news in a quarter of an hour and left the programme running. He wanted noise in the flat. Life. Music wouldn't do. Music was for moods. He wanted company.

After leaving Faruk he had gone to interview his friend, Ahmed. If he thought Faruk had been cagey, then Ahmed gave the word a new level of meaning. He reluctantly gave his version of events. Bereft of detail with phrases such as it all happening so fast, he painted a very sketchy picture. The boy, embarrassed about running and getting away, was also defiant. He was on the offensive, almost daring Dannaks to criticise him for not standing by his friend. When Dannaks said he had probably done the right thing and could not have made a difference he did not win the boy's empathy. Such was the depth of his shame. In the end Dannaks did not learn anything new. The boy's dreary voice alone said that he was sick of telling what had happened.

He had stopped off at Patel's on the way home and bought four bottles of bubbly. They were in a plastic bag at his flat door so that he couldn't leave without picking it up. He was going to give them to the E-Shift.

In the cubbyhole of a kitchen he looked at his six bottle wine rack and chose the cheapest red he had: a supermarket purchase. Monday evening was not a good time to over-indulge. It threw the week off balance. But he needed another glass. Just one. With something akin to self-loathing he opened the bottle. The pop of the cork was a wholesome sound. He found solace in the glug as he poured the wine. He threw the cork in the flip-top under the sink and put an upturned tumbler on the bottle. He wanted the wine to breathe, but he didn't want those pesky fruit flies drowning in it. He'd learnt his lesson; one time he'd used a tea strainer to get a clean glass. Dannaks brought the wine to his nose. The aroma was not enough and he took a meagre sip. It was too soon to drink, it needed to breathe, but he couldn't resist taking the sip.

He returned to the room a rejuvenated man. Putting the glass on the television guide on the coffee table he pulled out the Nobby Kabel file. Within minutes he was engrossed, the television a background murmur.

He went straight to the newspaper cuttings.

After coming to power in spring 1933, the NSDAP took control of the *Kripo*, restructuring and politicising it. The *Geheime Staatspolizei* (secret state-police), like *Kripo* and *Schupo*, abbreviated to *Gestapo*, stepped into the *Kripo's* work at the start of the War. Their job was to take on cases that were said to take advantage of the country's situation. Draconian prison sentences were dished out for minor offences such as stealing chickens or not blacking-out. Handing a couple of cigarettes to a prisoner of war could bring eighteen months imprisonment. As Germany faced defeat, the *Kripo* were ordered by the Gestapo to build a resistance network to operate under occupation. The network was to be made up of so-called "*Werwolf-Gruppen*".

Nobby Kabel was said to be a member of *Werwolf* HH. The double H did not represent the vehicle licence plate for Hamburg (Hanover had H and Berlin B). That was coincidence. The double H stood for Heinrich Himmler. Nobby Kabel didn't admit to belonging to a Nazi organisation. He wouldn't even say whether such an organisation existed. But Dannaks picked out a quote:

"We're still occupied. Our politicians are gutless puppets. But I and those like me have not lost our pride."

He was also the typical corrupt cop. He took from pimps, was on a number of gangsters' payrolls to forewarn of police operations, raid, etc.

He was sentenced to six years. Shortly after his release he was shot dead whilst apparently attempting a petrol station robbery. The policeman who shot him said Nobby Kabel had come at him with a knife. Was it really by chance that the patrol car arrived as Nobby Kabel was carrying out his robbery? There was some question of whether he was actually carrying out a robbery. Dannaks noted the shooter's name. Holger Markowiak.

He picked up the sheaf of papers he'd seen on Saturday. As he turned the pages he became lethargic. The more he saw the more futile it all seemed. All this information. And so little action. Oh, the misdemeanour here and there, but never the big one. Never the one that smashed these organisations. Here it was youths, vicious and unpredictable. With Raul there was structure. Structure could be analysed, pressure put on the weak spots, and with luck the foundations irreparably destroyed. But the youths of these gangs didn't have a central motive like Raul. Their motives were political or social; they were as varied as their ages. He was about to pack it all away when he saw the graph of right-wing activity. Something had especially bothered him about it. He thought it was the beautifying of the disturbances. Now he knew it was the monitoring aspect. This was the epitome of their work. It told them only whether they were better or worse than previous years. It didn't give them anything they could act on. It was a pat on the shoulder or pull-your-socks up graph.

"It's monstrous that such large gangs can roam about at will." Yes, it was.

At the station Dannaks heaved the plastic bag containing the four bottles of wine onto the counter.

"The poisoner making good?" asked the duty officer.

"It's the antidote," said Dannaks. "For the E-Shift."

The officer took the bag and there was a silence. Then he said: "I'll see they get it. But..."

"But?"

"I believe the chief wants the name of the shop." This could only mean a lightning inspection by the health authorities.

"I'll hear from him then," said Dannaks. He turned and headed for the stairs.

"Hey, Dannaks, come and look at this," said Wulff as he passed the third floor storeroom. He and Schuppenhauer were huddled over the PC that was also hooked up to the mainframe. This was their prized piece of electronic equipment. Unlike other stations and especially the *Polizeistern* where Dannaks had worked for Narcotics, this station trailed in technological clout. REX shared the photocopier and fax with the entire station. "We started on that box of stuff that was confiscated last week." He was referring to a raid on a right-winger's flat. *LKA* State security had given them the laborious task of sifting through the confiscated material. Dannaks looked at the game on the screen. "It's called KZ (*Konzentrationslager* – Concentration Camp). I think the object is to contain the prisoners."

"Process them," Schuppenhauer corrected grimly. "We just printed this off." He handed Dannaks a sheet of paper. It detailed how to make a pipe-bomb. "The Internet's the Wild West."

"It can only get worse," Dannaks said, wishing he had a wittier quip to hand. He was pleased that they had called him over. Other than Uwe, nobody in Narcotics had shared with him. He was blemished. Whether they respected him or not, there was no in-between; former colleagues had tried to have as little as possible to do with him. Time had distanced his past too. REX was a smaller tighter unit. These colleagues appeared willing to accept him. They appeared keen too, with the exception of perhaps one.

As if they could read his thoughts one of them asked: "How was your first day with De Niro?"

"Who?"

"Reinhart."

"Okay." But Dannaks wanted comradeship. "He's a little strenuous. Why did you call him De Niro?"

"Reinhart De Niro. You'll find out soon enough."

He went to the utility room and poured himself a coffee.

Reinhart was at his desk studying a page of protocol he had typed up. Dannaks shrivelled as he greeted the man. Naturally it was fair that Reinhart should check his own work, but it was the time he took doing so. They simply did not have the time for grammatically perfect protocols. Reinhart took a pencil and examined its tip. He picked up a sharpener, hunched over the waste paper basket and began sharpening it.

Dannaks slipped his jacket over the back of his chair. "I've got a commitment at three today," he said. "I haven't squared it with Frank, but it's something for Narcotics. It's not a problem, is it?" Even if it was a problem, he could not cancel. He would not cancel.

Reinhart was about to speak when the phone rang. He picked it up. "*Soko* REX, *Kommissar* Keller speaking." He smiled and then looked at Dannaks. "Yes, he is." He swung the moveable stand to Dannaks: "Homicide for you."

Dannaks spoke very little. The man wanted to check arrangements for the three o'clock search of Freddy's flat. As he spoke, Dannaks unconsciously drew a small circle in the top right-hand corner of his blotter. He began to write in the name Krohn, realised what he was doing, glanced up at Reinhart who was preoccupied and began casually cross-hatching the shape. He had read somewhere that shading empty shapes was a sign of frustration.

When the conversation was over Reinhart said: "Déjà vu."

Dannaks ignored him. "What's the order of the day?"

Reinhart was silent. He looked stumped. Either he was considering pursuing the fact that Homicide had called him at about the same time the previous morning or he was formulating an answer.

"I think Frank wants you to help Schuppenhauer and Wulff."

Dannaks tried to hide his joy. He sipped his coffee and began a list of things to accomplish.

10:04

The editorial offices of the Hamburger *Tagespost* were on the fourth floor of a modern plinth-fronted building, built in the post second world war fifties. It was situated firmly in the office quarter in the centre of Hamburg off the beaten shopping track and beyond *Ost-West Strasse*. Nevertheless, snack bars and *Kneipen* that undoubtedly thrived during the working week were nestled between these buildings or resided on their ground floors.

The fourth floor was archetypically open-plan with the standard glass box at one end for the chief editor. The cluttered desks were positioned symmetrically with enough space between them to create a grid-pattern corridor. Every desk was sandwiched with small cupboards or shelving space. Occasionally an additional squat cupboard bridged two desks. But there weren't enough of these to create a labyrinth. Tellingly, all routes running the length of the office to the editor's box were unimpeded.

The place was in full swing and quite noisy. Telephones trilled for pick-up; other handsets were wedged between necks and shoulders whilst the person typed. Couples pored over papers, others appeared to be in splendid isolation, feet up, reading hard copy and sucking on pens.

Craig felt that some places were universal regardless of where you were in the world.

Robert led, greeting co-workers on the way. Few paid Craig any attention.

Robert tapped on the frosted glass panel of the editor's door and opened it without waiting for an answer. Craig wasn't sure an answer would be heard above the hubbub.

A woman sitting behind a desk speaking on the phone gestured for them to sit in the chairs opposite.

"Ulrich, I've made my decision. That's how it is going to be. Let's hear nothing more about it."

She hung up and after greeting Robert she leaned forward and shook Craig's hand. "Diana Sohn," she said. She wore a charcoal skirt and a buttoned up white blouse. A matching grey jacket hung from a hanger on a coat stand near the door. Her auburn hair was scraped back, revealing a full face practically bereft of make-up. Her dark opaque eyes didn't pierce so much as absorb and gave an alert impression.

After some polite preamble about one of Craig's articles Robert had apparently shown her, Diana came to the point. "Our paper is interested in the article you propose to write. Robert has told me of your ideas, but I'd like to hear them from you. We can talk about money in a minute. Are you interested?"

"Yes, very."

"Okay, good. Talk to me."

"I'm going to use the attacked schoolboy incident. I was wondering whether I could do some small upfront articles."

"We have already reported that."

"I know. But I want to address the civil courage angle."

"Go on."

"This kind of thing has become so commonplace that – and no offence intended – the reporting of the incident was marginal."

"I'm listening."

"I think this is a good opportunity to rise above your competition. You know, lead the way in saying Hamburg will not tolerate racism."

She pondered for a moment. "It was still a minor incident..."

"And we haven't got all the details," said Robert. "What about using the *Imbiss* Molotov cocktail or even the pub attack on Saturday?"

"Those were just gang things. You know, feudal stuff," said Craig. "I think you should stick with the schoolboy. It's got the civil courage aspect. We should encourage that. Those lads who came to Faruk's rescue haven't been interviewed. Maybe–"

"They haven't been found," said Robert.

"They should be located and commended."

The door burst open. An exuberant youth looked in. "Oh, sorry Diana. I'll come back later." He began closing the door.

"When my door's closed, Siggy, you knock."

Siggy nodded apologetically and closed the door.

"Sorry about that," Diana said. "He's new." She let a moment's silence distance the interruption. "I see where you're going." Craig wondered whether she thought he was trying to milk the situation for more money. "Let me think for a minute." After a short silence she leaned forward. "What about a reward or prize for Faruk's rescuers?"

"That's great," said Craig. "It gives my upfront article more purpose and certainly positions the paper as a champion of civil courage."

"Yes," said Robert, "but we could attract all kinds of cranks."

"True," Diana agreed. "We need something that identifies

them as Faruk's rescuers."

"I could talk to him," said Craig.

"Okay," said Diana, sitting up and adjusting the papers on her desk. "Get something uniquely identifying from Faruk and write it up. We can get it out tomorrow, if you get it to me fast enough. Now, let's talk money."

15:00

Dannaks approached the man standing at the doorway to the St. Pauli house. There was no garden, the uninspired three storey terraced house opened directly onto the pavement. The only thing that distinguished this one from its neighbours was the colour of its door and window frames. It was green. Age and grime had taken its gloss. The building was tight and mean: three storeys high with sash windows. The man at the door was contrastingly colourful. He had yellow hair that could only be dyed, wore beige slacks and a white short-sleeved shirt with a bow tie at his neck. He looked more like a media personality than a Homicide detective. Dannaks was surprised by his youth. Were they getting younger or was he getting older? He saw Uwe, Lampe and two others from Narcotics approach. That was timing.

There were throwaway introductions and Dannaks missed the detective's name. The man spoke hastily but authoritatively. Dannaks saw that his bow tie was patterned with brown Tasmanian devils roaring and frolicking. Another colourful character. He glanced at Uwe who read his thoughts and smiled.

Dannaks's day had been dull. Most of his work had been at his desk. He tried to shift the wealth of minor tasks various members of the team had given to him. A lot of the jobs, confirming alibis and the like, were solved through simple telephone calls. One related to seized right-wing material. Another was a resident's complaint against the staging of a right-wing concert: they wanted to take the organisers to court.

This was the real work of the *Kripo*: laborious desk work, the routine shuffling back and forth of bits of paper. Being a detective was rarely glamorous. The stakeout on Friday had been an exception; itself the culmination of a case that had been painstakingly developed over many months. Mostly hours were invested in following up and documenting petty crime. Cases were developed and then, unless one of them turned into a major crime, were broken off or superseded by a more important one. Some

151

seventy-five percent of so-called petty crime never reached the courts. The *Kripo* built up files only to see them come to nothing. And the *Schupo* was frustrated, running around nabbing the same criminals over and over again. A liberal justice system, an over-reaction to the past, was trussed up by its own legal machinations and often resulted in lenient sentencing. All this did nothing to motivate the length and breadth of the force.

At some point Frank had called him into his office. There he had been made to give up Patel's address. He thought of giving the shopkeeper a warning phone call, but it was risky. Besides the health authorities would not move so quickly.

The noise made by six men trudging up the stairs rendered talk impossible. Only when they were outside Freddy's second floor flat did the Homicide detective, Dannaks had named Tasmanian Devil, turn to them. "Let's talk inside. I suggest we go in the lounge and organise ourselves from there." He then split the paper sticker that sealed the door with the key he used to open it.

The lounge was musty and still. Freddy's persona lingered. Uwe lifted a sash window. Fresh air and the sounds of outside were immediate intruders. They pillaged the stillness. But somehow, although evidence of Freddy was all around them, the open window emphasised his absence.

"As you know this was not the scene of the crime. We've been through here and satisfied ourselves that there's nothing of worth. However, this is an ongoing investigation. If you find anything, you'll have to show it to me." He considered whether he had more to say. "It's all yours. I'll be back in, say, two hours?" Uwe nodded.

After he left, Uwe allocated search areas. "I'll take the hallway and bathroom. You two, the bedroom. Dannaks and Lampe, you can do in here."

"Do I have to work with him?"

Uwe scowled. "You don't have to hold hands. I can draw a line down the room if you want? At least I'll know you're getting on with it and not gassing."

"What are we looking for?" asked one of the bedroom officers.

"Anything," said Uwe. "But I think he had a telephone book or diary. If we could find that–"

"Homicide would have found it," said Dannaks.

"They didn't."

"So we're looking for something that's hidden," said Lampe, taking off his jacket and tossing it on the sofa.

Uwe nodded. The others removed their jackets and put them on the sofa too. Only Dannaks kept his on. He could feel his skin begin to prickle.

Lampe went straight to the hi-fi and began pulling out the records. "Who has records these days?" he said to himself contemptuously.

"I do," said Dannaks, looking over from the bookshelf. He chose to omit saying that he didn't have a record player.

Lampe gave him a disgusted look and turned back to the LPs. "The only good thing is the artwork," he muttered.

Dannaks pulled out every book and looked on the shelf behind it, read the title and checked the cover before rifling the pages. One shelf was dedicated to tobacco tins with lids displaying soldiers and sailors from the Napoleonic era. There were glorious sailing ships too. Dannaks thought of the *Windjammer*.

Lampe examined each record, its sleeve and cover. Twenty minutes later he began taking the hi-fi apart. Meanwhile Dannaks left the shelving and began on the ornaments and hanging pictures: a flamenco dancer, an autumnal forest scene. He'd seen photographs of Freddy, Freddy with his son and his son alone. There was none of his wife.

Uwe came in. "How are you doing?"

"Another hour I'd say," said Dannaks, who was checking the underside of a corduroy armchair.

"Anything?"

"No."

"Lampe?"

"Not even some decent music to put on this antique," he said, keeping his back to them.

"I'll start on the sofa," said Dannaks, lifting the jackets and putting them on the armchair. Seeing that Lampe was suitably engrossed he gave Uwe a nod and patted his jacket pocket.

Uwe left the room taking out his handy. Dannaks removed the cushions and squeezed them. He then ran his hand along the inside rim of the sofa. Then he got down on his hands and knees and lifted the front edge of the sofa. Like the armchair the underside was a wooden-frame with stretched sackcloth. There was a lot of dust. Checking Lampe once more he wedged the diary between the frame and the cloth just behind one of the front legs. His nose tingled as he got up and went to the other end of the sofa. In the hallway he could see Uwe watching and waiting. "Give us a hand, Lampe," he managed before the sneezing fit began. Lampe looked over and sighed. As he went to the other end, Dannaks thought he had his sneezing under control. "Dust." He tried to furtively glance into the hallway. Uwe should call him in the next few seconds. As they tipped the sofa backwards Dannaks began sneezing again. "Put it down," he said, easing the sofa onto its back. He continued to sneeze and moved towards the door, leaving Lampe with the upturned sofa. The toilet flushed. His handy began to ring and he fumbled for it between sneezes. At the doorway he put the phone to his ear. "Dannaks." The line was dead, but Dannaks said: "I'll phone you back." Without turning he went to the bathroom. "He's a walking disaster," someone said. Uwe let him in and Dannaks grabbed toilet paper to blow his nose.

When he returned to the lounge, his nose tingling but under control, the sofa was still upturned. Lampe was at the hi-fi again, but with his jacket on.

Dannaks looked at the sofa. The diary was gone.

16:33

He sat on the bench in the underground cool. Posters warmed the tiled walls with clumsy advertisements. Sound-bites relying on photography of picture book simplicity. Few people were about. He pulled out a paper and turned to the article he'd given to Robert, examining whether editing had affected its original meaning.

Hearing the train he hastily folded the paper into his bag and moved to the edge of the platform. He watched the carriages whiz by, looking hard for Stefan. As the train slowed he walked towards the last carriage, all the time looking for Stefan. Most passengers favoured the end carriages because the station exits were generally located at the ends. Stefan was a surfer and would choose the last carriage.

But he hadn't spent the entire day riding the *S-Bahn* system. After leaving the *Tagespost* he had made a housecall.

Before ringing the doorbell, Craig again switched on the cassette recorder concealed in his jacket pocket; the small microphone was clipped to his belt.

A big man, with a chin beard that met a thin well-trimmed moustache, opened the door. His stony, grey eyes were uncompromising and he educed an overpowering aura of hard authority: granite to Suleyman's weathered hardwood.

"*Herr* Krohn?"

"Who are you?"

"I'm a reporter."

"What the Devil do you want?"

"I'd like to ask you some questions about your son–"

"I have no son." He was closing the door.

"Your son, Karsten. He's a–"

"He's no longer my son." The door was almost closed.

"Could he be responsible for the attack on that schoolboy?"

The man hesitated. Then the door swung open and before Craig could react the man's fist had his collar gathered under his neck.

"You don't listen, do you?" He shook Craig like a doll. "I have no son. How the hell do I know who attacked that piece of shit? Perhaps somebody didn't like the stuff he was peddling. Now I don't know which hole you crawled out of, but why don't you get back there before I give your mother something to worry about?"

Craig was shoved away, discarded. He almost fell. By the time he found his feet the door was slammed shut.

On the way to the station he had checked the recording, listening for any morsel he could use. There was nothing. Ahead of him lay another tiresome day searching for Stefan. He was running out of time. All he had was a number of trivial second-hand incidents and a good measure of pain. Perhaps he could use Sunday's chaotic right-wing concert? The idea didn't fill him with enthusiasm.

This desperation had compelled him to seek out Rüdiger Krohn. He was chuffed at his own resourcefulness. The police station had let slip one important piece of information. The man was not at work today. It was an opportunity Craig couldn't afford to pass up. The man's private address was not listed in the telephone book and the police had not given it away. Craig had called angling clubs claiming to be a representative of an international fishing tournament in which Krohn had taken part and won. Unfortunately, he went on to explain, the handwriting on his entry form was illegible. Perseverance won through and the fourth club obliged him with the police officer's address.

Robert had given him Karsten Krohn's address.

By now he was utterly sick of riding the S-Bahn. He'd read. He'd made notes. All the while the futility of his search gnawed at him. Not only did he have to pick the right wagon at the right time, he also had to have the right line. And there were six of them. The blurb said they covered 144 kilometres and 67 stations. Half a million passengers used an average eight kilometres of the S-Bahn on a daily basis.

He was looking for one person.

16:47

The Tasmanian devil, TD, returned to lock up. He looked flushed and, although Dannaks couldn't smell alcohol, he wondered whether the man had been drinking.

"Any luck?" he asked. They were gathered in the lounge.

The silence was short-lived.

Lampe pulled out a plastic evidence bag from his jacket pocket. "I found this."

The others were surprised. Dannaks was dumbfounded. The bag contained the diary.

"It's some kind of diary," he said handing it to the Homicide detective and going on to explain where he had found it.

TD nodded appreciatively. "Thanks a lot. Anything else? Anybody?" Everyone was still. "Then, have a nice evening."

With that they all traipsed out; TD locking up and resealing after them.

Out on the street they went their separate ways.

When Uwe and Dannaks were out of earshot, heading towards the former's car, Dannaks said: "Well, that's a surprise."

17:10

Craig said hello to Petra when she came in and then quietly returned to the small workroom. He was beginning to feel intrusive. Nothing had happened to make him feel this way. On the contrary she said she was glad of the company.

Craig worked until he reached a point where he had to use the computer to go on. Rather than start it up and bury himself further, he wandered into the kitchen where she was cooking.

"How's it going?" he asked switching on the kettle.

"Two minutes." The small table was already set.

"Smells good."

"It's packet."

"Still smells good. Can I make you a cup of tea?"

She nodded, all the while stirring the seafood paella in the frying pan.

Then they were sitting in front of their plates, the heat of the paella steaming the window.

They talked about Robert's workplace. Craig told her of Diana Sohn's idea of a reward for Faruk's rescuers. He had reached Faruk at his home and after telling him of the reward idea he had asked him about something that would identify his saviours. Faruk was silent for a while and then he said that there was something but he couldn't remember. He needed time. With this Craig had called Sohn and in spite of this they agreed to go ahead with the upfront article.

Craig then talked of riding the S-Bahn fruitlessly searching for Stefan.

"And if you don't find him?"

"I have some other ideas. There's a neo-Nazi, Karsten Krohn. I might approach him. But I have even less hope of getting him to talk to me."

Petra offered a sympathetic expression.

"I'll do the kitchen," he said, when they'd finished. "I have to call Faruk first."

Suleyman broke the fifth ring of the phone. He said he was on his way out.

"I'll make it quick. I really need to talk to Farrie. I'm doing a small article for the Tagespost. It should help get the march approved. But whilst I have you on the phone I need to clear up one point. Why the tests? It's not normal, is it?"

Suleyman was silent for a moment and Craig wondered whether exasperation held his breath. "A few days ago we get letter from school. They say abnormalities in assignments of certain pupils. And they want rounds of tests to confirm suspicions."

"By abnormalities, you mean cheating?"

"The letter no say."

"Could I have the name of the school? A phone number would be great, if you have one."

"My son no cheat. He better than that. And he knows what he get if I find he lying."

"Surely the whole class must take the tests?"

"My son and other foreigners singled-out."

"Why didn't you tell me this before?"

"I think no important. Beating of son is important."

"Yes, of course. Er, well, can I speak to him?"

17:16

"What now, Sherlock?" Uwe had asked, pulling out from his parking space.

Lampe handing in the diary had been a blow, and Dannaks had every right to feel despondent.

"I have another idea," said Dannaks.

"A back-up plan?"

"Not really. More another approach. If I can't bait the source of the leak, maybe I can go for the receivers. It harks back to what the landlord's daughter said at the pub. Something along the lines of it being monstrous that large gangs can roam freely."

Uwe nodded. "And?"

"What if they were tipped off?"

"You're talking about Karsten Krohn's gang."

"Yes. The 211ers." Karsten Krohn's gang had become known as the 211ers, itself a play on 311 used to represent the Ku Klux Klan. K being the eleventh letter in the alphabet led to the 3Ks being represented by this number. 88 represented Heil Hitler, 28 was Blood and Honour and 211 was Karsten Krohn.

"What are you going to do?"

Dannaks explained.

"Give it a rest," said Uwe, shaking his head.

Dannaks had heard worse and he had heard worse from Uwe.

Uwe dropped him at Meßberg as requested and Dannaks took the U1 to Alsterdorf. From there he walked round to the *Polizeistern.*

He went straight to the *LKA* 7 offices, which for the most part were empty. But he found one man sitting at his computer terminal. Although the door was open Dannaks knocked. He introduced himself, adding that he was of course affiliated with *LKA* 7 and that they were therefore colleagues.

The man said his name was Oliver König and that Dannaks should call him Oli. Dannaks proceeded to speak in the familiar form with him, but didn't give his own first name away, saying he preferred being addressed with his surname.

"I'm interested in the figures behind this," he said, showing him the graph of right wing activity.

"That's a *Verfassungsschutz* thing," said Oli.

The fact was that the further up the hierarchy a report went the more nebulous it became. And the *VfS* were up in the clouds.

Dannaks wanted the original details and they came from the frontline. Essentially the *Schupo* was the frontline.

Dannaks looked at him dully.

"Yeah, right. What I mean is that we do have our statistics, but some don't reach us. The *Schupo* also supply the data. And the VfS do their own thing too."

"Okay. Then what have you on the 211ers and Karsten Krohn?"

"Krohn? The son of–"

"Yes."

"I–"

Weske appeared at the door. Dannaks stiffened.

"Dannaks, isn't it?"

"Yes. Yes, sir." He shook his hand.

The handshake was firm, but – in keeping with his emaciated appearance – somehow brittle. Weske had been variously called Wespe (a play on his name, meaning wasp) and the undertaker. If he had looked fitter, one would guess the gaunt man to be a marathon runner or similar.

"To what do we owe this unexpected pleasure?"

Dannaks couldn't believe his bad luck. Not only was Weske still at work, he had also come down from his top floor office.

He felt Oli about to speak and piped up. "I wanted to find out about some gang moments. The details behind this graph." Would it be enough?

Weske's spindly fingers took the sheet. He studied it for a moment. A moment too long as far as Dannaks was concerned. There wasn't that much to the graph. And he had surely seen it already.

Weske and Frank had interviewed him for the job. He felt Weske was behind him going to *Soko* REX rather than joining *LKA* 7. Maybe he merely wanted to see how he faired. Or maybe he lacked confidence in him because of his past. On an individual level Dannaks didn't know his superiors well enough, to know who was a friend and who a foe.

Weske was particularly opaque.

"Any gang in particular?" he asked.

Dannaks mentally cursed and hesitated, wondering whether he could risk a lie in front of Oli. "Not really."

Weske nodded contemplatively. He looked Dannaks in the

eye as he handed back the graph. Then he glanced at Oli, giving him what could pass as a smile. "Okay. Don't let him keep you. See you tomorrow."

"Have a nice evening, sir," said Oli.

Oli returned to his terminal. Neither man spoke until Weske was definitely gone.

"Karsten Krohn, right?" said Oli.

"Yeah. Thanks."

He wanted to test Oli's allegiance, by making a comment about Weske. Something along the lines of: now there's a man in desperate need of a sense of humour or a hearty meal, but Oli spoke first and the opportunity passed.

"I can tell you when members of his gang were caught."

"He's never been caught?"

"No. Are you surprised?"

"Not really." Being the son of a *Schupo* chief would have inherent advantages.

Oli tapped on the keyboard. "There's not much."

Dannaks looked at the screen. "Give me the bigger incidents."

"Define bigger."

"The involvement of more than ten of the gang."

"Gang is also ill-defined. Some of them hang out in different groups."

"Just what you've got."

"I've only got the reports, dates and names."

"What you've got." Dannaks could see it wouldn't be enough. He would have to interview the arresting uniforms who had filed the reports. What he wanted would not be here.

19:15

On arrival Hasan and Cenk had respectfully put their lips and then foreheads to the backs of many extended hands.

"We wanted to talk to you yesterday," began Cemal in Turkish, when the two of them were also seated, "but Suleyman had visitors."

Hasan glanced at Suleyman and nodded.

"We are worried," said the older man. "You know why we have asked to see you rather than Murat?"

"Yes," said Hasan quietly.

Cenk suppressed the urge to fidget in his chair. Aside from

160

the fact that Murat would probably scoff and scorn, it was debatable whether he would have turned up.

"This is not an inquisition. I want you to tell us what all this is about. I want you to explain the purpose of this gang. And then I want you to tell us exactly what happened on Sunday evening."

Cenk looked at the gathering of men. There were a dozen or so in the room. No women were present. The Elders was how he referred to them. These were the men who moved about the streets dressed in the clothes of their homeland: pinstriped suits, flimsy trousers, thin cardigans, a hat or woollen cap. They were some of the oldest of their community. The majority of them were older than Suleyman.

These then were the community leaders. Their social standing was unquestioned. Age gave them their prestigious positions. They were the *hodja's* trusted men chosen by their common understanding. Except to pray they rarely met formally. More often than not they moved in social circles playing backgammon or dominoes drinking coffee or tea. Only when there was what they considered an emergency did they congregate to discuss the problem. This was not an isolated Anatolian village, although the concentration of Turkish people in the area gave them a sense of seclusion, but the same rules applied to those who respected their cultural ways.

"What this is all about," Hasan began slowly, "is the formation of a group to protect our community." Cenk noted that he'd chosen to avoid the word gang. He knew he had swallowed bile to ask Murat to take on his shift tonight. Hopefully he was behaving. Hasan would have to do Wednesday and Thursday.

There was some murmuring and stirring and someone tried to interrupt, but Cemal, with understanding in his wide craggy face, stilled them with an ever so slight wave of his hand.

Cenk prayed Hasan would present a reasoned argument.

"We decided to do this after the attack on Farrie." Cenk looked at Suleyman. Hasan had unsettled himself with clumsy phrasing. The opening 'we decided' was ill chosen. With respect to those about him, the 'we' were just a bunch of youths. Who were they to decide what was good for the community? Using Faruk as the reason was a ploy to connect with them. Of course it was true, but now it was said it seemed flimsy. So he reminded them of the hospitalisation of a grocer earlier in the year. "Erkan's beating was worse. And everyone agreed that the sentencing of those right-wingers was too mild. Our group is for protection, nothing more." Hasan's lips betrayed his nervousness: they always became slightly askew when embarrassed.

An elder with a shock-white beard was running a small string of beads between his forefingers and thumb of one hand first one way then the other. His motion ticked away silent seconds.

Cemal nodded his close-cropped, grey-haired head.

"That's the purpose of the group," Hasan went on. "What happened on Sunday evening was, er, something that I knew nothing about... Until after it had happened. I was not there." Seeing the end in sight, his speech quickened, but he made more mistakes. "The, er, gan– group is in two parts. I lead one and Murat leads the other. His group went to Bergedorf and attacked the snack bar." Pause. The beads ticked off three seconds. "I phoned him yesterday. He said things got out of hand. He was sorry." Cenk thought the last sentence an embellishment. He didn't know how well the elders knew Murat, but it was debatable whether they believed Hasan. "I wanted to keep tabs on Murat, so on Sunday I insisted Cenk went with him. That's why I brought him to the meeting. He was there." Cenk felt their attention shift to him. An elder, his eyes swimming behind solid dark-rimmed glasses, sent him a wisp of a smile. The smile was enigmatic and Cenk suspected something insidious behind his all-consuming eyes.

Hasan looked at Cenk paternally. "You'd better tell them what you told me."

Cenk's language of choice was German. If he thought Hasan had been nervous, then his re-telling of events gave the word a new meaning. His voice was at times controlled and at others excited. He went down cul-de-sacs and tied himself in knots trying to explain his actions. He attempted to weave a reasoned story but it unravelled from the start. He tried to justify his actions. He claimed he had no choice. Finally, he attempted to distract them with his heroism. He went back for Nazim. Here he floundered too, embarrassed by his courage which somehow cheapened in the telling.

19:34

Dannaks looked over the papers Oli König had printed. The reports were unrevealing. He knew he would be dissatisfied. What he was looking for would not be documented. Successful results were recorded. The one that got away would at best be hinted. Five stations had submitted various reports, but only two were of interest to him. Noting the incident details and names of the participating officers, but especially those who had filed the reports, he pegged the two stations to visit.

He also had a report on Holger Markowiak, the officer who had killed Nobby Kabel. There was nothing remarkable about him. He had completed his service, retired and died. But there had been enough suspicion surrounding the shooting for the BKA to take over the case. There was talk that both Nobby Kabel and Holger Markowiak harboured Nazi leanings. It was also put into question whether Kabel was actually carrying out a robbery. Whatever, the BKA took over the investigation and promptly buried it. Inquiries were evaded. Eventually a report was published that essentially claimed a lack of evidence.

Freddy had mentioned Nobby Kabel. He was significant. Why? Because he had been a bent police officer? Because he had Nazi leanings?

19:50

Cemal waited. His eyes were downcast, his wrinkled brow ridged with concentration.

"It is not often that we gather like this," he said eventually. "When we do, it is to discuss something that affects the well-being of the community."

The authority behind the Elders was inherent in the structure of the community. Ostracism in a small village in Turkey was unbearable. The Turkish quarter was segregated and like a village within the city. Intrinsic in the Turkish way of life was the importance of the family. And the good standing of that family within the community was fundamental. Therefore, although some youths flouted the elders and their ways, they were influenced and constrained by loyalty to their family and the standing of their family within the community. This structure was brought across by the first to arrive in the country and subsequently reinforced by the need to support one another.

"We are in a country that is not our home. We are in a country that does not accept our children, although born here as full and fellow members of the community. For them this is a particularly tragic situation. Most of them do not feel Turkish and are not permitted to feel German. Most of us in this room have tried to bring them up the Turkish way. For some this has been too difficult and they have returned to Turkey. For those who remain, remain as a part of a Turkish community. I think this is right. Our heritage must not be lost. We are not allowed anything else. Even Murat chooses to live among his own people, even though he – and many others of his generation – does not respect our ways. The truth is that we are in a situation were the actions of one affect us all. The idea of an organisation to protect us is not a bad idea. That is not at issue here. What is at issue is a gang that stems from our people and attacks in our name. This is criminal and we want no part of it. There are criminals amongst our people, but they are not members of this community and we do not harbour their likes. They have their own codex. There is no room for their kind amongst us. When these streets become too dangerous for our children to play and feel safe–"

"It's already happened," interrupted Suleyman.

Cemal nodded.

"Then we are lost. Here we are numerous. In reality we are few. We are an island. When the island is attacked or besieged we are lost. We do not have the numbers to truly defend ourselves.

"The attack on Faruk happened outside our community." He raised his hand before anyone could interrupt. "He is not the first and he will not be the last. But whatever happens, we must remember that we do not have the numbers to fight openly. Our fight must come from within the German population. We have a special, and sometimes fragile, relationship with the police. We have a special relationship with multicultural groups and social workers. These things are fundamental, part of the fabric of a society. We cannot afford to jeopardise our position. I believe that it is getting better here. There are enough German people on our side. But the minute we take up arms we lose a lot of them. And we become no better than the people we fight. We become the aggressors.

"Germany needs our youth. The population is top heavy and our youth pays their pensions. Without the *Gastarbeiter* Germany cannot function. The refugees are necessary too – and I have heard voices amongst our own, complaining about the effect they are having on us. This is foolish. They too are Germany's future and therefore our future. Their number is another issue. That is a problem for the Germans. Many will be sent back. These right-wing swine cannot stop the flow. They can fight and kill, but with each outrage they seal their own fate. Each step they take forces the Germans to rethink their position. I don't know how far it will go. I don't know how far the German population can be pushed. But I do know that the real teeth of Nazism in Germany were pulled when they lost the war. Our youth is Germany's blood and future. Therefore in the name of integration they will protect our youth. The press will protect our youth. The World image the Germans wish to project will protect our youth. Ultimately, Human Rights, the European Community will protect our youth."

He paused and then turned to Suleyman.

"How many sympathetic groups have contacted you?"

"I don't know. There have been so many." He thought for a moment. "Most of them are youth movements. Some are Left-wing extremists."

Cenk was glad Suleyman spoke in Turkish. He knew his German was diabolical.

"We stay well away from them. Extremism is blind."

"I have kept away from them. I have only maintained links with authorised media people."

"I know you are trying to organise a march. I don't know whether the attack on your son warrants such attention. Don't get me wrong. But I am not sure we need such unrest." He stopped Suleyman interrupting with a flutter of a hand. "But that's another issue. Now we must find a solution to our problem." He looked at Hasan. "Are you the leader of this gang?"

"Yes, I er–" He was unprepared for the question. "Yes. But the group is in two parts and I cannot control both."

"Murat controls one and you the other?"

He nodded.

"Why did you go to him in the first place?"

"He's always been on the fringes. And he's always wanted to be part of the community. I mean really part of it and I, er, thought that this would be a good way to bring him in."

"The fringes being his work of a shady nature."

Hasan grew hot. "Yes, I know. But he has never had a chance. I thought that this would bring him over to us."

"Black and white. Good and bad. Did it not occur to you that this might have been the opportunity he had been looking for? He is at best a hooligan. He could be worse: a gangster. Did you not think that he might have wanted power of this kind? Because of you he thinks we are behind him. You must tell him that he is on his own, especially when he carries out such attacks. We will not jeopardise our relationship with the German authorities."

Cenk wanted to say that they were condemning the wrong man. Oh, the attack on the snack bar was down to him. But the firebombing was Ponytail's doing. Had Murat known? If they thought Murat was a questionable character, what would they think of Ponytail? He was beyond the periphery of their community. He was criminal.

"I understand. It won't happen again. He thought he was doing the right thing."

"Firebombing is not doing the right thing. It is terrorism. Nothing to do with defending the people." Cemal looked at Cenk. "Have you no idea who threw the Molotov cocktail?"

He felt the heat in his face as he shook his head.

Cenk knew it was only a matter of time before the police interviewed him. The usual suspects had been approached and Murat had already been questioned.

Cemal looked at Hasan, who raised his shoulders.

"As to this gang affair, I am not against a protecting group. Your intentions were honourable, but suspect. Your involvement legitimises Murat's actions. Maybe you can tell Murat exactly what your function is. I doubt it. But everyone must know, otherwise you'll have every fool wanting to be part of it. If Murat doesn't abide by the rules, if he chooses aggression, then you must distance yourself from him.

"Finally, the man who threw the petrol bomb must be expelled and given over to the law. Find him and do it. Your gang is in danger of becoming a terrorist group. When that happens, you will have no sanctuary here. And we will not hesitate to expel you and give you over to the law. Have I made myself clear?"

Wednesday
08:58

Karsten ignored the doorbell. Whoever it was at this ungodly hour was persistent.

For a time he stared at the old Imperial War flag hanging above the bed. He smiled at the metal rings in the ceiling, similar to those used to hang baskets of plants; but these had another function and nothing hung from them. He stretched luxuriously. Then he brushed his palms along the side of his shorn head, listening to the rasp of sandpaper.

The ringing continued. Karsten tore the sheets back and stomped to the flat door. As he crossed the room he looked out of the window and searched the car park below for a woman to look at his magnificent nakedness. There was nobody. He took the intercom handset from the wall.

"Yes?"

"Karsten Krohn?"

"Who is it?"

"My name's Craig St. James. I'm doing an article–"

"You're a reporter?"

"No. I work alone. I'm–"

"Piss off."

"Just a few questions. We could do it like this if you want. I don't have to come–"

Karsten replaced the handset. He turned to the window again. Was it the shopping day of that peroxide from the second tower block? He waited. Smiled at his manhood. The bell rang again.

He snatched up the handset and strangled the visitor. "I said piss off. You ring once more and it'll be the last thing you do." He hung up again.

He waited. Maybe he should have asked if there was money involved. They could certainly use some. Jutta's salary and her short-changing *Ausländers* at the cash-till and pilfering were sorely missed. Not only was she no longer earning, they also had another mouth to feed. All that baby paraphernalia was daylight robbery; most of it was useful for only a few months. Now he knew why kids often went about in clothes a size or two too big for them.

The reporter was not a German. He sounded American. There was no movement in the car park, so he hadn't come by car. Unless he was still at the door or staking out the flat. That wouldn't be

167

something new.

He'd been cleared of involvement in the pub attack, but questioned about the beating of the schoolboy. Only a rubbish run could explain the presence of skinheads in that part of the city. A rubbish run was simply dumping a van load of unwanted and broken articles on their doorstep. It wasn't rubbish in the sense of refuse, but things that were normally expected to be taken to a dump: old mattresses, broken stereos, ironing boards, vacuum cleaners, that sort of thing. This was how they lived. Amongst the rubbish, a step away from the dump. The advantages of a rubbish run were two-fold. Firstly, you got rid of your rubbish. And secondly, but most importantly, the good German people saw what vermin lived alongside them.

None of his lads had admitted to attacking the schoolboy or even being in the area at the time of the attack. It was probably countryside boys. There were many of them out there in the sleepy villages.

He went to the kitchen and switched on the electric kettle. Then he went to the windowsill and took one of the two mugs hanging from the bent arms and clenched fists of the statue. After spooning coffee into the mug he went back to the statue and removed the second mug. He picked the bronze up, so that he could study the workmanship. Of course it didn't look anything like the owner. The only resemblance was that of age: the proprietor of *Die ruhenden Handschuhe* belonged to this era of bare-fisted street fighting.

Karsten checked his own scraped knuckles.

He had pushed the others so he could be the last to leave the building in the hope that all the bulls would be occupied. At the window he'd seen that there were too many of them. Wheeling about he'd gone upstairs. There he found a window with a reachable drainpipe, opened it, checked the sturdiness of the fittings and climbed out. One of his worshippers followed. "Coming?" Karsten asked. The youth hesitated. "If not close the window." He glared. The youth then climbed out. His trepidation could be seen in the caution of his movements.

Some time later they decided to risk entering the house and getting past any remaining police. They edged open the window and climbed in. When they were descending the stairs, Karsten spotted the bronze through an open bedroom door. It sat on a dressing table.

They were on the stairs, almost too late, when they heard the police conversing. Karsten said they should return to the roof. The youth reluctantly agreed. But Karsten didn't return to the window. The youth waited whilst he went to the bedroom for the statue. A sudden lull in the conversation, coinciding with a crack of the landing floorboards alerted the police. Karsten dashed to the window.

"Come on," Karsten hissed.

"I–"

Karsten pushed past him and clambered out, the statue rammed into his waist belt.

"Close it," said Karsten. "Properly."

And the youth slid the window down. Karsten heard him twist the latch closed. Good lad.

He heard the commotion. They questioned the youth. He said he'd hidden under a bed. He heard him say that he didn't think anyone else was hidden, but they would search the house anyway. They didn't think to unlock the window and look out.

Karsten had waited. He was practised at waiting and watching. Of course, a helicopter would have spotted him, but the bulls wouldn't use one now. It was all over. And earlier it would have been too noisy for the late hour. In any case it would have been too expensive. He knew very well how the police worked.

It had been cold, but with little wind. The commotion died and a couple of uniforms remained to guard the building. He waited until he thought they were sitting in their vehicle before descending the drainpipe. Too bad he hadn't brought his gloves.

On the ground he'd moved from shadow to shadow to his motorbike. He pushed it a good two hundred metres before starting it and racing off. He'd got home at six in the morning.

In the days between then and now he had catnapped his sleep deficit away. Nevertheless he would have liked a lie-in. In bed the day stretched out before him. Now, because of the reporter, he had the morning to fill too.

On paper he was unskilled, but he had built a reputation as a handyman. A carpentry firm sometimes sub-contracted him and gave him back-handers. Once in a while he helped wire-up a house. He even did the odd paint-job. To the authorities he was unemployed. To this society he was unemployable.

He'd put the day aside for working on his surprise. Jutta

would be back from her parents next Tuesday. He had less than a week. In two or three afternoons he could have it finished, but he needed more material and that meant money. Without a contract on the horizon another burglary was the only option.

He looked about the room. Her sewing box lay open by the wardrobe.

He wondered how long it would take her to notice that the larger safety pins were missing. The lads had liked that idea.

10:34

Karsten shoved the shelving to one side. There was just enough room here for him to get behind the stack of wood and bric-a-brac to the prize. It was unfinished. Stopped months before lung cancer claimed his mother. He'd left home by then. No doubt his leaving hadn't helped, but his father was to blame for everything. Everything. Especially her death.

The back was missing, but the curved pieces were with spines and the seat was made but not fitted. Now he would cannibalise it. She would understand. She would want him to do it: for the granddaughter she would never meet.

From rocking chair to rocking horse. All he had was a picture from one of Jutta's magazines. But it was enough. He was that good. Karsten knew wood. And practical arithmetic was second nature. Carpentry and fishing were probably the only things he had in common with his father. At least, the only things he'd care to admit.

He removed a tool from its place. Karsten was organised. But he would not be fanatical. His father had kept the original packaging of the tools he bought. He always packed everything away. His fastidiousness drove Karsten and his mother to despair. His father was a stickler for order too. Everything had its place. When he was younger Karsten had joined him in choosing the optimal position. Ultimately it was his father's decision. And that was that. Towards the end Karsten had moved things in the house: an ashtray went to the other end of the mantelpiece; an ornament would be turned; a desk lamp angled wrongly. But his game backfired when his father blamed his mother. Karsten challenged him and lost. His father had training and easily wrestled him to the ground. Now with National Service behind him, the outcome could be different.

He placed the pieces on the workbench and imaged the

170

rocking chair that would never be. The plan for it came from the western "The sons of Katie Elder." Attached to this film was his father: he too was a lumbering John Wayne of a character. His mother had been the little woman, at one time fiery, eventually fragile. Was he as much to blame for her demise? He didn't like to think about it. But she'd deteriorated as he'd grown. Every time his father and he had been at loggerheads she'd shrunk, cowering away from the titans in their increasingly frequent tussles. Until he'd left home at fifteen.

He now saw that as a schoolboy his self-mutilation had undoubtedly exacerbated the situation. Meddling teachers and contrastingly stern and sugar-sweet social workers had tried to get behind his cutting himself. SVV they called it: *Selbstverletzendes Verhalten* (self-injurious behaviour). At the time he didn't understand why he did it. They were his arms and legs and the cutting gave him pleasure. Full stop.

What had Jutta said when they had first met? "God, you've been in some battles. Who've you been fighting?"

After a moment he gave the only answer he had: "Myself."

He'd left home before his mother died. The SVV stopped the day he heard about her death. She hadn't committed suicide but thoughts that she didn't even want to live for him were buried deep in his psyche. Ultimately he believed that his father had as good as killed her.

Now he could see that he was doing the same with Jutta. It hadn't been a problem before. She was as hard as old boots and could handle a good bashing. He'd admired her for her strength of character. She was an exceptional Renée. She could be his equal: gods among mortals. But of late – he thought from the time of her pregnancy – she'd become soft: awash with hormones. Now she crumpled under him. And he despised her. And he despised himself. For he understood the change in her and he envied her connection with life.

There was a fine piece of wood for the horse's head. Chunky and silky and just like the seat. He'd sanded it, rubbed and oiled it until it appeared moulded. Why, he'd almost massaged it into its present supple state.

He'd had mixed feelings when she became pregnant. Procreation was a way of beating the enemy. Most German women had lost their way. Emancipation had led them astray to become frustrated dried up executive prunes, lesbians or both. But Jutta and her kind knew that a woman's biological purpose was birth and nurturing children. It was the Christian way.

Yet, sometimes he wanted to pick up the child by the ankles, both in one hand and smash it against the wall. All the worm did was sleep, suck and shit. Jutta had assured him that she'd grow. That didn't alter the fact that Jutta had changed. She had little time for him and was always too tired for anything. Their sex life was non-existent. Some said a baby brings parents together. He felt the opposite. The baby was a wedge between them.

Now he had time. She thought he needed time alone, but maybe she wanted to get away from his belt. Or maybe she thought her absence would make him appreciate her? Ha, he couldn't change. Gods don't become mortals. But she'd done it? Perhaps she had never been a god? Or perhaps women were flawed at birth, by birth: the womb being their Achilles' heel?

11:03

They were easy to find. They inhabited their own world in the middle of the busy station like frightened animals. They slouched together against a wall at the bottom of an escalator underground. And when roused they acted defiantly, reacting and overreacting unpredictably, oblivious to the general public or perhaps because of them. That's why they were left alone.

He broke into the group, addressing no one in particular. "Hi, I'm Craig St. James–" The two girls were as bedraggled as the four men. All had greasy rat-tailed hair, forlorn eyes, ill-fitting clothes, rounded shoulders and dying pride glowing weakly in their eyes, waiting for the opportunity to flare or fall. He sensed their suspicion. "I'm looking for a person named Stefan." They stared at him blankly. "He rides the *S-Bahn*." Nothing. "Do any of you know him?" The two girls suddenly got interested in a belt one of them was wearing.

A drawn-looking youth broke away. Craig saw him wink at the others. "Hey man, you're English aren't you?" He put his arm about Craig as if they were pals. Craig smelt his breath. He was little more than a walking cadaver and Craig wondered whether he had

172

Aids. All his features were pulled down like melted wax. Despite hunching over he was a good head taller than Craig.

He half leaned and half led Craig away from the group. "What do you want?"

"Stefan. He's a surfer."

"We're all surfers, man."

"Do you know Stefan?"

"I know a lot of Stefans." Craig ignored the looks of the commuters. The cadaver leaned into Craig's comfort zone, but Craig couldn't pull away. "I'm looking for the one who surfs the S-Bahn."

"What for?"

Craig sighed. "I want to interview him."

"For money?"

"Maybe."

"Interview me–"

"No, I–"

"I've got a story to tell."

"First Stefan."

"Stefan, Stefan, Stefan. Come on, man. Get real."

"What do you mean?"

"Show me something."

"When I get to see Stefan."

"You got a handy?"

"Yes." Craig had practically given up.

"Give it to me."

"Let me call."

"No."

"Why not?"

"Come on, give us your handy."

Despite his height Craig felt the man was a pushover. He gave him his handy. The youth turned back to the group. Craig followed closely. The group was on the ground, sitting in a loose circle. The cadaver bent down and spoke quietly to one of the girls. Craig waited. The girl looked at him and then tapped in some numbers.

Above the noise of the station Craig could not hear what she said. She handed it to the cadaver. He listened to her and then returned it to Craig. "He'll meet you at three at Halstenbek."

"Great."

173

"Fifty," said the cadaver holding out his hand. Craig cautiously took out his wallet and pulled out a twenty.

"That's more than enough."

Just then two station sheriffs came down the escalator. The cadaver and the rest of the group were up and away. The sheriffs walked after them.

Craig went above ground and pressed re-dial. The automatic message: "no connection under this number," greeted him. "Shit," he said aloud.

He went to a snack bar and ordered a coffee. No sooner had he sat down than his handy rang.

"Hi, Craig. It's Rob. How's it going?"

"Getting nowhere fast. I've just been ripped off and the coffee's crap."

"Ripped off?"

"I'll tell you later."

"It might cheer you up to know that the march has been approved."

Craig's civil courage article had appeared in the *Tagespost*. It had been tailored to the paper's style and the editor had removed some of the bite, but the jab at complacency remained. So Craig was not disappointed. Despite the lack of confirmation his mentioning of a planned protest on Saturday had not been cut.

"Great. Where?"

"*Rathaus.*"

"Good."

"And the length of Mönckenbergstrasse. All you have to do is find the numbers to make something of it. You and a dozen Turks–"

"You know better than that. Extended families and all."

"Okay, you and thirty Turks, not counting grandma and grandpa. It's still not going to be very impressive."

"We'll see. It's only Wednesday. The Left could get interested."

"You mean they'll hijack it and use it to have a go at the right-wingers at Deichtorhalle? Incitement is an offence."

"I'm not planning on doing a thing. But the Left wouldn't miss an opportunity like this, would they?"

"Too right, they wouldn't."

"Any resonance on my article?"

"Nothing, yet."

"It's someone from the *Schupo* for you," said Reinhart, pushing the phone his way.

On his way to the station Dannaks had bought a large cheese and salad baguette for lunch. When he said he was eating lunch in the office, Reinhart apparently thought that he too should show such enthusiasm for work and had exclaimed: "You've got to have a lunch break."

"Yes, you have," said Dannaks.

Reinhart may have heard an emphasis on the word you, for before leaving the office he added: "It's law."

Once he was gone Dannaks had looked up the police station and gone through the list of uniforms who worked there, looking for anyone who might know him. Satisfied that he was safe he had made his call.

As luck would have it the duty officer had said he would have to get back to him.

Now Reinhart was back at his desk examining the tip of his pencil. Their conversation had obviously occupied his thoughts whilst he was out, because when he returned he said: "You're one of those workaholic types." It went through Dannaks's head to say something like compared to him everyone was a workaholic, but he just smiled instead.

"Sorry about before," said the man on the telephone, "but we had a disturbance. How can I help?"

"Does *Polizeimeister* Witt still work there?"

"Christoph Witt. Yes."

"What shift is he on?"

"Lates."

"So the best time to catch him would be now or ten tonight."

"Yes. I could get him to call you. What's it about?"

"That's okay. I'll come in," he said and hung up. He didn't want to forewarn the man.

Reinhart was staring at him. His wrist turning as he sharpened a pencil.

"Shouldn't we be getting on?" asked Dannaks.

As Frank had said, short of murder, REX received all manner of cases. Reinhart and Dannaks were to visit a refugee home where there had been a rape. With men and women cooped up on these sites it was little wonder that trouble occurred. They were not permitted to work until they were accepted into the country and the process of deciding eligibility took months, sometimes years. Women and families were housed in separate corridors or houses. But the majority of refugees were single men and many of the women were subject to sexual harassment. Ethnic groups naturally formed hierarchies within these artificial societies and rivalry was rife. The situation was a powder keg with a short fuse. Indeed, many had turned to petty crime; a sure way to have their application declined.

"I was waiting for you."

Waiting was the word, Dannaks thought. The man could at least have been doing something useful; instead he had been idling his time away sharpening his pencils.

Reinhart caught his observation.

"Shall I do yours while I'm at it?"

"No."

16:33

Craig sat on a bench and pulled a magazine from his bag.

He had given up for the day, having convinced himself that he would have to make do with the notes he had gathered. He could make a last-ditch search tomorrow morning. He wasn't sure. In a strange way giving up was a relief.

The underground station was little more than a tunnel with a single central platform sandwiched between two rails. Because it had been silent for some time the sound of the train behind him, travelling in the opposite direction, caused him to glance up.

For an instant he saw the driver through the glass of the truncated face of the vehicle and, as he returned to his magazine, something on that side of the platform caught his eye.

There were a number of passengers waiting to board the train, but because of the billboards that divided the platform length-wise, he was unable to see them all. At the far end he sensed stifled movement that could only be youths or children restrained by an adult.

Craig wedged the magazine back into the bag and walked to the slowing train. He stopped and looked down the length of the platform. A neighbouring woman in her mid-forties broke from her mesmerised gaze and looked at him and, although he was looking beyond her, his eyes wavered.

They appeared when the train halted. There were three of them, shuffling with arrogant confidence towards the end carriage.

The leading youth grabbed the handles of the double doors and tore them apart. He and another boarded the train. A youth wearing a flak jacket and carrying a small limp rucksack followed them.

Craig followed the woman into the nearest carriage. Because they were separate units he would have to make his way down the train along the platform at the next stop.

There were not many people in the carriage, but there were enough to pose the uncomfortable choice of sitting near the woman in her mid-forties. She caught his eye and he saw the shimmer of a greeting.

Craig decided to stand.

The doors slid shut, rushing to a numbing close, and the train accelerated out of the station.

The carriages were of the old style, characteristic of the *S-Bahn* system: high-backed wooden benches that compartmentalised the interior. Unlike the *U-Bahn* carriages with their open-plan layout that resembled those of the London Underground.

At the next station he alighted and hastened down the length of the train. Just as the command for people to stand back came over the speaker system, Craig jumped into the front end of the last carriage.

As he walked down the aisle he could hear them boisterously talking and he wished he had brought somebody with him. Robert would have been a good choice, but a German would have been better. He noted the passengers in the carriage: an old man with a ragged face, two young men in suits and a woman, her daughter and a baby. The last carriage of the train had a compartment with extra space for bicycles or whatever. Here three benches of the wooden-slat type one would expect to see in a park lined the walls.

Craig stood at the entrance. "Hallo. I'm looking for somebody known as *S-Bahn* Stefan."

"Piss off," snapped the largest member of the trio.

"I'm Stefan," said the one in the flak jacket, stitched upon the shoulder of which was a confederate flag patch, a symbol of the Ku Klux Klan.

"My name's Craig St. James. I'm a freelance reporter. I'd like to interview you."

"Fuck off," said the big one.

21:58

After Dannaks identified himself, the duty officer behind

177

the Perspex called into the back of the room to fetch Witt. Dannaks couldn't see who left, but a few minutes later a younger man spoke to the man at the front. He nodded and waved Dannaks over to tell him that Witt was in the coffee room. He buzzed Dannaks through telling him to take the fourth left.

REX was housed in a similar station, but apart from the desk officer, he had no day-to-day contact with the uniforms. Having started as a uniform himself he knew only too well that they were at the front line. Alongside their service weapon they carried a telescopic truncheon and pepper spray. But respect for the uniform had eroded long ago. Some two hundred assaults on Hamburg police officers were logged annually.

Dannaks was tired. The rape case that afternoon had been strenuous. There had been too many babbling people. The need for interpreters rendered everything painfully sluggish. There were too many witnesses, too many contradictions, too many intrigues and it was difficult to know whom to believe. It was hopeless. They would have to continue tomorrow.

The coffee room was located next to the room of safety deposit boxes – resembling the squashed rectangular safes one would find in a bank. This was where the uniforms locked away their weapons. Six weary men were in some kind of banter. Dannaks had hoped to get Witt alone.

Calling it a coffee room was something of a misnomer. Indeed there was a coffee machine and appropriate paraphernalia between a microwave and a draining board and sink. There were also three Formica-topped tables. But oversized utilitarian shelves sported many large black kitbags. So that the place resembled a left luggage room.

Dannaks knocked on the open door and announced himself. "I'm looking for *Polizeimeister* Witt."

A big blond man said: "I'm Witt."

"REX is that *Ausländer* outfit, isn't it?" said another, sitting at the same table.

"You didn't say nigger to someone, did you?" said a third man, before Dannaks could speak.

"No, it's nothing like that. It's about this." He stepped into the room and handed over a printed copy of the report. He had thought of asking to speak to Witt alone, but on the fly he decided he had nothing to lose speaking in front of his colleagues. Indeed throwing a wider net could be rewarding.

Witt read and slowly nodded. "Yeah, I remember this." He put the sheet down and his colleague at the same table tried to read it surreptitiously.

"Maybe one of you was also there," said Dannaks, inviting them all to read the report.

"It's the motor club incident in Billstedt," said Witt. Then as the sheet began its round he asked Dannaks: "What's the problem?"

"No problem. I, er, just wanted to know whether you caught everybody that night."

"What do you mean?"

"I mean: did anyone get away?"

"Anyone in particular," asked the one at the same table. The idle way he asked was loaded with suspicion and Dannaks regretted his spur of the moment decision.

"No," he lied, also as indifferent as possible.

"Yeah, some got away," said Witt. "There weren't enough of us."

Dannaks knew that Karsten Krohn would not want special treatment. But he was now established and accepted – indeed a leader – amongst his right wing comrades. Perhaps now he would not be singled out because of his father. Dannaks really wanted to hear whether Krohn had been spotted, and had got away. He wanted more than that: he wanted to know whether they had let him get away. But he knew they would never admit to such a thing.

Dannaks waited for someone else to add something. His questioning look was met with blank expressions.

"Good," he said picking up the report that had been returned to the desk in front of him. "That's all, thanks a lot."

"Any time," said the one sitting at the desk with Witt.

Dannaks was outside the door, but distinctly heard one of them ask: "Who did he say he was?"

Dannaks walked in and greeted Reinhart who was finishing his banana.

As he hung up his jacket he wondered about Reinhart's manner. Normally he was a torrent of words. But today he was more than silent. What was it? Embarrassment? Guilt?

The day hadn't started routinely. The tiny hallway of his flat, sandwiched between kitchen and bathroom, was dull even on the brightest of days. To put on his shoes he always used the light. This morning it had lit, pinged and extinguished. Of course he dismissed the thought of it being an omen. But since childhood he always found it eerie. He made a note to buy a new bulb.

Reinhart got up and washed his hands.

Dannaks sat at his desk and pulled his files. He had a quarter of an hour to review his work before the morning meeting. He was struck by the odd feeling that something was wrong with his desk. He was an orderly person, but his desk seemed exceptionally tidy. The cleaners were ordered to wipe exposed surfaces, but otherwise to leave everything undisturbed.

Was it nothing to do with his desk? The flowers on Reinhart's own were no longer new, having appeared Monday, but Dannaks was not quite used to their splash of colour lending a different tone to their desks. Buying flowers each week fitted his colleague's dandy personality. Dannaks felt it an unaffordable luxury and yet there was something admirable in it. Luckily he was not allergic to them; otherwise there would be yet another reason for unease between them.

No, he could not pinpoint the source of what bothered him. Shrugging it off, he picked up a pencil to list what he would say at the morning meeting and then he saw that the cap of his black marker pen had not been pressed home. With felt-tips he was always careful to click the caps on securely. The top was on but not clicked secure. He idly clicked it shut.

The silence became a gulf between them and they sought refuge in their work.

Then Reinhart jarred the silence with the grate of his pencil sharpener. Dannaks thought he had turned the sharpening of his pencils into an art form. He could spend a full two minutes on each pencil. A ritual few twists of the sharpener, blowing the end and rubbing it between his index finger and thumb. Then inspecting and testing the strength of the tip on a scrap of paper. If it was too sharp and fragmented the process started again. He probably had the sharpest pencils in the Hamburg police force.

He stopped and Dannaks almost gave a sigh of relief.

Thinking about what else he should add to his list he realised what was wrong. The shaded circle he'd doodled on his blotter was gone. In actual fact the top sheet had been removed. He did not mind that somebody had decided to use it. But what if he had noted an important telephone number on it?

"Did you take the top sheet off my blotter?"

"No," he blurted too quickly.

Dannaks thought of following it up with a lecture on important phone numbers, but decided to let it go. Hopefully the message had been received.

They worked on in an impossible silence. A married couple after an argument.

Reinhart was an enigma. He trusted him about as far as he could throw him. What was his game? He showed little interest in his work and appeared to be happy doing nothing or the trivial and mundane duties. Yet he was continually making or referring to entries in his notebook. And he appeared to maintain two.

Dannaks dialled. The officer remembered him.

"I'm afraid it looks as if it's going to be a sticker," said the officer. "We've passed the psychological seventy-two hours."

"With this kind of murder you normally do, don't you?" Dannaks asked.

The investigating Homicide officer took a moment to consider. "It depends what you mean by a murder of this kind. You're assuming that it's an O.K. execution."

"The mutilation makes it look that way."

"True. But if there's one thing I've learnt in this game it's: don't assume anything." Dannaks could only smile and the man continued. "I can tell you we've all but ruled out a domestic killing. And considering the man's background it's a fairly safe bet that it's an O.K. murder—"

"In which case going over the crucial seventy-two hours is not unusual." Dannaks felt the man smile on the other end of the line.

"No." Seventy-two hours was a psychological barrier too. The trail grew colder by the hour, but if it wasn't solved within seventy-two hours then it wasn't going to get solved easily. And the longer the investigation ran the more likely it would be superseded by a fresh murder. Murders rarely got solved like they did in the movies. Such killings got solved through something else: another operation successfully breaking up a syndicate and somebody talking. "We've got another meeting with *O.K.* this afternoon, but– Right. I'm on my way. I have to go."

"Thanks for your time."

Dannaks replaced the receiver. No doubt more recent cases would supersede this one. Homicide was also responsible for collecting evidence in attempted murder cases. And attempted murder covered everything from pub brawls to back alley beatings and stabbings to bashings of the domestic nature. Faruk's attack was considered marginal and didn't warrant their involvement.

After hanging up Dannaks avoided looking at Reinhart. He knew he had been listening to his every word.

09:30

The main topic of the morning meeting had been Saturday's march. Dannaks and Schuppenhauer had volunteered. Wulff excused himself and Reinhart said he had an important dress rehearsal for his society's play. The première was next Saturday. Frank told Dannaks that because of the march their tearoom meeting with the Elders had been postponed.

The point that caused most agitation was that in the light of the forthcoming march Seven had taken on Faruk's case. Protest was fruitless. REX simply didn't have the clout.

He dismissed the others asking Dannaks to stay behind.

"Dannaks, remember I said I run a team?"

He was surprised by the question. "Yes."

"That means working together." What was he talking about? "Teamwork is based on trust. Do you understand?" Dannaks nodded. "Anything to say?" Surely he couldn't know about Freddy, Lampe or Nobby Kabel. Could he?

The thought helped Dannaks's puzzled look. "No."

Frank looked disappointed and dismissed him.

Dannaks closed the door and stood in the corridor for a moment. What was that all about? Maybe Frank was an odd ball after all. Moody. And to think he had thought of asking him about Reinhart's manner.

Cenk felt Hasan's disgust. He avoided Basha's cocky smile. Nazim's own cocky smile made him cringe.

Cenk flitted from one to the other including the officer standing in the corner, but he favoured the window and the tops of the trees. They weren't allowed to speak. Evidently the police didn't have the space to keep them in separate rooms or cells. Apparently they had a witness or witnesses. Who? Did they have the right-wingers themselves, a passenger or two from the train journey? Or worse, had somebody seen them in the act? Had somebody been hiding in the darkness? And of course they were gathered here at the same time for the sake of the witness: to cause them as little inconvenience as possible. Bringing them together also told Cenk that the police knew their identities.

The interviews had been done singularly, but more than one was to be in the line-up. Cenk couldn't work out their ploy. Maybe they didn't have enough line-up innocents to balance out the numbers?

The joke was that the main culprit was not present. Ponytail had not travelled with them.

Cenk stuck to their story. Half-truths are better than lies, Murat had said. Yes, we took the train to Bergedorf and rode back on bicycles. It was part of a game, organised by Murat. Each pair was given a sheet of clues to a route home. On the way they were to answer questions on the sheet. The last act of the game was to eat the sheet.

Hasan and two others from his group that evening didn't offer this story. They said they were nowhere near the snack bar that night. They'd patrolled their own neighbourhood.

Two by two they were called away. No one returned. Hasan and Bilal went first. Then Murat and another. There were strangers too. And Murat would say that this meant that the police had nothing and had simply hauled in the usual suspects. This didn't stop Cenk from wondering whether this was a clever ploy by the police to disguise the fact that there was a grass amongst them. They had been rounded up pretty quickly.

Nazim and Cenk were then called out together. They were escorted into a room and positioned against a wall opposite a long mirror. There they waited looking at their own reflections and the reversed number on the card they held. Minutes passed. They were told to step forward, turn to the right, turn to the left and then step back in line. Then they were led out of the room.

They were told to stand outside a door at the end of a corridor. A uniformed man stood at the door too. When they got there Murat came out. He smiled and, despite the uniform with him, he winked. Nazim was called in and Cenk was left to wait outside. Four minutes later the door opened and Nazim came out. He beamed but thought better of the wink. He too left silently. Cenk went in. There were two men in the room. One sitting and one standing. The one standing, a notepad in his hand, pointed to the chair opposite the seated one. Cenk sat down. A disconcerting mirror stretched almost the width of the wall behind the man. Cenk found himself taking furtive glances at it.

The seated one did all the talking.

"Before I start, let me tell you that you are entitled to legal representation. But then this will all take longer and this is an informal interview. And none of your friends wanted anybody."

"I have nothing to hide," said Cenk.

"Good. Then you won't mind if we record the interview. It's just for the sake of protocol."

Cenk shrugged.

He switched on the recorder and gave his name and that of his colleague, the date and time. He then asked Cenk his name, age and address. Finally he repeated what he said about legal representation and asked for Cenk's consent.

"Have you heard of a gang called the *Schwarzer Freitag*?"

Cenk nodded.

"Please answer for the recording." He then repeated the question.

"Yes."

"Are you a member, or have you ever been a member, of the *Schwarzer Freitag*?"

"No."

"Do you know who the leaders are?"

Cenk shook his head before quickly saying: "No."

"Do you know any members of the *Schwarzer Freitag*?"

"No."

The man was silent for a time. "Okay. That about winds it up." He reached over for the stop button of the recorder. "By the way—" he began as if an afterthought had come to him. Cenk knew that this idle question was important. He'd seen enough TV detective shows to know that this one could be the most important one of the entire interview. When it came he was totally thrown. "Do you know why the gang called themselves the *Schwarzer Freitag*?"

"I, er, think it was something to do with that beaten schoolboy."

The man considered for a moment before verbally ending the interview and switching off the recording.

The next two were waiting outside and Cenk managed a wry smile.

He went down the corridor and an officer opened an outer door for him and stepped outside with him. Nazim was waiting. The officer nodded Nazim over. "Before you go I have something to say." He tapped a cigarette on a metal lighter. "You look like clever boys. So you might listen to me." He put the cigarette between his lips and flicked open the lighter. A long flame waved. He lit up and savoured a long drag. "We've got your names. We'll be watching." He stared at them. Then he pulled on his cigarette again, closing his eyes on the smoke. He leisurely looked up and down the corridor. "Now fuck off."

Outside Nazim forced a laugh. "They've got nothing. And that just now. The hard cop bit. What an idiot."

Cenk couldn't see Hasan or Bilal or the others. He was not sure who the idiot was. The bull, Nazim, himself...

"Don't tell me he got to you," said Nazim.

"No, he didn't," Cenk flared. "But I didn't expect them to be on to us so quickly."

Hasan and Bilal appeared. Murat and the others had gone.

"Shall we wait around?" Cenk asked.

"No," said Hasan.

"You think someone talked?" asked Nazim, as they began to walk.

"What?" said Hasan. The pavement ran alongside a main road and the traffic was loud.

"Cenk said he was surprised they were on to us so quickly." Cenk thought that perhaps one of the Elders had given them away.

"For something like that they don't hang around." Hasan looked sick. "What did you think?"

"Murat," Cenk began, "said that they tolerated the fire-bombing of refugee homes."

"They didn't–"

"Nobody got hurt," said Nazim.

"You two still don't get it, do you?" Hasan shook his head. "We have to be damn careful. They think we're terrorists. But that doesn't frighten me as much as what others might think."

"What do you mean?" asked Bilal, who had seemed deep in thought. "Who?"

"Other terrorist groups. Real terrorists." He looked at their faces. "They might contact us. Want us to join them. Or they might want to join us. We have to watch ourselves. And not lose track of what we're about."

Cenk thought that they'd already lost their track.

13:00

"You're hovering about like an expectant father at a delivery," said Robert, rising and taking the sheaf of paper. "Make me another coffee."

"This is my current baby." Craig flicked on the kettle. "Are you any different?"

Robert grunted and left the kitchen.

Maybe Robert was different. He whipped off copy on a daily basis with practically guaranteed publication.

Craig spooned coffee in two mugs and then stood at the window waiting for the kettle to boil. Today was a strange day. The sky was bright but clouded: grey substituting blue. Far off streaks of blue cracked the grey sheet. A shower had swept by. The road below glistened. The cars swished onward.

"Fuck off," the big one had said.

"What are you afraid of?" asked Craig.

"Not you," said the vicious looking one.

"I heard you were looking for me." Stefan had obviously picked up on Craig's English accent.

"We don't talk to reporters any more," the vicious looking one persisted.

Stefan ignored him. "Is there money in it?"

"Fifty."

"Each."

Craig laughed cynically. "Twenty. Each."

"Okay. But no pictures and no taping."

Craig nodded, although he was unhappy about not being allowed to record the interview. He was annoyed at himself, because he should have concealed his recorder and microphone. The equipment protruded from his bag of magazines.

The kettle clicked off and Craig poured water in the mugs. He wondered how far Robert had read.

"*S-Bahn* Stefan: racism in Germany" was the title of the piece and the title the paper would use. They would enlarge and sharpen both esses to resemble the Nazi SS insignia.

> *On Friday last week, Faruk, affectionately know as Farrie, was attacked and beaten by a group of skinheads. He had spent the evening shooting pool with his friend Ahmed and they were making their way...*

Craig went on to describe the attack on Faruk.

> *The German people have an open abhorrence of warfare, evident in the softly-softly approach of the politics of the country. Although apparently healthy, this virulent public condemnation of violence could be founded in a disturbing fear of themselves. That's what these skinheads will tell you. Who then, are these youths attacking foreigners in the name of Nationalism? How widespread is their cause? Do they really have a silent majority behind them? How organised are the extreme right in Germany? Is there a danger of history repeating itself and Nazism rising once again in this country? Should the rest of Europe have cause to fear?*
>
> *Before tackling these questions the first question has to be: why now? Part of the answer lies in one of the stalwarts that periodically plague a country: unemployment. Unemployment does not necessarily precipitate racism. Many things fuel the fire of frustration. Racism simply comes to the fore.*
>
> *During the break-up of Yugoslavia the refugee problem brought out old and suppressed or unreported resentments. In this respect the refugee problem and attacks on those seeking, or securing asylum in Germany exacerbates a problem that has always existed under the surface.*
>
> *Farrie's case illustrates this fact. For the refugee problem no longer occupies centre stage. Some racism is fundamental. But why? A good place to look for an answer would be the foreign population, the so-called victims of racism. In particular the Turkish population of Germany. They should be among the most integrated foreigners. Some have lived in the country for decades and many were born here.*

Robert skimmed over the next few paragraphs, which were a potted history of the Turkish people in Germany and especially in Hamburg.

Farrie's father said that prejudice was in the German language and, although he could not furnish his statement with examples, there are some glaring examples in any good lexicon. A direct application can be seen in the verb türken, *for instance, which is slang and means to fiddle, diddle or fake. Something that is faked is said to be* getürkt.

A plastic bag is sometimes referred to as a Turkish brief case.

Craig wrote about the concept of the *Gastarbeiter* and how it had initially been thought of as a temporary arrangement. He described their arrival and touched on some of their hardships.

In common with the industrious Germans the Turks are a hard-working people and were initially employed as a labour work force. They took on the work many West Germans did not want and consequently became a service class, which in turn became an under-class. They are the largest minority and as far as the xenophobic elements of the public are concerned, represent the greatest threat. But the lack of integration goes deeper.

Integration comes with its own complexities. For what is integration? Undoubtedly natural assimilation is inevitable. But both sides abhor the associated cultural erosion. Rather than observing a cultural enrichment, elements of each society see only a diluting of tradition.

One can spout statistics that the Turks are the largest foreign population representing 30% of the 5 million foreigners in Germany and that this figure, around 1.6 million, is approximately equal to the population of the second largest city in Germany and Farrie's home: Hamburg. It is said that the third largest Turkish city after Istanbul and Izmir is Berlin. The very fact that these statistics exist exemplifies the segregated attitude of German society. The question arises: when will 2nd and 3rd generation Turks be treated as equal citizens of their country of birth?

Since the attack Farrie has suffered bouts of sickness and migraine. Despite this, the authorities dithered over agreeing to allow him to take tests which contribute to his continual assessment, crucial to his leaving-certificate.

On Saturday there will be a solidarity march for Farrie in the centre of Hamburg. Unfortunately this coincides with a rally by the Far Right, who are to protest outside the Deichtorhallen which is hosting the Cohen exhibition of Nazi atrocities. Various Left wing groups have announced that they will oppose the rally. Their opposition has not been approved by the authorities and they will be seen as the agitators. One does not need a crystal ball to see that some of these Left-wingers will use Farrie's march to legitimise their presence. And then the meaning of the march will be lost. Indeed, a gang calling themselves *Schwarzer Freitag* – Black Friday – has appeared and seem bent on revenge.

But perhaps the German people need such an escalation of events. In today's ever more violent society the beating of a schoolboy and the authorities' procrastination over him taking the tests does not warrant a protest march. The general feeling is that this is an isolated incident carrying little weight. Yet, this complacency hints at an acceptable norm; an acceptable norm that paves the way for more horrendous crimes. There was a Molotov cocktail attack on a snack bar renowned as a right-wing meeting place. The Schwarzer Freitag *have claimed responsibility. Racist murder is with us too. Thankfully the list of victims is relatively short. Two right-wingers have been killed so far by a killer the Press have coined the Hangman. Yet, these and past killings cause short-lived outrage. Lain at the doorstep of the madness of youth. Surely the breeding ground deserves treatment? Surely, more effort should be spent on integration? To achieve this means not only tackling the perpetrators of racist crime but making a direct assault on apathy.*

Racism is not harmless. It is insidious. It hides behind national pride and patriotism. A renowned right-wing extremist with the colourful name of S-Bahn Stefan offered a classic example of this attitude.

What does Stefan think of the foreigners in his homeland? Was he simply another bored youth looking for expression? Was he and his friends interested in right-wing politics? More than anything, were his views merely exaggerations of a silent majority? If so, was this then the reason for the apparent apathy of the German people?

The interview took place on a train. He was sitting with two of his friends in the last carriage. The one introduced as Blade had just finished scratching the carriage wall. "Hamburg grüSSt seine Gäste." (Hamburg greets its guests the German word for greet drawn with the sharp SS symbol). The third member of the group was called Günter. He was the largest: a lumbering hulk of a youth. He was not the brightest of the trio, and perhaps because of this one felt the most sympathy for him. Blade was the wild card in the pack. He tended to be restless and disinterested in what was being said. Only occasionally did he show that he was listening. Whether he was bored because he was highly intelligent or because he wanted action was hard to gauge. He had the shortest hair too: a marine crew-cut. Added to the dark eyes set slightly too close was his stocky muscular frame. Stefan was the one who knew who he was and if not where he was going, aware of where he was at.

"Deutschland den Deutschen" ("Germany for the Germans") and "Ausländer raus" ("Foreigners out") were not slogans the trio used during the interview, but the two sentiments were behind everything they believed.

Most of what Stefan said boiled down to the same reasoning, which is condensed here. The liberal helping of expletives that punctuated his speech has been removed.

"Only Stefan spoke, then?" said Robert.

"The other two may have interjected one-liners," said Craig, "but yeah, it was all Stefan. I've cut his repetitiveness. He could have told me all he had to say in half the time. I also cleaned up his foul language. But maybe I should have used it. It would have undermined his viewpoint. I don't know. Tell me what you think."

The first question Stefan answered was whether considered himself a racist.

"It's not about racism. I don't believe in racism. What it is, is a question of culture. You don't seem to realise that they don't want to be part of Germany. You talk about the Turks. They're the worst; they've made a little Turkey here. It's cultural. They want to come over and spread like a disease. They want to invade and turn us into them. It's not immigration or anything to do with being refugees. It's invasion, full stop. They want Islam to take over. They want to destroy

us.

"You reporters and left-wingers speak of integration, but you don't see that they're not interested in integrating."

All three youths had a common denominator of distance in their eyes: a cultivated void. It was a dullness they had refined and probably thought cool. Judging from their dress and their Vietnam veteran thousand-yard-stare it was obvious they were at war. The three boys were eighteen or nineteen years old. They were dressed similarly in a mishmash of slate blue, khaki and camouflage. Blade had a belt buckle sporting an Iron Cross. But the real threat was in the hardness of their eyes and the aggression that lay in their distance. It was tempting to reach out and humanise them. To do this one had to understand them. But their views were too alien for empathy. In the end abandonment was the only option before the interview turned into a repugnant diatribe.

What were his views on a multi-cultural society?

He laughed and the others joined him with smiles and chuckles. Although one got the impression that Stefan's companions were not sure they could justify their chuckles and laughter. When Stefan began to elaborate, Günter and Blade nodded.

"Look at the state of Britain today. Better still, America. The place is a shambles. What a bloody mess! The blacks and Hispanics have brought that country down. They're even losing their language.

Emotion was not completely absent. Stefan's eyes would blaze with fanaticism, as if such conviction made his argument more convincing.

"That's your multi-cultural society. It's not too late for Germany. Hitler had the right idea. He just went a little too far." The six million should have been deported rather than killed. "There's no doubt about it, he was one of our greatest politicians. Not like this pack of gutless, wishy-washy cowards we have now. Letting all these Ausländer drain our economy and foul our streets. Today's politicians are worried about their careers. Sucking up to the International community. Frightened of their own shadows."

Here he touched on a point that seemed to be shared by the general populace. Because the Germans are a proud people,

191

they respect, even need, convincing leadership. The contradiction lies in their fear of manipulation and dictatorship.

"The politicians know that these foreigners are here to take our jobs," Stefan continued. "But because they have this misguided idea of proving that Germany has changed — and they'll go on trying to prove it unless we stop them — they'll keep letting them in. That's what's behind our Asylum laws. The people are speaking and the politicians are not listening."

He paused before picking up the thread again.

"I don't approve of the violence," he said quickly. The others averted their eyes. "That's for idiots. But people want change and there'll be trouble until there are changes."

Politicians working within the confines of democracy have careers that rely on representing, or better still anticipating, the will of the people. The uncertainty in Germany today is a reflection of the conflicting signals they are receiving from the populace. Furthermore, the new states of Germany have swelled the voters with a will that is divisive.

Craig wrote about the forty years of prosperous living that had lulled the West Germans into a state of self-satisfaction. The result was that West Germans resented and secretly mocked their relatively poorer neighbours from East Germany.

For emphasis he mentioned that Hamburg was a West German city.

Herein lies the rest of the answer to the predictably poor attendance that will be seen at Saturday's march. People are reticent. Their reticence should not be interpreted as condoning the violence, but there is no obvious air of condemnation either. The politicians, unable to gauge the strength of feeling in the silence of the people, denounce xenophobia but undertake no action. Inaction by the government is taken to mean that the problem is not so serious: isolated incidents. Why should people protest the limited actions of a minority? Consequently nothing is done by the people or the government.

"They're taking all our jobs," said Blade, in one of those rare moments when he showed that he was paying attention.

Don't you think that they're filling the job vacancies that the Germans themselves don't want?

The social structure, biased toward the German citizen,

contradicted Blade's statement. If the jobs were there for the taking, then the way the German system worked, a German would fill the position. This is not to say the German citizen is obviously more privileged in the community. On the contrary, he or she has to negotiate the same confounding bureaucracy for which Germany is deservingly infamous. The difference is that a German has more of a chance of battling through the official gobbledegook than a foreigner, because ultimately it was not set up with the foreigner in mind.

"They work for peanuts," said Blade.

This was true. Indeed Germany had a thriving black market problem. Then, weren't the German employers to blame? For they chose to employ the cheap workers rather than their own people.

Stefan came to Blade's rescue. "Those employers are the leftists and capitalists." This seemed a contradiction. "You're right, they're to blame. Maybe they're just stupid and don't realise the true situation: the true feeling of the German people. We'll get them too. Don't worry. Like I said, we'll have our day."

What of the progressive nature of society? The world is changing and merging. It doesn't look like it can be halted. What about living together?

Again Stefan was amused. "You're missing the point. Look what happened to the American Indians and the Aborigines. It's history. You can see it. They had their lands, their ways and cultures. They were invaded and killed off. You couldn't get away with that today. People are more aware. You have to do everything with more subtlety. The foreigners know that. They're not stupid. But it's invasion just the same.

"It isn't only that we don't want them. They don't want us. All this talk about integration is bullshit. They don't want to integrate.

"In Germany we still have a chance to remain pure and Christian." Again he had touched on something fundamental. Religion aside, the Turks were victimised because their culture was not as European as the Italians, for instance. His voice took on a superior tone. "From the guts of the system we'll rise up. We are the people. I'm not interested in playing the political game. I don't want to be part of this corrupt political

system."

Having decided that our conversation had come to an end, Stefan abruptly announced that he wanted to do some surfing.

He smiled and the two small earrings in his left ear glinted. One was a stud, the other a dangling crucifix.

He got up and pressed the red emergency button that unlocked the doors – a feature of these trains to allow passengers to evacuate a moving train. Then he calmly yanked them open. His long straw-blond hair aggressively shaved only at the sides whipped with the rush of the train. Blade and Günter remained unmoved. Stefan climbed out onto a stepping board near the wheels, closing the doors upon himself. He then reached up and held the guttering that ran the lower edge of the curved roof. Stefan grinned before he stepped up onto the outside handles of the doors. Holding the guttering with one hand he swung his free arm wide, a broncobuster at a rodeo and yelled at the top of his voice: "Yeeeee haaaar."

When he returned to his seat he explained that he was twelve when a friend introduced him to Bahn-surfing. From then until now he had been doing it on a regular basis. Why? For the buzz. At first it had been the exhilaration of the act itself. The danger lifted the stress from his life. Then came the thrill of being caught. Recently the transport management had employed more guards or sheriffs to watch the trains. Primarily, this had been to safeguard passengers that travelled at off-peak times or on lonelier stretches. Nonetheless Stefan's chances of getting caught had increased. He boasted that he had sprayed his name and swastikas on some carriage rooftops. His ambition was to do a handstand up there. Finally he admitted that he was growing bored with surfing and was looking for other ways to get his kicks.

If he wasn't already an active member of an extreme right-wing group, it wouldn't take a clairvoyant to see that this would be his next step. Then his talk of getting kicks would probably take on a new and more literal meaning.

Stefan is unemployed but he is not unintelligent. He does not come from a broken home, but spends a lot of time away from home. And he is not from East Germany, where, it is said, suppressed Nazi feelings are finding expression.

Unification not only meant East Germany ceased to exist; West Germany ceased to exist too. The problems in Germany are the problems of a new Germany. A time of great change is always a time of stress. And in times of stress a scapegoat is inevitably sought. It is the nature of the scapegoat that is telling. When there is economic instability, high unemployment, recession and so on, the populace tend to blame the government, but they also turn on the minority. In Germany this is the foreigner.

The German social structure does not encourage racial equality. There is an economic class system with the West German at the top, the Ausländer at the bottom and the former East German sandwiched uncomfortably in-between.

A short time later the train stopped at a station where the three of them jumped off and shuffled towards the exit. As the doors closed Blade about-turned, gave a straight-armed salute and shouted: "Sieg Heil." He laughed, goose-stepped for a moment and then jogged after the others. It did not seem to matter which station it was. They were going nowhere. They were just hanging around, waiting.

In the next article Craig St. James will present arguments as to why there is unlikely to be a so-called Fourth Reich.

"Not bad, Craig," said Robert. "A little dark. It certainly makes the last sentence an enigma."

"Then they'll want to read the next instalment. The darker it is, the more shocking the light."

"Cut the Turkish history, condense the rest, you know, repackage it, Diana will run it."

"Now?"

"After you've emailed it — you're not doing anything, are you?"

"I'm having dinner with Carina."

"It's not even two. What are you going to do? Psyche yourself up for the next four or five hours?"

"Yes. Yes. I'm just a bit burnt out, that's all. You'll have to check my translation."

"Deal."

"By the way, are there any serious contenders for the reward?"

"Ha, I forgot to tell you. We've had about a dozen calls, but they didn't get the location right. Fame and money. It's a hell of a carrot.

"Figures."

"Two groups appeared serious, but they didn't get past the key question."

Faruk had told Craig that one of his rescuers had been wearing a black woollen Jack Wolfskin jacket.

14:15

They had got nowhere with their rape case that morning and were forced to break and continue tomorrow.

Dannaks felt that they'd now truly drawn the arse card: the worst of the assignment chits.

Germany had an inordinate number of asylum-seekers. Many may not have targeted Germany as their host country and were simply caught passing through. The country was a transit land: poor East travelling West. But there were those who had come up from the South. Immigration had been overwhelmed and a private company had been contracted to help with the paperwork.

During their time housed in enclaves of hastily built prefabricated houses off the beaten track, whilst their cases were being considered, the asylum seekers were subject to the law, like everyone else. If their application and any subsequent appeals failed or they broke the law and were considered undesirable, they were deported.

And Reinhart and Dannaks were at Hamburg airport to oversee a deportation. The deportees often injured themselves and sometimes the uniforms were heavy handed. Injured deportees couldn't travel.

The detectives were not alone. In the room separated from other travellers was a social worker, fussing about her charges as if they were children on an outing. Six uniforms and two immigration officers tried to look official. Somewhere two medics were also at hand, but they were not in the room.

Dannaks found the whole thing degrading. He couldn't imagine what the twenty people in front of him felt. The plane was taking them back to Sudan. All were black and all the Germans were white. Most of these downtrodden people were young men in their early twenties. But there were families too. One man was pleading with the social worker in broken English. Dannaks grasped that he was agreeing to be sent back, but that his wife and two little children should be spared. "They kill me and my children no future." Dannaks looked at Reinhart whose English was much better. The blood had drained from his face.

Craig leaned back and rolled his shoulders. Repackaging and translating the article for Robert had taken his mind off Carina for a couple of hours. He manoeuvred the cursor to the printer icon and clicked the mouse. Robert's laser printer sprang into life and Craig heard it suck in a sheet of paper.

He left the room as it began to print. In the kitchen he saw the newspapers he'd bought during his walk. Robert had still been in the flat and they'd read them together. Faruk's plight was mostly dwarfed. The pieces were vehicles for the announcement of the march. And the likely clash with the Right. The march was rolling and had gathered too much momentum to be stopped. The Left, the Greens, human rights campaigners and the popular press had taken up the issue. Some had begun digging up previous attacks, emphasising that Faruk's case was the tip of an ignored iceberg. The extreme elements of the Left were trying to stir up further support by portraying the education authorities as representatives of the oppressive establishment. The boy's teachers had broken their silence and a decision had been reached about the tests. A doctor had spoken out. He maintained that although it was difficult to be one hundred percent certain, Faruk had received injures of such a superficial nature that it was hard to believe that the beating and his migraine and sickness were related. He suggested the boy seek psychiatric treatment.

At six Craig made his call. Faruk answered.

"How are you feeling?" he asked after identifying himself.

"Better, but not brilliant."

Craig struggled for more idle talk. "Tell me, when your mother came in the other evening she said Aloha. That's a Hawaiian greeting, isn't it?"

"Yes," he appeared embarrassed.

"Why?" Faruk grunted and Craig went on as lightly as possible. "You must admit it's not what one would expect from a Turkish family."

"I suppose not."

The short silence worked for Craig and Faruk explained that the greeting harked back to an incident some years ago. It had been winter in Hamburg and they had no heating. Leila and he had complained bitterly about the cold. Their mother had soothed them with stories. One in particular had remained. As a young girl she had seen a film about a tropical island where it was always warm and one did not have to go shopping because everything grew on trees. Everyone was happy. When they met they always greeted each other with "Aloha." Leila and he had adopted the greeting using it whenever there was reference to the cold. But their mother had played along and now, all these years later, although the two children had dropped its use, she continued to say it in her singsong voice.

"And what did your father think of this?"

"He didn't understand."

"I didn't think he would. Can I speak to him?"

"No. It's Thursday the whole family's out."

"Out?" Craig heard a key pushed into the flat door.

"Visiting. The families take turns in entertaining."

"You didn't go?" Craig looked up as Petra came in carrying two bags of shopping. They nodded and smiled.

"Too boring. Besides, I'm not well."

"Yes. Of course. You know that the march is going ahead?" He could hear Petra emptying the bags in the kitchen.

"Yes."

"Look, I've finished my English article and I've written another German one from it. I know this may sound like a strange question, but I need to know, so that everything fits together. I didn't ask you when I saw you, because I didn't know about it until I spoke to your father later. This week you were supposed to take these tests to find out who had cheated and who had not."

"Yes."

"I've heard they've allowed you to take them later. That's great. What I wanted to know was why you went out last Friday to shoot pool and talk?"

"I don't understand."

"I'm asking: why weren't you studying?" Petra looked down the corridor and rocked a hand near her mouth, as if drinking from an invisible cup. Craig nodded and she disappeared again.

"We'd been doing that all week and we had all weekend too. You can't study all the time."

"No, I guess not." Pause. "Okay, thanks a lot. Get well soon."

He hung up and called ahead of himself. "You should have

told me you were going shopping. I could have helped out."

She looked up from the sink, where she'd just filled the kettle. "I thought you'd be too busy."

"I finished a couple of hours ago." He pulled two mugs from the cupboard. "I've been doing the piece for Rob. But I still could have helped. Let me pay for it at least."

"Don't be silly. You are not even eating with us tonight, are you?

"No. Carina's cooking."

She smiled and he did too. "Take us out for a meal."

"You're on."

"Who were you talking to?"

"Faruk. Actually I wanted his father, but he was out. Apparently the families get together on Thursday nights. They take turns entertaining."

"Probably a hangover from the Muslim weekend. Thursday is their Saturday."

20:03

Dannaks drew a breath before entering the *Windjammer*. Perversely, part of him hoped that the red-faced man would not be inside. Going in alone was reckless. He had no allies and no one to rely upon as a witness.

He found a snack bar and got himself something to eat and drink. He sat alone in the back of the place, near a machine that let you, a muscle-bound Jake Dangerous, slug it out with Armour man. He watched the looping routine, introduction, previous high-scorers with equally improbable names, then the combatants prowling, fists flying and drop kicks, big Jake raising his arms in triumph, insert coins flashing urgently, over and over again until he got sick of it.

The mundaneness of eating and drinking and the game machine gave him a pause.

His reverie took him on to the *Henker*. The blows to the head may not have been caused by a blunt instrument or a kick whilst Kai Doermer's and Markus Jensen lay on the ground. They could still have been flying kicks. Jake Dangerous flying kicks. But Homicide had checked out the members of the kick-boxing clubs and karate schools. Naturally the motive was all-important. Find that and you were half way to finding the killer. But the only thing the two victims had in common was that they were right-wingers. There had to be something else. That was the importance of victim profiles. Maybe they had upset someone important in the right-wing ranks? Maybe they wanted out? Maybe their killer was a right-winger, after all?

For now he had another pressing problem to solve. Freddy's murder was clearly down to Raul: tying up loose ends. But Freddy's last words to them had been a clue, not to his murderer, but to something deeper.

Dannaks was stumbling along, but the path he had chosen was the right one. He knew he was heading for trouble, but he couldn't turn back. Anyway, he didn't really know where he was going, so he had absolutely no idea which way was back.

The machine reminded him that he needed to buy a light bulb and as luck would have it he found a place still open and managed to buy one. In its thin cardboard box it bulged his outside jacket pocket.

Parting the heavy curtain dashed his hopes of not finding Red-face.

A glance at the bartender told him that he was as welcome as last time. "Stormy tonight," he smiled. The barman remained stony-faced. Undeterred Dannaks made a beeline for the red-faced man's table. As before, they were playing cards. The room was not crowded but it was already heavy with smoke. Entering the room had probably notched up a few percentage points on his chance of developing lung cancer.

He had decided that threats and attempting to befriend the man were out. Honesty was his only choice. The man would give nothing away in front of his companions. Dannaks would have to get him outside.

He boldly knocked on their table. It was a ritual one performed amongst friends, used when it would be too disruptive to greet individually with a customary handshake.

The red-faced man was the first to speak. Again he did not look up and concentrated on his cards.

"Is this becoming a bulls' pub, Udo?" he asked loudly, his question directed at the landlord. No answer.

"I want to ask you one question," said Dannaks.

"No, I won't be your boyfriend."

"It's to do with your dead friend."

"A snitch is no friend of mine."

Was this true? Had Dannaks totally miscalculated? So it was on the streets that Freddy had been an informer. It was a factor he'd not accommodated in his equation.

The man looked up. "What's the matter? Had a tiff with your girlfriend?"

"Last time you said I was the girl."

"Maybe you're lesbians."

"You're not my type. Too much rouge, remember."

The man stiffened. When he spoke his voice was full of menace.

"Are you alone?"

"It looks like it. Why? Do you fancy me all of a sudden?"

The man gave a sinister smile.

"You've got no friends here, bull. Provoking me from behind your badge—"

"A, I'm not provoking you. I'm trying to solve the murder of one of your friends. And B, I don't see a badge."

"You're a stupid man, then."

"You're eye-sight's improving. You recognise my gender."

"Shall we go outside?" Red-face asked.

"You don't want to kiss in here?"

"We'll need some more room for the type of contact I have in mind."

"You and your cronies?"

The man stilled a friend with a glance. Then he mimicked Dannaks.

"A, they're not my cronies, but my friends. And B, I don't need any help."

Dannaks stepped back as the man placed his cards face down and slowly stood up. He hadn't realised the man was so big. He was a head taller than Dannaks. He also looked heavier.

"Wait for me. This won't take long."

20:05

"What does he want?" asked Cenk, following Nazim to the back of the house. He hoped it wouldn't take long. He had promised Hasan he would patrol. Yesterday he'd patrolled with him. Only Nazim, Bilal and another accompanied them. Nazim and Bilal had already said they couldn't make it tonight.

"I told you, he didn't say," said Nazim, stopping and giving him his best annoyed look before brightening. "Maybe Leila's there?"

"I doubt it." But he hoped word would get back to her. "And now?"

Nazim looked down at the cellar window. The window was at their feet. Black metal bars caged it. "This must be it." He crouched.

"Why we can't go by the front door, I'll never know." But he knew Faruk's father didn't want the likes of them – *Schwarzer Freitag* members – visiting his son even if he was out. Here the neighbours looked out for one another. Nosiness was encouraged.

Nazim grabbed the metal frame and found that it did indeed lift by half a centimetre. Opening it like a door was relatively easy. The screws in the wall took some masonry with them, but the holes were well established and the crumbly-looking cement hard. The window itself was not locked, simply wedged in place and required a couple of shoves at the edges.

Nazim smiled.

They climbed in and stood in the dullness for a moment, letting their eyes accustom. Nazim was feeling jubilant and strode ahead.

"Wait," said Cenk. "I can't see."

"I can."

Cenk doubted he could see any better and fumbled unsteadily forward. They were in a corridor. "Here are the steps," said Nazim.

"Slowly."

He heard Nazim climbing.

"This is crazy," said Cenk.

"What?"

"Nothing."

Then there was a shaft of light. Nazim had opened the door at the top of the stairs. Although he'd only opened the door a crack Cenk could see him beaming.

Cenk crept up behind him. "There's nobody there," Nazim whispered after a moment and pulled the door wide. They climbed the stairs of the house as stealthily as possible, all the while ready to duck down, until they reached the top of the house. The door at the top wasn't locked and they found themselves on the roof.

"Wow," said Nazim, going to the parapet.

"Get back. Someone might see you."

The view wasn't spectacular, but unusual. Rooftops as far as the eye could see broken only by a spire or taller building.

"Come on," said Cenk.

"Yeah, this way," said Nazim. He walked to the edge and looked across the gap to the adjacent building. The gap was no more than a long step or a short jump, nonetheless the drop was awesome. Two planks formed a bridge. "Do you think they're safe?"

"Yeah, Ali uses them."

"If he can do it, so can I," said Nazim. "It's like Indiana Jones, isn't it?"

"Must be a safety precaution in case of fire," said Cenk, wondering how long they'd been exposed to the elements. Maybe the wood was rotten? Ali was lighter than them because he was at least five years younger. Before he could speak Nazim had stepped up. He laughed nervously.

Cenk watched the sag of the wood as Nazim walked across in two steps. "It's a piece of cake," said Nazim from the other side.

"Not so loud," he scolded. Cenk gave himself no time to think and strode swiftly to the other side. "I hope this is important," he muttered. "What a palaver." They went to the door and cracked it open. Again they waited and listened.

Then they descended the stairs to the third floor of the four-storey house.

Ahmed opened the flat door. He greeted them and as they removed their shoes Faruk appeared. He smiled uncertainly. They too greeted one another.

"Nobody here?" asked Nazim.

"No," said Faruk. "Ahmed's banned from the house. But when my parents are away..."

"Why's he banned?" They entered the lounge and sat.

Faruk looked surprised by the question. "My father thinks he let me down."

Ahmed grew awkward. "Why don't you say it? He thinks I'm a coward."

"He doesn't think that. I told him you didn't let me down. I wanted to run too." He looked at his hands. "My father will get over it. Give him time. I know how to handle him." Cenk doubted Faruk. He had heard that Suleyman had a cast iron hand over his family.

Silence fell upon them. "Do you want something to drink?" Faruk asked suddenly.

"Later," said Cenk.

"I'll have a cola, if you've got one," blurted Nazim.

Faruk made to leave the room. "Cenk?"

Cenk nodded. Whilst he was away nobody spoke. When he re-entered Nazim and Cenk muttered their thanks, but let the silence question him.

"I suppose you're wondering why I wanted to speak to you," Faruk began.

Cenk nodded and Nazim spoke. "It better be good after that assault course we've just negotiated."

Faruk paled and looked to Ahmed for support. "Well I– we thought we could talk to you. About the gang. We don't know Hasan. He's the leader, isn't he?"

"Yes," Cenk said quickly, before Nazim could speak.

"We heard about the snack bar. And we thought that maybe you could cool it a bit."

"What do you mean?" said Nazim.

"He means," said Ahmed, "that we think the gang is a good idea. But it's not good, if it stirs things up."

"That wasn't us," said Nazim. "Well, it was. I mean, we were there. But it wasn't our idea."

"You're right," said Cenk. "It was stupid. Hasan has had a word with those responsible."

"Only after Cemal spoke to him," said Nazim. "And you."

"That's not true," said Cenk barely containing his temper. "Hasan phoned Murat at work on Monday. Before we saw Cemal."

"That's what he said."

"It doesn't matter. You agree that Hasan was against it."

Nazim couldn't bring himself to nod. He just raised his eyebrows.

Cenk turned to Faruk and Ahmed. "I'll speak to Hasan."

"You know as well as I do, he can't do anything," said Nazim.

"Maybe." Now he was the one not willing to admit the truth.

"What does he mean?" asked Faruk.

Ahmed jumped in. "He means Hasan's not in charge. Murat is, right?"

Cenk mulled over the question.

"Yes," said Nazim.

When Faruk spoke his tone was solemn. "My father doesn't

approve. He thinks the gang is dangerous to what the march is about."

"Why?" asked Nazim.

"Look," began Faruk, choosing his words carefully, "we were attacked. But they didn't kill us. They were just a bunch of drunks. We don't want to start a war. We–"

"You can't make peace with them," said Nazim triumphantly.

"We don't want revenge."

"Nor do we," said Cenk, "but it's not just about what happened to you. It's all that's gone before. And we want to stop it from happening again. You're right to–"

"Maybe they'll kill next time," blurted Nazim.

"But you called yourselves the *Schwarzer Freitag*," said Faruk. "That's a reference to what happened to me – us."

"The trigger," said Cenk.

"The final straw," said Nazim.

Faruk seemed desperate. "Yes, but I want this to blow over. The march is bad enough."

"What do you mean?" asked Nazim.

"I don't want to be responsible – I don't – we don't want to be in the limelight."

"I'd love to be in your place," said Nazim. "Not being beaten up. I mean, having a gang formed for me. And my name in the papers. Reporters calling. And–"

"Is there something you're not telling us?" said Cenk. He watched Faruk blanch. He watched him look at his hands and he saw the sideways glance at Ahmed.

His expression was hard when he looked Cenk in the eye. "No."

20:19

A glance at the barometer behind the bar, confirmed stormy weather. He was the first onto the dark street. The red-faced man followed.

Dannaks felt numb. Or had profound depression suspended his feelings? He certainly didn't feel brave. Maybe there was no such thing as bravery? Maybe there was only stupidity: pride and cornered cowards?

"That's far enough," Red-face said. Dannaks stopped and turned to him. The eyes of the piggy in the upstairs window were not

205

flashing. Dannaks took this to be an omen: he wasn't returning.

"One question, that's all."

"I have my answer prepared."

"You're supposed to have been his friend."

"I was and I still am. Slip me your number."

Dannaks took out a visiting card from his outside breast pocket. The man engulfed his hand and the card with his own.

"Look over my shoulder. Is anybody looking?"

He could hardly look over the man's shoulder even on tip-toes. So he looked past him and before he could answer a fist slammed into his cheek driving him onto the hard road. His fall was eased by the man maintaining his hold on his hand with the card. Nonetheless something cracked in his side.

Above the ringing in his ears he heard Red-face say: "Stay down."

20:21

Craig entered her flat behind a bouquet of flowers and a bottle of sparkling wine. "Hi," was all he managed.

She grabbed the gifts. "Shoes off and don't come in the kitchen," she said and hastily retreated to the kitchen. He gave a stunned smile and took his shoes off. All thought of speaking vanished when he heard her curse "shit" over the sound of sizzling.

He padded into the lounge. The table was set: navy table cloth, aquamarine serviettes, blue-rimmed plates, a glass pitcher of water, blue pattern tile coasters, and a candlestick holder with two new tapering electric blue candles. The carpet was functional grey. Potted plants and a standing lamp broke down the corners of the room, defining the living space. The sofa was an old dumpling of fat cushions, unsuitable for anyone with back problems. A matching winged armchair, optimally angled for the television was probably her favourite position. Framed Paul Gauguin pictures brought colour to the plain walls.

The overall tidiness and thought in design of the room was feminine and he was thrilled.

He looked out of the window, listening to her busying herself. Her view was that of the building opposite. But she had a little stone balcony the size of a single mattress. The balcony wall was lined with a long tray of flowers. A plastic drop-leaf table was fixed to the wall and two garden chairs stood either side of it. The view was poor, but the balcony was high enough from the road below to afford a sense of privacy.

"It's not much," she said.

He hadn't heard her come into the room and swung round. She looked away from the balcony and met his gaze.

"It's great." He was taken by her presence. He could just fall into her hazel eyes. And her lips were wicked, hair strangely lank. But it was the spot of gravy or sauce that caught him off guard. "Great for breakfast," he bubbled, hurriedly moving on before she read anything into his words. "Great for an evening tipple." She was bemused. He was using the word great too much. "Just great." He beamed and she smiled and then he laughed and she chuckled shaking her head.

Before embarrassment encroached them she spoke. "What would you like to drink? Your bottle is in the freezer." His alarm drove her to explain. "Just for a while." She seemed to search for her words and then gave up. "Water, beer, wine, red, white?"

"Wine would be gr–" he stopped himself. "Fine."

"Red or white?"

"Whatever you've got open."

"Neither." She waited as if she'd issued a challenge.

"White," he surrendered. He felt a tinge of distance. "Wine would be fine," he repeated. "My mum always says that if you say something that accidentally rhymes then you can count the words and discover who is talking about you. Wine would be fine has four words. Someone with a name beginning with D is talking about me." He stopped and she smiled. "Oh shit, oh sorry. But yes, someone with a name beginning with D is talking about me also rhymes. That means someone–" he mumbled through the alphabet "– with the letter K is talking about me."

"I am not talking about you." Her surname was Kowalski.

"No." For an instant he felt foolish. "You've got, er," he reached forward as if to touch the fleck on her chin, but reverted to pointing instead.

Her eyes widened. "What?"

"Sauce or something," he smiled. She relaxed and smiled as she touched the sauce. He felt he had won points by not touching her. The English gentleman.

"I'll be back in a minute." She fetched the wine, after making a detour to the bathroom. He opened the bottle and they drank a glass together.

And the evening was cast. He felt he could say nothing wrong. Their conversation gushed as if they had a lifetime to explain. They skated through their likes and dislikes, childhood incidents, mixed English and German when it suited them. Their effervescence overwhelmed; sweeping aside cultural differences and quashing awkwardness.

The conversation moved to holidays and they to the sofa. She had a photo album on her lap and he was leaning close to her. On the surface he was looking at the photographs, commenting on each and every one. All the while he enjoyed her perfume teasing his nostrils, and breathed in her body warmth, could barely hold himself back from touching her long fingers, but paralysed by the tension in the air. He made a quip about one of her previous boyfriends and she threw herself back, laughing and shaking her head with joy, hair swaying. For a flash he was reminded of a baited fish on a line, but the excitement of the now left no time for examination. The album slipped and they both grabbed it. Their hands touched and they were electrified. Eyes melted, skin magnified, breath was held. The album fell to the floor. They kissed. Her hand went to the back of his neck and then on up into his hair, the kiss became more passionate, almost painful, a clash of teeth, a small withdrawal, tender smiles, eyes sparkling with consent. Then they were all over each other, devouring each other, clumsily undressing, falling off the sofa; the album shoved away, glasses of wine almost toppled. Clothes were thrown aside. She was in black suspenders and stockings and his penis hurt as it pushed at his boxer shorts. He mumbled something about finding paradise. She laughed, not with derision, but with glee. He helped her push down his underwear, which had snagged on his erection. His penis sprang out and he felt relief, she grasped it and smiled wickedly. He was pulling down her knickers, dispensing with the stockings and suspenders, feeling the smooth length of her leg under the nylon as he took down her black knickers; bunching the lace topping that matched her stockings. He wanted to look at her, to admire her, but he was overcome and she would not have it. She pulled him onto her and gasped as he pushed himself inside her.

20:34

All the way home his cheek smarted and fixed his thoughts on what Red-face had to say. Visiting the second police station was in the balance. He wasn't really in the humour.

Only when he was turning the flight of steps that led to the floor of his flat and *Frau* Schumann opened her door did he realise where he was.

"Oh, *Herr* Dannaks," she said in pain.

His brow furrowed. She looked as if she was about to cry. She gestured to his door. He climbed the remaining steps and turned. The large swastika in red spray paint stopped him in his tracks. Thoughts congested his mind. When he heard *Frau* Schumann sniff his attention zeroed-in on her. She was still in her open doorway.

He went over and hugged the little old lady who seemed at once small and frail. He was lost for words and could only mutter a half-hearted litany of: "it's okay."

"What does it mean?" she asked, easing away and producing a tissue from somewhere, wiping her eyes and holding it to her nose.

"Nothing, just kids, I'm sure."

She looked into his eyes and he knew he had not convinced her. Something akin to betrayal dried her tears and she became ashamed. She must have noticed his bruise because her expression again changed.

"Oh, *Herr* Dannaks, I see you've had some trouble. Come in and I'll dress it for you."

"No, thank you, *Frau* Schumann. That's very kind of you. It's not as bad as it looks."

"I hope it wasn't one of those boys from the corner. Did you try to arrest them?"

"No, I–"

"Well, it's outrageous that they should pester schoolchildren."

"Yes. It is outrageous. You'll understand if I go in to look at this."

She peered closer. "Of course, we don't want it going gangrenous."

For a moment he thought she was talking about the door.

"No, it's okay, really."

"Did you get it from them?" she nodded at the swastika.

"I don't think so."

"Oh, *Herr* Dannaks, you do have some enemies."

"Yes," he said, using the lull to turn his back on her, "I do." He pushed his door.

"I have some ointment."

"That's very kind. But thanks."

She gathered herself together and he knew her disappointment. "I think I'll have a stiff sherry."

"Should I come in with you?" Although he'd been trying to get away guilt had got the better of him.

She paused a beat to examine his sincerity. "No." And the light returned to her eyes as she brushed his hand.

Dannaks smiled. He'd been forgiven.

"Good night, *Herr* Dannaks."

He smiled. "Good night, *Frau* Schumann."

He watched her go inside and close her flat door.

He about-faced and stared at the swastika. It was classically drawn with starting blobs on the top lines. It wasn't perfect, but it wasn't a hasty scrawl either. He pushed his key in the door and felt for tampering. He turned the key and let the door crack open. There was nothing to show entry.

The common landing light went out and he froze. He reached over to the red glow of the switch and started the timer anew.

He flicked the light switch in the flat. But of course it didn't work. He unconsciously moved his hand towards his hip, stopping and telling himself that his gun was in his office drawer. He entered the room and searched for an immediate weapon. No baseball bat, no broom, absolutely nothing was within reach of the flat door. He looked over his shoulder at *Frau* Schumann's closed door. Could she be looking through the peep-hole? He thought not. So he bent down and slipped off his left shoe. It wasn't much of a weapon. His brother's wife had said they looked like plastic imitations of real shoes. Patel had sold him a brown pair too. Oh, they were airy and terribly comfortable. But they lacked substance. There was no weight in the heel. Both pair had cracks at the back of the ankle were he used his finger to slip them on. He left his right shoe on should he need to kick. He felt like a modern Neanderthal before his abode and he sincerely hoped *Frau* Schumann wasn't looking. Kids indeed.

He pushed the door wide and listened. His flat was mausoleum still. He stepped in and thought of saying something about being a police officer or I know you're in here. Instead his arm rounded the bathroom entrance and pulled the light-switch cord. He pushed open the door there too. This light shrivelled the darkness of his lounge-cum-bedroom and he hobbled in, flicking on the kitchen light and then the lounge. He checked the lounge, which offered very little for his brother's children's attempts at playing hide and seek. The kitchen was no better. He pulled back the shower curtain and returned to close his flat door and lock it. Only then did he take off his remaining shoe.

He slipped off his jacket and carefully hung it up. Rolling his jaw and then shifting his chin with his hand he went into the bathroom and stood before the mirror. Just under his left eye was a bruise with a purple centre and a rose penumbra. Any higher he'd have a black eye, any lower and his jaw could have been put out of whack. He had no ointments or creams and although the skin was not broken he washed his face in tepid water.

The man had taken his card, so he had something to say.

Priorities, priorities. He went to the front windows. The warm air made him gasp. His kitchen and bathroom were common in size and the fact that they were windowless. The rush of night traffic competed with the wind rushing the leaves on the trees. He found ice and broke two cubes into the only flannel he had. He wrapped them and put the cold parcel to his cheek. A wave of depression engulfed him and he threw the flannel and ice in the sink. The clatter jarred. He returned to his jacket, taking it into the kitchen and lay it on the work-surface. Then he sighed and pulled out the flip-top bin from under the sink. Over the open bin he carefully turned the outer pocket inside out. The box was almost flattened, but the filament and most of the shards of the broken bulb were still inside. Tiny pieces had found their way into the pocket corners; others were snared on the lining. Meticulously he picked out every one, resorting to tweezers for the difficult pieces. Eventually he was satisfied he had them all and tentatively ran the flat of his hand over the pocket before pushing it back inside.

This was what had cracked when he hit the ground. He'd have to do with a darkened hall for a little longer.

He re-hung his jacket and then opened a kitchen cupboard. The bottle of Dulwinnie was next to the jar of coffee. He fetched a crystal tumbler, one of five from an original six from his brother some Christmas ago. He watched the level of the amber liquid as it flowed into the glass. With the tumbler in one hand and the envelope in the other he went into his bedroom. Of course he only had one room.

The sofa bed was out.

He wanted to phone Uwe. He wanted to convince him and himself that he wasn't chasing shadows. But Uwe would not appreciate a call at this time. His sparring partner was a nine-to-five man.

Depression took him again and a tear surprised him. Pull yourself together, man.

He favoured the floor next to the coffee table rather than the sofa bed. For a moment he wondered whether he'd done enough for one day. Why not enjoy the whisky? Watch a bit of television? Unwind? What was the point of going to another station? It could wait.

What did the swastika mean? Should it mean something? He answered the second question first. Only his door had been smeared. Not *Frau* Schumann's or as far as he knew anywhere else in the house. So a prank was unlikely. He'd been targeted. This led to a partial answer to his first question. It was a message. More, it was a warning. Okay. Then who and why? Again the logical question to answer was why. Motive first. Why? Reinhart? He had definitely torn off the top sheet of his blotter. Was he spying on him for Frank? No. That was too outlandish. It certainly wasn't a REX prank either. This was serious. So why? All he had done so far was go after Lampe. And then what could Lampe gain from such puerile activity. Hardly revenge. And why a swastika? But that wasn't all he'd done. He'd visited the police station. Okay, so let's assume he had rattled a cage. Surely this was an over-reaction? He toyed with reporting it, but that could blow his investigation. Ha! What investigation? Of one thing he was certain: he was doing something right.

There was another aspect to the swastika, other than being a warning. Whoever had drawn it knew where he lived.

The long-planned Right-wing gathering at the Deichtorhallen near the main station and the Left-wing challenge made a clash inevitable. The *Polizeipräsident* concluded his introduction to the briefing in the large conference hall of the *Polizeistern* by unnecessarily adding that the cohorts from the media would exacerbate the situation further.

Nobody asked whether permission for the march or the demonstration could be revoked, but he had given them reasons why not.

City Hall wanted to make a statement. The case of the Turkish boy had received too much attention. The procrastination of the education authorities leading to similar occurrences being brought to light had made the thing too big to be cancelled.

The Right-wing gathering was a legal meeting that had been approved some time ago. Trying to revoke it would do more harm than good. "Volker Herbst has put it together and he knows his rights. He'd love the opportunity to present himself as a victim and wave Article 8 in our faces. But it wouldn't get that far." Article 8 of the Basic law guaranteed citizens the right to gather at any place, any time and in any way. "You know how slick politicians can be. He knew his chance of protesting in the centre was nil. Now he's getting mileage out of the fact that although he's drawing similar numbers, the Turkish march was given the centre of the city and the prominence. As I said at the beginning of the briefing, these decisions, wise or otherwise, have been made." Dannaks knew that the Polizeipräsident walked a tightrope of sounding as if he was on their side whilst being party to City Hall's decisions. Falling out with the mayor was never wise.

He then handed over to Willy Fischer, who was being groomed for the *Polizeipräsident's* position. He went through a check list that had been given to the organisers of the Right-wing gathering. Breaking any of these rules meant being removed from the area or arrested.

- *Bomber jackets and white-laced paratrooper boots, uniforms or parts of uniforms were banned.*
- *The number of flags was not to exceed one per five demonstrators.*

- *When the police were talking, megaphones and loudspeakers were not to be used.*

- *All weapons, or anything that constituted a weapon, would be confiscated and lead to immediate arrest.*

- *The right to deter access to the demonstration area remains at the discretion of the police.*

- *Unhindered public access to the exhibition must be allowed at all times.*

- *The duration of the demonstration would not exceed four hours commencing at midday.*

Police presence was to be necessarily high, in itself provocative, and yet it was imperative that they remain impartial. Not only were members of the *Kripo* and a majority of *Schupo* present, there was also a backup contingent from the border police. 1,200 officers from neighbouring states were supplementing the Hamburg force of 1,400.

The next speaker, Saturday's commanding officer spoke. He made the point that the challenge would swell the numbers. City Hall wanted the marchers in front of them, in the square before the building and then Mönckebergstrasse: the main shopping mile. Strategically confining and protecting the protesters in this stretch of the city centre was a nightmare. There were many entry and exit points, especially through shops that backed onto the Spitalerstrasse precinct. Innocent shoppers would aggravate managing the march.

The uniformed men were to line the route. Dannaks and other plain-clothes officers were to mingle with the public and report. If necessary they'd be called in to control the outskirts of the march.

Frank and Schuppenhauer had travelled with Dannaks and sat on either side of him. When the meeting adjourned Frank stayed on with the other heads and Dannaks and Schuppenhauer returned to the station.

"That's a hell of a shiner you got," he said of Dannaks's bruise.

"It's not as bad as it looks." He didn't elaborate and Schuppenhauer didn't press him.

He was with Reinhart for an hour to visit an old woman who claimed to have inside knowledge about a right-wing group. She was a cleaner and said she had discovered lots of material stashed in the cupboard of an antique shop. The information was useful but not earth-shattering. She had refused to speak to the

Schupo and insisted on speaking to detectives. What was interesting for Dannaks was Reinhart's performance. His acting skills had come to the fore again when she had complained about her arthritis. He lied by saying he was a sufferer too and suddenly he was moving carefully. This empathy won the woman's confidence and she painted a much fuller picture than they could have expected. On the way back to the office Dannaks complimented him. Nonetheless there remained a crevasse between them and Dannaks could not find a way to broach the subject of their differences. He'd thawed to the man, but he wasn't ready to trust him.

Early afternoon, Dannaks got a call.

"Just listen," said the caller. "My name's Orth. I was in the coffee room when you visited Wednesday night. I am at the Präsidium. I could meet you at the play area of City Park at about five thirty."

"I know it. I'll be there." The man hung up.

The man had chosen a public place, so the likelihood of a trap was slim. But Dannaks remained concerned. He searched his memory of the faces in the coffee room, but couldn't conjure them all up, let alone which one could be Orth.

To befriend Reinhart the odd thought of asking him to back him up jumped into his mind. The idea brought a smile to his face. Reinhart was hardly the image of the muscle he might need. You could only take acting so far. He dismissed the idea when he remembered that the man would undoubtedly be at rehearsals. And what had Schuppenhauer said that morning? "Hasn't he told you that today is what the English call poet's day?" After a theatrical pause he explained that poet's stood for: "piss off early, tomorrow's Saturday".

13:04

Behind the man was a striking poster of the Crucifixion. Underneath were the words "*Ausländer raus?*"

Over the telephone the spokesman had sounded official and organised, but here in their office, Craig was reminded of the working chaos of a Students' Union room.

The spokesman, a tall lanky man by the name of Klaus, sat on the other side of the cluttered desk. About his neck, tucked under the collar of his blue denim jacket, was a black and white keffiyeh. He wore a white T-shirt with a faded blue Che Guevara resembling the man on the poster behind him. Also in the room was a chubby little dark-haired fellow. Looking like one of the Blues Brothers, he was

215

dressed in a shabby dark suit, patterned shirt and narrow woollen tie. He busied himself in the background but remained half-aware of the conversation.

One of the things that gave Craig the impression that he was back at university was the wealth of literature and posters. There were numerous gay rights magazines, Green Peace leaflets, human rights fliers and workers' rights articles piled high in corners or littering the desk. Posters covered every available inch of wall space. Serene ones demanding the saving of forests and whales contrasted with shocking ones against nuclear power, vivisection and hunger. Most radical of all was an old police-wanted poster of the RAF (Red Army Faction) and the Baader-Meinhof gang.

Klaus was a chain-smoker and Craig wondered whether the posters were there to protect the walls.

Craig asked him about the views of his group.

The smoker spoke generally at first. He said that many people thought the leftists had died with the fall of the Wall. He admitted that they had lost some credibility at first, but his group and the Left as a whole were again gaining respectability.

"Do you think that the current revitalisation of the Left is largely a reaction to the antics of the Right?"

"No." He took a drag on his cigarette. "I believe that people are beginning to realise that the Left has other things to say. For instance, that the rights of the workers are still – and will always be – an issue."

"Tell me about the challenge."

"The press have typically exaggerated my statement. I didn't make a challenge. It was a warning. What I said was that should anyone from the Right try to disrupt the march, they would be in for a big surprise."

He took another drag on his cigarette.

"Actually the warning was Spiff's idea. I'm just the spokesman."

The Blues Brother nodded, all the while continuing to open or seal cartons of pamphlets.

"We want to bring them out and show people their true colour. The Right must be confronted."

"Is violence the way?" said Craig.

"Confrontation doesn't mean violence, but occasionally there's no other way. The foreigners are underdogs here. They rarely claim their rights. That's where we come in. This country is in danger of becoming authoritarian. We're here to fight that tooth and nail. Peacefully if possible. But if not, then..." He met Craig's eyes. "Why do you think nothing's being done about these Right-wing outrages? I'll give you a clue. Unlike them, we don't receive a forewarning of a police raid."

The conversation digressed. "Your country is employing Aids as a racist weapon. Your airports are screening European students from Africa or the Third World." At first Craig debated his points, until he realised the man's head contained an endless list of such human rights violations.

Eventually Craig got away. When he was out on the street he sighed relief and relished the fresh air. For some reason he could not get the incongruity of the phrase 'fighting for peace' out of his head. A few days ago the statements would have overjoyed him; grist to his mill. Now it all seemed extreme and somehow banal.

Klaus represented the other extreme. Oh, he wasn't quite a left-wing extremist. But was he the type of person Craig wanted to see more of?

After sending his first article he naturally had an energy-low. But his attitude was under the influence of his budding relationship with Carina. He was no longer as fervent as when he'd arrived. There was a skirmish going on in his mind. Their relationship was consuming him and he was having difficulty focusing on his goal.

14:03

In the lounge above the sofa was a large-framed poster of a man that exuded a mixture of tranquillity and resolve. He was poised in a stance reminiscent of Napoleon. Both arms were bent. His right arm resting firmly on his hip, the other across his front hanging easily but not limply at the same level as his waist. He was turned slightly so that the white of the circle with the black emblem on the red armband on his left arm was only partially visible. Too much of the contrasting black upon white would detract the overall peace that emanated from the picture. For the man was in a warm light brown uniform on a black background with the red of the armband lending to the overall ambience of the picture. The expression on the face was one of intensity: the eyes looking into the distance. This far-off look gave the impression of an intelligent man deep in thought. His eyebrows were crooked and he was contemplating problems. All was not well. But these problems, although grave, were not insurmountable. His posture, the stiffness in his back, his stance, and his look said that he was prepared to shoulder the burden of leadership. It was taken as implicit that it would require the people's dedication, support and sacrifice. Underneath were the words: "*Ein Volk, ein Reich, ein Führer!*" (One people, one realm, one leader).

On the sofa sat two muscle bound skulls. Kutnik and Steiner: lugs with a combined IQ that didn't exceed room temperature.

"All you need to know is that he's a polyp," said Karsten, placing a photograph on the coffee table. "That should make it easier." He saw their amusement. Idiots.

"Five thousand each," he said, clamping his square jaw shut against protest.

The skulls sucked from their beer bottles that looked insignificant in their big hands. They tried to appear impassive, but Karsten could see the glow of money in their eyes. Skulls were easy to read. Simpletons. They were the worst of the right wing movement and its bedrock: unchangeably loyal.

Karsten could see that they wanted to look at each other.

He sat in the easy chair on the other side of the coffee table as if interviewing them. They'd done similar jobs, but few as extreme or daring.

"I'd say," began one, looking at the puny bottle in his big fist, "that this was worth more. He is police." He dared a glance at Karsten and then his partner, before returning to Karsten. The other one looked up.

Karsten thought about his reaction behind a smirk. They couldn't read him. Would he bend or blow? He wanted to keep five for himself, but this was an exceptional job. And perhaps he owed it to these two morons because of Saturday night's foul-up. These two had been pulled in, caught outside the pub. Charges pending.

"If the end result is anything less," Karsten reiterated, "you'll get less. You understand?" Slight nods. "Five-five," he said. It would leave him with four and as an intermediary he wouldn't get his hands dirty. If they were to go down, they'd go down quietly: unchallengeable loyalty.

There was triumph in their faces. One drained his bottle to hide his joy and the other placed his empty on a beer-mat on the coffee table. He knew that the table was one of Karsten's prized works.

He knew they wouldn't say no to a second drink, but he wasn't going to offer. He simply waited. There was nothing else to discuss. They knew the rules. Money after the job was done.

Sure enough, they began to feel uncomfortable. They got up together, one sliding the photograph of Dannaks from the coffee table into his pocket.

Karsten remained seated: important like a don.

The two left, closing the flat-door quietly behind them.

He heard their footsteps on the concrete stairs and he heard the glee in their murmuring. He waited until the house door closed. Then he picked up the empty bottles and took them to the crate in the kitchen.

Skulls. Most of his gang were skulls. Simple boneheads. It was probably what made him stand out. He was clever. Too clever for them. Most would go to Volker Herbst's show tomorrow and disrupt the march. The gang wanted him there and Herbst wanted him there, but Karsten wasn't inclined to play second fiddle. Herbst would use him for his clout and street credibility. He'd been after him for a long time.

"United we can get somewhere," he'd claimed. But Karsten knew he meant Volker Herbst could get somewhere. After all the party was named after him: part of his ego trip. And why wouldn't he help him? Because Herbst reminded him of his own father. Physically they were similarly big-boned men, but they were not the same. Herbst was a toad to his father's lumbering John Wayne figure. Herbst was red-faced and puffing, his father pale and confident. Mentally they could be kindred spirits. His father was less fanatical but equally convincing.

He knew he was an anomaly. Yes, his father was a ranking police officer. But that wasn't what set him apart. He had been on a couple of the organised camps, but they'd been little more than drunken Boy Scout meetings. It was a chance to wear a uniform and play soldiers. But because of his hate for his father he was ambivalent about uniforms. He had his Fred Perry shirt, something from Masterrace and the obligatory white-laced Doc Martens. But he tended to dress how he liked.

Others had approached Karsten asking him to stand as a figurehead. But he didn't want that kind of prominence. It meant bureaucracy and coming to heel. He was answerable to no one but himself.

His father was trussed up in an appalling hierarchy. A few idle remarks had almost cost him his job. Karsten had been interviewed and had drawn fame by saying what his father thought but could not say. "I don't deny the holocaust; I just don't think grief should be turned into a business." He'd shown them the numbers on his wrist: his concentration camp tattoo. They'd written about the subtle undermining of the past, whereas he wanted to show them that he was a victim too. And this fame had given him the prominence he had until then avoided. Others adopted the tattoo. He enjoyed the fame and the leadership. Leadership came naturally. But he fought becoming a cog in the machinery.

Then there were those hanged boys. If it were possible they were below the skulls. They hadn't the muscle. One had been a moron, the other a boy with a big mouth. They weren't even cogs. And nobody missed them.

No, he was more, much more. Way above everyone. Light-years ahead of the men who'd just left. They were the simplest cogs in the machinery. Willing to do anything to remain a part of the machine. Willing, for instance, to commit murder.

17:25

Dannaks had alighted from the train at Borgweg at ten to six. The brisk walk through the city park to the children's area had him in a lather. The park was in a state of flux. After-work groups were settling down on picnic cloths with bottles of wine; families were setting up grills. There was a steady stream leaving the park too.

The rape case that afternoon had been strenuous. There had been too many babbling people. The need for interpreters rendered everything painfully sluggish. There were too many witnesses, too many contradictions, too many intrigues and it was difficult to know whom to believe. It was hopeless. They would have to continue tomorrow.

At the children's area there were still a few straggles of children, mostly with mothers, sitting on the benches. Dannaks rounded the pool. On the fifth bench nearest the wall of trees he saw the man. He was of average build and wore steel-rimmed spectacles. He was clean cut and looked like an insurance salesman.

Dannaks sat down on the bench leaving enough space for two people to sit.

"Orth?" asked Dannaks, looking straight ahead.

"Yes."

Dannaks watched a slip of a girl on a swing. The shadow of a cloud stole the warmth and contrast of light and dark. A mother fussed over her baby in a pram. Dannaks's skin chilled with the sudden change in temperature. A woman with a worried expression was watching them as much as her two children. Maybe she thought they were paedophiles? Why would two men sit on a bench overlooking the children's playground? But then under the trees there was a lone youth in a baseball cap. He was the pervert. And on cue he moved back into the shadows. Then he started walking.

"I am not telling you anything. And we are not meeting here."

Dannaks leaned forward and nodded.

"I am not like you. I like my work and my colleagues. But... Sometimes – I mean sometimes – it doesn't happen often – I don't agree with what happens."

A raven descended upon a deserted spot near the pool. Two small boys chased it. It hopped and then flew onto the top rail of a climbing frame twisted into the image of an elephant.

"You mean bending the rules?"

Orth didn't answer and Dannaks was tempted to look at him.

"Yes."

"At the motor club?"

Again the long silence. A large cloud blocked the sun and cast the area in an unpleasant coolness.

"There weren't enough of us," began Orth.

"I understand." He couldn't see the youth in the baseball cap.

"Some right-wingers got away."

A family walked by, the father carrying a young child on his shoulders.

"But they could have been caught."

"Maybe."

"Was Karsten Krohn one of them?"

"I am not like you," he repeated. "I'd never go against the lads."

"I know." He waited. "Did Krohn get away?"

"Yes." Orth rose and walked off. The cloud passed and the returning warmth was welcome. Shadows were elongated representations of their objects. The shadows of two climbing frames became Dali-inspired elephants on stilts. The raven was now on the slide Dannaks knew from photographs. He looked over at the ship and then the slide and tried to imagine the scene the two joggers had found in October. Two boys raced past and scrambled up a sturdy tent of rope netting. One reached the top of the central pole before the other. "Winner!" he shouted. The loser touched the top too. They descended. A children's playground was an assault course. He tried to imagine the scuffle at the ship, the fireman's lift, trudging through the sand to the slide, Doermer's feet dragging now and then. A waif of a girl was at the top of the slide. She slid down. The killer was an athlete. The skipping rope, even the tangerine, supported this assumption. Could he be a soldier?

17:44

Incredible as it seemed Dannaks was in no doubt that he was being followed. Why would someone want to watch his movements? The swastika could be shunned as the antics of a prankster. Being followed was immediately serious. He tried to shrug off the thought that it could be a hit. But the more he thought about it, the more convinced he became that he would have to catch and interrogate the man.

His heart began to thunder.

To think that the insignificant and pure chance event of a woman stumbling had alerted him to the possibility of being followed.

The man must have picked him up from work and followed him to the city park.

Dannaks stopped at the kiosk at *Borgweg U-Bahn* station, glad to be sheltered from the gathering clouds. He'd seen them in the park, way off, but threatening like an encroaching army. Others had seen them too and were packing up early. He looked at the magazines and eventually wandered back onto the street. The sky was dark, but still it had not started to rain. He couldn't see the tail. He had hoped he'd enter the station so that he could confront him. Dannaks ordered a crepe and lemonade and stood at one of the tall tables on the pavement. As casually as possible he looked up and down the road and then over to the waiting buses and parked cars. He couldn't see him. The man was good.

Dannaks had left the park and had been on his way to the station. A middle-aged woman with a shopping bag had crossed the road from the bus and was in front of him. A few people were walking this stretch of pavement. Quite unexpectedly, when he was practically alongside her, the woman toppled forward, as if she had caught her foot. She and Dannaks would later inspect the ground for a protruding edge of paving stone. Although she held onto her bag her groceries spilled out. Dannaks and another pedestrian assisted her. As he crouched he noticed a man stop in his tracks and suddenly crouch to tie a shoelace. His baseball cap hid his face. He'd not been close enough to help and he had done nothing unusual. But Dannaks thought him familiar. He had seen his black jeans, his dark blazer, but especially his shoes.

The woman left admonishing herself: "How stupid, how stupid," all the way down to the platform. Dannaks saw her off, stopping at the station kiosk at the top of the steps.

He finished his crepe and downed the last of his lemonade. He still couldn't see the man. Wiping his mouth allowed him more time. Big isolated raindrops began spotting the road and pavement. The bus on the other side of the road, beyond the parked cars in the central isle, moved off. Nobody was on it and nobody was at the shelter. But there, as he followed the bus behind the parked cars, he saw inexplicable movement in a rear-view mirror of a mini-van. He scrutinised the mirror. Again movement, something round and blue and then curved, peaked, a cap, a baseball cap. His tail was crouching between the parked cars on the other side of the road. Even if Dannaks got close he didn't think he could catch him. There were too many obstacles.

The rain grew earnest.

He threw his garbage in the bin and entered the station.

There were only three or four people on the sheltered platform. Where he stood he had a commanding view of the steps he had just descended. They were the only way in and out of the station.

The growing sound of an approaching train did not completely drown the footsteps of a prospective passenger descending and then stopping halfway. Again, doubt caused him to wonder whether the person had just remembered to buy a ticket from the machines opposite the kiosk.

A gust caught the rain and he moved away from the edge of the platform. There was a flash and seconds later a long rumble as the train slowed to a stop.

Dannaks boarded the nearest carriage, the second to last. The lights were on and the darkness made it seem like ten o'clock at night. He missed the stand-back call because of the drum of rain and an ongoing conversation. But he heard the call firmly repeated as a latecomer apparently dived for the closing doors.

He instinctively knew the latecomer was his tail.

At Kellinghusenstrasse he should have crossed the platform to the connecting train; instead he alighted and descended the steps to the kiosk below. He stood at the window inspecting the display of magazines and waited. A lot of people had their backs to him. They waited at the exits for the rain to ease.

Only a grubby homeless man selling *Hinz und Kunz* (equivalent to London's Big Issue) met his eye. Dannaks shunned his guilt and watched the steps. He didn't have time for niceties.

"*Hinz und Kunz*," said the voice meekly.

The homeless man was standing next to him. So much for conspicuously ignoring him. He appeared to be holding his last copy and Dannaks reached inside his jacket for his wallet. Then he glanced at the man; seeing him properly for the first time. He looked weary with slack shoulders, but otherwise relatively handsome in a rugged friendly gardener sort of way. "Here. Keep the change," said Dannaks taking the magazine. Succumbing to a feeling of guilt for ignoring the man, he apologised. "I'm looking for someone." The man nodded and gave him a half-hearted smile that revealed the terrible state of his teeth and completely destroyed his handsomeness. He'd heard it all before. Dannaks tried to smile but the man was already fading away.

He heard the connecting train arrive. Then one left after the other. People began coming down from the platform. An old lady, descending the steps behind a small tartan trolley, was staring at him. He wondered whether she wanted help, but she appeared to be doing fine. When a lad also coming down the steps offered his help she politely refused. But she was smiling sympathetically. Dannaks looked beyond her. The man was not among the travellers. Had he flown? The woman was still smiling. Dannaks put on an exaggerated "leave me alone" look. Still she had him in her sights. He stared back. Did he know her? At the bottom of the steps she turned her tartan trolley behind her and to his horror she came straight towards him.

"I'll take that, young man," she said, when she stopped in front of him.

"What?" Exaggeratedly looking beyond her to show he was occupied.

"That," she pointed; he looked down at the magazine in his hand. She had her purse out.

"No, it's not for sale."

"Don't be silly, my boy. I know how bad life is for you."

"No, you don't understand."

"I'll give you extra for it."

"Okay, here take it."

"Oh no, no." She'd found some coins.

She pressed the money into his hand and he let her take the magazine. She smiled, chuffed by her good deed, and moved off, the tartan trolley following her like an obedient dog.

Dannaks knew his sweatshirt and jacket were worn, but he'd always thought them acceptable. If he'd been a mite quick-witted and hadn't been so distracted he could have shown her is identification and told her he was undercover. The thought of telling Uwe and hearing the probable reaction along the lines of "great disguise" flashed through his mind. Undercover vagrant.

He climbed the now deserted steps. The platform was clear. The rain was easing and there was a break in the clouds. He had a five-minute wait ahead of him.

By the time his train arrived there were others on the platform. The doors opened and Dannaks hesitated allowing the others to board. Then he moved forward. As he did the periphery of his vision registered a familiarly clad figure emerging from behind the waiting room. He snapped his head round, but the capped figure entered the neighbouring carriage under the cover of others. Not before Dannaks glimpsed the side of a training shoe. The stand-back call came and Dannaks boarded the train.

Dannaks was convinced. There had been no reason for the man to miss the earlier connecting train. It was the same man. The striped training shoes, dark jeans, hoodie and baseball cap.

The worrying thing was that the man had remained on the platform. He had not followed him down to the kiosk. This meant he knew Dannaks wanted to change trains. He'd taken a risk, of course, but ultimately it meant he knew Dannaks's route home.

There was no getting round it; Dannaks would have to tackle him.

17:48

Craig had seen the change in the advertised subject of an afternoon chat show and had recorded it. Although Carina had expressed only mild interest, after dinner, they were both settled upon the sofa when Craig pressed play. As always he had a pen and paper close at hand.

The show's presenter, who also chaired the debate, outlined the topic, giving a potted history of Faruk's ordeal, the education authorities' procrastination over allowing him to take some tests, the ensuing media coverage of other abuses, followed by the march and finally the left-wing challenge. Then he introduced the guests. There were four in all. Two were politicians, neither of whom were big-league players. One was a minor right-wing politician from the CDU (Christian Democratic Union - conservative party) the other was from the SPD (Social Democratic Party - labour party), and known to hold particularly leftist views. The *Schulleiter* (headmaster) of Faruk's school was present and there was a social worker who worked extensively with the Turkish community. Also in attendance was a small non-participating audience to add a bit of warmth to the proceedings. The cameras panned back now and then to take in the debating group within this silent jury of three dozen or so.

The first half of the show, in contrast to the second, was mainly routine. The intermittent sparring was generally a clash of personalities and ideologies and often covered a moot point. But one of the highlights came at the very beginning of the discussion.

Presenter: We all understand that there has been some controversy over these tests the boy was meant to take. We'll come to that later. I would like to open by asking you to explain these tests, as they were not strictly normal.

Schulleiter: I'd like to start by saying that what happens in the classroom should not be the subject of a public debate. Having to explain what is essentially our handling of a specific problem undermines both the credibility of the teacher's decisions and that of the school as a whole. In addition I should say that I had, and have, the full backing of the education authorities. And in protest and as a display of solidarity we'll be gathering at the school playground at eleven o'clock tomorrow morning. (Because of what would transpire at the march their tame gesture would be rendered all the more meaningless.) In answer to your question, the recommendation that the pupils take a test was put to me and under the circumstances I agreed.

Presenter: For the sake of clarity, what were these circumstances?

Schulleiter: It had become obvious through erratic results amongst other things that within a small section of the class there appeared to be some cheating. I don't want to go into details, but it seems that a certain group of the pupils bought assignments or help from some of the cleverer ones. We were not certain whether this buying was with money or extortion. Rather than humiliate these cleverer pupils I agreed to special tests being carried out for the entire class. They were given the week to prepare.

(There was some shaking of heads and comments on the state of the classroom today.)

SPD Politician: Isn't it true that the majority of the pupils said to be cheating were the foreign students?

Schulleiter: I believe so.

SPD Politician: Don't you find that strange?

Schulleiter: No. I don't find that strange at all.

SPD Politician: It's normal then?

CDU Politician: You're driving at the possibility of racism in the classroom.

SPD Politician: What do you think?

Schulleiter: It's not a question of racism, but of ability.

SPD Politician: Are you implying that the German pupils are more intelligent than the foreign ones?

CDU Politician: Don't be ridiculous.

Schulleiter: You're forgetting one very important fact and that is that the entire class were subjected to the tests.

The direction of the conversation then took a turn and became dull. The presenter interrupted the person speaking and announced a commercial break.

"It started well and then just petered out," said Craig, staring unthinkingly at the flashes of mundane advertisements.

"I find it boring," said Carina who had picked up a magazine from the coffee table. She would read it for a time before becoming engrossed in the second half.

"Coffee?" offered Craig, pulling himself to his feet.

"Decaffeinated."

He nodded and left the room. When he returned, cups in hand, the second half had just begun.

Presenter: Welcome back. We are debating...

I want now to turn to the march itself and the implications of this left-wing challenge. (To the social worker.) You were very quiet in the first half of the show. Can I ask what you think the march will achieve in view of the fact that the schoolboy has been allowed to take these special tests?

Social worker: The real meaning behind the march is not the tests. Or the individual incident of the beating of the boy. It is about integration and what I thought this debate was supposed to be about... (The social worker spoke about the Turkish community being an integral part of Hamburg, emphasising that they were isolated and not integrated.) This is what we should be discussing and this is what the march is about.

Schulleiter: I don't think that's the message of this march at all. If it is, it's hidden. The media have fired this thing up, putting us, the education authorities, in a bad light. That's why I am here. To set the record straight. This march has gained such momentum that it has to go ahead, despite this outrageous challenge from the Left. The whole palaver is totally unnecessary. It's going to cost this city. Police time and money—

CDU Politician: It's fired-up, as you so put it, by the irresponsible challenge from the Left. I find it absolutely ridiculous that this march is going ahead. (He spoke at length of a juvenile culture encouraging disorder and the disruption of the fabric of society.)

SPD Politician: What of the right of the individual to protest? You seem to forget that they pay taxes too.

Social worker: Freedom of speech is paramount in a democracy.

Schulleiter: You're losing the perspective. We're talking about a schoolboy who is involved in something—

SPD Politician: What something?

Schulleiter: Involved in something—

(The SPD politician attempted to interrupt again).

Presenter: Please let him continue.

Schulleiter: All this is academic. The boy can take the tests. But they're only to confirm— (sigh) In his particular case it is a foregone conclusion...

SPD Politician: Are you saying his performance in the tests is irrelevant?

(The conversation went around and around, until the *Schulleiter* was cornered.)

Schulleiter: Well...er...by and large.

CDU Politician:The outcome of these tests will not have a great effect on his end results? (Stirrings in the audience.)

Schulleiter: I am under that impression.

CDU Politician:Yes or no?

Schulleiter: Yes.

Social worker: How absurd.

SPD Politician: What did you mean earlier by involved in something?

Schulleiter :   (hesitant) Well, this, er, beating. It's—

SPD Politician: What about it?

Schulleiter: As far as I know the boy is a bit of a tearaway.

SPD Politician: What do you mean tearaway?

Schulleiter: Street kid.

SPD Politician: Isn't that prejudiced and totally irrelevant to his classroom performance?

Schulleiter: It would be if it were not true.

CDU Politician: I think what he's trying to say is that the march should not go ahead, for the simple reason that there are no grounds for it.

SPD Politician: I still don't know what the boy was supposed to be involved in.

(At this point a lot of to-ing and fro-ing went on before the *Schulleiter* again lost his composure.)

Schulleiter: Obviously gangs or sects.

SPD Politician: Obviously? Why obviously?

Presenter: Yes, I'm not sure we are following this. (To *Schulleiter*) Could you elaborate?

Schulleiter :   (again hesitant – turning the atmosphere electric) It– (clears throat) It came to our attention that the boy had some scars.

(Louder murmurings from the audience.)

CDU Politician:What kind of scars?

Schulleiter: Like burns.

CDU Politician:Where?

Schulleiter: A sensitive area.

(Further unrest in the audience.)

SPD Politician: How did you come to see them?

Social worker: I don't think we should be discussing this.

Schulleiter: They were noticed in the shower after physical education.

Social worker: I really must protest. This—

CDU Politician:How did he get them?

Social worker: That's enough.

Presenter: Yes, I think that if you don't wish to answer then we shall leave it at that.

      (Silence)

Schulleiter: It's out now. (Pause.) I don't know how he got them. You should ask our social worker here. He said that he had an accident, but they looked purposeful. That's why I thought he was in some kind of sect. You know, some gang thing. You people don't work with kids. Most of—

CDU Politician:(to social worker) Can you shed any light on these scars?

Social worker: (reluctantly and then to *Schulleiter*) I consider your attitude most unprofessional.

SPD Politician: I agree.

CDU Politician:Are you going to answer my question?

Social-worker: No.

SPD Politician: I find this conversation taking on a disgusting tone. Everyone seems to have forgotten what we are supposed to be discussing. To answer questions about these marks – if they exist – avoids the real issue. No doubt it'll come out in the press within the next day or two.

Presenter: We're running out of time and I'd like to end by asking each of you to give a (emphasises next word) *short* answer. I want to return to the issue of the march and the implications of this left-wing challenge. Should the march go ahead?

CDU Politician: Under no circumstances. It is absolutely ridiculous. We're talking about a demonstration in the centre of Hamburg on a busy Saturday.

Social worker: Naturally. As I said before, in a true democracy everyone has the right to free speech. We're not talking about the beating of a boy or the shameful stalling of the education authorities. This is about integration. The question–

Presenter: I must hurry you along.

Social worker: The question we should ask ourselves is: had this been a German schoolboy–

CDU Politician:Oh no, you're not beating–

Social worker: Had it been a German–

CDU Politician:– that drum again.

Presenter: Please let him finish. You've had your say. But we have no time.

Social worker: – would we be asking the same questions? Would the education authorities have hesitated over allowing a German schoolboy the right to take the tests? The–

The programme credits began to run across the bottom of the screen.

Presenter: I have to stop you there. Very, very quickly. (This last sentence was directed to the remaining two speakers.)

Schulleiter: This march is meaningless. It's a waste of time and money and will do nothing for the relationship between the Turkish community–

Presenter: Sorry.

SPD Politician: The march is to go ahead, so all this is academic. All I can say is that it would have been interesting to have the boy's father in the studio. Then we could have heard the true reason for the march. We would also have discovered the truth behind the marks and–

Presenter: Sorry, I have to stop you there. (He quickly signed off with a plug for next week's show.)

"What do you think of the scars?" asked Carina.

"I don't know. I'll ask Faruk about them tomorrow."

"Maybe he is not so innocent."

"Maybe. If they exist."

"You think they were part of a gang initiation or something?"

"Maybe," he said irritably. "I don't know."

"The sparks were flying," said Carina, verbally backing off.

"There would have been more sparks had Suleyman or a member of the *Schwarzer Freitag* group been there. Or someone from the left-wing group that made the challenge and a real right-winger, Volker Herbst, perhaps a skinhead or Stefan."

"At least they are talking about it. That is what you wanted."

"True. But look what time it was broadcast."

231

She gave him a you-will-never-be-satisfied look.

18:09

The train pulled into Klosterstern. Dannaks moved to the door of the carriage and waited for the stand-back call. When it began he sprang onto the platform and stepped into the last carriage.

Each carriage had two sets of double doors on either side. Inside, a central aisle ran its length separating single seats on one side from double seats on the other. These padded seats faced each other as if a table should be between them.

He saw the man at the other end, near the second set of double doors. He was seated facing into the carriage, looking out away from the platform, his face hidden by his cap and his elbow resting at the bottom of the window, a hand cradling his chin. The seat in front of him obscured his shoes. Something bothered Dannaks about the cap. It wasn't the cap itself; there was no motif, nothing unusual, a worn grey or denim baseball cap. Then he had it: the man's ears seemed prominent. Yet, they were not outsized or jugged. But there was something more.

Although he appeared to be looking outside, the darkness combined with the light within the carriage increased the mirroring effect of the windows.

There were eight people in the carriage. Two were sitting together, the rest were seated with the customary psychological space.

Dannaks made his way down the aisle. Still the doors remained open.

Although he did not look at him directly Dannaks knew the man was aware of his presence.

He heard the crackling noise of the intercom akin to a microphone being picked up. There were some shouts and the scuffling of feet. "*Einsteigen, bitte* (Board, please)."

Dannaks was distracted for a moment. He glanced at the latecomers charging across the platform. Dannaks looked back at the man and caught his eye before he whipped his gaze back to the rain outside.

The latecomers, two teenage girls, congratulated themselves on catching the train. They entered the carriage at the double doors nearest the man. As they glanced about for a suitable place they attempted to quell their excitement and regain their composure. Their loudness, rendered all the more intrusive by the stifled atmosphere in the silent carriage, caused them embarrassment and they giggled

232

uncontrollably.

Choosing to move into the carriage away from the man, they saw Dannaks standing in the aisle. He had not stopped moving, but the appearance of the newcomers had caused him to hesitate. The girls exchanged glances and smirked.

The order: "*Zurück bleiben, bitte.* (Stand back, please)" was issued. One of the girls, in attempting to suppress her mirth, issued a pig-like snort. This sent the other into raptures. They were moving out of the aisle, bent over and drunk with laughter, to some vacant seats when the man made his move. He shot up and bolted for the doors. Dannaks brushed past one of the girls as he lunged after him. "Hey!" said one of the girls. The man's timing was impeccable and he slipped through the closing doors. Dannaks crashed against them and this caused the girls further mirth: the brush-past apparently forgotten. But Dannaks muttered an apology.

As the train pulled away, he saw the man smirk. Even then Dannaks did not get a good look at him. He noticed his dark hairy arms and knew that he was not blond. This meant that he had no or very little hair on his head. That was why his ears appeared prominent. He was a skinhead. Although Dannaks had only seen the side of his face, he thought he would recognise him again.

20:05

The patrolling that evening was routine and uneventful.

Hasan's group repeated Sunday's performance.

Basha's group rode about for a while before diving into a pub for an extended pause. Then they took a roundabout route home.

Ponytail was absent.

Neither team was particularly happy, but talk of the march and the challenge sustained them.

20:18

There was nobody behind him and he slowed the bike when he turned the corner. This was a 30 kilometre per hour zone. Before he passed the house he kept his head as still as he could as he looked to the right and left. The helmet and visor camouflaged but hindered his scrutiny. He took in everything. Details he'd noted in a dozen or so drive-bys in the past weeks were checked.

Then he was passing the target. This time he dared to turn his head. A fluttering glow in the front room meant that the television was on. The upstairs landing light was on too.

The motorbike took him beyond the house but he didn't

accelerate away. He brought the speedometer needle up so that it wavered at the 30 kilometres per hour mark.

He'd come back later when it was dark. He knew the rhythm of the house. He knew the rhythm of the street: quiet suburbia. He'd come back, park his bike and walk to his hiding place. Of course it wouldn't be that simple. But he was a spider. He could be fast, fast and stealthy. But he could be unbearably patient and still. Fishing had taught him patience. Staking out places and occasionally stalking his victims had taken his patience to greater heights. Tonight he'd go beyond stalking. Tonight he'd go through the motions. Tonight was the final rehearsal.

The weather forecast for tomorrow was the same as tonight. Perfect.

He couldn't wait. Weeks of work would culminate in a sting. And the thought of the sting gave him a buzz that was sexual.

21:45

Dannaks climbed the stairs to his flat. He had not come straight home. Instead he had walked. His general direction had been home, but he had been too wound up to go to his flat. He contemplated a brisk walk about the Alster. He sought distraction and even thought of going shopping. Some shops were still open. He glanced in shop windows of the Lange Reihe, the main artery of St. Georg. But he didn't really look. This road accommodated an international hotchpotch of shops. There were antiques and curios, Indian and Asian shops, Chinese and Italian restaurants, pubs, cafés, a loud US-style fast food bar all stars and stripes and miniature Statue of Liberty. Competing for attention with eye-attracting inventiveness were chemists, hairdressers, small supermarkets, grocers, bakers and opticians. The eating places were open and their roadside tables were occupied. Off this road were residences, blocks of flats, old and new, interrupted by yet another restaurant or local that survived solely on its speciality, often as a meeting place for Greeks, Turks, Iranians, Russians, Spanish and Portuguese. Here the sleaze of the side-street prostitution and drug addiction was being pushed further away by a slow gentrification. St. Georg was becoming terribly chic. He left the activity for one such side road and found himself standing outside the segmented window; each segment was yellow bottle end glass, a swirl in the middle, opaque as amber. The *Narzisst's Eck* (Narcissist's corner). He hesitated. He didn't want to get drunk. He didn't know what he wanted. All he knew was that he didn't want to be alone or in conversation. He went in.

Karl-Heinz greeted him. Dannaks knew his critical look.

"Whisky cola," he said, putting him out of his misery. Karl-Heinz gave him a lopsided, almost disapproving smile and turned away. He prided himself in being able to guess what Dannaks needed. Whisky cola meant frivolous filler.

"Any quick nosh?" he asked.

"A packet of crisps?"

Dannaks smiled. He was returning to the human race. "Anything else?" he asked, leaving himself open for a "if you want to eat, go to a restaurant" comment.

"Uta could do you a sandwich. Ham and cheese?"

"Fine."

He barely noticed his drink and was surprised to see the empty glass on the table. And when had he wolfed down those sandwiches? Hadn't he only just nodded to the regulars Hagen and Frauke and sat down?

He went to the bar and paid. This time Karl-Heinz had him figured out. "Work?"

Dannaks nodded and smiled wearily and then left.

He was pulling out his key when *Frau* Schumann's door cracked open. With a watchdog like her, how could someone have defiled his door? He turned to her.

Still she wouldn't let him go. "I wanted to tell you that *Herr* Scholz couldn't get it off." She pointed to the swastika, which was now pastel pink. *Herr* Scholz was the resident caretaker responsible for communal areas. "He said he'd have to paint the entire door. He said he didn't know who was going to pay for it." Dannaks had seen the notice on the house door calling for more vigilance.

"Don't worry *Frau* Schumann. I'll sort it out with him."

He had, of course, spent too long in the *Narzisst's Eck*. His original intention had been to bide his time before making his way to the second police station. But the tail had thrown him. The swastika was bad enough. He felt like a fish out of water. Flapping about, gasping and expending vast amounts of energy getting nowhere. And naturally he was getting somewhere or at least drawing attention to himself. He was upsetting somebody.

Saturday
09:20

They were sitting in a snack bar in the Wandelhalle arcade in the main station. As always the main station was a hive of activity, but they'd found a corner in the utilitarian snack bar to eat their filled bread rolls and drink coffee.

Uwe had already remarked on the bruise Red-face had given him. "I told you all you'd get was a bunch of fives. You're really a mug."

"Thanks for your sympathy. He took my card."

"In case he wanted a punch bag for regular boxing sessions?"

"Ha, ha," Dannaks groaned. He chewed a mouthful of bread roll. "He wanted my card. I think he has something to say."

"I'm with you so far. You're getting bashed about for doing nothing."

"Almost true." He sipped his coffee. "Lampe is getting transferred although we've got nothing on him. They think I'm putting something together."

"It's the potential, you mean. They know what you're capable of." Uwe digested the idea. "I still don't get it. What—"

"I almost caught someone following me."

"Is this the voice of paranoia?"

"Are you going to listen?"

Uwe put down his roll and held up his hands in surrender.

Dannaks explained going to the Polizeistern and then police stations in search of information about the activities of the 211ers. He told him about meeting Orth and concluded by telling him about being tailed.

He had phoned Orth that very morning and warned him that someone may have seen them together. Dannaks had reasoned that Orth himself would have nothing to do with the tail. But he couldn't completely rule out that someone from his station was behind it.

"I was tailed. Take that for a fact. And I think my tail was a skinhead."

"Are you sure?"

"Fairly. There's more." Dannaks waited for a prompt, but Uwe merely sipped his coffee. Dannaks chose to eat. He watched a backpacking couple unloading more gear than was humanly possible to carry around a small table.

"When I got home Thursday evening there was a swastika painted on my door." He furnished him with more details.

"But you haven't got anything. Why would they overreact?"

"That's my weak link. I–"

"Link? Let me guess, to Rüdiger Krohn?"

Dannaks was silent.

"Okay, okay." He pulled an invisible zip across his lips, but then said: "Who do you think did it?"

"I'll answer that in a minute. There's something else you don't know–"

"Do you actually do any work in REX?"

Dannaks ignored him. "Let me ask you a question. Was it coincidence that the pub was attacked on the night of our stakeout? What if they thought they were free to attack with impunity?"

Uwe shook his head. "We were onto those skinheads pretty sharpish. They staged their attack near the stakeout. Even their timing was bad. So that blows your logic out of the water."

"I said: what if they *thought* they were free to attack with impunity? The change was last minute. The pub is a long way away from the original stake-out location. Their information could have been old."

"It's all flimsy, but I'll go with it for now."

"You know that the leader of this gang is Karsten Krohn."

"He wasn't caught."

"It doesn't mean he wasn't there."

"You're now going to say that Rüdiger Krohn is the leak. Come on Dannaks, we've been there. Nothing was established. It's common knowledge they don't get on."

"What better cover?"

"It still doesn't make sense."

Dannaks was silent, hoping his friend would see it his way.

"Uwe, I was tailed by a skinhead."

"You've got nothing and you know it. When we have a large pre-arranged operation we pull in the *MEK*, riot police, sometimes the border police and customs officers. Word gets around. The leak, if there is one, could be anywhere."

Dannaks replied with silence, popping the last piece of bread roll into his mouth.

"It still doesn't make sense." Dannaks didn't have an answer. "Let's lay this out chronologically. Correct me if I'm wrong. Tuesday you point the finger at Lampe. It doesn't get you anywhere. But you go to Seven looking for information on Karsten Krohn and the 211ers. Wednesday you visit a police station in search of more material." Dannaks nodded. "Thursday you visit another station and you go home to find a swastika on your door. Friday you try to catch someone – a skinhead – tailing you." Uwe paused, although he made it clear he was not finished. "The only thing that could have rattled them is you fingering Lampe or asking about Krohn. I can understand them tailing you. But really the swastika doesn't make any sense. Why would they over-react? Are you sure one of your REX colleagues isn't fooling around?"

"No, I'm not sure. But it goes against what REX is about."

"It still sounds like a prank or panic."

"Or a warning."

"It's that without a doubt. But you've got nothing in the hand. And you've done – sorry, accomplished – very little."

"Maybe. But they don't know that."

"What next?"

"I don't know. As far as I can see whatever I do rattles their cage. Sooner or later they're going to make a mistake."

"Or you'll end up a lot worse than you are now."

Dannaks huffed cynically.

Uwe checked his watch. "I'll get this," he said, getting his wallet out. He had been allocated the Cohen exhibition. Dannaks would be further away, on Mönckebergstrasse near *Rathaus* square.

"You know, I saw this exhibition last weekend with Annelore." Uwe smiled wearily. "I can't get over the irony of it. Here we are protecting an exhibition of atrocities carried out by – amongst others – the police." Dannaks raised his eyebrows questioningly. "A good part of it is about the Polizeibataillon 101. Amongst other things they were responsible for mass executions in Poland. These ordinary police officers, originally hairdressers, clerks, harbour workers made up firing squads that had no compunction shooting children. One shooter specialised in killing children, by teaming up with his neighbour who shot the mother. He justified his position by reasoning that no child could live without its mother and he was simply releasing them."

09:32

When Craig emerged from the main station he was surprised by the activity. The numbers meant that many were unaware of the march or had not heeded the papers, radio or television, advising people to avoid the centre. The only sign that this was not a normal shopping Saturday was the congregation of police vehicles at the top of Mönckebergstrasse outside the main station.

He'd left Carina in the Wandelhalle shopping arcade. She didn't want to go to the Cohen exhibition at the nearby Deichtorhallen. He was pleased. She was still cold about his research and he had taken to mentioning his work as little as possible.

Like Thursday night, last night had been another one of furtively sleeping, waking to ravish one another before slumping into exhausted sleep. He was tired, a junkie buzzing on the adrenalin of their passion.

The exhibition was less than five minutes walk from the main station. He found he was able to look down from the pavement at a forecourt in front of what looked like light aircraft hangars. A wealth of youths hung about the entrance. He spotted Volker Herbst talking to an exclusive huddle. Apparently nobody wanted to see the exhibition today. Nobody appeared to be going in or out. Surrounding this group of two hundred or so, were uniformed police officers in full riot gear. They were stiff and menacing. Craig reckoned there were at least two officers per protester. But nothing was happening. Everyone was just standing around. Craig dismissed the idea of provoking an incident by trying to enter the building. It wasn't on his itinerary. He'd told Carina he'd be a quarter of an hour at most.

He took out his camera and quickly snapped a few shots before returning to the main station.

"Was it worth it?" Carina asked when he found her in the bookshop.

"So-so. There's nothing going on," he answered, knowing that he would not have to elaborate. "Shall we go?" Craig felt responsible for the march. He had pushed it through and incorporated it in his article. Although it was not due to start until ten thirty, there were already isolated knots of people. They were not shoppers. They were left-wingers loitering: easy to spot in their black garb; a chimney sweep convention.

Craig had heard that bigger demonstrations had stopped the traffic on the busy Ost-West Strasse, which ran parallel to pedestrian Mönckebergstrasse. Today's route was strictly confined to the length of this street, from the *Rathaus* to the main station, a distance of about a kilometre.

On their way to meet Petra and Robert, Craig took out his camera and photographed the police presence: two large army-green armoured vehicles with double-nozzle water cannon. They resembled fire engines more than the armoured personnel carriers he had seen employed in Northern Ireland. Television reports would later say that they carried nine thousand litres of a water/tear-gas mixture. Two heavy-duty windowless vans were there to transport the arrested. Five small buses were full of policemen and policewomen. There were numerous Peterwagen. A group of thirty police officers were checking their riot gear. Two officers talked and examined their video cameras.

Nobody had any idea how many people would turn up, but the police were plainly leaving nothing to chance.

Shortly after 10:00 a.m. they met Petra and Robert. The four of them walked down the road towards the gathering crowd at the *Rathaus* square. Police vehicles and personnel were present here also.

Craig was surprised to hear that no one had claimed the rescuers' reward. Of course he would have read about it in the *Tagespost*. Like Robert he assumed they were out of towners. Robert said that Diana Sohn was not upset about holding on to the paper's money.

The pale copper-green spires of the *Rathaus* were striking against the pastel blue sky. The building dominated the square. Craig had been stumped when it came to describing it for an article. The building was a motley of styles that because of their sheer clutter tended to make it appear – at first glance or to the uninitiated – baroque.

As they drew nearer, the incongruity of the situation became apparent. In the street they were amongst shoppers who were going about their business. Further down there was an extraordinary gathering of people with banners and flags. Mingling with this latter group were cameramen, reporters and photographers.

The banners carried loud slogans. *Nein zur Gewalt. Gib' dem Haß keine Chance. Wir schämen uns, dass ein Schüler zusammengeschlagen wurde. Die Wurzeln des Hasses wachsen im Klassenzimmer.* (No to violence. Give hate no chance. We are ashamed that a schoolboy was beaten up. The roots of hate grow in the classroom.)

Craig spotted Suleyman at a centre of attention. He was wearing slacks, a tired limp-collared shirt and a blue woollen cap resembling something a sailor might wear. Many were hustling for a place near him. Craig excused himself from his friends and fought his way through the crowd to Suleyman. They shook hands and above the clamour he managed to ask after Faruk.

"He feel better, but I not think he fit for this." Whether true or not it was a clever move. To appear not well enough to attend carried more weight. No one else from his family was present.

"Look around," Suleyman gleamed, shouting to make himself heard. "There be three or four thousand people here."

Craig's smile would have been weak, except for the fact that there was a certain heady atmosphere at the heart of the gathering. He estimated fifteen hundred to two thousand, but there was no point in quibbling.

Carina appeared at Craig's side.

"It is too much public. Cancelling would mean uproar. We'd make sure of that." Suleyman grinned. "You missed the mayor." Apparently he had got in an early point-making photo opportunity with Suleyman before the march began. Now nobody of prominence was present.

Television cameras had been set up atop their purpose-built vans; other cameramen shouldered theirs and mixed with the gathering.

No one in particular started the procession. There was some unspoken consensus and the mass surged up the road.

Craig dropped back to walk with his friends. He had wanted to ask about Faruk's scars but it was neither the time nor the place. Moreover, he thought the question had already been put to Suleyman and he would have the answer sooner or later.

"Was that Suleyman?" asked Carina.

Craig nodded.

"He certainly lives up to his name," she said.

"Oh?"

"Suleyman means conqueror or oppressor in Turkish. And he looks like a strict man."

Craig thought that he would have ordered Faruk to remain at home. "It's probably because he's been through a lot."

Mercifully, the effort required to make oneself heard allowed them to fall silent.

He shot surreptitious photos and scribbled details as they walked. There were many Turks, of course. But there were a lot of Germans too, both young and old. There were women pushing buggies carrying babies and there was even a small group of schoolboys. Was Ahmed present? On the whole there existed amongst the marchers a leisurely atmosphere that contradicted the protest.

Some shoppers looked on half-interestedly; most went about their business.

Lining the pavement every twenty metres was a huddle of uniforms. Near the *Rathaus* there were more.

The procession came to a halt a few metres from a line of one hundred or so chain-linked uniformed officers, one of whom carried a loudhailer. Behind this line were the main station and the Deichtorhallen.

Everyone stopped.

Petra spoke, asking something to the effect of "what now?" Nobody chose to answer. Craig was only half-aware of her. Apprehension had sharpened his concentration, excluding everything unrelated to the goings-on at the police line.

Whether anything was being said at the front he could not tell. There was some chanting. *"Stoppt den Haß. Integrieren statt Ignorieren."* (Stop the hate. Integration instead of ignoring.)

Then there was movement at the front and the people began to shuffle away from the line of officers. They began to turn and the head was absorbed into the body and the tail of stragglers became the new, and perhaps for some, reluctant head.

And so they all traipsed back in the direction of the *Rathaus* square. On their way Craig pointed out a man walking ahead of them. It was the stringy left-wing extremist group leader, Klaus. In black he looked as if he was auditioning for the part of Hamlet. He was smoking.

At the square the procession gathered as if someone was to give a speech.

10:36

Dannaks was positioned on Mönkebergstrasse nearer *Rathaus* Square. On the other side of the road was Burger King and behind him was McDonald's. He was loosely partnered with Schuppenhauer. They were to observe and report. So far nothing had happened.

Dannaks had skived off for a quarter of an hour to buy a light bulb. It sat in its box in the same pocket as its predecessor. His partner had gone to McDonalds for breakfast. The march was scheduled to run until two. He knew that group dynamics could push them beyond this deadline. But he had nothing else to do and the extra cash was always welcome.

"Hey you," said the boy. "Quick come with me." He looked rough, like a small pit-bull. His clothes were shabby, one size too big: a hand-down.

"What is it?" But the boy was going, beckoning him on. "Wait." Dannaks flicked his transceiver on. The boy turned a corner and was gone. Dannaks hastily searched for his partner in the window of McDonald's. He looked back to where the boy had gone. "Damn." He pocketed his transceiver and went for the corner. When he got there it took him a moment before he spotted the boy on the opposite side of the road.

Although he was only a street behind Mönkebergstrasse the contrast was pronounced. There were few shops, even fewer people, and little traffic. Dannaks felt his gut constrict. The boy was gone again. Why had he picked him out? Why not a uniformed man? Had he seen his transceiver? Nevertheless, why not a uniform? Dannaks ran across the road, a palm to the horn of the oncoming car. He heard the driver berate him as he slowed at a corner. The buildings here were four to six storeys tall and close enough to deprive the pavement of sun.

The boy appeared between two buildings no more than twenty metres in front of him. "Here," he called pointing behind him. Dannaks hastened. He looked between the buildings. There was a body on the ground.

"Get help," he ordered, taking in the scene. Although the boy was gone he shouted, "And then come back here." He moved briskly to the body. A man. Nothing else lying around. Not a tramp. A corpse? The light behind him changed and déjà vu struck him. Did the corpse move? He turned to see another man, also a body builder, standing behind him. He was about to tell him to get help, but his mask and the way he filled the entrance sent other signals. There was movement and Dannaks turned to see the corpse confidently rise from the dead. He was also wearing a *Totenmaske* (death mask). Plain like the tragedy and joy masks, the yin and yang of the theatre, these masks were deadpan, straight-mouthed and porcelain-white like those worn at ice-hockey games.

The corpse was a skinhead. That same wild dog irrationality salvaged the situation. Could he take them on? Only life-threatening circumstances allowed the use of his service weapon. This was one.

He went for his gun. They had anticipated his move and were on him with surprising speed.

He had no chance. The light bulb was not the only thing to crack.

10:37

There was hesitation filled with more sporadic chanting and then the procession started up the road again towards the police line in front of the main station. The protest was being carried out in a civil manner and it looked as if the right-wing groups had stayed away. Or the police were doing an exceptional job containing them.

Craig noticed that there were fewer spectators among the shoppers. The novelty had worn off.

Again the crowd reached the line of officers and again after a few uneventful but strangely tense moments they turned back. This time Craig was able to see the faces of some of the policemen. Most carried a cornered-animal expression: a dangerous mixture of fear and threat. A threat that could easily be mistaken for challenge.

They were turning when Craig saw a man in black, wearing a sleeveless vest that showed off his impressive biceps. Craig spotted others who were similarly clad. Their red headbands set them apart from the left-wingers. Having noticed them he wondered why he had not seen them earlier, their dress was conspicuous.

He moved closer to Carina. "I'll be back in a minute," he said, and wound his way swiftly through the slow moving crowd.

"Excuse me; are you a group or a gang?"

Everyone ignored him. Then a stocky one turned to him. "We might be the *Schwarzer Freitag*."

"Could I perhaps interview you? Not now. After all this."

The man beamed.

Craig was taking down his name and telephone number when the interruption came. A voice shouted for them to go back to their own land. It was a stab at the heart of their protest. He looked to the pavement from where the shout had been issued. Bunched together stood a dozen aggressive-looking youths.

Murat finished giving his telephone number and then gave the youths the finger. Craig felt the black-clad figures gather. He checked the whereabouts of Carina and the others and realised that they were blissfully unaware of the heckling. But as he looked over he saw on the far pavement a group of four skinheads. Behind them, way back, were the police.

244

There was further harassment, but nothing more than harsh words. The procession moved on.

Craig quickly scrawled the rest of Murat's telephone number and then excused himself.

The gathering stopped at the square and after a longer pause moved off again. This time the movement was at a slightly slower pace. The knots of skinheads and right-wingers at the pavement did not have the numbers for an all-out battle. To venture into the road was tantamount to a direct confrontation. This did not reduce their hostility; no doubt assuming that few marchers would be willing to return the aggression. There were noticeably fewer stragglers amongst the protesters. Some people had disappeared, notably the women with buggies. The schoolboys remained.

The police had seen the changes and were moving in tight groups along the pavement to support their dispersed colleagues lining the road. Some were conversing with the hecklers.

Looking ahead Craig saw that the line of officers at the main station had been replaced by a wall of clear plastic shields held by truncheon-carrying police officers in full riot gear. They had donned full white helmets with visors, rendering them faceless, almost inhuman and Craig could not help but feel a tinge of aggression towards such staunch authority.

"What did you want to see them for?" Carina asked. She looked hurt.

"Interview."

From nowhere and everywhere grew the chant: "*Nazis raus.*"

"You'd better get out of here, things could turn ugly."

"And you?"

"I'm staying."

"You'd better go too," Robert told Petra.

A flash point of violence occurred further up the procession. Strangely, the pavement and the road remained psychological barriers for the opposing groups. Craig saw that some left-wingers had left the road and were fighting with skinheads. He saw camera teams move in dangerously close and realised that this would show the march in a different light. For the fighting, brutal though it was, was more a skirmish on the fringe of the body of peaceful marchers. Yet, on television this incident would make the entire thing appear out of control.

The police were quick to move in. They went in hard,

indiscriminately grabbing anyone who appeared to be part of the fight, wrestling them to the ground and pinning them there until reinforcements came to help man-handle them back to the trucks.

Craig was impressed by the speed with which they quashed the fight. Nobody was badly injured. It had been all fists and boots. One knife had been pulled by a left-winger and Craig was surprised that more weaponry had not been in evidence.

The heckling had turned to chanting and clusters of aggressors on the pavement were extending their fists, or the first two fingers with the thumb, in unison. The latter was a cross between the straight-arm version of the black-power and the Nazi salute and represented a K of the dead neo-Nazi leader Michael Kühnen.

Robert said he'd had enough and the girls agreed. "I'll hang around," said Craig.

Carina didn't speak but scowled as if willing him to change his mind. "Take care," she eventually said, but didn't kiss or reach out to him.

Near the police line, where there were no right-wingers, Carina, Petra and Robert slipped into the thinning number of shoppers, many of whom had taken shelter as if from rain in the entrances of large department stores. The number of marchers had also thinned substantially.

Craig was on his own.

10:43

The protesters were still at the police barrier when a voice from a loud speaker mounted on one of the police vehicles advised them to disperse. The voice stated that they had said what they had come to say and that it was time to go. Their safety could no longer be guaranteed.

Some left the crowd at the edges of the line. Others were simply infuriated by the advice, taking it as an authoritarian command and shouted abuse at the police.

Craig checked his watch and scribbled some notes.

Eventually the gathering turned from the station to once again run the gauntlet of Mönckebergstrasse, for this is how it appeared. The situation was ludicrous. All they were doing was walking up and down the road waiting for something to happen.

Although the majority had left, there were still more marchers than right-wingers. Mothers and children had disappeared. The schoolboys were gone too. Dark skins and the *Autonomen*, professional protesters, in their standard black remained. As time went by the marchers were whittled down to a hard core of protesters.

The chanting was continuous and monotonous and because it came from the marchers and the right-wingers, unifying both groups, it was garbled. Then the whopping sound of the rotor-blades of an unseen helicopter drowned their words.

Miraculously the journey to the square passed without incident.

10:47

They were moving en masse towards the police line. Some of the left-wingers had covered their faces with balaclavas or handkerchiefs or the standard-issue Palestinian black and white keffiyeh.

Murat was about fifty metres ahead of him. He had decided to position himself closer to Murat. But the protesters had become so densely packed that it was impossible to reach him. Though not shoulder-to-shoulder, most wanted to walk in the centre of the road. Craig felt vulnerable despite the numbers. He couldn't see Suleyman.

Behind him a right-winger grabbed a protester and pulled him onto the pavement. As more right-wingers moved in on the victim, protesters broke ranks and counter-attacked.

Craig looked in the direction of where he had last seen Murat and saw a scuffle instead. He decided that Robert had been right. Things could only get worse.

The television cameras focused on the sporadic skirmishes and Craig looked about to see who else was observing the incidents. The procession was bitty. There were a few curious bystanders on the fringes. Astoundingly there were people ignoring it all and going about their shopping.

Craig spotted Murat. "Come on you bastards!" he heard him shout. His eyes were sparkling as he kicked a fallen right-winger.

Craig was pushed closer. He saw Murat at the doors to Barkhofpassage give his pursuers a further come on. The others, his colleagues and spectators, seemed taken unawares and gaped incredulously.

When they were almost upon him he turned and kicked the glass door aside. He charged through the dispersing huddle of spectators on the other side. Craig followed the right-wingers after him. The short shopping passage was narrowed with restaurant tables. People scattered people and those seated people were returning to

247

their drinks and meals, a new topic like a news flash taking their conversation. Craig moved almost unhindered in the wake of the right-wingers.

Emerging through the double doors onto the open pedestrian precinct, Craig turned left and edged his way through yet more tables of people. Some diners were protesting, but most cowered, shielding themselves, their possessions, food and drink. The precinct was full of shoppers, either blissfully unaware of the scene on the other side of the building or resolutely ignoring it.

Murat was clear of the tables coaxing his six pursuers towards him with his palms upward, a swift movement of his fingers gave them the come on. Craig watched him spring into a cat-stance. The leading youth stopped short and extended his arms to hold back his friends. With a motion of his hands he signalled for them to fan out.

Craig wondered whether the spectators thought this was part of a show, a distraction from the perplexed buskers: a four-piece band standing lamely with their instruments hanging. Their audience had turned to the restaurant entertainment.

Murat changed his stance. His attackers would converge on him simultaneously.

The shoppers were huddled in doorways or pressed against shop fronts watching from a safe distance. Occasionally someone would break the safety margin and walk briskly past. They openly ignored the confrontation; their infuriated expressions leaving their disgust in no doubt. A few passed derogatory comments, but no one neared the group.

When the fight began nobody in the audience moved. They were transfixed. Some craned their necks to get a better view. Handies were raised to film the spectacle.

Predictably they came at him at once and he went into a flurry of action. During the exchange one of the skinheads fell onto an empty chair. He picked it up and brought upon Murat's blocking arm. This and other blows must have convinced the Turk that he was getting hurt. He could win, but at what cost? When he decided to flee most of the skinheads were down.

Craig smiled when one or two of the spectators began clapping and hooraying. They fell silent when three of the skinheads got up.

Craig watched Murat sprint down the paved precinct that eventually converged with the pavement of Mönckebergstrasse. He followed the skinheads giving chase.

Ahead of him was the entrance to the *U-Bahn* system: a covered shelter with words stating that it was the entrance to the U3-line at Paulstrasse.

Through the parting shoppers he could see police on the steps leading down to the trains. A few of these officers had seen the Turk, but the majority were looking into the entrance. Two positioned themselves to stop him and were shouting something. Murat hesitated. The skinheads were closing in.

Craig watched him hurtle into the two officers. He struggled and they yelled at him. Other police officers joined in the tussle. Their attention was diverted when the first of the skinheads arrived and Murat brusquely wriggled past them and hurtled down the steps into the station.

Sunday
01:00

He had parked his bike at midnight a good ten houses from his target building in the shadow of a high wall. The lights were on downstairs in a neighbouring house and there was the shimmer of a television. He walked on the opposite side of the road and slipped into the darkness between two houses. From there he watched the lit house for a while before turning his attention to his target.

These were detached family houses. Some had alarms, but his did not. A large Japanese people carrier sat in the carport in front of the house. He let a car go by before nipping across the road and rounding the car. He crouched and waited. He squeezed the door handle. It was locked.

His target house was an exception. His rule was no kids and no old incontinent people. And strictly speaking he had not broken his rule. There were no kids or old people living here. The couple were a few years older than him. The woman was heavily pregnant. Therein lay the risk. She would have a weak bladder. But on one of his surveillances he had seen the man unloading a pram. That had clinched his choice. The others he had been staking out could wait.

Of course, should anyone wake and confront him they'd get slammed in the face before he scarpered.

That was something else about avoiding old people. If necessary he would punch anyone. But he had been fond of his quirky gran. Only when her Alzheimer's was too advanced did he abandon visiting her.

He was completely in black: his tight biker's balaclava was black, his small rucksack too and he'd smeared his cheeks with boot polish. Like a shadow he bounded down the side of the house in dark soft-soled shoes. He used his penknife to ease the latch of the garden gate. He slipped through and leaned it closed behind him. At the back wall of the house he again waited and listened. Then he crept up to the kitchen door. All was dark, but he carefully peeked in. He slid off his rucksack and pulled open the drawstring. He took his glass-cutter out of its felt bag and a rubber teat a little like the suckered end of a toy arrow. Then he stood, licked the surface of the teat and pressed it on the glass near the door handle. With the cutter he inscribed a circle. He held the teat and tapped the glass until it came free. The glass grated as he extracted it and he again waited before repeating the process with the second pane of glass.

Then he carefully put his hand in the hole. He turned the key slowly, pulling the door to himself to reduce the clack of the latch. There was hardly a sound. He opened the door and he was in. Like the back gate, this door was also left open, leaning closed. There was no breeze but he placed a pan on the floor to hold it in place.

He then went and unlocked the front door, leaning it closed too. With his exit routes secured he took his time investigating all the ground floor rooms, staying near the walls, before creeping up the edge of the stairs to the bedrooms. Hugging the walls reduced the chance of noise, especially on the stairs. All the doors were ajar. Perfect. He went into all the rooms, doing the couple last.

Their lights were invariably out by half-past eleven. By one they were deep in the land of nod.

Looking in on sleepers was invariably the height of his creeping.

06:53

Dannaks drifted in and out of consciousness. Each time he woke he had to rediscover his whereabouts; each rediscovery coming progressively quicker. Knowing he was in hospital, knowing he had survived was not all consciousness brought. Delirium was an anaesthetic. By Sunday morning his waking moments were longer. His head was a motorway. Juggernauts bounded up and down crevasses of pain. Lying still confined the routes to his head. To move made him aware of other junctions. Some were congested with dull agony; others were pile-ups of untold injury and trapped screams.

He thought Uwe was at his bedside some time Saturday afternoon. But he wasn't sure. There were two other occupied beds in the room. One patient appeared to suffer from sleeping sickness, whilst the other was a television addict.

Pain woke Dannaks and forced him to move, resulting in more pain. Only exhaustion rescued him until the next waking bout. He'd caught some television that evening. Or had it been in the night? An arm like the angled light in a dental practice supported a small television. The nurse helped him with his headphones. He was in St. Georg hospital, she explained. House C.

Some of the television stations extended the news to append coverage of the clash of extremists, the subsequent rioting and looting. Others had cobbled together specials. Whatever, the programmes were mainly a hysteria of images; it was far too early for in-depth analysis or meaningful discussion.

"I came here to buy something," protested the acne-ravaged skinhead, "but because of my haircut the bulls wouldn't let me."

"I came out of the shop," said a bomber-jacketed youth, "those bleedin' marchers laid into us."

Was Frank on television or sitting talking to him?

"The police didn't stop us," began a large-framed lad. "Then again they didn't see this" – he pointed to his shorn head, then grinned at the biker's helmet he carried – "because I had this on."

The mayor and a number of politicians voiced their abhorrence. There was even a one-line statement of repugnance from the Chancellor.

The question that was uppermost and said something of the rather pedestrian lifestyle of the majority of the populace was how this could have happened in their city. Berlin, yes, but surely not here? Hamburg had its trouble spots, but they were on the fringes of society, where such flash points could be expected. But in the city centre was outrageous.

Inexorably he was keelhauled back to the attack.

He'd reached his gun, unclipped the holster. He'd seen it skitter across the ground as a blow surprised him. They had moved damned quick. He swung out. Connected, hurt his hand. Another blow from an unexpected angle. Another part of him shouting for protection. The dull flash of rings or a knuckle-duster. He threw out another fist, which didn't connect and left him vulnerable.

Then the blows literally rained down on him. He wanted to melt into the hardness of the wall. He wanted to fit into the small space perfectly. And he pushed himself into it trying to make himself small; pressing himself in with his elbows clamped at his sides and his hands ineffectually covering his head.

He tried to cry out but the air was pummelled out of him and all he could manage were hurt grunts.

Incongruously, his mind was active all the time. He knew that to fall to the ground would expose him to their kicks. Kicks to his head would be particularly damaging. For some reason he felt he could sustain the injuries to his body. He tried to get used to them and told himself to absorb them. Ignore the pain, it would soon be over. But the blows continued and he felt his knees weaken.

Bizarrely he wondered whether Jake Dangerous had been modelled on one of them. Yes, he was on the receiving end of a computer game. Fist-sized hailstones were battering him down.

He even tried to think of something else. The boy beckoning him on. What had he looked like? A little bulldog. How old was he? Thirteen? Fifteen? Features; he needed features. The corpse. What had he looked like? Big. All these thoughts shattered as they formed, shredded with every blow.

The march became a riot when opportunists attempted to loot a shop. Seasick cameramen tried to capture it all. Whether the perpetrators were right-wingers, left-wingers, Turks or another group was unclear. Things rapidly degenerated into a free-for-all and it became hard to distinguish the various groups. Adding to the melee were the security guards, shop assistants and occasional public-spirited bystander.

A police chief ineffectively called out over a loud-hailer for the crowd to disperse. He was just going through the motions. "We expected trouble, but the scale of it has taken us by surprise," he said. "We had to withdraw the helicopter. Someone fired a signal rocket at it." He gave the order for a round of tear-gas to be fired into the knots of the trouble.

The attack eased up only to resume more vehemently. Now someone was kicking his legs.

He wanted them to stop. He wanted to ask them to stop, but he could not move. He could not ease his face from the wall. If he did, one blow on the back of his head would smash his hands and face into concrete. Anyway they would not have heard him; they were in a frenzy of violence.

He tried to move along the wall, towards the entrance, light and life, but the blows intensified.

Energy was being drained from his legs. He was going to go down.

There was a shot of a policeman with a wide calibre snub-nosed rifle with a shoulder stock. He broke it open and inserted the grey capsule. He fired capsule after capsule 45 degrees into the air. The canisters clattered and rolled and pumped out brown clouds.

A group of police wearing droopy-snouted gas masks moved upon a mob. They strode forward in a line, batons whacking their shields in unison. Their dark uniforms were strapped down hard, encased in moulded black-plastic body armour. They were no longer individual officers. They were no longer human.

The attack continued. He thought he could grow accustomed to the pain and so diminish its severity. But it was not like that. His back and sides were aflame. Somebody had gone over him with a blowtorch and now he was being stuck with knife points: eruptions of pain on a landscape of soreness.

Then he did not think. He just wanted to be away. He wanted to be asleep, unconscious, unaware, and dead. He wanted not to be. He was succumbing to the hail and storm.

A nurse was holding him down. Had he been fighting her? He slackened. Apologised.

His knees gave way and he crumpled to the ground. All the while he kept his hands over his face, elbows clamped at his sides. As he went down, tender skin scraping the gritty concrete wall, a kick caught his testicles and he vomited with the excruciating pain that numbed and spread.

His attackers jumped back, no doubt in disgust.

Dark thoughts rose from the depths of his mind. One was monstrous, terrifying. It was a dark and all consuming and wreathed in pain. They were going to kill him.

Features? He wouldn't need them. He wouldn't need anything.

"As the trouble escalated we were ordered to stop almost everyone," said a police spokesman. "People were advised to shop elsewhere. The order to completely seal off the area came later. I've heard cries of persecution and discrimination, but look at the stuff we confiscated." The camera panned back and drifted over the usual collection of knuckle-dusters, knives, piping and chains. Then there were the heavy-duty socks containing cans or torch batteries. By far the most outlandish weapon was a rucksack full of raw potatoes bristling with screws and nails.

He was curled up on the ground. The blows continued, but their frequency had eased off. His attackers were tiring. He could hear them panting and grunting with exertion.

There was a pause. Another kick. A flash reminiscent of his childhood bike accident. He'd fallen and felt the click in his foot. There were shouts. Footsteps. Urgent voices. A soothing voice. Someone familiar. Pain. Terrible pain and movement. Rolling on a ship. The sky changing to an endless corridor of dulled strip lighting. Whiteness, like the flash. An unblemished girl's face. And then darkness and hurt and unbearable loneliness. The breathing of others. Vague shapes and vague noises, stillness and darkness.

10:09

"What did the doctor say?"

"I don't remember," said Dannaks. His brother had been with him for little more than ten minutes. Although they had more material for conversation than usual, the awkwardness had begun to make itself felt. "A nurse said I was lucky."

Dannaks was now the only patient in the room. The sleeper and television addict were gone. The latter had left about nine o'clock. They'd exchanged nods.

Shortly afterwards a police officer had taken an initial statement. Someone would take a lengthy one on Monday. Stressed by taking so many statements – Dannaks wasn't the only victim of the rioting and he certainly wasn't the only police officer – the officer spent little time with him.

"Do you want me to get him?" Jürgen asked.

"Who?"

"The doctor."

"The doctor's a woman. No."

His brother wearied before perking up when he pulled out two sheets of paper. They then rode on the crest of the children's drawings: a horse from Adriana and a plane from Tobias. Jürgen had not known the extent of Dannaks's injuries and had kept his family away.

"I'll bring Verena and the kids later. You don't look too bad."

"The real damage is under the sheets." The look of horror forced him to elaborate. "It's mostly bruising."

"Do you want anything?" The merest of pauses and then a wicked smile. "Hard-boiled eggs? Nuts?"

Dannaks laughed and winced, Jürgen laughed and looked concerned. The offer was straight from a Laurel and Hardy episode they'd seen as children. The bond between them had been stronger then. Of course they'd squabbled, but there'd been allegiance against the perceived injustices of their parents.

Uwe had contacted Jürgen. Jürgen had told Dannaks that one of his new colleagues had saved him. He thought his name was Schuppenhauer.

The humour dissipated, but the bond remained. "Do you want anything from your flat?"

"Actually, you could get me something. A light bulb." Jürgen's shock twisted Dannaks in an agony of chuckles. After he'd wiped his eyes and calmed he explained. "Forty or sixty Watt will do."

They were content to be silent for a while.

"I don't suppose you want to tell me what happened?" A top brass assistant had seen him at eight. A uniform was at the end of the ward, ready to stave off resourceful reporters. Officially he was a casualty of the rioting. Five uniforms had also been admitted to hospital. Cuts and bruises. Some stitches. All had since been discharged. The brass couldn't understand how he could have let himself be lured away. They didn't believe that he'd been singled out and he wasn't going to tell them anything. They put it down to bad luck.

Dannaks gave his brother the official version. Whether he believed him or not didn't matter, he at least had something he could tell Verena.

11:11

The front pages were plastered with veritable black pillars: headlines with the common screaming denominator of abomination. "*Hamburg: Gefährlichste Stadt Deutschlands*", "*Schlacht im Zentrum*", "*Elf Stunden Gewalt*". ("Hamburg: Germany's most dangerous city", "Battle in the city centre", "Eleven hours of violence").

An icy breeze smarted their cheeks.

They were sitting in a rented *Strandkorb* (a purpose-made up-ended wicker basket with an in-built bench large enough to seat and shelter two people) on the beach at the Baltic Sea, an hour's drive from Hamburg. They had stopped at the main station to pick up copies of the British paper containing Craig's article along with numerous German papers.

The city centre had been brought under control by Saturday evening, but isolated incidents continued elsewhere.

Craig left after seeing Murat disappear. He'd phoned him four times that evening, but no one answered. He'd spent as much of the time as he dared watching television with Carina.

"Surely the challenge shows the anarchists just wanted trouble," said Volker Herbst, his beefy-red face filling the screen. "I told everyone to stay away from the march."

"If he did, he said it too late," said Craig. Of course it was debatable whether his plea would have stopped the majority.

"People should realise that they're the real threat," he went on, his ample jowls quivering over his collar. "They're the ones disrupting and smearing society. They're the shame of the German people."

"He looks like a pit-bull terrier in a suit," Craig had remarked.

"I am absolutely sick of this," said Carina. "I am glad we are getting out of Hamburg tomorrow. We are going?"

"Yes," answered Craig curtly, annoyed more by the promised day-trip than her interruption.

The cameras had naturally focused on the fighting. On the periphery of the fray Craig could see people standing about and he was reminded of what Carina had said of his article. "When you put something under a magnifying glass you get a distorted image."

These scenes, the clouds of tear-gas drifting over the familiar sights of Hamburg, figures dashing this way and that and the cameras moving erratically as the cameramen tried to capture the action, portrayed the march as a fully-fledged riot. For Craig this was superfluous detail, straying from the main issue and the meaning of the march. Indeed, there had been no march. The isolated skirmishes and localised incidents had given way to something more substantial. The heart of Hamburg was under siege.

Lost was the initial adventurous atmosphere. Lost was the menacing tautness at the police line. Lost too, the headless mutating mass looking for direction. The pictures and discussions implied a mob with purpose. At times the body of people had been shown as an irresistible beast, lumbering forward in an inexorable sweeping orgy of destruction. Only later, almost as an afterthought, did they speak of the reason for the gathering. In a short television interview, Suleyman, who had been whisked away like a VIP at the first sign of violence, was questioned whether a boy's right to take a test sanctioned a demonstration. Surely it only aggravated racial tension? Why hadn't he cancelled the march when the education authorities relented? He said they were protesting an indiscriminate attack. The streets weren't safe for a non-German. The actions of the education authorities showed another more insidious form of prejudice.

"Did you not say he has been here for thirty years or so?" said Carina.

Craig bristled. He knew where this was heading. "Just because he can't express himself eloquently in the language, doesn't mean he's a barbarian."

Neither wanted confrontation. Eventually Carina had dragged Craig away. By then even he was sick of it. Now Carina had her magazines and he could scrutinise the papers.

For the most there were stark photographs vying for prizes. There was a picture of a youth wearing a motorcycle balaclava hurling a stone at a shop window. A boy holding his bleeding forehead, scarlet rivulets like exposed veins clawing down his face. Other pictures depicted the mayhem just as graphically. But some taken after the event were just as poignant: damaged cars, trees, street lamps and shops, splashes of blood on the pavement.

Each group flew the flag of victimisation. A police officer, who wanted to remain anonymous, admitted that he sympathised with the right-wingers. He understood their frustration. The refugees received furnished accommodation and money, he was quoted to have said, when there were already enough unemployed and homeless in the country. "The youths are bored and frustrated. They drink and end up in jail for causing a disturbance."

"A lot came for fun," said another police officer. "It's a buzz that breaks the routine."

A social worker concurred. "The youth of former East Germany feel betrayed and sold-out. Unemployment is high because their businesses have been closed-down because they're unworkable, out-of-date or require too much money to refurbish them to be competitive or meet European Union or environmental standards. There's an air of hopelessness. The issue is compounded by snobbery on the part of the *Wessis*. They regard everything from the East as worthless or antiquated. Communism is dead and is being buried and with it all that was East German. Full employment, for instance, was one of the ideals of communism; the free market has only brought unemployment."

Volker Herbst was being threatened with prosecution for public incitement. Supposedly he'd said: "We're forced to gather here, but we have every right to be in the city centre. In fact we have more right than those Turks to gather in the city centre. And as a German citizen we have the right to move freely. So I'll tell you what I'm going to do when I've finished here. I'm going to go shopping."

The Minister for the Interior and mayor gave the standard rhetoric. The *Polizeipräsident* agreed. Yes, they had known of the possibility of trouble. No, it had not been considered wise to call off the march. No, the police had not gone in too early too hard. The right-wingers had assembled and agreed to disrupt the march. The left-wingers had issued the challenge. Looters and opportunists and society's professional disrupters in league with the extremists had been waiting in the wings.

In another paper there was an interview with Suleyman. Prudently, because of his poor articulation the paper had reported and not quoted him. He said that his son did not belong to a sect or gang. He had no scars on his legs. He was thinking of taking legal action against those who had made the accusations. Craig thought it suspicious, even out of character, that he was only thinking about taking action.

"There's a lot of heat over what happened yesterday," said Craig having difficulty folding away the paper in the breeze, "but very little light."

"Brrr, we could do with some of that heat here." Carina snuggled up to him.

11:15

"Well, *Kommissar* Dannaks," the doctor began. "It appears you have no permanent injuries. Two broken ribs and some bad bruising." She was a handsome woman. The wrinkles at her mouth spoke of humour and severity. "For a while we thought you had a ruptured liver. You're lucky you didn't take more blows to the head." Maybe she could tell he was besotted because she distanced herself. "You're not a sporting man, are you? I think the extra padding helped." He was crestfallen. "I'd like you to stay a further night for observation."

"I don't have to?" He was sitting up in bed. Her young entourage of three, obviously in training, were mentally noting every word.

"No, you don't have to. You can discharge yourself. I advise against it. If you do, you've got to promise to take it easy." Yet, her last sentence was not delivered as an adult speaking to a child. Her trainees would take years to master such tact.

He raised a hand, swallowed the spasm of pain in his side, and saluted weakly. "I promise." Her smile was cursory and he felt embarrassed. Thoughts of a relationship with her moments earlier were already light-years away. The pain moved across his back and settled as a dull ache at his left hip.

11:58

Karsten closed the bedroom door leaving the spoils of the burglary spread upon the bed. He'd left the television on, having watched the rioting on the news. The volume was barely audible.

He buzzed them in and opened the flat door. Then he went to the kitchen and cracked open a beer.

He'd missed the rioting. That kind of dumb action was for boneheads. He had needed the earlier evening to psyche himself up for his job.

His booty lay on the bed. He'd already pocketed the cash. As usual he wished he had taken more, but his rucksack had been full. The electronic organiser, handies, watches would sell easily. He was keeping the baby paraphernalia, baby-clothes, bottle-warmer.

It wouldn't make up for the money Kutnik and Steiner had lost him. They hadn't finished the cop. Because of that he'd been told that half a job deserved half pay. Idiots. By far the most stupid thing they had done was to use one of their own sons to lure the detective into the alley. The cops wouldn't get anything on the boy. He could say he genuinely thought a man was in trouble or that he was given money to fetch someone. Nonetheless the cops could trace the boy to the father and then to him, Karsten. Skulls.

He wasn't happy. He didn't want to see them. At best they were fringe 211ers.

But now his inner circle members were coming to whinge and show him their wounds.

He was sitting in the easy chair when they sloped in. The first three took the sofa. The remaining two stood for a moment before descending to the floor near the coffee table. One had his hand in plaster, another an arm in a sling, two had bruises in the face, one walked as if treading egg-shells and another winced as he sat on the sofa.

Karsten looked at them scornfully. He waited. Skinhead or not, every last one of them was a skull. Yet, they were his boys. The news on television had shown him that they had taken a licking. And the pub fiasco last weekend was fresh in his mind. He'd lost points there. Too many had been arrested. Telling them he'd been given duff information could not help. He felt no guilt for what had happened. Guilt, the same as worry, was for the weak. He'd learnt long ago, that guilt for what had been done and worry for what might happen were utter time-wasters. But he felt he had to make it up to the boys. If only for his own sake. They didn't know this and he wasn't going to show it. Let them squirm first. Let them beg.

"You were right," began the most outspoken of them.

"As always," said another.

"Herbst said he had nothing to do with you," said Karsten.

"He wanted us to break the march."

"Of course he did. But he's a politician. What he wants and what he says are never the same. So he doesn't want anything to do with you until next time. He'll bullshit you with talk of being most useful to you when he's in power and that's why he needs an official face. I've said all this before." Yes, he'd said it all before, but these guys hadn't gone to the rally for Herbst or to protest the exhibition. They hadn't gone on to the march for what Herbst had said; they'd gone for no one but one another. Comrades in arms.

Karsten was not against marches and protests. Last year he had protested against globalisation, finding himself standing alongside Leftists. It was a crazy world.

Their faces dulled over.

"What do you want?" he asked, although he knew the answer. Make them squirm.

No one spoke and Karsten glared.

"We thought we'd hit back," said Wolfram.

"Okay."

"Really hit back," said another brashly.

"Okay."

Wolfram spoke calmly, but Karsten could feel his exasperation. "We thought we could fight them again."

"I don't see anyone capable in front of me."

"Superficial. The others are okay."

"Two are still in hospital."

"You can swing a baseball bat with a broken nose."

"You want more of the same from those Kung Fu clowns?"

"We weren't ready."

"You know what to do," said the brash one.

Karsten let them stew. He looked at the television and picked up the remote control from the coffee table. Let them wait. He switched off the volume and began surfing the channels. He stopped at a documentary. Watched and waited. Realising what the programme was about he turned up the volume and all heads turned to the television, those on the floor shuffling for better positions.

A Negro refugee was complaining to the reporter about accommodation conditions. He moaned about the crowding. He complained that two showers for twenty were not enough.

"Didn't know you used them," murmured Wolfram. Others smiled.

The cameraman focused on the appalling state of the toilets and the refugee said that they were always broken.

"They'd be better off with a hole in the ground," said

Wolfram.

"And turn Germany backward," said Karsten angrily. Smiles disappeared. "We don't want nigger-land here."

Interviews with people who lived nearby followed. Some were understanding, but many were not and spoke out. One said that the refugees put used toilet paper in the bin and not in the toilet. There were complaints about the smell. "They're always hanging around the street, loitering." Another said: "They play their music too loud and my baby can't sleep. It frightens the children too. But you can't communicate with them." Yet another: "They have another way of thinking. Hygiene is not important to them."

"It makes me sick," said Wolfram. Karsten knew Wolfram's story. He was an *Ossi*. He had poured all his energies into renovating the house his parents had left him. He had wanted to sell or rent it to a rich *Wessi*. The local council had set up a refugee home nearby and the value of his property had plummeted. He sold and lost on his investment.

"Integration is media's buzzword," said Karsten. "Well, integration is the slow murder of the German people. Death by a thousand *Aufenthaltsgenehmigungen* (staying permissions)."

Karsten switched the television off. When he spoke, he spoke quietly, each word hard. "But I'll tell you something else. You should have listened to me. Breaking heads in public and singing *'Deutschland über Alles'* is for idiots. You can only get arrested. And what for? People have to realise that our cause is just and that means proper targeting. We're not a bunch of purposeless drunkards. We're supposed to represent the vitality and courage and strength of Germany. We are Germany's rightful future and its only hope of a proud identity." He relished the silence. "And now you and the others come whining to me for revenge." He looked at the glowering outspoken one. "Programmes like that make me sick too. Television is on their side, not ours. Attacking refugee homes is a mistake. They're poor bastards. Oh, they should go. They must go. But these Turks, they've got too big. They live here and they don't intend leaving. They came over as guest workers feeding off our hospitality. Well the guests are unwelcome. So, yes, we'll hit back. All we have to do is get a message to them."

"I know one of them," said the one with his arm in a sling. "He went to my school."

The part of the Baltic coast that they walked was sandy, but the scene before them was a wind-swept one. Unruly bushes almost the same colour as the dirty sand separated the beach from the road. The sea itself did not look inviting. The water was an unattractive grey. Certainly nobody was swimming.

They had made love last night but they had also slept well. Their passion was satisfying but harnessed. Their relationship was settling or they were succumbing to their exhaustion. Whatever, the full night's sleep had done them good welcome.

"I can understand the existence of rockers," Carina began. Before the walk she had set aside her magazines in favour of the papers. "That's music and film and other things, but how did skinheads come into being?"

"They evolved from the street-gangs of London's East End at the end of the sixties," Craig began. "Their shorn heads were a matter of practicality for street-fighting. And their rough and tumble clothing was meant to protest their poverty as much as their readiness to fight." The breeze gusted into a bracing wind. "It was a reaction to the changes in society at that time: a contrast to the long-haired colourful hippies and the smart young architects and computer programmers. Actually, they weren't politically right wing, merely reactionary.

"Today's skinheads are also reacting. I think the public and media politicised them with neo-Nazi attire. And since the boots were the right size they chose to wear them."

Carina and Craig walked for an hour, snacked, returned to their *Strandkorb,* read and talked, packed up, walked for twenty minutes before finally collapsing at a restaurant table, they'd reserved earlier, where they ordered an impressive fish platter.

When his brother arrived Dannaks was dressed and sitting in the foyer at the front of the hospital.

"I could have walked," he said. He could feasibly have walked home, but he would be gasping after ten paces. He felt strangely vulnerable and feather light. Fragile was the word.

"I'm here now," said Jürgen. The growing awkwardness waited to be overcome. "I've got the vacuum cleaner in the back." Dannaks had asked him to bring it. There was no room in his flat for one of his own and he didn't want to bother *Frau* Schumann.

By the time they'd reached the car Dannaks had betrayed himself. His steps were as measured as his breathing. The light seemed aggressive, the activity on the road brusque. He was aware of his frailty. Perhaps he should have stayed another night. Then he could have seen the doctor again. He was fooling himself to think that she would be interested him. Every patient probably fell for her. He smiled to himself: maybe some literally fell for her, to end up in the ward again. Of course he was kidding himself. She was in the fast lane, earning five, maybe ten times as much as him. Then again, she worked shifts and you couldn't hold down a relationship with that kind of give-all job, so—

"Shall I help you with the seat belt?" He couldn't bring it across his chest and he let his brother clip it home.

They were silent during the journey. Dannaks wanted talk, however banal, but they'd used up all their pleasantries.

Between Dannaks's flat and St. Georg hospital was the Lange Reihe. Off this road were a series of bewildering one-way streets. Parking was at such a premium that you were often disgorged back onto the Lange Reihe so that you could start your assault anew. Frequently the only hope of parking was catching someone vacating a place.

If Dannaks had been able to walk his brother would have left his car in the hospital car park. Instead he dropped him and the vacuum cleaner outside his apartment building and left in search of a parking place. Dannaks sat on the steps outside the door.

The day was glorious: not a cloud in the sky. But spring wasn't yet ready to give itself up to summer. Dannaks was glad of his jacket. The steps became uncomfortably cold too and he stood.

When his brother returned ten minutes later Dannaks was propped up against the wall. "I went back and parked in the hospital car park."

As always the stairwell was dim by comparison and although it was broad daylight they had to switch on the lights which exposed the dinginess. Dannaks felt his brother's disapproval. His was no seedy pad, but the air was present. Jürgen had a two-storey semi-detached house with a cellar and a small garden for the kids. Space, neighbours, lawn mowers and chitchat across the fence. Dannaks had habitation rather than a home. His abode started behind his flat door and extended for twenty square metres: too small to be called humble.

Jürgen led the way, lugging the vacuum cleaner. Dannaks followed aware of each careful breath taken with every step. Why hadn't he chosen a place with a lift?

At the door Jürgen noticed the faint but obvious swastika. "Bringing your work home?"

Dannaks noticed the change in the light at *Frau* Schumann's peep-hole.

"Kids," he said. He grew depressed knowing he was fooling no one. He wanted to show his appreciation, not distance himself.

He opened the door and flicked the switch. Nothing happened. He switched on the kitchen light.

"The light bulb?" said Jürgen.

"The very one."

"Sorry, I forgot. We've spares in the cellar. I'll bring one by later."

"No, you've done enough, thanks."

His brother didn't press him. He didn't want to stay for a drink either. He wanted to get back to his family. Away from his estranged brother's postage stamp flat with the swastika on the door. He came into the room as far as the sofa bed would allow. Dannaks wanted to hastily make up the sofa, but he wasn't up to haste. Instead he edged his way over to the window and opened it to the traffic and fumes.

They stood in the room. "I owe you one." One what? He'd proven himself an unreliable baby-sitter.

"Okay. Now take it easy. I'm sure you're not supposed to be out. Use the week to get some rest." Then he double-checked Dannaks's face. "You're not going in tomorrow, are you?"

"I'll see how I feel." He reddened.

"You can barely walk."

"I'll see how I feel," he repeated for want of better defence.

"Still after your gold-plated gravestone?"

Dannaks smiled weakly. He already felt low; now his brother was kicking him.

Jürgen shook his head. Then he went to the vacuum cleaner and began pulling the cable to plug it in.

"I'll do that," said Dannaks.

"Don't be silly."

"I've got nothing else to do."

"That's how it should be." He continued to extract the cable.

"Jürgen, please."

His brother stopped, frozen by the plea. Then he stood. "Dad's stubbornness on top."

They looked at one another, each an enigma to the other. Dannaks wondered why his brother wasn't bored. Cushy job at the insurance company, wife and kids, house, a holiday a year in the sun and a life mapped out to the end of his days. Boring and enviable. What did he, Dannaks, have? Hardly a cushy job. No wife, no kids, no house and he had to be forced to take his breaks. The sun and his skin were not the best of friends. And his work was not always boring or enviable.

He could live his brother's life as much as his brother could live his.

Jürgen looked about the room. He was about to say something. Dannaks suspected a jugular attack along the lines of a woman would do you a world of good. That always made him bleed. His brother had once jokingly called him the last leper of St. Georg. The district got its name from the asylum that existed around 1200 for Middle East crusaders suffering from leprosy. That too had hurt, but not as much. Instead his brother's shoulders suddenly slumped.

"I'll call to see how you're getting on. And pick up the vacuum cleaner. You should phone mum. And dad too. They don't know, but the kids might let slip."

"Give my regards to Verena and the kids."

And then he was gone. And although Dannaks wanted him gone he felt empty. He switched on the television and turned up the volume to ride the traffic. He went to the kitchen to see what the refrigerator had to offer. Not much. He'd make do with blue cheese and toast. He found a lone onion that was more sprouting tentacles than body, but he could tease a few pieces out.

He uncorked a bottle of Merlot.

12:55

"I had a choice," said Basha, "I could ride into the station and jump clear before the train stopped or I could jump clear with it moving." Cenk noted the pause as Basha checked their captivation.

"Of course, those right-wingers were idiots," he digressed, "they should have tried to cut my fingers."

Cenk thought it strange that few of Basha's colleagues were present. Most could be said to come from Hasan's group. Maybe they'd already been given audience?

After welcomes they'd talked about the march, most of the time repeating what they'd said in smaller groups. Now, holes were filled. Like the rest of them Cenk had spent the night in a cell. Bilal had been his companion. They'd been interviewed and a doctor had seen them. Skinheads had been locked up in neighbouring cells and there had been some verbal slagging before exhaustion took them. He'd slept fleetingly. At seven in the morning they'd been given a cup of coffee and sent on their way. Basha said: "The skinheads got out before us. I bet they got breakfast. Maybe a ride home too."

The lawyer said they could expect to be fined.

Cenk's father said that he was proud that he stood up for what he believed. Had he not been on nights he would have joined him at the march. His mother silently disapproved.

They'd agreed to forgo patrolling that evening. None of them had the energy for it. They thought the right-wingers would be licking their wounds anyway. Nonetheless lukewarm statements of remaining on standby were voiced.

Cenk realised now that Basha had held back. They'd all told their stories. He'd waited for them to be told, so that they could pale into insignificance against his own.

This was his moment. He was a hero. He'd rescued Hasan and him. He'd rescued Nazim too. At the march when the scuffles began they'd become separated; like the two groups within the gang. Hasan had gone down immediately. He told Cenk he'd been winded. In any case he stayed down and Cenk had moved to protect him from a kicking. Nazim was in a tussle of his own and Cenk found himself fighting two youths. He saw Basha chop an attacker down, another was on his knees behind him, pressing an arm to his ribs and trying to cover a bloody nose. And Cenk had wanted him to come over and for an instant they made eye contact. Then someone was onto Basha and Cenk blocked a blow to the head, but not a kick in the shin. Suddenly Basha was there, taking Cenk's opponent on. Basha didn't duck as the flash of a knuckle-duster came to meet his head in a roundhouse punch. He dipped backwards. The momentum of the swing brought the man off-balance and it was a simple matter for Basha to slam the top of his foot into the man's exposed flank. Cenk heard ribs crack and watched the man go down. Basha made it look so simple. He stepped over to help Nazim, smiled at Cenk as he gave Broken-ribs a back-kick in the face. The smile said that he was enjoying himself.

It was too easy. There was none of the clumsy grappling that Nazim and Cenk were involved in. And certainly none of Hasan's grovelling. For Basha there were only decisively quick, clean movements.

Basha downed Nazim's man and was then at Hasan's side, helping him up, relishing the heroic moment. He looked Cenk in the face. "Get him out of here." He nodded over Cenk's shoulder. Half a dozen right-wingers were coming at them. Further behind them Cenk could see many uniforms.

"Come on you bastards!" Basha shouted. His eyes were sparkling as he emphasised his intentions by kicking Nazim's fallen right-winger.

"It was all instinct," Basha went on. "Part of the training."

Basha had taken them through Barkhofpassage, passed the diners in the precinct, through a police line and down the steps of the U-Bahn station. Cenk knew the station. The steps went down to a corridor, which was relatively long with a couple of bends before opening out into a hall with a low ceiling and a forest of tiled pillars. He ran past right-wingers at the high tables of the underground snack bar. They'd been kept underground by the police. They'd followed him to the nearest platform where a train had just come in. There was no other exit. The call to stand back came and the doors began closing. He was too far away. He looked at the right-wingers. The doors closed. He sprinted and leapt at the doors of the accelerating train. He stopped to bathe in the awe of his spellbound audience. They were with him, hanging onto the handles of the closed doors, being carried out of the station, through the tunnel and up and out into dazzling sunshine.

During the telling of the train journey, desperately holding on to the handles, his eyes lit up as he re-lived the moment. His excitement gutted his cool image. His face glowed with animation and he looked crazed. Efforts at being matter-of-fact were wasted. Cenk thought the experience had altered him. He had enjoyed the fight. He had played the hero and pulled it off. He was the hero. And the idea of being a hero was an elation he could not disguise.

As the story sensationally unfolded he no doubt saw the captivation of his audience slipping and his telling of it deteriorated as he tried to hold his listeners. He ran over parts of it again, blunting its edge.

At some point he lost his footing and had to rely on the strength in his arms alone. Of course he'd tried to open the doors, but this was an U-Bahn train whose doors had compressed-air locks. Then he was grateful the doors couldn't be opened because there were right-wingers inside. Too many for him to tackle. It sounded like a trainload of right-wingers. Cenk had seen some of the evening news on the television in a back room of the restaurant where he worked. There hadn't been that many right-wingers.

Cenk knew the line and knew that the tunnel became impossibly narrow. But he was willing to swallow this part of Basha's story. He said he had to press himself against the train and the wall brushed his jacket. But when he said there were right-wingers inside the train pushing the blade of a knife between the doors, trying to cut him, Cenk was forced to reconsider. Hasan's face too was clouded with disbelief.

"I decided to jump off the moving train. It wasn't going as fast as trains can go, but it was going fast enough for me." He smiled and looked for smiles and confirming nods. Rödingsmarkt was the next station set on the raised level of the line. The train slowed to climb the curving rail fly-over: a metal bridge that spanned a number of roads and travelled down to the harbour on this elevated level. "So I jumped. That's how I scraped on my knee." He wore a long sleeved track-suit and shorts.

"I skipped the rails, climbed onto the wall and walked off in the opposite direction."

"I'm amazed you could hold on to the train," said Hasan.

"I haven't got spaghetti for arms like him," said Basha nodding at Nazim. Cenk cringed. It was an unnecessary remark, especially since Nazim was his most avid supporter. The hurt was visible in Nazim's eyes. But then, Cenk felt Nazim needed to be brought down. At the march he had worn a black headband too. Cenk had said he looked ridiculous and thought Basha would tear it from his head.

At that moment Basha was buzzing and he didn't see his audience. His eyes looked beyond. When he spoke, his voice was far away as if he were thinking aloud, as if his words weren't really for them. "For all that, I know I can do better, much better."

"What do you mean?" asked Cenk.

"What?" asked Basha, shocked.

"What do you mean you can do better?"

He seemed stunned and took an age to answer. When his answer did come it was accompanied by a triumphant smile. "Next time I'll treat them to my flying double-kick."

13:01

He was glad he hadn't turned his bed back into the sofa on Saturday morning. He lay down, found a comfortable position, consumed and watched television. But each comfortable position remained only comfortable for a frustratingly short time.

The doorbell rang. He got up wincing and cursing. Had his brother returned to insist on vacuum cleaning? It rang a further two times before he reached the intercom.

"Yes?"

"Albrecht," said Uwe into the intercom. "We tried the hospital first. I should have known it wasn't as bad as they said."

Dannaks buzzed him in. He'd said we. That could only mean that his wife, Annelore, was with him. He looked into the flat. With the bed out it was a mess. The vacuum cleaner took up more space. And with the coffee table there was standing room only.

He opened his flat door and plastered a smile on his face to hide his shame and pain.

Annelore led. She was a no-nonsense woman with piercing blue eyes. They harpooned him even in the dullness of the landing.

"You don't look too bad," she said.

"In this light," Uwe added. Annelore gave him a severe look.

"How bad did they say it was?" said Dannaks, shaking their hands and gingerly backing into his flat.

"Within an inch of your life?" Uwe gave him a moment, but he was backing into the lounge, taking care not to fall on the bed. "No quip?" Dannaks was beginning to wish he hadn't answered the door. "It is bad."

"What are you doing out of hospital?" asked Annelore, ignoring the untidiness.

"Mending."

"Sister Dulwinnie or Balvanie?" asked Uwe, closing the door.

"Nurse Merlot."

"Not ready for the hard stuff? I–"

"Should you be out of hospital?" asked Annelore brusquely. "Should you be drinking?" He didn't like her matronly expression and her perfume assaulted his nostrils. She was an attractive, intelligent looking woman. Dannaks would call her fine, maybe dignified, rather than beautiful. "What's the damage?"

"I, er, opened the bottle for later. I wanted to let it breathe."

"It's probably doing that better than you," said Uwe.

He nervously looked at them both. "I've a couple of cracked ribs and bruising."

"Lucky," said Uwe.

"I don't feel it." He envied their sharing.

"Well you are. So, what happened?"

"Do you want to sit down?" asked Annelore.

"No, it's okay." He felt hot and clammy.

"You look pale," she said. "I'll make tea."

"No, I'll do it." A spasm of pain stabbed his side.

They hit some kind of stalemate. Then Annelore suggested he made the tea with Uwe in the kitchen, whilst she vacuum cleaned.

"No. I'll do it. If I'm going to be cooped up here I've got to have something to do." He suddenly felt dizzy.

"I think you'd better sit down before you fall down," said Uwe.

"There's a stool in the kitchen."

"Good. Come on then."

"But the bed—"

"I can manage," said Annelore.

Uwe stepped aside and Dannaks gingerly went into the kitchen. "You can hardly walk." Uwe followed. "Sit down." Dannaks sat. "Where's the tea?"

Dannaks told him. He heard Annelore fussing in the lounge and made to get up. Uwe blocked the doorway. "Sit down. You're not going anywhere."

"What are you going to do? Give me a tea bag whipping?"

"The state you're in it'd be enough. I don't suppose you possess a teapot. Thought not." He opened a wall cupboard, fetched three mugs, and put a tea bag in each. He put water in the kettle. "Stay here. I'll help her with the bed."

When he returned Uwe said: "Tell me what happened. I'll tell Annelore later." The sound of the vacuum cleaner filled the flat. Dannaks told him of the boy and the skinhead in the alleyway. "You seem to have a penchant for alleyways." He recalled the Saturday morning chase after the stakeout. "When was it?"

"I don't know exactly. Before the trouble started, if that's what you want to know."

"Trouble was brewing a long time before it erupted."

"Uwe, I was targeted." Uwe poured water into the mugs. Dannaks couldn't read his silence and ploughed on. "It wasn't an accident. A kid picked me out." He sucked in a breath as he shifted position on the stool. "They wanted to kill me in that alley. And remember this, they were skinheads. Why now? What have I done other than point the finger at Lampe or Karsten?"

Uwe yo-yoed the tea bags. Although the vacuum cleaner was still going, Uwe moved closer. "They might try to kill you again."

"They might."

"What are you going to do now?"

"Get well."

14:07

Ulrich had worked with *HVV* (*Hamburger Verkehrsverbund* – Hamburg transport association) all his life, but he had heard nothing like this before. He wasn't talking but steering the tourist barge under the Kennedy Bridge. The front was out from under the bridge and into the sunshine when it began.

He was preparing his favourite manoeuvre: swinging round in his swivel chair to face his passengers and explain that the New Lombards Bridge, built in 1952, had been renamed in 1963 in honour of the assassinated American president.

He had checked for boats ahead and set the wheel.

The sound was a rapid banging, completely out of sync with the rhythm of the engine. He glanced in the mirror at his passive passenger-audience seated at their tables and suspected that one of what he termed the bubbly-set – youngsters with an effervescent sparkling wine attitude – at the open end of the vessel had climbed upon the roof. They weren't interested in his spiel. By the looks of them, telling them that Curd Jürgens lived in a villa on the Alster, would merely result in querulous expressions, testifying that they'd never heard of the actor. Whoever was on the roof was not content to walk. No, they were performing an incoherent tap dance, indeed a frantic thudding.

He swivelled round earlier than usual and looked up, but didn't immediately locate the source of the disruption. The horrified gaze of an elderly woman led him to a dark shape heading to the back of the boat as it moved forward.

The thudding ended as abruptly as it began when the roof wanderer reached the end of the boat less than three seconds later. Ulrich realised that the person had drummed on the spot and the boat had moved forward. He heard the commotion amongst the bubbly set, a girl screamed, others yelped and the men shouted. Then one of the men barged into the entrance and yelled for him to go back.

Hilda was daydreaming when the banging began. After shopping with her companions – enjoyable, but always an ordeal because all four of them had different wants – she was glad of the opportunity to sit and put down her bags. She was chuffed to have acquired a window seat. This was the first and most relaxing leg of her homeward journey. After alighting she would have a tedious bus journey ahead of her. She could have taken the U-Bahn to her bus stop, but the boat was a much more pleasant way to travel.

She too had never heard anything like it and thought the ship was hitting something under the bridge. Flashes of the vessel sinking, the panic, whether she could save her purchases, whether she could save herself in the icy water – she hadn't been swimming in ages – whether the bright young girl in the family of four would make it. All this shot through her heard like a hurricane. As the sound grew she could see the darkness through the Perspex roof. The frantic shape was almost overhead when she realised that the banging was the movement of shoes desperately trying to find hold on the curved edge of the roof.

Whoever was up there was scuffing their soles on the Perspex leaving terrible black streaks.

The noise of the propeller and the joviality of the group standing outside at the end of the boat dampened the thudding. Thorsten thought the noise was some kind of strange echoing effect under the bridge. Not unlike the metallic rush in a tunnel, he was aware of it, but took it to be one of those inexplicable things. He would put it down to resonance. Only as they emerged from under the bridge did the thudding become real and imperative.

Even then he was preoccupied with Anika's smile. He knew he would have to make his move soon, certainly before Lukas moved in.

Anika yelped and Claudia screamed. Thorsten turned to what had caused their reactions. On the edge of the roof was a scrambling body. The boy was hanging by the neck, something yellow was stuffed in his mouth, his face was scarlet, eyes inhumanly wide, legs kicking, arms pinned behind his back. An instant in twisted profile revealed the yellow object to be a broken unpeeled banana. In a moment he would be hanging freely near them without the roof of the barge. There was not enough time to haul oneself onto the roof and perhaps reach the rope. Lukas moved to grab the boy's legs, the movement of which had changed from scrambling to kicking in unison like a frog. Lukas would only be able to hold his feet for a moment. In mere seconds he would be beyond the vessel, hanging freely, the kicking subsiding to twitching and finally stillness.

Thorsten shouted inside to the driver. "Stop! Go Back!"

He slept badly. He hardly slept at all. At six o'clock in the morning he'd had enough. He struggled up and hobbled into the kitchen, made himself a cup of instant coffee, found a nub of yellow butter in its crumpled wrapper, toasted some dry bread that had begun to curl and spread butter and marmalade on one slice and peanut butter on the other. His head was split in two.

For the first time in years he watched morning television. He caught vestiges of the wake of Saturday's rioting. At six thirty the news headlines were repeated. A well-known S-Bahn surfer named Stefan had been killed at the Kennedy bridge yesterday afternoon.

He had heard of Stefan through his work with Narcotics. Stefan rode the train system with his companions, sometimes together, sometimes separate, delivering drugs to order. Rarely did they meet directly with the punter. They were distributors. Which of the trio carried the drugs was never the same. Using handies, their arrangements were never fixed and extremely flexible. This made him exceedingly elusive. A team had been trying to break into the network for a number of months. They had taken more than a year to understand it.

Dannaks remembered looking out of the window and seeing the traffic at a standstill. His view of Kennedy Bridge was obscured by trees, but the flashing lights of emergency vehicles told him the location of the commotion. He thought there had been a traffic accident. Now he assumed that Stefan had been killed in a drugs dispute. The police spokeswoman would not comment on the speculation that the *Henker* had struck again. At the mention of the name Dannaks froze, his hand with a piece of toast poised near his mouth.

Just his luck. He had been waiting for the *Henker* to strike again so that REX might be called in to assist. And now that it may have happened he could hardly walk.

He decided to wait for the seven-thirty news and went into the bathroom, caught sight of his back in the mirror as he was getting into the shower, felt like crying as he drew the plastic curtain and found solace in water that was a mite too hot.

The doctor had said that his ribs would take four to six weeks to heal. To his surprise he'd not been bandaged. The only treatment he'd been given was painkillers.

The thought of being holed up in the flat all day, perhaps venturing out to do some shopping, depressed him. There was little to do. Annelore had done the vacuum cleaning. His gratefulness had been hidden behind an endless sneezing fit that had him in tears of pain. His hurt racking him with echoes of his shudders. They'd made him stick his head out of the window for air. She'd changed his sheets and made his bed anew too. He'd done the laundry last weekend. Oh, he could busy himself in the flat. But any household chores he could think of, offered little diversion from his agony. He hoped the seven o'clock news would confirm that the *Henker* had struck.

In his underwear he drank another cup of coffee in front of the seven-thirty headlines. He watched in vain. Once again there was little on the previous reports.

Dannaks picked up the remote control and blanked the screen. The silence in the room was instant. Now the sound of rush hour nudged at his windows. He got up and turned his back on the room, parting the curtains slightly to peek at the shunting vehicles below. Although the sun wouldn't make a direct hit on his flat until midday, he winced at the brightness. He let the curtains fall back again, dulling the room in keeping with his demeanour.

For a long time he stood looking into the room, listing all the jobs he could do. He even began prioritising them. He stood until pain forced him to move. Then he went to the kitchen and fetched the stool that was really a small stepladder. He returned and had to move the vacuum cleaner. Soreness throbbed at his chest as he moved it away. He swore. Then he positioned the steps in the vacated area. He stepped up and reached for the velvet case on the top of the wardrobe, biting his lip at the fire that shot across his shoulders.

He nearly stumbled before touching the floor and was grateful when he half sat and half fell on the sofa bed. He unhooked the lid and opened the box on the coffee table. The pristine .38 revolver looked unused. He found the Smith & Wesson 36 "Chiefs Special" more solid than his standard issue weapon. Checking the time and the immaculate state of the weapon he decided to service it later. He loaded it, pushed it into its ankle holster, and took four attempts to strap it to his leg.

Then he struggled with his trousers. Putting on his shirt was an equally painful experience. He went to the flat door and knelt to put on his shoes. A shot of pain in his left side brought tears to his eyes. He groped for his shoes, knocking them off their rack and he wished he'd at least switched on the kitchen or bathroom light. With no overhead light and the curtains drawn it was quite dark.

Struggling to blindly tie his shoe laces, ripples of pain shot through his body and he teetered on the brink of falling. With one shoe hastily tied he used the wall to help himself to his feet. Hurting and sweating he tried to calm himself by breathing steadily, instead he began to hyperventilate and it was all he could do to stumble back into his lounge and crash with a grunt of pain on the bed.

He was going nowhere.

08:47

Was this what he wanted? Yes, he wanted to give the German people a wake-up call. But this! Perhaps it was mere coincidence that he had based his article on Stefan.

For an instant Craig saw the lad sitting in the train: "I've heard you were looking for me. Is there money in it?" Then he was outside and yelling: "Yeeeee haaaar."

Carina had left for work and although they had arranged to meet for lunch she had telephoned and told him the news. He dressed, went out and bought the papers.

They had much in common with Sunday's editions: bold blocks of black lettering screaming outrage.

The front-page headlines fell into two categories, but were essentially repetitive. The first type was: A city in chaos gripped by panic. The chaos referred to Saturday's rioting and the panic referred to the second type of headline: Serial killer strikes again. *"Eine Weltstadt schämt sich"; "36 Stunden Gewalt"; "Mord auf der S-Bahn"; "Bahnsurfer ermordet"; "Henker schlägt wieder zu"* (A world city shames itself; 36 hours of violence; Murder on the *S-Bahn*; *Bahnsurfer* murdered; Hangman strikes again).

Craig reasoned that Stefan's killing was premeditated and nothing to do with his article.

He was sipping a cup of coffee in Carina's kitchen, the papers spread before him, when the telephone rang again.

"Hi." It was Robert. "You've heard about Stefan?"

"Carina called me."

They spoke of the murder and the weekend. Then Robert came to the point. "The police want to speak with you. They've got your – Carina's – number. I didn't have your handy number nearby. They're probably calling as we speak. I wanted to warn you."

"Thanks," was all he could manage.

"There's a lot of interest—"

"Your paper gets first bite."

Craig thought it strange that Robert didn't react, but he let it go. "Do you think it's coincidence?"

"Your article and his death? Of course not. Other articles featured Stefan. He was already a bit of a celebrity."

"Perhaps." He was not convinced.

"You want to come in or do it on the phone."

"I don't know. I'll talk to the police first."

09:23

"Albrecht," the voice answered breathlessly after the fifth ring.

"Dannaks," he announced. "Bad time, Uwe?"

He tried calling Frank but his phone had been engaged.

"I'm at work. It's never a good time." He caught his breath and continued before Dannaks could speak. "How are you feeling?"

"Sore. But better. I've got a hangover's headache without the alcoholic fun to mull over." He paused. "I saw the news earlier."

"Is that the reason for the call? I haven't much time."

"Is it a drugs thing? Or was it the *Henker*?" Dannaks knew that Uwe could be overheard and gave him the multiple choice option.

Uwe was silent for a moment. "The latter."

"Thanks."

"I'll call y—"

"I've got a favour to ask."

Uwe grunted instead of groaned. "Go on."

"Can you check evidence control? I want to know who's looked at Freddy's diary."

"Your diary?" he asked, lowering his voice. "You mean the one Lampe handed in?"

"Yeah."

Again Uwe silently considered. Then he sighed. "Hold on."

Dannaks heard him tapping a keyboard.

"Here's grist to your mill."

"Yes."

"Rüdiger Krohn took a look at it."

Dannaks felt triumphant.

"When?"

"Friday."

"Ha."

"What does it mean?" Uwe asked.

"I don't know yet."

"You really are tired of living. If– What? Yeah. Okay. I've got to go. Catch you later."

"Yeah," he said, but his friend had already hung up.

Dannaks put down the phone, but remained standing even though his side was aching for support.

Homicide may have decided the diary was a hoax. But Krohn may not have known. Even if he had, curiosity had got the better of him and he had looked at it. There was only one reason for him to look at it. He wanted to see if he was implicated in any way. He could not have been within Freddy's radar unless he was connected to Raul in some way. Anybody connected to Raul who had heard about the diary would want to check it. But that was such an obvious move. Was Krohn that stupid?

He picked up the phone and sat on the edge of his bed.

This time Frank's phone rang.

"Neumann."

Dannaks tried to sound jolly. "Dannaks. Hi Frank."

"How are you?"

"Fine, Frank. Fine."

"Do I have to ask again?"

"I've got a headache."

"And?"

"And my side aches."

"I came to the hospital. But you were unconscious. I'm surprised you're out."

"One of the few advantages of being a bit flabby around the hips," he joked, still trying to sound flippant.

Frank wasn't taking the bait. "I heard something about broken ribs and a ruptured liver."

"The liver's fine," he said. "Enlarged and overworked, but fine."

"Well, you've got this week to recover."

Dannaks was deflated. "I, er, thought I might come in tomorrow."

"I'll pretend you didn't say that."

"Maybe before the week's out?"

"You've heard about the murder."

"Yes."

"It wasn't really a question."

"I, er, heard it was the *Henker*."

"And you want to know whether REX is helping."

"I–"

"Give me some credit, Dannaks."

"Sorry."

"Yes, is the answer. Reinhart has been seconded."

"R–"

"But that doesn't matter to you."

"I don't suppose you can tell me anything about it?"

"No."

"The Kennedy Bridge is pretty public," he continued. "It means he's getting audacious."

Frank remained silent. He obviously wasn't going to talk.

Dannaks sighed. "Frank?"

"I'm still here," he answered. "I've got some questions." Dannaks's deflation turned to fatigue. "You sound up to it."

He mustered his energy once again. "Fire away."

"Tell me what happened."

He told him about the boy leading him to the alley and then the two masked attackers laying into him.

"Would you recognise your attackers? I mean any distinguishing marks. You know what I am asking."

"No."

"But the boy who delivered you to them?"

"I think so."

"Good." He heard Frank take a deep breath and instinctively knew that the real questions were about to come. Frank's opening word was a giveaway tag. "Now, why you?"

"I don't know."

"Think."

"I don't know."

Frank showed his exasperation in his sigh.

"Then tell me what you are doing in your spare time."

"What?"

"Dannaks I may be wrong, but I don't believe you were attacked because of something you're doing for REX. I know you are doing something on your own time." Had Reinhart said

280

something? "I get the feeling you don't have much of a private life. I don't know what you're up to — your unfinished Narcotics business — but you're jeopardising this *Soko*."

"I'm not."

"Let me decide that. You just admitted you're doing something on your own time. I want to know."

In a monotone Dannaks began with Detlef's suggestion, going on to the search of Freddy's place and planting the diary. He admitted that Lampe's transfer had stumped him. He mentioned what the girl at the pub had said about such large gangs roaming at will. He spoke of visiting the station, his meeting with Orth and being followed. When he spoke of the swastika painted on his flat, Frank interrupted him.

"When?"

"Thursday."

Frank said nothing for a while. "I can't get it out of my head, that whoever is behind this is over-reacting."

"Take my past into account." Dannaks heard Uwe's words: "They know what you're capable of."

Frank digested the idea. "The swastika on the door was a warning. The attack—"

"Wasn't a warning. I was lucky—"

"Lucky Schuppenhauer saw and followed you."

"Yes. Could—"

"Just a minute. Let's cut to the quick. You're looking for a leak. Perhaps in Narcotics. Perhaps not. A leak that helped this Raul. Right? Okay. Instead you think there may be a leak to right-wingers."

"Or both?"

"Why not? Either way that part could be a REX assignment."

He hadn't told him that someone in power was behind Detlef's suggestion. And he certainly wanted to keep his investigation covert. "If you make it official the target could crawl back under a rock. We may get a bone thrown to us. To keep us quiet. Just like Raul's been playing it. But—"

"I get the picture," said Frank. Dannaks sensed that he had more to say. "One more thing. You weren't listening when I told you that I ran a team. I don't care what you think of your colleagues." Oddballs. Or was he talking specifically about

Reinhart? "They're a team nonetheless. REX has no room for loners." Was Frank setting him up for the push? "This isn't finished."

"Okay, Frank." He didn't disguise his resignation. "Could you put me through to Schuppenhauer? I'd like to thank him."

10:24

The fish weren't biting. But Karsten had time.

He had not yet explored the fishing possibilities in former East Germany. There were sufficient locations in and around Hamburg. Schleswig-Holstein had a lot of beautifully situated lakes containing perch, pike, carp, tench, bream and other whitings. And the brooks and rivers of the Lüneburger Heide offered catches of grayling and trout.

Fishing had not escaped the notorious German bureaucracy and a government fishing licence was required and then a local permit. Fishing rights belonged to individuals, societies, local authorities, towns or the government. There was a cumbersome wealth of rules to be obeyed. One had to observe minimum fish sizes and closed seasons. There were regulations governing fishing methods and allowable baits. Even the number of fish caught was controlled.

Of course Karsten didn't bother with all that. He didn't believe in permits, rules, authority. He fished where he wanted, when he wanted. He confronted trouble or packed up. His motorbike was ideal for quick escapes. His panniers were large enough to hold all his fishing gear with room to spare for a good catch.

His father was a member of some of the associations that leased the numerous waters of Hamburg, but even he bent the rules, swinging his official weight when it suited him.

"Are you a guest of the hotel," the man in the suit had asked.

"No," his father had answered. "You're disturbing the fish."

"I'm afraid you can't fish here," said the man, bristling at his father's arrogance. "The lake belongs to the hotel."

An eight-year old Karsten, fishing alongside his father, shifted on his stool. His mother sat away from the bank knitting furiously.

His father regarded the man for the first time, allowing him a false sense of triumph. "The hotel owns the lake?"

The man nodded.

His father nodded too, before quietly asking: "Don't you think some of it requires fencing off? You get families in your hotel, don't you? Young children?"

The man stood in stunned silence for a moment. "That's the hotel's business and none of yours. Now get off my property before I call the police."

His father expressed his irritation with a strong sigh. He sluggishly got out his badge and allowed the man a moment to pale, before giving him a cold wide-eyed stare and spitting: "Go away."

The man turned crimson before wheeling on a heel and returning to the hotel.

The memory was from the golden time of his childhood. His mother and father seemed happy and the world seemed in order.

The golden time now seemed short, but it probably lasted till he was about nine years old. By then he'd begun to answer back and stick up for his mother. More often than not it earned him a belting. His father had a strong will and a short fuse. His mother yielded every time. Her advice to avoid confrontation only rankled Karsten. She found solace in silence and a cigarette. And her silence made Karsten disrespect her. He loved her, certainly more than he loved his father, but he began to despise her too. She must have noticed, because there was a phase when she'd make a quiche, his favourite, almost every week. But he saw how the joy left her face in the pallor of her skin. The colour drained from her cheeks. Her face became ashen. It was almost as if a colour film was being turned into black and white. Like in the Wizard of Oz; only here the twister was a pillar of smoke leaching the colour from his world. He was sixteen when she died of lung cancer. When she was diagnosed she was smoking countless packets a day. Karsten knew that his father was behind her ever increasing consumption and in this way he had bullied her to death. He had visited when his father was at work. For he had moved out well before she became bedridden. On her deathbed she gasped that it was one of those things; that she was to blame, and that he should not blame his father, but he wouldn't hear it.

He had attended her cremation, arriving late, and standing at the back near the door, well away from the pitiful congregation seated in the first three rows.

His father had driven her to smoke and eventually she had become smoke.

Karsten took a long drag on his cigarette. He smoked not because of any death wish. Or some form of solidarity with his mother. He smoked because he simply didn't care.

The plop of water brought him back to his fishing. He looked at his rod perched arm's length away. He liked the space and his own company. Fishing was his form of meditation.

His own company reminded him that Jutta was returning tomorrow. She and the baby would shatter the silence and Jutta would be endlessly tidying up behind him. The state of the flat would depress her. Maybe they'd fight straight away. He hoped not. He wouldn't lose. He never lost. But she'd be crying and the baby would join in and he'd have to get away. He hated their whinging.

Detectives had come for him at nine in the morning asking where he had been early yesterday afternoon. He told them he had been at home with his buddies, the last of whom had left at three. He had called a couple of them, after the detectives had left, to make sure that was what they said.

The sun was a badge, shiny and ineffectual. When the clouds obscured it the breeze was chilly.

There was nobody about and he looked at his watch. Somehow he'd lost interest. He had hoped for a good catch to fill the freezer. At least something for Jutta to cook when she arrived. But he had nothing. And his thoughts had invaded his enjoyment.

Two of the boys were watching the Turk they'd singled out. They needed to watch him. They'd have to take him tomorrow. Karsten smiled. If they liked the safety pins, wait until they saw what he had in mind for the Turk.

Yet, what he intended would not deliver the kick he needed. Deep down he was profoundly bored. Like a drug the deed needed to grow for the heights to become higher.

He had smiled as the sign toppled. The pole and shield lay on the grass. They'd badly bent the metal triangle, but hadn't been able to tear it from the pole. And despite their efforts at obliterating the paint on the ground, the extra wide parking space was rarely taken. In any case the cripple was gone: mission accomplished.

Karsten and four of his friends had come upon the wheelchair-bound woman after a drinking session. He knew her by sight: She lived in a neighbouring block.

"Hey, one got away," he had said loudly as the invalid locked her car. Apart from them the parking area was deserted. "Horst, have we got any of that Zyklon B left?" The boys laughed as they swaggered up to her.

The woman, having no time to wheel away or re-enter her vehicle, faced them.

Before she could speak one of them suggested that they take her for a ride. Her sour expression had prompted Karsten.

"What's the matter wouldn't you like us to push you home? We'll save your arms."

"Leave me alone," she snapped.

"Don't be ungrateful," Karsten said in an overly pained voice.

Her expression became a mixture of fear and anger.

"Don't look so sad. It's not often that a woman—"

"An ugly one at that," one interrupted.

"— gets the attention of so many men. Come on smile." He waited. "Look boys, she's not smiling."

"Leave me alone."

"You've got to smile—" and he turned to one of his friends. "Give me your can." The youth hesitated and Karsten impatiently twitched his fingers. The youth delved inside his denim jacket and drew out a can of spray-paint.

"Leave me alone." She had shielded her face.

"You sound like a broken record. Get her hands," he ordered, vigorously shaking the can.

Two of them pulled down her arms down. She screamed and someone from afar shouted.

"I'd close your mouth," Karsten advised holding up the can. He then calmly sprayed a bright red banana of a smile on her mouth. "You talk and it won't be paint next time."

Then they scarpered.

That had happened in the seemingly carefree early days. Although he was still young he seemed so much younger then. That kind of buzz had been enough for him. It was still enough for most of the lads. Now he needed more. Much much more.

He looked at the rigid line of his telescopic fishing rod. The fish weren't biting today. He grunted and nimbly stood his lighted cigarette upon his bait container. "Fuck you," he hissed at the water.

He pulled over his knapsack. Checked again that there was nobody about and then pulled out the object in its oilcloth. He placed it on his lap and glanced around before peeling away the cloth. He'd cleaned the revolver last night. Although he only had fourteen bullets he wanted to test it. He hadn't fired it for more than a year. He knew the markings by heart but studied them as if they were hieroglyphics, as if there was portent between the bland words on the barrel. "Sturm Ruger & Co. Inc Southport Conn USA." He turned it over. "Ruger GP 100 .357 Magnum Cal." An extreme right-wing group, trying to recruit him, had sent it to him. They asked for it back. He'd said no and never heard from them again.

He picked it up, relishing its weight, its latent power. Stretching his arm and looking down its length to the branch of a tree on the opposite bank he squeezed off a satisfying click.

Fuck the fish, he thought and pulled out the box of bullets.

At fourteen years old, when his mother was out, his father had shown him his service handgun. He'd unloaded it and passed it to him. Karsten had pointed it at his father.

"Never point it at a person," he snapped.

"But it's not loaded."

"No matter what you think, treat a gun as if it is always loaded."

This had been his first lesson. Other lessons followed. When loading and unloading never point it at a person. Before firing, check that there are no blockages. And, although it sounded silly, always use the correct ammunition.

His father had been full of lessons. His mother and he had been bombarded by them; good or bad they were lessons to be learned. Unquestionably learnt.

He pushed a bullet into a cylinder chamber. Looking around one last time he got up, picking up the ancient cushion he'd been sitting on. He held the cushion against the end of the barrel and squeezed the trigger. Click. He squeezed again. Despite the cushion the boom was sufficient to make him swear with delight.

He realised the cushion was on fire, regarded it for a moment, then laughing, he threw it like a Frisbee across the lake.

10:28

Oli König had called ahead to check Dannaks's availability. Homicide would normally have interviewed him. But all the teams were busy. They had asked Seven to do it. And Weske, thinking they knew one another, had chosen Oli. They agreed to a ten-thirty interview. He arrived early.

They sat together on the sofa which Dannaks had laboriously changed from his bed. This feat alone had almost persuaded him to take another shower.

Oli retrieved a file from his briefcase and placed it closed on the coffee table before them.

"I was interviewed in hospital. Did you see the report?"

"Yes. But it's very skimpy. And, er, if you don't mind me saying, you were drugged up."

Dannaks conceded the point.

"You said they were wearing death masks?"

"Yes."

Oli opened the file and took out some sheets of pictures of death masks that looked to have been taken from the internet. Three sheets in all. The multitude of forms nonetheless overwhelmed him.

"Wow. They all look so similar. I think my attackers wore the same type. They, er, weren't elaborate or colourful. They were quite plain. White, plastic-coated – or at least they weren't matt. The mouth was straight. That's all I remember."

He pointed to a few candidates.

"Okay," said Oli returning the sheets to the file. And picking out more pictures. "I know you didn't see their faces. But could either of these two have been present?" He placed the two photographs next to each other in front of Dannaks.

They looked formidable: heavyweight bruisers who would look at home as bouncers, veritable pillars sandwiching the door to a roadhouse.

"It all happened very fast. Their build is right. But I'm sure these are not the only two built like anabolic advertisements."

"True." Oli picked up the photographs. "But these two come as a pair."

Before Dannaks could wonder why these two had been singled out Oli picked out another photograph, careful not to let Dannaks see it. "And now we come to the boy. You saw him."

"Briefly."

Again a photograph was placed before him.

Dannaks picked it up. His gut reaction was yes. The bulldog features were present, but the context and animation absent. And the more he stared at the photograph the less certain he became. Despite his observation training he knew he had to be certain.

"My gut reaction is that's him. But I couldn't testify to it."

Oli nodded.

"Who is he?"

"He's the son of one of the two I just showed you. Steiner."

"You are joking."

Dannaks realised the resemblance to one of the bruisers. He knew his mind would start to fit them in the picture. Again he knew his recollection would not hold up under the scrutiny of a court cross-examination.

"Kutnik and Steiner aren't the brightest of the bunch."

"Can we get the boy?"

Oli shook his head. "He's thirteen, too young to be held criminally responsible. If we do get him to admit he led you to the alley he could claim innocence. He–"

"But they were wearing masks. There's nothing innocent about that."

"He could say he didn't see any masks. And despite his father's stupidity, he and Kutnik will have alibis."

"Other right-wingers."

"Yep."

"No point, then."

"Not really."

In the ensuing silence Oli packed up the file and slipped it in his briefcase.

"We'll get this officially written up when you're back at work. Any idea when that might be?"

Dannaks wasn't paying full attention. "Monday."

"Yeah? That's quick."

He refrained from saying he tried to go in this morning.

Oli stood. Dannaks struggled to his feet.

"I can see myself out."

"One thing," he began. The effort of rising had forced an intake of breath that had hurt his chest. "Are Kutnik and Steiner members of Karsten Kohn's gang?"

Oli gave him a lopsided smile, as if he had been waiting for the question.

He nodded slowly. "Like a lot of these gangs there's a hard core and then those on the fringes. These two are fringe members." He waited a tick. "We need to know what you've been up to."

10:58

They interviewed Nazim first. The two homicide officers took him to the back room office of the shop. His father went with him. Cenk was left to take the delivery and watch the till. He often helped out in Nazim's family-owned mini-market. It broke up the day and brought in extra readies and the occasional perk such as a packet of this or that, fruit or vegetables that weren't shifting. His mother worked in the school-kitchens and his father was a night watchman.

His parents were always pleased when he brought something home. This was one of the big plusses of being Nazim's friend. Not everyone got on with him. Yes, he was naive. But he was sincere and he made Cenk laugh.

Being a security man, Cenk's father encouraged the karate classes. He was proud. His mother never voiced an opinion. Cenk knew she was uneasy about it. Nazim's father was ambivalent. He certainly wasn't pleased about having the police in his shop.

"You're on," said Nazim, emerging from the back room office. Cenk tried to read his face. He looked pale. An officer was behind him and Cenk muttered that he'd almost finished. Of course the police wouldn't give them the chance to collaborate. Nazim gave him a surreptitious wink.

"This way," said the officer. He was glad they had come for him now. He could have been in all sorts of trouble had they wanted to interview him this evening in the restaurant.

Cenk struggled to remember the officer's name. He had seen their identity cards but shock had obliterated their names.

Nazim's father returned to the till. "All right on your own?" he asked. Cenk nodded.

In the back room there were only two chairs and a small desk. Otherwise shelving of stock, stacks and towers of crates shrivelled the space. The officer following Cenk opted for an upturned crate. Cenk sat opposite the other officer at the desk.

The officer, on the crate on the periphery of Cenk's vision, held a notebook and pen. But Cenk's attention was fixed on the man in front of him. Cenk gave his name, date of birth, address and occupation. They asked him about his hobbies and paid particular interest to his karate club affiliation.

The tone changed a mite and they asked him about his whereabouts around two o'clock yesterday. He told them he was at Murat's flat and gave them the names of those also present as witnesses. Instead of asking more about the gang they asked what he was doing for dates in October and February. The dates threw him and he admitted that he couldn't remember. Maybe he could find out. Later he would learn that these were the exact times and dates the *Henker* had struck. They then asked whether he had access to a motorbike. They knew he didn't legally possess one.

"I want you to tell me what you know of the *Schwarzer Freitag*."

Cenk's mind spun and after a while the officer raised

questioning eyebrows.

Cenk shuffled and took a deep breath, glanced at the officer with the notebook. "It's, er, it's a group to protect us – our community – from attacks."

"Attacks?" said the officer mildly.

Cenk didn't recognise the officers. Surely they knew all this? They'd been interviewed after the snack bar incident. "Yes. Faruk was attacked by skinheads."

"Ah, yes. The schoolboy. What Saturday's rioting was all about?"

"That–" Cenk strangled his own words.

"Yes?"

"That wasn't our fault. It was a peaceful march until those right-wingers laid into us."

"Of course." His agreement was unconvincing.

"So you are a member of the *Schwarzer Freitag*. Correct?"

Cenk reddened. What was the right answer? They must know. "Sometimes."

The officer smiled. "A rather coy answer."

"The truth," protested Cenk, feigning indignation.

"Who thought of the name *Schwarzer Freitag*?"

"I don't remember."

The man stared at him.

"I don't remember."

The man sighed and reached down and put a briefcase on his lap. He opened the top and pulled out a manila envelope. He lifted the flap and fingered the edges of A4-sized photographs. He looked at Cenk, as if deciding what he should see. Cenk wanted to see them all. He wondered at the theatrics. Surely Nazim had seen them? Why had the man put them away? Why the big deal choosing what to show him? Nonetheless he adopted his most blank expression.

The officer made his choice and put it squarely in front of Cenk. It was a black and white photograph taken during the march. Hasan was already on the ground. He could see himself taking on a right-winger. Nazim looked drunk or asleep. His eyes were closed. Off to the right he located Murat, Ponytail and others.

Maybe dressing similarly had not been a clever idea?

"As a – shall we say? – part-time member of the *Schwarzer Freitag*, you should have no trouble identifying other members." He added: "Full-time or part-time."

Cenk studied the photograph. His first move was easy but he wouldn't make it before he knew how to go on.

After a while the officer prompted him.

Cenk placed his finger on Nazim.

"I'd like you to say their names as you point."

Cenk gave Nazim and Hasan away.

"What about the one with the moustache?"

Cenk nodded.

"Point to him and say his name please."

Cenk gave Murat away.

"The one with the ponytail?"

Cenk froze. Then he shook his head.

"What about the one next to him with his hand up?"

Cenk felt compelled to give the man one more. So he gave Bilal away too. He said he didn't know the others.

The man slid the photo back into the envelope.

"Who's the leader?"

"Hasan."

"Anyone else?"

Cenk was surprised by the question. "No."

"Did he think of the name?"

"No."

"But you said you didn't know. So it could have been him."

"No."

The detective considered for a moment.

"Could the name have existed earlier?"

"No. It's to do with the attack on Faruk, last Friday."

Pause.

"Where does the gang meet?"

"On the street."

"You don't have a favourite place?"

"No."

"Was the gang responsible for the Molotov cocktail attack last Sunday?"

"I don't know. I wasn't there."

"Where were you?"

"Out."

"Where?"

"Walking around."

"Walking the streets?"

"Yes. Protecting."

"As a part-time member of the *Schwarzer Freitag*?"

"Yes."

"So the gang was roaming the streets nowhere near the snack bar in Bergedorf?"

"Yes."

"Who else was with you?"

"Nazim," he said quickly.

"Hasan?"

"Yes, Hasan."

"Murat?"

"I, I don't remember. Maybe."

The officer looked at his colleague. His tone became less official.

"Cenk. I can call you Cenk, can't I? You seem like an intelligent young man. Not street thug material at all. You mix with street thugs you become one."

Cenk closed down. The man must have seen it in his eyes for his tone became official again. "As we see it the *Schwarzer Freitag* has the makings of a terrorist organisation. You're a member. There's no such thing as part-time. You're in or out. And in my book you're in. Take my advice; get out before it's too late. Last week a fire-bombing, next week a murder." He mesmerised Cenk with a hard stare.

"Where were you yesterday?"

He was unprepared for the sudden change. "I was at home."

"You didn't go out?"

"Yes, yes I did. I went to Murat's."

The man asked him when and for how long. Who else was present? Didn't they roam the streets last night? Why not?

"Listen to me, son." Cenk cringed at being called son. "We know who you are. We'll be watching you. Take my advice. Stay off the streets."

16:13

"The last time I wore make-up was at a student gender-bender bash," said Craig.

The woman powdering his cheeks and forehead with a brush suitable for fingerprinting explained that it was to stop his skin shining under the glare of the studio lighting.

The police had interviewed him late morning. He had not been able to furnish them with anything useful. He had bristled when the officer concluded the interview by asking if he could tone down his next article. It was possible the killer had targeted Stefan after seeing his article. Craig didn't like being told how to write. Should the police be told how to police?

For the impending television interview he had been given the sheet of five questions so that he could compose his answers beforehand. What he couldn't quite fathom was why they had told him the conversation would take between ten and fifteen minutes. He had asked and been told that the pre-recording for this evening's local news transmission would be edited. The five questions would be answered in so many minutes and no more. He was aware that a question not on the list he had received was highly likely. Such programmes liked to get a reaction and lend the whole an air of spontaneity. Those sorts of questions normally came towards the end of the interview.

Craig felt prepared for all eventualities. What transpired was totally unexpected.

As he predicted the prepared questions were cordially asked and comfortably answered within the first five minutes. Then the woman announced that they wanted to show a clip of Stefan's parents.

Craig blanched when the one minute of film was over. Of course the entire thing was crass.

Stefan's parents were filmed face-on sitting on their sofa in their modest living room. His father looked grim and remained stony throughout. His mother was tearful, her voice cracking under the strain of talking about her dead son.

The only time the camera left her was to zoom in to the framed photograph of a ten year old Stefan she held on her lap. He was on a bicycle broadly smiling.

Her broken voice spoke of a sweet boy who had always loved trains since his first Lego train set. She admitted that he had rough edges – but what boy didn't? Craig was appalled by the fact that she appeared to believe her boy had remained the one in the photograph. He had to stop himself from shaking his head in disgust. In only one point was he in total agreement with her. She said no one deserved such a horrific death.

When the presenter asked for his reaction he latched on to this one statement. "I am deeply sorry for their loss and extend my condolences. Murder is terrible."

"Do you think your article contributed?"

"Certainly not." He scolded himself for his knee-jerk reaction and forced himself to calm down.

"The killer may have read it."

"The killer may have read a lot of things. As I understand it I am not the first to interview or write about Stefan."

17:34

Dannaks was unaccustomed to unannounced visitors. So when his flat bell rang he flinched, sending such shudders of pain down him that he cursed.

If he stopped to think about it he would realise he never had so many visitors in one day. If he analysed further it he would conclude that he never had so many visitors in any one month.

He hobbled to the intercom and pressed the talk button.

"Hallo?" he said.

He heard a far off voice, barely audible above the hiss of traffic. "It's Reinhart."

Dannaks buzzed him in and hastened as best he could back to the room to roll up the puzzle he had been half-heartedly piecing together.

By the time Reinhart rapped on the flat door, Dannaks felt wretched and clammy under the armpits.

Opening the door Dannaks was confronted, almost accosted, by a bouquet of flowers.

"Hi colleague," Reinhart boomed.

Dannaks shrivelled as he stepped back to let him in. "Hallo. This is, er, a surprise."

"I knew you lived nearby. Frank gave me your address. Here, take these." Reinhart's boisterousness overwhelmed him as he backed into the kitchen grabbing the proffered flowers. "And this." He pushed a manila envelope at him. "It was sticking out of your post box." Reinhart then saw the line of shoes and dropped down to slip his own off. "I hope you don't mind. I thought I'd drop by after work."

"Nice of you to come," he lied, turning his back on him, putting the envelope on the kitchen stool and looking for something to put the flowers in.

"You don't look too bad."

"It's all under the surface." He began filling the sink with water. "This'll have to do for now."

"No vase?" said Reinhart, as if a vase was a household essential.

"I, er, can borrow one from the neighbour, *Frau* Schumann."

"Is she in?"

"I, er, don't know."

Without putting his shoes back on Reinhart padded out of the flat. "Next door?"

"Yes," he called after him.

Dannaks took a few deep breaths. He heard *Frau* Schumann's bell ring. And then he heard Reinhart's voice. He smiled as he imagined the two of them in conversation. Their voices receded and Dannaks left the kitchen to look across to *Frau* Schumann's flat. To his amazement the door was closed. He shook his head and smiled at the thought of the two of them in conversation. Who would talk whose head off?

A good ten minutes later Reinhart pushed open Dannaks's flat door.

"I got the vase," he said.

"And a good chat."

"She's a nice old lady."

Dannaks nodded. "I made tea." He had also tidied up some more.

"Great." The kitchen offered as much room as the hallway so Reinhart gave the vase to Dannaks.

They took their tea to the lounge.

"Oh, your flat is smaller than hers," said Reinhart. "But you've got the view. And what a view."

Most people were surprised – even appalled – by the size of his flat and tended to overcompensate by praising the view. Dannaks no longer cared. He'd heard it all before. In fact he preferred the insulting quips which came later and were a measure of friendship. Reinhart wasn't there, yet.

In the short time Reinhart had been with *Frau* Schumann Dannaks had come to terms with Reinhart's visit. In truth he was now quite pleased.

They engaged in a short preamble that covered Dannaks's well-being, current office events and touched on Stefan's death.

"What fruit?" Dannaks asked referring to the *Henker's* calling card.

"A banana," said Reinhart. "Skin and all."

"I don't suppose you can tell me anything?"

"Not really. I don't know anything anyway. Of course REX bagged the donkey work. You're better off here." Dannaks didn't agree, but held his tongue.

Eventually they came back to Dannaks's health, more specifically, why he was singled out.

"How long have you got?"

"About an hour."

"Okay. Make yourself comfortable. I'll tell you everything." He took a sip of tea. "From the beginning then. As you know I joined as a *Schutzpolizist*. After training I was posted at a station for a few years. That was fine. Then I was transferred to Rüdiger Krohn's station. Wilhelm Fischer–"

"You mean *Meister Proper* Willy?"

"Yes, the very one. He got promoted to Krohn's level and got his own station."

"And never looked back."

"Right. Krohn's station was one of Hamburg's toughest. Naturally, being a red-arse I had a lot to learn. At first everything was fine. Over time I came to realise that my concept of justice contradicted that of some of the men. I believed – and still do – that if a hundred guilty men remained free to protect one innocent from being sent to prison, then great. Some believed the opposite: better sacrifice one innocent and bag a hundred criminals."

"Rough justice."

"And statistics."

Reinhart nodded contemplatively.

"I could turn a blind eye to some of the corruption. Payment in sexual favours, that sort of thing. Some of the lads beefed themselves up with steroids. On the streets you can't blame them. I think they were getting the drugs illegally. Okay, it's not heroin, but all the same it's dealing with drug dealers. It's a fine line. It's not addiction but it could mean a weak spot... But yeah, I admit I could ignore it."

"So it wasn't corruption that got you?"

"No. What got me was the police brutality. Human rights abuses. Don't get me wrong. I am talking about a minority. Most of the lads were in order. Out of one hundred and twenty I'm talking about a group of half a dozen who played too hard."

"Like what?"

"No permanent or lasting injuries. Forcing salt water down

suspected couriers to get them to spew up the packets of drugs. Beatings, slapping about. Insect spray in the face."

"Negroes I presume."

"The majority of dealers are non-nationals."

"Sometimes it's all that's open to them."

Reinhart's radical attitude surprised Dannaks, but he continued. "I heard about the lads laughing about an *Ausländer* phoning for help and being told to phone again when he could speak German properly." He sipped his tea. "To be honest I only ever saw a slapping. I went to Krohn–"

"Didn't anyone else ever complain?"

"Not as far as I know. Most turned a blind eye." He saw Reinhart's surprise. "You've got to understand the situation. You came straight into the *Kripo*. In the *Schupo* there's a great feeling of comradeship. On the streets you need to rely on your colleague. It's a tough world. Sometimes even strong-arm tactics backfire. You heard about the criminals wearing razor blades under their collars? That was their answer to rough handling by the police. But bastard or not every one of us is a bull and we all get the same treatment. Spat at, called Nazi-swine. It's a baptism of fire. And that's the stuff that bonds. To go against your own is just not done. It's a code of honour. I was new and like the others I tried to swallow what was going on, but it began to make me sick. Others hadn't liked it either, but had learnt to stomach it. Time on the streets rubs away soft edges. Anyhow, they came to terms with it. When I started rocking the boat some of them secretly confided in me."

"Covering their arses."

"Perhaps. It doesn't really matter. I went to Krohn and he said he'd handle it. But nothing happened. He called me in a few days later and said he'd spoken to certain individuals and cautioned me not to take it further. His boys got results. They took a lot of shit and some of it stuck. If he took everyone who stepped over the line to task he'd have no one left. There were limits, but they were limits that he set. He had a station to run. He had results to get. He would judge what was minor and what was not." Dannaks paused. "Everything was fine for a few months. Then I stumbled on something I couldn't let go."

"I was on a Narcotics bust. The arrests had been made and I was given the job of gathering up a stack of plastic bags of heroin that were on a table. One of the bags was split and I didn't have any tape to seal it. A detective gave me a children's plaster. How appropriate, I said, a pink elephant. It's a hippo, he said." He looked at Reinhart. "It is important." Reinhart showed no emotion. "There was another slit in the bag which had been covered by two pieces of Sellotape. They formed an X. This bag's seen better days, I said and the detective smiled. We packed up and that was that. A couple of weeks later I saw the plaster in a bin at the station. I thought it strange. The evidence should have been shipped to the *Polizeistern* by then. We raided a brothel that same day and yes, you guessed it, we found heroin. The guy was an underworld face, but not a dealer. He screamed set up. I saw the two bags and bingo, the Sellotape cross. He was right. He was being set up."

"Better sacrifice one innocent and bag a hundred criminals."

"Correct. At first I didn't know what to do. When we got back to the station I made sure no one was around. Then I took the plaster out of the bin with a set of tweezers and popped it in an evidence bag. I knew whose bin it was, but that didn't mean anything." He pondered a moment.

"I went to Krohn again. He said he'd handle it. But I knew he wouldn't do anything. As far as he was concerned I was a troublemaker. I didn't tell him about the plaster. I just said I knew. Word got round. I'll spare you the petty terrorism. As you can imagine the atmosphere at the station became tense." Dannaks sipped some tea. "Krohn began manoeuvring and started a campaign to blacken my name. I was an agitator damaging his troops' morale. He asked to speak to me one evening. He wanted to know what I had. Did I have hard evidence? I gave him nothing. That's what he expected, but he'd accomplished what he wanted. Keeping me late. It was dark when I left. Five balaclava'd men attacked me."

"I can see you've got something against Krohn, but the thugs could have known he was going to keep you late and then it's nothing to do with him."

"I don't believe in coincidences." Dannaks regarded Reinhart. "It's possible, I suppose. But Krohn turns a blind eye to his minions' antics so I consider him as guilty as them."

"You didn't recognise any of the attackers?"

"I knew who they were." Pause. "Far from silencing me, the attack merely acted as a catalyst. I contacted the *Kripoman* who'd given me the plaster. He's a friend now. Uwe Albrecht. He took the plaster and told me to go to DIE. The funny thing about the plaster is that he doesn't have any kids. But that's another story." He stopped long enough to kick out the idea of digressing. "DIE came in and took Krohn's station apart. I don't know how he did it, but Krohn got away unscathed. Well, his career was stopped in its tracks. He's got as far as he's going to get. But I hadn't realised the extent of this 'code of honour' network. After all, I was a newcomer and Krohn was long established. The plaster had a good fingerprint of one of the men. But things were getting nowhere – or maybe they were – but very slowly. The evidence bags were counted – one was missing. The upper echelons were embarrassed that evidence had been pilfered, but they wanted to keep it behind closed doors. There were ongoing investigations against specific officers for malpractice and mishandling a foreigner whilst in custody. DIE said there'd been enough bad publicity and agreed to exercise discretion. I think behind my back the ground was being prepared for my dismissal. If I was going to be discredited and dismissed I had nothing to lose. So I gave them an ultimatum. I gave them two days after which I was going to the press. The press got the story the following day. I didn't leak it, but that didn't matter. The damage was done. Six of Krohn's men went down. I was offered a transfer to the *Kripo*. I'd passed the necessary examinations. To save face they wouldn't let me join the Homicide, which was what I'd been working towards. That's how I came to be with Narcotics."

"It's no consolation, but I think you would have been ideal for Homicide."

"Thanks," he replied automatically. "Do you know what they said, when I asked about Homicide? They said they couldn't offer me a place because of my allergies–"

"What allergies?"

"Dust, grass–"

"Grass?"

"The green stuff. Not the stuff you smoke."

"Small mercies," Reinhart said with a wicked smile.

Dannaks smiled too. "They said they were afraid I'd sneeze all over the evidence."

"Human after all."

"What do you mean?"

"When you arrived, I thought you were a robot."

"What?"

"You didn't radiate warmth and friendship."

Dannaks smiled. "I guess not."

Reinhart pondered. "So here you are in REX with yours truly. But you *have* been working on something else."

Dannaks explained what he had been doing.

"And you think the swastika has something to do with it?"

"It's not unreasonable."

"You're tempting the Devil. If I'd been through all that once, I'd certainly not go through it again."

"Yeah. I'm crazy. But I feel it is unfinished business—"

"You're out to nail Krohn?"

"Not entirely. I sold myself out last time. I took the *Kripo* job, the soft option. I turned my back on all the corruption. Krohn's authority was diminished and the chances of him moving upward are the same as me getting on Homicide. Others were warned or transferred."

"But you suspect Krohn's behind this warning?"

"Who else?" Reinhart had no answer. "I went after Lampe. His cousin, Heinrich, works for Krohn. Heinrich was one of the officers I put under investigation. So Lampe and I were natural enemies in Narcotics. After going for him that swastika appeared on my flat door."

"You said this all started after you went after Lampe. But you were doing something else, weren't you?"

Dannaks explained going to the station and asking about the motor club incident. He couldn't deny that someone there could be responsible for the swastika.

"Since it is confession time," Reinhart began. "I'll come clean about your blotter. I did take the top sheet. I, er, got so used to being alone in the office, I always arranged the flowers there. Anyway, the vase left a ring of water and I wasn't sure how you were going to react."

"Tell me how you can afford flowers."

"You are a suspicious one. My sister is a florist."

Dannaks smiled.

Reinhart glanced at his watch. "I've got to go."

"I don't suppose you could do me a favour?" Reinhart was on his feet and Dannaks rose too.

"Name it?"

"See if there's any more post.

"Up and down those stairs again?"

"I'll give you the key."

"Oh," Reinhart exclaimed. "I almost forgot. Someone called today. I said you weren't available. He wouldn't leave his name and he said he was only going to give you one more try."

"I know who it is. Give him my home number."

17:50

Craig listened to the answer machine. Rather than make return calls he forced himself to sit in front of the computer. He lacked the incentive he needed to work on the second article in the series and found himself instead shuffling the information.

He had been through a media ordeal. During telephone interviews he had virulently defended his article. A number of times he skated on thin ice and admitted that he had painted a fundamentally black and white picture. He tried to explain that this had been intentional because he wanted to quash a lot of assumptions about Germany in his second and third pieces. Ultimately, he fell back on the fact that if extremism was being discussed and recognised as a problem, then it was halfway to being solved.

His handy interrupted him. For a moment the caller's name didn't mean anything. "Murat? Oh, yes. I saw you at the march. You gave those skinheads a good pasting."

"You saw me?"

"Yes. I was impressed."

"Me too." He laughed. "Listen, I haven't much time. Do you still want to interview me?" Craig thought of the detectives' interest in the Turkish gang.

"Yes."

"Tomorrow. Seven o'clock at my place."

"Okay. Give me your address."

Craig hung up and made a cup of fruit tea. Could Murat be the *Henker*? The interview a trap? It seemed unlikely. He'd got his home address.

With pen and paper to hand he listened to the recorded messages again.

He was on the telephone when Carina arrived. It was all repetition and he wished he had recorded a statement. Yes, he felt terrible about Stefan's death, but did not feel guilty. He had reported what the boy had told him. Of course he wanted his condolences expressed to the boy's parents. No, he was not a left-wing agitator. And he had no idea who killed the boy.

Craig replaced the receiver. "That's the last call," he said, blowing sharply through thinned lips.

"Put the answer-phone on," she said, from the sofa.

"I'll turn the volume down too," he said switching over to answer-phone.

She nodded with a smile. Looking at her he felt comfortable. As if he'd arrived. There was still excitement in the air. Parts of her were enigmatic and thrilling. "You'll be on TV in about twenty minutes." She pointed the remote control at the television.

"Yep."

The phone rang. "Let it ring," she said.

He smiled and began to turn down the volume. However, his curiosity slowed him.

Suleyman began to leave a message. Craig hesitated, looked to Carina, who frowned and shook her head. He lifted the receiver and she looked to the ceiling.

After introductions Suleyman told him what had happened over the last few days. He said the telephone had not stopped ringing. Craig empathised. The number of crank calls had become intolerable and they'd changed their number.

"Farrie went school today. He was sick after lunch. They send him home. He has migraine." Suleyman cleared his throat. "Now they are playing."

"What do you mean? Who?" asked Craig, trying to sound concerned for somehow it all seemed trivial.

"As soon march over—"

"Who?"

"The school."

"Have they said he can't take the tests?"

"No, opposite. He can – must – take next week."

"Well, er, if he's well enough to attend school—"

"That is what they say. I am wonder whose side you on."

"I—"

"He got headaches. He not recovered. He can't. He tell me he can't. And them – the bastards. The minute the—"

"But that doesn't make sense. It's too risky for them. This thing hasn't died down. You were on television yesterday. You've got publicity. They wouldn't—"

"They have."

Pause.

"Suleyman, I don't see what I can do?"

"You write it. That was good article. My daughter translated."

"That good article possibly led to Stefan's death."

"Yes. Stefan." He had obviously not expected the remark and was caught off-guard. "Even him don't deserve that."

"Deserve what?" asked Craig. He had a feeling that Suleyman knew more.

"Death." Neither of them spoke. Craig was about to sign off when Suleyman said: "But don't that stop you writing truth. The Germans won't listen unless hard hit."

There was another silence. This time Craig filled it by bringing the call to an end with a statement that he would find out more about Farrie's situation and that he was on television in a few minutes.

When he replaced the receiver he let out a loud sigh and turned off the volume.

19:54

Reinhart was out of breath when he returned with the post box key and a wad of flyers.

Dannaks thanked him, shut and chained the door.

The flyers went straight in his kitchen bin.

He examined the envelope. Just his name and address, typed. No sender, logo, but most intriguing of all, no stamp.

In the lounge he opened the windows and looked over the water, now black as oil. Flickering lights at the banks were spots of warmth. The cars near and far shuffled along. People going for a drink or a meal. People like Annelore and Uwe.

He switched on the television. Sitting on the sofa he picked the edge of the envelope until he could get a finger inside. He ripped it open and pulled out a folded sheet of A4; a glossy pamphlet fell out too. The logo gave the game away before he had the sheet out. It was a sports club. Junk after all. His attention wandered to the television. He placed the lot on the coffee table.

Twenty minutes later, the programme no longer holding him, he got up to prepare something to eat. He took the post to the kitchen bin. Over the open flip top under the sink he paused. The name printed on the letter was not Dannaks. It was Krohn. He looked again. Was he hallucinating? He stared hard and checked the envelope again. It was addressed to him. He forgot his hunger and spread the papers on the kitchen worktop.

There was no logo on the envelope and considering the contents this was surprising. Of course, this envelope was not the original. That would have been addressed to Krohn.

The Romulus and Remus centre was an exclusive members' only club, established more than thirty years ago. The embossed emblem at the top of the letter was a coin or stone disc with a Roman head in profile. No, two grey heads looking the same way, one overlapping the other, Roman noses, pupil-less eyes and laurel leaf crowns. The pamphlet carried the same emblem but in gold. Romulus and Remus were abbreviated to R&R to associate the club with rest and recreation.

The letter was addressed to Krohn. The date was three years old. A three-year-old letter? On the reverse side was an unfilled general application form. Dannaks picked up the glossy pamphlet. The small print said it was four years old. A members' only club. Membership attained strictly by recommendation. Two existing members were required as sponsors. Then there was a form to fill out and you were in the club for a probationary half-year. On offer was nothing special: sauna, solarium, Jacuzzi, massage and swimming, a gym. Nothing special. But of course that wasn't what was on offer here. It was the clientele that was important. It was who was on the neighbouring exercise bike; who was pumping iron on the next bench. This was what members' only meant. This club offered a fast track into a chosen facet of society. The list of founding members at the foot of the letter told him nothing.

He re-read the letter and scrutinised the pamphlet. What did it mean? It was a clue. His next port of call. That was all he could make of it. So, who sent it? Detlef? Unlikely. He wouldn't be so cryptic. That only left the insider. He was a good possibility. What about Krohn himself? No, that was ludicrous. Then how had the insider got hold of the private invitation? Somebody close to Krohn. Yes. Detlef had said the insider was too close to help. Dannaks had never thought he could be that close. Who could it be? He mentally went through Krohn's colleagues. One name became insistent. Wilhelm Fischer. The master. Willy Fischer. Was he the insider who was too close? They had worked together. Willy had climbed the ranks and appeared to have severed all contact with Krohn.

He was drinking his first coffee of the day when Carina telephoned.

"I hate to spoil your day like I did yesterday," she began.

"Déjà vu," he said, his heart nevertheless missing a beat.

"You should get out and buy the papers again. They have printed parts of your article. The English one."

He knew only too well that pieces taken out of context could be misconstrued. On top of that was the danger of a slip in translation.

"And?"

"It makes you sound pretty harsh towards the Germans."

"Shit. This is ridiculous. The second article is going to look like a back-out. I said I wanted the first to be hard and the following two to explain it all away. They've only got one side of the coin."

"It gets worse. Stefan's parents are going to sue you."

Craig's jaw dropped.

"They say their son was never like that and hold you responsible for his death."

He closed his eyes for a moment. Defamation put paid to the idea of working Stefan's death into his next article.

"One reporter supported them. He said Stefan sounded like a second Hitler."

"The boy was a misguided adolescent going through a rebellious phase. I wrote what he said—"

"His friends say he never said that."

He saw Günter and Blade in his mind's eye. "They didn't have a clue what we were talking about." He took a deep breath. "Okay, I wrote what it boiled down to. He didn't explicitly say it all, but I don't believe I strayed from his beliefs. I didn't quote him, but I didn't put the words into his mouth either." Pause. "All I did was write what he conveyed."

"You do not need to explain to me. I know."

"Here we go again," he said.

"What?"

Her lack of comprehension irked him momentarily. "Today is starting like yesterday. I'm going to have to talk to the media again."

When he replaced the receiver he thought of what the police officer had told him the previous day. "Play it down," he had said.

Craig could almost laugh if it were not so tragic.

He remembered what Carina had said after his talk with Suleyman the previous evening. "You are becoming personally involved." He had agreed. His involvement was reaching a stage where he was becoming part of the news he was trying to report, undermining his objectivity and credibility. Had he not read somewhere, about a foreign reporter at a march in Northern Ireland trying to incite violence, his car boot packed with truncheons and sticks and placards? Craig had not gone that far. Yet, he could not help feeling that his article had contributed towards Stefan's death.

14:24

Dannaks asked him how the investigation was going.

"Slowly," said Reinhart. The telephone line crackled.

He waited a tick for Reinhart to elaborate. "Have you, erm, heard of a club called Romulus and Remus?"

"Yes. It's a top-notch sports club. Sport and leisure club. Members only."

"Anything else?"

"What do you want to know? That it has right-wing leanings?"

Dannaks perked up. "Does it?"

"Yes. That's why I know about it."

"Have we files?"

"Nothing of worth. The club's squeaky clean. There's a lot of money behind it. And power. I think it started as a conservative club. But it changed over the years. Attracting more of the extreme right."

"Anything else?"

"Not really. The founding members are twins. They spend most of the year in Majorca."

"You said right-wing leanings; do you mean Nazi tendencies?"

"I wouldn't go that far. Like I said they're squeaky clean. But you can bet your bottom dollar Volker Herbst is a member. Why do you ask?"

"Somebody I know got an invitation."

"Somebody you know?"

"Yeah. Never mind. Thanks."

14:12

Karsten could see Jutta was making an effort to hide her disgust. The flat was a mess. No place for a three- month-old. Full of energy, she'd swept into the flat, annihilating her surroundings, kissing him and beaming, acting out some rehearsed scheme.

306

She acknowledged the fruits of his burglary. He had long ago told her that it was only a crime if he was caught. "Otherwise it's just shopping. I'm just stealing from the rich and giving to the poor and deserving. And it just so happens that we're the poor and deserving."

Within thirty minutes her demeanour succumbed to the state of the place. Now she was tidying and cleaning, every wipe of her cloth a swipe at him. He always thought she had a cleanliness tic. He knew that she hated it when a customer touched her when handing her cash at the till.

He smirked as he played with the gurgling baby, letting it grasp his nicotine-stained finger.

Why couldn't it have been a boy?

He began to fiddle with the standing mobile under which Eva lay. He idly twirled the suspended plastic sunflower with its mirror centre.

He was too absorbed to let Jutta's frustration reach him. He was in playback reliving the Turk's struggling, hearing his muffled scream. The foreplay had been exquisite. But like sex, once the deed was done, the high waned and a sense of disappointment set in. Torture, by definition, should be a prolonged experience. But the hammer had to come down sooner or later. Once the bite supplanted the bark, all that was left was to bite again and again and again.

It had been too easy. They had picked him up at the office block and shadowed him in the van. He'd taken yesterday's route home. So they drove ahead and ambushed him in a side road. Bear took him from behind, pinning his arms down. They tumbled into the back of the van and the others smothered him. The lads had gone heavy and Karsten had to stop them. By then the Turk was unconscious; the chloroform-soaked gauze, procured from the hospital where one of the lads worked as an orderly, had done its work. They'd taped his mouth and threw him out in an abandoned warehouse. Karsten coldly explained what they were going to do and what he was to tell his friends. "Lucky you're a window cleaner and not a concert pianist."

The child made a noise and Karsten returned. Jutta thought the baby would bring them closer together. She'd been wrong. The child was a burden. It sucked at her and it sucked at them, the worm gobbled away their freedom, lapped up their money. Now Jutta had started talking about getting a car. Of course the motorbike was impractical. She had to pay for a taxi to bring her from the station. More money.

He held the baby's ankle; let his finger feel its fatty calf.

"I'll be out tonight," he said, more to the baby than to her.

She stopped scrubbing the stampede of beer bottle stains on the windowsill and turned to him.

"We've only just got back. Our first evening."

He watched the baby and felt her stare. When he slowly looked over to her, she quickly turned away and continued madly scrubbing. The light from the window effectively silhouetted her, but he could see the glint of tears in her eyes. The light played on her body and he saw her curves returning, her full breasts leaning over the sill. He felt a twinge between his legs. "I should be back before nine." Her shoulders lost some of their tension and her breasts sagged, stomach bunched, hips spread: a dumpling again. Maybe he wouldn't make it back before nine after all.

He tightened his grip on the baby's leg and it fell silent and looked startled. Then its bottom lip quivered and it began to cry.

He got up and went to the kitchen as Jutta rushed to her.

15:04

Dannaks was so startled when the phone rang he snatched it up. "Dannaks."

"At bloody last."

He recognised the voice immediately. When Reinhart had said that someone was going to give him one more call Dannaks knew it could only be Red-face from the *Windjammer*.

"First of all let's get one thing straight. I'm not going to be your informant. This is my first and last call. I'm doing this as a favour to a dead friend. What do you want to know?"

"When we first came to the pub what did you mean by 'new shoes'?"

The man paused as if wondering whether to answer. Was he about to lie?

"About a week before he died Hermann said he thought he was being followed. He thought it was an undercover bull. In retrospect he was bound to say that to us. Perhaps who he was spying on had caught on? I don't know."

"And the shoes?"

"That's all he had seen of his tail. The man was wearing black training shoes with a light blue zigzag on the side."

"Did he say anything else about the man?"

"No."

"Is there anything he said or did that might lead us to his killers? It doesn't matter how insignificant, anything?"

"In the *Windjammer* you said you had one question and I've already answered two. But the answer is no. There's nothing else."

"I know what you said earlier about not wanting to talk, but I would–"

"Then I'll spell it out for you. If you come to the *Windjammer* looking for me again we'll do some real kissing. And I'm not talking about that peck on the cheek you got last time. I'll put some real passion into it."

"Well, should you change your–"

The man hung up.

"Thank you."

15:58

Craig felt as if he'd again spent the entire day on the telephone. One reporter tried to cajole him into making an inflammatory remark against Stefan's parents, but Craig found it surprisingly easy to remain level-headed. Some of his acquaintances in the press assured him that the boy's parents had nothing.

Later that morning Craig telephoned Faruk's school and enquired about the boy's examinations.

"I'm authorised to speak for the school," said the secretary. She didn't attempt to hide her exasperation. Cutting to the quick told him that she'd run over the same conversation many times. "The school relented just before the march because it was felt there was no choice. The media made sure of that. We set a date and the family are griping that it's too soon. Look at it from our point of view. Administratively, the sooner the better."

"Yes, but he's been ill."

"Should he be given longer than the others to prepare?"

"I think–"

"Look, from what I know of the boy – and I'm only the secretary – he doesn't have a hope in hell of passing. But I didn't say that."

Her breathing steadied in the ensuing silence.

"You say you've personal contact with the family," the secretary began. "Can't you convince them that it's in everyone's interest to get these tests over and done with? We really don't want this blown out of proportion."

"I've no real influence over them and no right to say anything."

When he put down the telephone he cursed. Rather than extricating himself he really was becoming more embroiled.

His handy rang and he jumped and scrambled in his jacket for it. "Hi, it's Murat. Listen, I'm sorry, I can't make it for seven."

"Okay. No problem." He wasn't upset by the cancellation. "I'll get back to you."

18:00

As the three of them walked down the corridor, Cenk reflected that a little over a week ago they had made their way to Basha's apartment. Ten days ago to be precise. So much had changed.

Nazim had parked the grocery van in the multi-storey car park on Paul-Ehrlich Street. They'd walked to the main gate, picking up Hasan at the bus stop as arranged. They followed the path to the main building. There were buildings to their right, and grass and woods to convalesce on their left. As they passed the circular car park near the main entrance Hasan said: "I want to break up the gang."

"No chance," scoffed Nazim.

"Things have got out of control," said Hasan. Then he added the old Arab saying: "The magic has taken over the magician."

Cenk was wounded and confused. Hasan's sense was needed in the gang. Why, it was also his turn to patrol tonight. "Before you say anything to the rest of them, let's hear what Bilal has to say."

The main building of Altona general hospital was like a high-rise office block, a box of panatelas with lots of glass, slim and tall but with more length than height.

They entered the main reception entrance and were directed to Chirurgery III.

There was an air of settling down at this time. The hustle and bustle had dissipated and the ever-present pervading hush was giving itself up to solemnity. They only saw one nurse at a trolley of bedding in the corridor.

"Most nurses are real bunnies," said Nazim. "But I hate hospitals."

Cenk nodded.

"It's probably because one only comes to them at times of tragedy," offered Hasan.

"Rubbish," said Nazim. "When I was younger I used to play

310

in the cemetery, running between the gravestones. That's a place of tragedy."

Hasan smiled weakly.

Cenk decided not to take the bait and suggest that Nazim may have been too young to appreciate the significance of the place. Instead he said: "I don't like the smell of the disinfectant."

A nurse appeared ahead of them.

"Yeah," agreed Nazim. "It's pretty strong. They probably use it to mask the smell of blood." There was a moment's pause. "And some people can't handle the smell of blood."

Cenk took this as a slight directed at Hasan. "And some people talk through their arse," said Cenk.

The reprimanding look of the passing nurse silenced them.

In this state of dynamic tension they approached Bilal's bed. He was in a room of about ten beds, all of which were occupied. Basha, Ponytail and another member of the gang were already present.

After greetings Bilal spoke, repeating his story for the newcomers' benefit. "They got me on the way home from work. A big one grabbed me from behind. I didn't have a chance. Before I knew it I was in the back of a van. Then loads of them – *deos* (roll-on deodorant: skinhead) – thrashed me. I nearly choked on chloroform. When I came round I was tied to a chair. Their leader was a big blond *Horst* (idiot). He– He had a hammer." He paused to swallow back an emotion. His eyes glazed and widened. "He spoke about Saturday. How we'd given his boys a good licking. He said the *Polypen* (adenoids – slang: police) held them back. He said we should sort it properly."

"Sort what?" said Hasan. Either everyone was too shocked to speak or nobody had an answer. "There's nothing to sort."

"He's offering the chance of a fair scrap," said Basha.

"Fair? What's fair about a scrap? I think this whole thing has gone far enough. We should stop now."

"Stop what?" asked Ponytail, viciously calm as always.

"The patrolling. The gang. It's getting out of control."

"It's getting to where it has to go," said Basha.

"No, we–"

An Asian nurse interrupted them. "If you don't lower your voices you're going to have to leave."

They were silent until she left.

"How can you argue at my bedside when I'm like this?" Bilal hissed, holding up his cast-encased hands. "They did this to me to tell you to meet them tonight at seven."

"For a scrap?" asked Basha.

"No. To make arrangements. A spokesman and five others. For a scrap on Friday."

"It's madness," said Hasan.

"He said come if you've the leather."

Hasan shook his head.

The nurse reappeared with a security man in tow. "This man needs rest now. You have to leave." They got up and moved away. She moved in and fussed about the bed. They nodded and waved and raised clenched fists to Bilal as they left.

"Bloody BMW," said Nazim, referring to the nurse's flat-chested boyish figure and meaning *Brett mit Warzen* (board with nipples).

When they were outside but near the entrance Hasan said: "Let's move away from here."

Basha led and Hasan followed. Whereas Hasan walked Basha strode like a confident youth: the swagger of someone ten years his junior.

Cenk knew Hasan wanted a reasoned discussion. He also knew he wasn't going to get one.

"You should have held your tongue," scolded Basha, stopping at the edge of the circular car park. Cenk felt the portent of the moment. He was struck by the serendipity of standing almost exactly where Hasan had earlier announced that he wanted to break up the gang. They stood in a loose circle. An occasional person passed by, wisely choosing to ignore them.

Hasan defied the group with eyes deadened with resolve.

Cenk knew Hasan was out. He knew also that he himself would have to make a decision about where he stood. And he'd have to make it here and now.

More had happened than had been said. Basha was bubbling. Much as he had been after the march. Cenk sensed a change in Ponytail too. As if Bilal's injury had tipped him over the edge and he'd ascended to a new level of threat. Cenk feared for Hasan.

"If you want out, then get out," said Nazim, looking nervously at Basha and Ponytail. "Just don't try to bring us down."

Hasan glared at him and skimmed over the faces of the others. Cenk chose to look at his shoes. "You fools. Today they break someone's hands with a hammer. Tomorrow they'll break someone's head." Then to Nazim: "It's not a game."

"Nobody said it was," snapped Basha.

"The police are already on to us."

"And who brought them on us?" asked Ponytail, a toothpick rigid between his teeth.

"Whoever threw that Molotov cocktail." The group froze.

"They've nothing," said Basha eventually.

Hasan spoke in a quiet reasoning tone. "If you go to this meeting we lose what we stand for."

"We lose what *you* think we stand for," said Ponytail.

Hasan was visibly weakened, but fought on regardless. "If you go, you'll become like them."

"O you who believe, fight the unbelievers who are near to you," said Basha.

Hasan was outraged. The quote from the Qur'an was the basis for the duty of *jihad*.

Strangely he chose words from the Bible. "Yeah, an eye for an eye today. Tomorrow an arm and then a head. This is where you'll end up."

"In the car park," said Nazim giggling foolishly.

Hasan glared at him.

"The challenge is there," said Basha, "and we're to honour–"

"Honour? There's no honour in street fighting. You'll just become thugs like–"

Ponytail blew out his toothpick and stepped forward. His keen features were complemented by his choice of dark blue tie upon a sharp white shirt. Cenk had never seen him so smartly dressed. But the suit he wore in no way civilised him. A contrast made him look more dangerous than ever. Cenk thought that he had come from, or was going to, work.

Cenk may have given the appearance that he was elsewhere; Ponytail's move showed that he was highly attentive, for he mirrored Hasan by involuntarily tensing himself. He did not flinch so much as tightened.

Ponytail said nothing. He just stood in front of Hasan. Basha spoke. "It's irrelevant what you think. You're out. It's what you want. Your conscience is clear. The–"

Even now Hasan dared to provoke the situation. "You're looking forward to scrapping." A flicker of a smile appeared on Basha's face.

"Maybe," he snapped. Then he beamed at the others. "After all, we're the *Schwarzer Freitag.* We'll give those racist shits the blackest Friday."

Cenk didn't know where to look. Nazim nodded. Ponytail gave a sinister smile and the other member of the gang, who thus far had only contributed at Bilal's bedside, gave a short laugh.

Ponytail took another step closer. He now stood inches from Hasan. The atmosphere was electric and Cenk felt Hasan brace himself for a blow.

"Only us," Ponytail began with slow contemptuous precision, "in this car park – and Bilal – know of this challenge. We–" he paused "– are not going to tell anybody. If word gets out and the bulls turn up, we'll know it was you. You heard Murat, you're out."

There was an awful silence in which no one breathed.

Ponytail's face twisted with loathing.

Cenk thought he was about to go on talking, when he spat a large gob of spit in Hasan's face. Hasan remained riveted to the spot. Cenk watched the frothy saliva edge its way towards his mouth. His lips were clamped shut as he let the viscous stuff reach them. Hasan was stone.

The silence intensified.

Ponytail huffed, shaking his head ever so slightly, his mouth contorted with revulsion. "You have a woman's face."

He stepped back.

"Let's leave the yellow sow to wallow in her stench of fear," he said.

Although no one actually moved before him they appeared to leave together.

Cenk didn't look back.

Nazim spoke as they drove, but Cenk wasn't listening. He was glad he'd got away without having to position himself. He imagined Hasan still standing there with the spit on his face. Cenk wiped an imaginary wetness from his mouth. It worried him that Ponytail had called for them to leave. Basha had said nothing. Maybe Hasan wasn't the only one losing control.

18:42

The discreet brass shield, akin to that of a dentist or doctor, proclaimed: "Romulus and Remus. Exclusive club, members only." The solid panelled door was on the outside of an indoor shopping mall. Dannaks pressed the bell and heard a distant buzz. The door latch clicked and he pushed it open. Although it was heavy it moved with ease.

He found himself in a short corridor opening onto a small room. The walls were pastel yellow, veined like marble. The plasterwork was brilliant white. Shaded wall lighting subdued any garishness. Two three-seat black leather sofas lined two walls and sandwiched a door. A coffee table offered a selection of serious glossy magazines. Their covers were dominated by rifles or handguns; there was a hunter in Bavarian black and green and a Robin Hood feathered hat. The rest of the room was given over to a generous reception cubicle, the front of which carried a larger version of the club emblem. Dannaks decided it was a coin; the two profiled heads were looking to something slightly raised to the right. Of course their eyes were pupil-less like Roman busts, yet visionary and eternal.

A bright young thing sat in the spacious cubicle. She gave him a gorgeous smile that was infectious. Dannaks suddenly felt apprehensive. He didn't want to get her into trouble, but he needed to get as much out of her as possible.

Although the application on the reverse side of the invitation hadn't been filled out, there was a chance Krohn had joined the club. It was a gamble Dannaks had decided to take.

"Hallo," said the bright young thing as if he were the regular patron she looked forward to seeing.

Unconsciously he straightened, pulling back his shoulders and tightening his stomach. His aches reminded him of his state.

"I received this." He opened the letter and she leaned forward. His finger covered the date and he made no effort to give it to her. Her hand came up, flawless pearly pink nails; she wore a silver thumb ring. She smiled and didn't attempt to take the letter from him. He smelt her perfume and felt stirrings.

"Good for you," she beamed. Was this really a sports and leisure club? She was gorgeous: an aspiring model making up extra money. Or was she a high-class hooker and there was more emphasis on leisure here? She leant back on her perch and he folded the letter and put it back in the envelope. "May I call you Rüdiger?"

He nodded. She wasn't going to ask for identification. His natural social uncertainty was working for him. Her small rectangular badge resting on her shirt above her left breast said that she was Alexandra.

"Shall we deal with formalities first, Rüdiger?"

"I'd rather get a feel for the place first."

"You've not been here before?"

He shook his head and dared a boyish smile.

"Welcome to R and R, Rüdiger." Her teeth were perfect. "I'll tell you what," she began conspiratorially; "I need to go to the little girls' room." Her smile was wicked and Dannaks felt the warmth creeping up his collar. He didn't know what she meant, but her intimacy put him off balance. He wasn't used to such blatant flirting, especially from someone half his age. She ignored his smouldering and pressed a number on her telephone. "Can you take the desk for a while, Werner?" She stood, smiled again and smoothed the front of her short cheerleader pleated white skirt.

The corner door, between the leather sofas, opened and Werner entered. Dannaks didn't need to be told that he was a trainer or masseur. His muscles rendered his club T-shirt and shorts, skin-tight in all the right places. He had a handsomely angled carved face and Dannaks wondered whether he was real or had been cast: moulded to order for R&R. Genetically perfect.

He strode to the reception cubicle and Dannaks felt vulnerable and flabby. But he had no time to feel inadequate; Alexandra took his hand and led him to the corner door. The door opened onto spiral stairs like a lighthouse. She led and he felt awkward holding her hand: a little boy with his mother.

When they reached the bottom she said she'd only be a minute and left him. The stairway was in the corner of another area. Seats with large cushions surrounded a central pillar. There was a side-table with a coffee and tea maker, cups and saucers and a platter of assorted biscuits. A large water dispenser stood nearby. Fat-bladed swords were mounted horizontally on the walls next to each corner. The blades were inscribed. One said "Exit" and pointed behind him. The others indicated the way to massage and sauna, pool and workout, and changing areas.

Dannaks guessed that the mall had given up part of its underground car park to the club. There was little sound, just classical music coming from somewhere and the echo of water too.

A man in a toga emerged from the massage and sauna corner. He was a fit-looking fifty with prefect grey-hair. "Evening," he said. Dannaks nodded. The man went to the water dispenser, pulled a paper cup and filled it. He stood and drank silently, the machine glugged for him. Then he padded off towards the changing areas.

Alexandra returned. This time she didn't take his hand and he was both glad and disappointed. "The changing areas aren't so interesting; we can look at them if you like." He mumbled that it was not necessary and followed her to pool and workout. They walked a short corridor before coming to a large open plan room. In front of them were all manner of exercise machines. He estimated thirty or forty machines for the five men. The men were in ordinary sportswear. One wall was glass behind which a pool glinted under subdued burgundy lighting.

Dannaks followed her to the entrance to the pool, aware of the sideways glances of the men at the machines. For him? For her? He couldn't tell.

They stood in the pool area near the glass wall. The change in temperature was marked and his skin tingled. A man was swimming easy laps. Another two sat on stools in the water at a bar. Two adorned cocktails stood in front of them. The word decadence came to mind. So this was where the big league rubbed shoulders. He didn't recognise anybody. Hopefully nobody recognised him.

"Nice," he said, nodding his approval. Alexandra seemed pleased. But he really wanted to get away from the thick air and its warmth. She smiled and surveyed the area with renewed appreciation.

He began to smell the chlorine and his eyes smarted. His skin prickled and he knew that if they didn't get out soon he was going to break out into a terribly embarrassing sweat.

Mercifully she suggested moving on. They returned to the stairway and he relished the coolness and asked to stop for a drink of water. She served him. He drank self-consciously. The sweat attack had not come, but his self-consciousness threatened to bring it on. When he finished his drink he realised too late that she was taking him to sauna and massage.

Massage was also warm, the air heavy with oil and cloying talcum powder.

"If you want I'll get you a toga and you could go to the sauna and steam rooms."

He tried to hide his abhorrence. "No, I've seen enough."

"The steam rooms are something else. There are hot tubs and there's a huge whirlpool too."

"No. Thanks."

"Are you okay?" She was looking straight at him.

"Fine. Warm, that's all."

"Of course. Let's go then."

They climbed the stairs and entered the reception area. Werner stopped reading a magazine and returned to the depths. Dannaks waited for the door to click behind him before speaking. By then Alexandra was well into sorting out registration forms.

"Just a minute," he said leaning over the edge of the cubicle surface.

"Yes?" But she didn't look up.

"Do you think I could look at the members' list?" There was no getting round it. A direct approach was the only approach. Not honesty like at the Windjammer. Then again, she wasn't going to ask him to step outside. Although a kiss from her...

This stopped her and she confronted him with a perplexed look.

"I don't know my sponsors," he explained quickly. Then he grew confident. "That's why I've never been here before."

The situation hung in the balance.

"But why do you want the list?"

"I'd like to know who wants me in."

Again she watched him. Then she raised her eyebrows. "Why not?" she pressed a key on the keyboard of the computer in front of her. He couldn't see the screen. She gave him another queer look followed by a smile and a shake of the head. Then her nails clipped on the keys. She looked puzzled. Then nodded and tried another combination. Again the puzzled look. Then she slumped back. "I can show you a list, but it won't just be the current members. It'll have those who also left us in the last two years, I'm afraid."

"Can't you print it?"

"Oh no. That's definitely against the rules. You can't come back here either. Here, I'll turn the screen."

He had to lean over the counter to see the screen properly. She placed the keyboard in front of him and pointed out the scroll button.

He looked down the names. They were sorted alphabetically. Politicians from all persuasions were present. He recognised a businessman and a celebrity or two. Wilhelm Fischer was on the third page. In brackets next to his name was the word lapsed. On the fifth page he almost missed Volker Herbst. Rüdiger Krohn and his son were not on the list. The latter was no surprise. This place was way outside his league. Lampe was also not on the list.

Despite his side aching at being pressed awkwardly into the counter he returned to the top and went through the list again. He spotted Holger Markowiak's name. His membership ended with the word deceased. He scrolled back, but didn't find Nobby Kabel. By the time he had finished going through the four to five hundred names, having found nothing else, he was aware that Alexandra was waiting for him.

"Thanks," he said, handing back the keyboard. "How long has R and R been around?"

"Oh, about fifteen years." That explained Nobby Kabel's absence. He was dead before the club had been founded.

Whilst he had been scanning the list she had been sorting through an introductory package of forms. "I'll need your ID card or passport," she said.

"Maybe I could fill all that out at home?"

She looked him full in the face again. He felt bad. "No. I can't let you have any of this material."

"Oh?"

"No. It's club property." She thought for a moment.

He felt like a rat. "I'd really like to think about this."

For a second he thought she was going to lose her temper. She placed her hands firmly on the forms. He hoped his rotten feeling was working for him. He felt beaten and embarrassed. "If I was younger I'd ask you out to dinner." She blushed. Had he overstepped the mark? It was the first expression he'd seen other than breezy joy. "As a way of thanking you for the list."

She chuckled. "You're sweet."

"Thanks," he smiled, suppressing the urge to kiss her on the cheek. He backed off and headed for the door.

"See you soon," she said.

"Yes," he said half-turning for another look at her. She was again advertising her dentist's excellent work.

18:47

Although it was not dark, the six men arrived at the building site each carrying a torch. They were early. Everything was in place. The observers signalled one right-winger was already in the enclosure. The six had learnt the torch signal Basha had agreed with the observers should they require reinforcements.

They heaved back the standing partition of wire netting that served as an entrance for the workmen. The rest of the site was bounded by fixed netting approximately three metres high. Ponytail and another did not enter with them. They ran the wire-meshed boundary of the site and clawed their way over the top, so as to approach from the rear.

Those at the hospital car park made up the meeting party. Those, except Hasan, of course. Basha expressed his reservations about Nazim to Cenk. Cenk, himself, was flattered and puzzled that Basha didn't have reservations about him should it come to a fight. This was his first inkling that Basha saw him as a replacement for Hasan. He said he liked Cenk. He knew Nazim was his friend, but he was brash, perhaps only a part-time thinker. Whereas Cenk had a good head. He had potential.

Cenk followed Basha through the concrete shell of a building. There were no fixtures or fittings. They emerged onto a large space that would presumably become an enclosed courtyard.

A large man with short blond hair stood alone. Cenk decided he was the man with the hammer.

Basha moved to meet him.

"You ninja boys haven't got round to climbing a fence quietly," said Karsten when the two men stopped just beyond striking distance from one another. "I said six. Hopefully there are only two of yours behind me."

Basha gave a sly smile and nodded.

"And where are your five losers?"

"I'm alone."

"Sure," said Basha, glancing about.

"There will be no violence today," said Karsten.

"And Bilal – the man whose hands you broke?"

"Ah, yes." Karsten remained impassive. "That was an answer to our broken bones."

"We took casualties too."

"True. But we took more. And you did look good with all that fancy Kungy Fuey stuff."

Cenk sensed the stalemate. He held his breath in readiness for action. If there was to be violence it would occur now. The breaking of Bilal's hands had been a cruel and unnecessary act and if not Basha then certainly Ponytail might seek revenge.

Basha spoke and the tension eased.

"You want to scrap because of what happened on Saturday?"

"Partly. You've gained a reputation pretty quickly. Your gang's known. You could even say, famous. The *Schwarzer Freitag*. You need reminding of your place."

"And make a name for yourselves by thrashing us?"

Karsten was amused, but then his mood changed and he spoke contemptuously as if Basha had missed an obvious point. "No name, *Kanake* (wop). We need no name. You need teaching. That's all. We crush you."

Basha remained cool. "How?"

Cenk looked on incredulously. It was as if the two men were arranging a football match. He had managed to get off work this evening, but Friday was always busy at the restaurant.

"Fifty of yours against fifty of ours. Small weapons, but mainly hand to hand."

"Fifty?"

"Why not? There are more of you than us in this city."

"Okay fifty," said Basha.

"It'll be foolish with less."

"How do I know you won't be more?"

"The same way I know that you won't."

"What's that?"

"Respect."

"Respect," said Basha slowly.

"You Turks have done Germany a service. We're grateful. But the rebuilding is over. Now it is time to leave. It's our country—"

"I've heard this shit before. Where's the respect?"

"We respect you more than the Poles or Rumanians, Gypsies, homosexuals. You have honour and pride. I know you'll turn up with the right number. I know you'll respect the rules. We will fight on street terms. Here, on mutual ground."

The two men confirmed the time of the fight and agreed to honour the rules.

"I was here first, so I'll leave first," said Karsten.

Basha nodded and glanced at his group. Ponytail had slipped away.

Karsten moved slowly through the four that stood in front of him.

When they were out of earshot Nazim glossed over his fear by asking Basha in a whisper whether they should attack.

"We'll get our chance on Friday."

19:17

321

"Hallo stranger," said Robert. Craig had moved all his stuff over to Carina's place. They agreed that he hadn't moved in, but it seemed silly traipsing back and forth between flats.

"Don't be like that. Not now."

"Getting hounded too much?"

"Something like that."

"It's a real shame you made an Outright Sale Agreement. I don't mean because of the money. I mean because you could have controlled what was published. Huh, we could have translated it." Thankfully the translations had been good and although specific pieces had been chosen and gave his writing a darker tone, Craig could not say that he had been misinterpreted.

"Spilt milk."

"Yeah. I've got some news. You remember two groups claimed to have rescued Faruk. Well, a lad in one of them came back. He remembered he was wearing a different jacket. There'll be a picture of them receiving their reward from Faruk in tomorrow's paper."

19:25

Karsten strode like a god. And the weapon in his pocket could strike them down as surely as a bolt of lightning.

He smiled to himself when he noticed the three bursts of light. The Turks had reinforcements within striking distance. The thought of them realising that he was alone gave him an extra kick. Maybe they'd also be fooled into thinking Friday would be a fair fight.

He got on his bike and drove to the allotment. Jutta would have to wait. The gang were well into the four crates of beer. They became less rowdy when he called them together. He told them what he'd arranged. "There'll be at least a hundred of them. This is your chance for payback."

"Didn't you say fifty?" said Wolfram.

"Yes. But I expect they'll play by our rules."

"I didn't know we had any rules."

"We haven't."

19:35

When Dannaks left R&R a taxi pulled up in front of the door and a slick business-type in his twenties got out.

Dannaks held the front passenger door open: "Are you free?"

"Not any more. Get in." Dannaks glanced around. Looking over his shoulder had become second nature. He climbed in and the

322

driver set the meter. "Where to, chief?"

Dannaks opened his wallet and showed the man a slip of paper.

"You could walk that."

"I've done my walking for today. Anyway I'll not be stopping for long. You can wait and take me home."

"Okay, chief."

Dannaks looked at the note. He was only just round the corner from Romulus and Remus. Round the corner. His name had not been on the list. There were too many questions. And there was only one person who could answer them.

"That was one hundred and thirteen, wasn't it?" They were driving at a crawl in deepest suburbia: pristine chocolate box terraced houses, small and compact with fenceless front gardens giving the impression of more space. Dannaks consulted the paper. The driver switched on the overhead light.

"Yes," he said, looking up and recognising a figure well ahead of them opening the door of a car. "That's him."

"What?"

"That man getting into the Opel. Can you drive a little faster?"

"A little. This is a thirty kilometre an hour zone." The taxi accelerated to 35 kilometres per hour and Dannaks could see that they were not going to catch him.

The Opel left the curb and moved away.

He looked at the meter and decided on an upper limit of twenty euros. Twelve to go.

"Follow him."

"It's your money."

He took a sideways glance at one hundred and thirteen. The terraces had given way to large detached houses. Regardless of his rank this one looked beyond a policeman's salary.

A few minutes later they were on the main road, but two cars separated them from the Opel.

The Opel turned right at a set of traffic lights that changed to amber. Dannaks watched the car disappear as they came to a halt behind the two vehicles in front of them.

"What now?"

Dannaks didn't answer. The meter showed almost sixteen euros. "Go right. If we don't see him, you can take me home." The lights eventually changed and the two preceding vehicles went straight on.

"Where are we?" Dannaks asked, noting the parked cars and sudden lack of buildings on one side of the road.

"Bramfeld Lake."

As he answered Dannaks spotted the Opel. "Pull over."

The driver glanced at his rear-view mirror, pulled to the parked cars and flicked on his hazard warning lights. He switched on the overhead light and made to stop the meter.

"Wait," said Dannaks. "With luck I'll only be a minute or two. You can wait can't you?"

"I can wait, but I'll still have to charge for this ride." He pressed the button on the meter. "That'll be sixteen eighty."

"Eighteen."

"Thanks. Receipt?"

"Yes." If he couldn't use it someone else might.

"I'll stop up ahead for five."

"Okay."

Dannaks got out and followed the pavement onto the path. The bushes opened up onto the lake. The wind was spitefully cold here and he held the lapels of his jacket closed. It wasn't dark, but the shadows were long and starting to merge. There were other hardy souls about. Even the wayward sounds of children playing at this late hour could be heard. But the wind drowned all speech.

The path appeared to go round the lake and Dannaks had to choose a direction.

Was this what Detlef did? Go for lonely contemplative walks?

He went right, breaking into a mild jog, as much to keep warm as to catch Detlef. His body protested with a salvo of pain in his left side. Seconds later the pain became unbearable. He couldn't even walk fast. His pace slowed until he stopped. He was out of breath, racked with varying degrees of pain. He turned round and went back. He passed the path leading back to the main road and continued on in the other direction.

Up ahead was a bench with two figures sitting on it. He decided that this would be his turning back point. With luck the taxi driver was still waiting. The wind rushed again. In its wake was a calm that let voices be heard. Dannaks stopped and scrutinised the figures on the bench. The one nearest him was Detlef. But something held Dannaks back. He stared past Detlef at his companion. His eyes widened and he moved to his left, out of their field of vision, to get a better look. There was no doubt. Detlef's companion was Rüdiger Krohn.

"Back in the land of reason," said Uwe not rising from his desk or greeting him. Dannaks nodded to other colleagues who bothered to acknowledge him. "You're early."

Seeing Detlef with Rüdiger Krohn had completely thrown him. All Dannaks could do was go back to the road. He barely heard the taxi driver say that another thirty seconds and he would have gone. Then he was alone in his flat, not remembering paying the driver or entering the building. Only after going to the toilet and catching his expression in the mirror did he emerge from his disorientation. Symbolically he splashed cold water over his face. Then he began to organise his thoughts. What could such a link mean? Detlef and Rüdiger. Were they just friends? Was it a set-up? He wasn't Detlef's favourite detective. Could it be that Detlef and Rüdiger had teamed up to get him?

Needing to bounce his thoughts against another mind, he picked up the telephone and called Uwe. There was no answer for ten rings, the number at which Dannaks normally gave up, but he persisted. At nineteen Uwe answered.

"Yes." That one word was loaded with anger. Dannaks hesitated; he couldn't simply hang-up. He realised that it had turned eleven-thirty. He hadn't checked. The two whiskies in the flat hadn't helped his judgement.

"Dannaks," he announced. "Is it a bad time?"

Uwe was silent. Was he counting to ten? "You're the master of understatement."

"Sorry."

There was a loud sigh.

"I wouldn't call unless it was important."

"If it's work, it's not important. Get a life, Dannaks." In the background a female voice spoke and Uwe sighed. "Sorry, look–"

"No, I'm sorry. I wasn't thinking. Can we meet tomorrow? For lunch, say?"

"Yes. Let's do that."

Dannaks hadn't slept well. He couldn't help feeling he was being set up. He thought he had been hunting Krohn. The opposite was true. He'd been the prey all along. Why hadn't he seen it? He had never been at the top of Detlef's favourite persons' list. Yet what had he done to incriminate himself? It was all so bizarre. Krohn knew he would go after him, so he couldn't be the mysterious sponsor. Then someone else wanting to get Krohn and Detlef was tipping him off. How did they get hold of Krohn's letter of invitation? Unless it was someone from R&R. The only name that could fit was Wilhelm Fischer. But as acting police vice president he had the resources to launch a properly manned, albeit covert, operation. Then why Dannaks, alone?

To Uwe's remark about being early – just after half past eleven was early for lunch – Dannaks could have replied that they had not set a time. However, he wanted his friend's allegiance.

They chose to take the stairs to the underground garage.

"Has Annelore forgiven me for last night's intrusion?" He'd interrupted either a love scene or an argument.

"The question is whether I've forgiven you." A love-scene, then.

"And?"

"I haven't decided, yet."

"It depends on what I have to say?"

They walked the rest of the way in silence.

Dannaks yawned and flinched. Yawning hurt.

Uwe shifted the car into gear and pulled out of his slot. As they headed for the exit he spoke. "Chinese or Asian?"

"Chinese."

"Are you back at work?"

"No," he said, adjusting himself in his seat to dull an ache.

"You want to start talking now?"

"Let's get some food down our necks first."

Dannaks almost regretted asking Uwe to meet him. Was Uwe interested? Then who else could Dannaks tell? Frank? Reinhart? Were Uwe and he drawing apart? Not working together could cool their friendship, but surely not so soon.

They drove over a large metal plate, part of some road works, and the jolt sent a sharp pain up his left side.

Shortly thereafter Uwe parked the car and Dannaks had trouble getting out and walking.

"You're still in a state," said Uwe.

Dannaks smiled wearily.

The Chinese restaurant was familiar to them. A midday menu offered six set meals.

After ordering, Dannaks asked Uwe about the department and current cases. Uwe clipped his answers to the minimum. He was more interested in what Dannaks had to say. Perversely Dannaks avoided the main reason for the meeting and spoke of Stefan. During this time the hot and sour soups arrived. They'd barely finished slurping when the waiter began arranging the table for the hot plates. The various dishes arrived and they were left to help themselves. Only then did Dannaks speak about the R&R invitation and going to the club. He drew out seeing Detlef with Rüdiger.

Uwe stopped eating, his laden spoon poised mid-air. He put it down and sat back. Still staring in disbelief he wiped his mouth with his napkin. They stared at each other and Dannaks nodded away any vestiges of disbelief. Uwe picked up his shandy and Dannaks tipped some more sparkling water into his own glass.

"Well..." Uwe began, but didn't get any further.

"That's what I thought."

"You've got me there. I don't know what to say."

"How about: You're being set up?"

"Do you believe that?"

"Not really. It's too bizarre." Dannaks went over all his thoughts and the more he said the more he came to realise that Uwe couldn't help him. "The funny thing is, one minute later, I would have missed Detlef, and one minute earlier I would never have known about Krohn."

He snapped open his fortune cookie. Did anybody eat these things? He read the strip of paper. It was in English. "Donkey's lips do not fit onto a horse's mouth."

"Mine is no better: Play a harp before a cow," he translated. In German it also made no sense.

Dannaks said he would ask his colleague who was an English expert. Reinhart would be pleased. But Dannaks felt that these Chinese sayings had not fared well in their English translation either.

"I'm sorry," said Uwe, when they were back in his car, "maybe you're right about Detlef and Krohn setting you up. But that would make me as paranoid as you. It's over my head."

Dannaks nodded. He was on his own. He had known that sooner or later he would have to go it alone. But the circumstances were out of his control. Simply put, he was out of his depth.

Perversely he was thinking about his fortune cookie. Was he

looking at it all wrong? He needed to step back and get some perspective on the thing. That's why he'd gone to Uwe. He had hoped Uwe's distance would enable him to see the bigger picture. Dannaks was too close. He was in the thick of it and didn't know how to step back.

When they got out of the car at the underground car park of the *Polizeistern* Dannaks spoke to Uwe over the bonnet as he locked up. "And have you forgiven me for calling?"

Uwe smiled, but didn't answer.

17:32

The room was Spartan. Everything was stylised but radiated little warmth. The furnishings were modern and hard. The furniture was done in a black satin finish with chrome and brushed steel. A black leather settee stood behind a black coffee table with cylindrical chrome pipes for legs. It stood upon a black oval rug with a large scarlet triangle. Yet, Ponytail's flat was frugal. No sentimentality; no family photographs. The pictures on the walls were abstract and enigmatic. They were Japanese or Chinese prints with simple lines and pastel suggestions of colour.

The only hint that the man was human was an English paperback on the coffee table. It was Ernest Hemingway's: *For Whom the Bell Tolls*. Rather than make him human, the presence of the book only served to make him more of a mystery.

Cenk and Murat had come from the building site. From their rooftop vantage point they could see that the fight could be nothing other than a free-for-all. There seemed to be too many materials to hand: sand and stones, tubing and metal rods.

"How many have we got?" Cenk asked.

"Twenty-seven, give or take."

"It's not enough."

"I know. I'm hoping seven or eight will come from Berlin."

"We need more than fifty," said Murat, surveying the half finished buildings through the binoculars. "*Sol Birlik* thinks they might be able to dig out more."

"*Sol Birlik*?" Cenk didn't know what to think. True, they needed every man they could get, but was calling in left wing extremists the right thing? Everything was moving too fast. And moving over their heads.

Nevertheless the location of the fight was a closely guarded secret. Those at the meeting with the right-wing leader had agreed not to disclose it to anyone, not even other *Schwarzer Freitag* members.

"Problem?"

"No." Cenk didn't want to think about it. "If they arrive before us they could hide an army in there."

"They could ambush us before we arrive. There are plenty of places on the way."

They were silent for a time.

On the way to the site that afternoon Cenk had asked Murat why he had chosen him for company. Why not Ponytail, for instance?

"I said we'd see him afterwards. He wants to talk to us."

"How did you meet him?" It was a question Cenk had longed to ask.

"I saw him sparring. He was a guest at our club. He was magnificent. I had to recruit him." Murat was silent for a tick. "He's not really interested in our cause. He's got other interests. The big boys call on him now and then." By 'big boys' Cenk knew he meant professional criminals. To his disappointment Murat didn't expand upon the statement. "But you, you have potential." He turned to Cenk. "You could be a leader, *Lan*. I know Hasan is your friend and he is a leader." He waited a moment. "But he wasn't our kind of leader. He's the politician type. Do you know what I mean?"

Cenk nodded, not sure what to make of Murat's candidness. And as to his own leadership potential he didn't know whether to feel flattered. Did Murat believe what he was saying or was it part of a ploy to win him over?

"Surprised eh?" said Murat.

"About what?"

"You thought I was a mindless bone-crusher."

"I didn't."

Murat had told everyone that there was no point in patrolling. The right-wingers were not going to pull anything before Friday. Nobody pointed out that another gang could attack before then.

Ponytail had opened his flat door and turned his back on them. He went down a corridor and they followed. When they were in the lounge he greeted them. Then he said he wanted to finish up. He stepped up onto the coffee table and grabbed a chrome bar that was attached to the ceiling like a strip light. Murat and Cenk stood by limply. He shuffled his hands to the leather straps at either end of the bar. He unwound them, letting wooden rings hang. Then he grasped them and hung, his feet only six centimetres from the floor. He began to lift himself, the straps creaking under the strain. He held a crucified position for at least a minute, before pulling himself higher. Then he hung from the bar for a moment to recover. Ponytail hooked his feet upon the bar and hung like a trapeze artist. He winked at them before doing sit-ups.

And now they sat in his lounge, waiting for him to finish his shower.

"Nice flat," said Murat.

Cenk smiled, but couldn't agree. It certainly made Murat's place look juvenile. As if he could read Cenk's thoughts: "Do you like my posters?"

"Er, yes," said Cenk. Rambo and Bruce Lee had looked out from the walls of his flat.

"You can have them." Another tentacle of friendship.

"Thanks," he said a moment too late. He saw them in his mind's eye and began giving them away to Nazim.

The swish of the shower continued.

"I'll tell you something," Murat whispered, leaning towards Cenk, forcing Cenk to lean towards him. "I think he's losing control."

Almost on cue the shower was extinguished. Murat smiled. Cenk tried to make sense of the sounds coming from the bathroom. Why couldn't he shower later? He knew they were coming.

The door opened and he strode into the room. He was stark naked and Cenk could only stare before averting his eyes. He was horrified. The man reminded him of an insect. Without fat his skin was like parchment stretched over his muscles the very texture of which was visible. Cenk had never seen anything like him. Murat was stocky, chunky by comparison.

"Okay?" he asked.

"Yes," they said and Ponytail walked on.

Murat turned and, although Cenk had decided to remain still, he too turned and watched Ponytail go into his bedroom. When he opened the door, Cenk caught a glimpse of what looked to be a shrine at a dressing table. Murat's position on the sofa meant that he would not have seen it. Ponytail pushed the door behind him and it came to a standstill a centimetre ajar.

They turned back and looked at each other. Neither spoke, but Murat gave him a lopsided grin. They heard the opening of drawers.

Ponytail returned in what looked to be black silk pyjamas. The trousers were baggy and gossamer with a piece of white cord for a belt. His top was equally light, a V-neck T-shirt affair. No buttons, zips, frills or fuss.

"It's like a morgue in here," he said smiling.

It was the first time Cenk had seen him smile. And it didn't fit. He looked even more sinister. His thin mouth locked, curving at the ends and the whites of his eyes disappeared. Cenk found something dead and fish-like in his fixed grimace and the darkening of his eyes.

He went over to his sleek Bang and Olufsen stereo and pressed some buttons.

"You like Billie Holiday?"

He turned to them.

Cenk froze.

"I haven't heard much of her," said Murat.

Cenk thought of joking that he thought she was a tennis player. "I, er, saw the film."

"Ah, they didn't play the gutsy stuff." Despite this Ponytail appeared pleased. "Listen to this." He turned back to the stereo and skipped tracks.

Ponytail stood and closed his eyes. Cenk locked onto the pattern of the bowl on the table. He didn't look at Murat.

The room was filled with a soaring trumpet and a piano. Cenk was reminded of a B-movie set in South America. The trumpet died and the piano continued; each key was pressed individually as if the player was tuning up. Then she sang. Her voice was low and measured. She sang each word independently, slow and affected, so that she was almost talking. And the piano continued, reduced to punctuating her words. The trumpet returned only to give out to the piano and her words again. And her voice was higher, crying rather than singing.

Whatever it was, was mercifully short. Cenk caught only a few words. His English wasn't so good. Trees, blood, leaves, eyes. Even if he didn't understand what she was singing, tragedy was obvious. He didn't really want to know more. Something so torturous could not be enjoyed. He didn't know what to say.

Ponytail switched over to the radio, but turned down the

volume to the threshold of hearing. He turned. "It's about the American deep south, what the Ku Klux Klan did." His mouth twisted into a resemblance of a smile.

He scooped a handful of sunflower seeds from the bowl on the coffee table and put his hand to his mouth. They listened to him masticate.

"The blacks should have ganged up. Like we're doing now," he said.

Murat nodded.

"You know, most of the Turks have lost their pride," said Ponytail. "They've been sweeping up after the Germans for so long they've lost their honour too. Most of them are just paid slaves. Part of a service class. Tending to an underclass." Cenk had never heard him talk so much. Nonetheless his words service class and underclass seemed borrowed. "That's why the Schwarzer Freitag is important." He looked at Cenk. "Hasan was right about one thing. We can't afford to become thugs like those skinheads. We must be better than them. And do you know how we can be better than them?" Cenk shook his head. "By regaining our honour. We must be warriors, not thugs. We must be samurai."

"Right," said Murat.

"I'm talking real honour."

Murat nodded. Cenk was confused.

"The Schwarzer Freitag must instil fear and pride. Not everybody can join. We need an initiation. A code of honour. It's too late for this Friday. But afterwards we have to get organised. We have to have ranks."

"Like an army?" Cenk regretted his words the second they were out.

"No. Much more." Ponytail was becoming animated. "Soldiers like samurai. Discipline and all. But like a samurai capable of the ultimate sacrifice in the name of honour. Do you understand?"

"Yes." Murat nodded approvingly.

Cenk was unsure.

19:22

On the train Dannaks had scoured the papers for something more on Stefan's murder, but there had only been a reheating of stories of the *Henker's* previous victims.

Faruk was featured in one paper. He was photographed presenting an oversized cheque to a youth. He looked either wary, frightened or embarrassed; Dannaks couldn't tell. Whatever it was, he certainly wasn't comfortable.

Lunch with Uwe had taken its toll. He was so preoccupied with getting home he forgot to buy another light bulb. By the time he put the key in his flat door just after two he was exhausted.

As he bent to take off his shoes in the semi-darkness, a spasm of pain crumpled him. Grunting he pulled himself up. His shoes were no longer orderly lined but he couldn't be bothered righting them and disgustedly threw the ones he had been wearing amongst them.

Despite medication he uncorked a bottle of Merlot and poured himself a good measure. In the lounge he opened the window. The noise of traffic filled the room yet it remained airless and stuffy. He stood at the window looking over the lake reflecting the white, red and neon, moving, winking, shimmering and showing no signs of settling.

By the time he got to work a light sheen covered his skin and he felt wrecked. Although his face wasn't badly bruised – Redface's punch was fading – he caught some odd looks on the train. And he'd been the one looking from face to face, wondering whether he was being followed.

Dannaks wasn't prepared for Frank in the corridor after negotiating the stairs.

"What are you doing here?"

"That's a nice greeting, Frank."

"You still look a mess. You're supposed to be recuperating."

"Is it let's-not-be-nice-to-Dannaks-day today?"

"I'm trying to be nice. Get home. You're on sick leave."

"I'd rather stay."

"Okay. I already heard you were at the presidium yesterday. But you're getting nothing other than desk duty." Dannaks nodded. "Get properly landed and be in my office in ten minutes. I'll give you something to do. Oh and Dannaks, is the footwear a new fashion?"

Frank was gone before Dannaks could react. He looked down and saw that his left foot sported a brown shoe, his right a black one. He'd put his shoes on in his darkened hallway.

He delicately walked into Schuppenhauer and Wulff's room.

"We weren't expecting you," said Wulff, who was placing his motorbike helmet and gauntlets on the windowsill.

"You ought to get home," said Schuppenhauer, seated at his desk.

"I prefer being here." He held his right hand out to Schuppenhauer. "Thanks, again."

"Sure," he said, rising to save Dannaks moving. "I'm just sorry I didn't catch one of them. They knocked me over getting away. But then I was more worried about you."

Reinhart was at his desk mumbling to himself, reading a notebook that he snapped shut when Dannaks came in. "Morning," they said simultaneously. Dannaks squirmed out of his jacket, trying to hide his hurt.

"I wasn't expecting you today."

Dannaks didn't have an answer. He unlocked his desk drawer and took out his service weapon. He pulled it out of its hip-holster and checked the clip.

Reinhart left the room and he knew he had gone to talk to Frank, although he couldn't hear what they were saying. He returned with a smug look on his face, but he didn't say anything.

A few minutes later Dannaks was waiting for Frank to finish a telephone conversation.

"Reinhart was just here. He thought you might like to be involved with investigating Stefan's murder." Dannaks brightened. "Don't get over-excited. I'm sure it's fairly banal. Are you up to it?"

Reinhart was fussing with the flowers in the vase on his desk when Dannaks returned. He swung round and Dannaks thanked him.

09:23

"There's word on the street of a fight," said Frank. Dannaks had briefly run over his ordeal and the team had reported on their current tasks. "An organised clash between Turks and skinheads."

"Bloody stupid," said Schuppenhauer.

Reinhart appeared not to be listening.

"A throw off from Saturday?" asked Dannaks.

"I don't know. It wouldn't surprise me." Frank looked at his notes. "The Schwarzer Freitag and 211ers are associated with this information. But sources believe it's bigger than them."

"Why not let them tear each other up?" said Reinhart.

"Because we're not talking about a backstreet brawl between twenty or so youths. This is big. Perhaps in the hundreds."

"Shit on toast."

Dannaks smiled as much at Frank's statement as Reinhart's reaction.

Frank addressed Reinhart. "What has Homicide for you today?"

"Reupke–" he looked at Dannaks and interjected: "from Homicide – called to say he wants us to re-interview some British reporter, who wrote about Stefan a few days."

"When?"

"Two o'clock."

"Okay. Dannaks will go with you."

"I'll bring him up to speed."

Dannaks filled the short silence. "I saw that they found Faruk's rescuers. Have they been interviewed?"

"I interviewed them," said Wulff. "They said they wouldn't recognise Faruk's attackers. They couldn't even describe their

336

clothing. Except for the textbook stuff. White-laced paratrooper boots. They just saw the backs of them and didn't catch up."

"No one stopped to help Faruk?"

"No. When they got back Faruk was gone."

Silence consumed them again.

Frank demonstratively picked up his list and allotted Schuppenhauer and Wulff further tasks. When he finished he asked Dannaks to stay behind.

"I've a meeting with Cemal Atasoy and other community leaders at five today. I'd like you to come along. Remember, I wanted you to meet them last week. Do you think you're up to it?"

"Yes." Dannaks made a note.

12:58

The café was functional and empty. Outside it had not looked uninviting. The attractively low prices should have warned them. Inside it was obvious that the windows needed a clean. It was hard to tell whether the grime on the glass was on the inside or outside. Probably both, thought Dannaks. Three tall tables and a long shelf running the length of a wall had been resurfaced beyond repair. A number of bar stools, the yellow sponge of which bulged out of splits in the plastic seams, rescued one from the sticky linoleum. This was not a place for indulging.

The two detectives had viewed the food in dismay. Hunger drove them to purchase baguettes that looked relatively fresh and least likely to carry salmonella.

They hadn't seen anything else and thoughts of going elsewhere were curtailed by the fact that they weren't far from the reporter's flat.

Reinhart carried two coffees to Dannaks who'd taken their chosen baguettes and positioned himself on a stool at the shelf nearest the window.

Their drinks were in thick, worn cups chipped at the edges. The liquid resembled real coffee only in that it was hot and wet. Specks of black powder floated on top and ringed the rim.

The man serving them looked as if he'd stepped off the set of some zombie film. The ravaged skin of his face, his dark panda eyes, sunken and weary, the stubble peppering his cheeks and chin and his wiry unruly hair rendered any make-up artist redundant.

Dannaks felt wretched. He knew he ate unhealthily, but this was the pits. The baguettes were like chewing gum. This was

337

standard police fare. For many the snack bar was the only choice. Not only were they cheap, but also quick. Of course nutrition was never mentioned. For bachelors like Dannaks who didn't really cook this was dangerous. Where they currently found themselves was beyond gallows humour joking.

For a while they ate silently. Then Reinhart began without prompting.

"Stefan was killed at Kennedy Bridge. I'm sure you know it." Dannaks nodded. Running parallel to Lombards Bridge that marked the inner Alster, the Kennedy Bridge about fifty metres away marked the outer Alster. The bridge supported four lanes of traffic, two lanes each way. "The traffic comes in waves. What you might not know is that the traffic light configuration of the roads is such that there's a twenty-five second lull on the bridge on the side of the road Stefan was killed. At that time of day traffic would have been light. There'd have been no traffic stopped on the bridge itself. We should have more witnesses, even if it's a bit of a racetrack."

He stopped to tear off a piece of rubber baguette with his teeth, looking like a lion pulling on sinews. He chewed longer than he would have liked, his mastication becoming more pronounced and deliberate towards the end.

"The best witnesses are the motorists who have come forward. We're hoping for more. Of course what they saw are only drive-bys. But the succession means that we can roughly piece things together. There were some pedestrians and some people sailing but they were too far away. We also have the testimony of those on the tourist barge. Stefan's earlier movements before arriving at the bridge have been filled in by his friends."

Dannaks rolled his jaw, which ached from chewing.

"The drivers saw Stefan leaning against the railings. They also saw a biker, in full leathers and helmet, not far from him. Some say they also saw a large dark bike. We've got no reliable description. No distinguishing patterns on his outfit, no licence plate for the bike. Not even the type of bike."

Reinhart paused to use a finger to make a space on the rim of the cup for his lips. Dannaks had used a teaspoon to idly skim off the floating specks. He awaited his colleague's reaction to the taste. The look of horror satisfied him.

After placing his cup back on its saucer he continued.

"The biker – our killer – had some rope at the railings. Yellow, standard stuff you can get at any retailer. Forensics is not hopeful. One driver thought he was setting up a bungee-jump or a climb. Another thought he was putting together some kind of protest banner. Anyhow, he set it up, waited for the next lull and went for Stefan. We don't know exactly what he did. Witnesses say he kicked or hit him with something. They all agreed it was a blow to the head. Once down he dragged him to the rope, tied his wrists behind his back with one of those plastic cable binders, wrote on his head with an indelible felt-tip marker, put the noose around his neck and chucked him off the bridge."

"What did he write?"

The coyness and dramatic pause irritated Dannaks.

"SF."

"SF?"

"Yes."

"What's it mean?"

"You tell me. Nobody knows. The same was found on Jensen's forehead."

"*Schwarzer Freitag?*"

"They don't think so. The timing is wrong. It's possible, though."

"Wasn't there any fruit?"

"Yes, sorry. He rammed a banana down his throat." Reinhart tackled his baguette again.

"The fall should have broken his neck," he continued. "But he hit a tourist barge."

"It contrasts the Jensen killing."

Reinhart nodded. When he'd swallowed, almost painfully, he said: "Efficient and expedient." He took a sip of ersatz coffee.

"He brought his own stuff too."

"Yes. The rope and cable binder. It's the rehearsed precision that impresses me. We're talking broad daylight and twenty-five seconds or less. He incapacitates his victim, ties his hands, marks his forehead, attaches the noose, rams a banana down his throat, lifts and drops him over the railings. All in twenty-five seconds."

They ate in silence.

"The letters SF weren't anywhere at the first hanging."

"Not that I am aware of."

"All the more reason to believe that it was a chance killing."

Reinhart nodded uncertainly.

"People knew about the fruit, but Homicide was trying to keep the letters out of the press. They still are. But there were a lot of bystanders later. And a lot of them had handies. To some extent Stefan's hair hid the letters. But it's just a matter of time before it gets out."

A youth, equally ragged looking, appeared out of nowhere with a broom and began sweeping the far end of the room. Dannaks thought by the way he shuffled he was using the broom more as a crutch. All that was missing was the playing of Michael Jackson's Thriller.

In disgust Reinhart shoved his plate with the half-eaten baguette. Dannaks had persevered and almost finished his. But he too had given up.

"One question," said Dannaks, knowing it was time to leave. "Why was he on the bridge at that time?"

"His friends say he had an interview that he was keeping to himself. They were annoyed that they had not been invited. And Stefan wanted to go alone. All forms of media have been contacted: television, radio, papers... Nobody had arranged to interview him."

"The lure of fame brought him there."

"Yes."

"Come on, let's get out of here. Before more of the owner's relatives rise out of the floor."

13:11

Carina had time to return to the flat for an extended lunch break. She brought the papers with her.

His successful television defence, and the fact that Stefan's parents had dropped their case against him, had rejuvenated his enthusiasm to write. The dead boy's parents had been all but discredited by the majority of the media. Not only had they delved into Stefan's past showing the validity of Craig's article, they also disclosed Stefan's father's right-wing affiliations. If that wasn't enough, the fact that Stefan had been a drug-pusher didn't help. Craig knew that as long as he kept his head there was a good chance that he would come out unscathed, if not on top.

They were lying on the bed, cooling. The bedding, like their clothes, was discarded, thrown to the floor in the conflagration of passion.

"I have got to go," Carina said, making no attempt to move.

340

"Ah, the police won't be here for another three quarters of an hour." Although things were settling he had agreed to meet the police for a second interview at two.

"You have to finish your second article."

"Yes," he said wearily. The British features editor had spoken to him. His first article had met with mild interest, generating a few letters, but nothing of worth. Saturday's riot had been internationally reported. He wanted Craig to hype the remaining articles with references to the rioting, Stefan's death and the serial killer.

Craig felt he was walking a veritable tightrope, for he suspected the police were again going to ask him to tone things down.

Half an hour later he was alone in the flat in front of his laptop. He worked for the best part of an hour. Then he caught the early afternoon news. In the short regional programme there was coverage of Stefan's funeral.

A blustering, red-faced Volker Herbst made a predictable speech, touching on the boy's innocence, the press's smear campaign and police apathy. The country needed a strong – Right – hand to bring everyone into line. The charge of incitement against him was losing steam simply through lack of proof.

Craig sympathised with Stefan's parents. But the attendees shed such an ambiguous light on the funeral that his overall feeling was one of detachment.

Thankfully the procession and service passed without incident.

13:57

"It's what we call a fresh eyes interview," said Dannaks. "Unfortunately, we'll probably ask a lot of questions you were asked last time."

Craig nodded.

"You can help us in a number of ways," said Dannaks. "Firstly, have you thought of anybody who might have done this? Perhaps you interviewed somebody..."

Craig shook his head.

The three of them were seated at a dining table in the lounge. Dannaks was glad they were at the dining table. If he'd sunk into the sofa he would have needed help getting up. This wasn't the lad's apartment. The feminine touch was obvious in the carefully chosen

341

ornaments; the furniture was aesthetic rather than practical. The give-away was that his name wasn't on the door.

"What do the letters S and F mean to you?"

Dannaks put the man in his late twenties, early thirties. There was something refined about him. He didn't slouch and seemed to have his wits about him. Even his casual attire was smart. His overall demeanour spoke of a good education. Dannaks's shabby dress made him feel inferior and although he always put it down to not caring, he realised that he could have problems with his self-worth.

He answered after a while. "Other than the *Schwarzer Freitag* nothing."

"Are you sure?"

Again he pondered.

"Yes."

"Then I want you to tell us all you know about the *Schwarzer Freitag*. You were the first person, as far as we can gather, to mention them. Please bear in mind that this is in connection with a murder investigation."

Dannaks glanced at Reinhart who was poised over his notebook. His face was cast in stone. They had agreed that if the Englishman's German was poor, Reinhart would interview him in English. The bizarre thought that he had brought the wrong notebook shot through his mind. Date, time, place. "When the interviewee was asked about his whereabouts on the night in question, he answered: To be or not to be, that is the question."

"There's not a lot I can tell you," Craig said. He spoke precisely, relating how he had heard of them and approached Murat on Saturday. "As far as I can tell, they are the Turkish answer to neo-Nazis."

"Ready?"

"Ready to take on the skinheads."

Dannaks wanted to say that he should tell him something new. The Left fighting the Right, the Right fighting the Left; it was always the same. And whichever way it was cut the police were in the middle. They were there to be accused by the Left of being heavy-handed or by the Right of letting the underbelly of society get out of hand. And the citizen who sat on the fence didn't think much better of them. They were treated more like the LA cop than the British Bobby. The public had a short memory too. With a Hamburg crime statistic of one thousand victims a day you would think the police would at least be respected if not liked. "Would you recognise any of them if I showed you some photographs?"

Craig huffed. "Maybe." Again a silence grew. "What's all this to do with Stefan's death? I thought that was what you wanted to talk to me about."

Dannaks smiled. "Probably nothing." He picked up the brown envelope he'd placed on the table. "I'd like you to look at these," he said, pulling out a wad of large black and white photographs. They were shots from Saturday's march and rioting.

Craig pointed out Murat and Ponytail. "What happened to Stefan and the others?" he asked as he handed back the photographs. "The papers weren't too explicit."

Dannaks answered with silence. He didn't want to alienate him, but his Che Guevara T-shirt spoke volumes about his leanings. He probably thought the police were heavy-handed, perhaps blind in the right-eye. "I read your German article and your English one. I didn't have time to read it all, I'm afraid. My English is a bit rusty. *Kommissar* Keller, here, helped me out. I noted that it is to be one of a series."

"Yes."

Dannaks sensed his guardedness, but there was no other way to approach it. "Our reporters have linked your English article with Stefan. It's more substantial than the German piece you did. Parts of it have appeared in the German press. We can't stop that. You've said that your article is a series. Would it be possible for you to tone down your next one? It could help us defuse the situation. I'm not telling you what to write, I'm just asking you to carefully consider what you put on paper."

"You want me to play it down?"

"We want you not to play it up."

Craig gave a wry smile.

"Better still, if you could delay it..."

Craig shook his head. His smile undermined his apologetic look.

14:10

The chair fell away, clattering upon the floor; the straps creaked under his weight and the easy sway of his taut naked body. His muscles defined themselves and the veins in his hands and forearms protruded. To adjust his position, but more to assert his strength as if he could somehow escape his bonds, he pulled himself up. The straps creaked in protest and one of the rings turned with a squeak. He relaxed again.

A cord was tied about one ankle and pulled to the door handle; another tethered him to the bed. Karsten hung spread-eagled.

He was also blindfolded.

He hadn't said anything, but he hoped Jutta wouldn't go for her safety pins. Not that he couldn't handle pierced nipples and foreskin again. He didn't want to break the spell by explaining what had happened to the big ones.

Eva was asleep and she had better stay that way. He could hear Jutta moving and hung in silent expectation. How he relished his vulnerability. He needed this subjugation, this sensation of fallibility.

Jutta had also been tied up, but on the bed. Depending on her mood she could handle the pins and the caress of razor blades, but she had not been able to graduate to the belt or stock. These were his domains. Now he didn't believe she could handle any of it.

She was in the room and he heard the rasp of a match being struck. He then knew she would start with hot candle wax. Maybe she'd run the naked flame over selected spots? It wouldn't be enough and he felt up to asking for a gag for some real pain. Could she dig up one of her bursts of cruelty? Cut and sew.

Like exercise the pain brought exhilaration: a bolt of adrenaline. Like exercise he felt cleansed and refreshed afterwards. But there was more. Much more. Endorphins swamped him too. He grew with the experience. He rose above the humdrum reality of everyday life. He became Godlike.

Yet, recently, this feeling had diminished. The kick was not as it used to be. Jutta's enthusiasm had waned and routine had crept in to cap the heights. He had to relive past sexual heights to bolster the current one. His exhilaration was tainted by the realisation that he had to make an effort to become Godlike.

16:55

The meeting with the so-called Elders took place in a Turkish tearoom, full of bristly old men in drab attire. In dress-sense Dannaks felt quite at home. Some were playing dominoes, but most were simply chatting. The tearoom was slightly larger than a good-sized room of a house. It was basic: bare floorboards, white-washed wood-chip textured wallpaper, a few framed landscapes, the Turkish flag an eye catching splash of red and white, a basic kitchen clock, four-legged square tables and basic wooden chairs. A corner bar imprisoned a

344

grizzly man with tufts of wiry grey hair poking out of his open-necked shirt. Behind him the wall was plastered with magazine pull-outs of dark-skinned football teams.

The hodja, Cemal Atasoy, met them outside and was ritually greeted by everyone when they entered the room. Dannaks and Frank were acknowledged. They went to a table were two men were already seated.

Dannaks followed Frank's lead and drank tea. Other than introducing himself he did not contribute to the conversation. When they left Frank had to agree with him that the half an hour had given them no information. Dannaks went further; he felt the Elders were an anachronism. "I get the feeling, they're losing their authority."

"It's difficult to say," said Frank. "They bring their children up differently. The community sees to it that they become proud of their heritage. They learn Turkish history. Folk tales get passed on. They study the Koran and follow the Islamic faith." Frank took a deep breath. "And then there's that sense of 'us and them'. Many of them feel apart and not a part. The Elders and their direct descendants may have spent twenty or thirty years, or all their lives, in Germany, but they remain Gastarbeiter. Things are changing. The youth are being assimilated into German society. There's the rub. I don't suppose the Elders have much say over the likes of the Schwarzer Freitag."

19:04

The owner gave Cenk an irritated look as he handed over the telephone. The restaurant was getting busy. A party of sixteen people was due to arrive at seven.

"Hallo?"

"It's Hasan."

"Yes. I'm busy."

"I've heard the fight's on. Are you going?"

"Yes."

"You know it's madness."

"Of course. But something has to be done. Bilal's hands are broken. This is not like Faruk. This is a direct challenge. Not going to the fight doesn't mean that the right-wingers will give up. It will continue and get worse."

"It'll resolve nothing. Things can only escalate."

"That's what I just said. They're going to escalate whether I go or not. And I have to go for peace of mind."

"Do you?"

Cenk faltered.

The restaurant door opened and a train of people came in. The owner and another waiter hurried to show them to their seats.

"We can't resort to street fighting. When–"

"I've got to go."

True, Ponytail had not reacted well to the news that they had so few volunteers for Friday. Cenk had suggested recruiting the Left. Ponytail had chewed him out with more talk of honour. This was a Turkish affair.

19:05

Dannaks stepped up onto his kitchen stool he'd placed in the hallway next to his orderly row of paired shoes. He fumbled in the dullness – the kitchen, bathroom and lounge lights were on. Eventually he had the bulb screwed in. He climbed down and checked it worked.

He'd bought it at Patel's, where the shop owner had taken him aside to tell him that someone from the health authority had been yesterday and found nothing of consequence wrong with the hygiene of his kitchen. The sandwiches Dannaks had distributed must have been a one-off. There had been no other complaints.

20:26

After the detectives left Craig had turned down the phone, switched off his handy and spent all his time writing his next article.

The detective who had spoken had not looked well. His bruise reminded him of what he looked like a week ago. The man had looked fragile too, as if every movement was pain. His pasty skin said that he didn't eat well.

"Hopefully this'll redeem me in your eyes," he said handing her the ream of paper.

"You never dropped in my estimation." She smiled.

They were slumped on the sofa in the living room. One didn't sit on Carina's sofa.

A burden had been lifted from Craig and his mood lightened the atmosphere in the flat.

"I've already sent it, but it's not too late for fine tuning."

"Cry Nazi" was the working title he had chosen for the piece.

He sat looking at a magazine, but remained restless, half-watching her for reaction. Imagining what she was reading.

He began bluntly by stating that Stefan had been murdered on the day his article came out. He wrote that whoever killed the boy was

346

as bad as the right-wingers who were the topic of his series. Craig had heard that the *Henker* could be responsible, but he didn't want to get sidetracked. He then tied in the march and ensuing riot to his first article, before launching properly into the theme of the series.

"I like the beginning, although it takes the bite out of what you say later."

"It's important to keep things in perspective," he said. "Reporting is about news. And news is about out-of-the-ordinary incidents. You can try to be impartial and present a broader picture, but reporting creates a caricature, not the character, of a country."

"You could expand this and make it a little clearer." Carina pointed to the paragraph.

"Politicising the right-wing outrages," he read, "which are often the actions of disillusioned youths seeking expression, legitimises them."

"One sentence is not enough."

"Okay."

"You talk about caricature and then do this piece on the German psyche."

"Yes, yes," he said testily. "But I need to show that the Germans are not like the British. There is a national character."

"Okay. It is not clear to me how you distinguish that from national identity."

"Germans lack a sense of national identity. Patriotism and pride – not economic pride – are tainted by history. It's easier for most Germans to say: *We are not...* Only the Far Right dare say: *We are...*"

"I will have to think about that," she said. "This bit about German assertiveness being mistaken for arrogance is good. That's what a lot of Brits think. I am glad you did not say we have no sense of humour. That really infuriates me."

He laughed.

"What's so funny?"

"I was going to say you should laugh it off."

She gave him a queer look. And he chuckled to himself. He spoke before she could think he was mocking her. "Anyway, you've got a sense of humour." He let her dwell a moment. "You're going out with me."

She laughed. They kissed.

They made love and missed the beginning of the film they wanted to watch.

It was after eleven when the film finished. Craig left to go to the toilet and Carina zapped round the channels.

After his toilet he stood in the lounge doorway, watching the glow of the television on her face. "I'm going to bed."

"I will be there in a minute," she said, not taking her eyes off the television.

He nodded and returned to the bathroom to brush his teeth. Twenty minutes later he was in bed reading. It was almost midnight and he was beginning to wonder why she wasn't coming to bed when she called him.

"Craig, quick, quick, come here."

21:48

"Aloha," called Zeynep, as she unlocked the door and entered the flat. Ali called out too.

All was still.

She frequently returned home before her husband, who often remained at the Thursday evening get-together for a further game of chess or backgammon or simply men's talk. Ali needed to be put into bed.

Faruk had told his parents he would stay in and study. Perhaps he was asleep.

The television could not be heard and there was no music. Strangely the flat seemed more than empty: it was vacuous.

Ali sat on the floor and fought to remove his shoes. Zeynep slipped off her shoes and took off her jacket. Leila followed. Then Ali struggled to pull off his little jacket whilst Zeynep hung hers on a coat hanger. He threw his jacket upon the chair nearby and was away. Leila scolded him and picked it up and placed it on a hanger in the cupboard.

They heard him go to the lounge.

Zeynep was entering the lounge when Ali dashed across to his shared bedroom. She was halfway across the room, heading for the kitchen to check on the lentils she had left to soak, when she heard him yelp.

The yelp froze her and his subsequent screams for her snapped her out of her docile frame of mind.

She dashed to the bedroom and saw him near the doorway, looking into the room. Leila was behind him – a hand to her mouth.

Ali was crying and looked at her as she approached. He was terrified. Leila didn't move.

Ali, his eyes imploring her, began repeatedly calling his mother, although she was standing next to him. "Ahn-neh, ahn-neh."

What happened then was governed by shock for Zeynep would recall nothing of the next few minutes. Only when the neighbour entered the room a minute later would she momentarily come out of her fit of despair. Zeynep screamed. She fell to her knees, and screaming and crying she began hitting her thighs and ears with closed fists. When she was a teenager and her mother's father died, her mother had done the same.

Little Ali looked on helplessly as his mother rocked back and forth hysterically screaming and thumping herself. Tears blurred his vision and he cried loudly. But it was he who heard the doorbell ringing. And he who went to the door to contend with the catch.

Leila was simply incapacitated, stunned into immobility.

The neighbour entered the flat. He asked Ali what was wrong. It was practically a rhetorical question because he did not wait for an answer and without removing his shoes strode on in the direction of Zeynep's wails. Ali was too distressed to answer anyway.

He saw the stunned girl and the raving woman on the floor thumping herself and then he saw her other son. He was hanging by a cord tied around his neck, itself tied to the light attachment above the bed. A piece of plaster had broken away and hung from some ceiling paper. His face was drained: the pallor of death. His half-lidded eyes were pupil-less and rendered all the more chilling by the skin-coloured tape that sealed his mouth. This had the horrendous effect of making it look as if he had no mouth and concentrated the scream in his eyes.

The neighbour knew the boy was dead but he nevertheless climbed upon the bed and vied with the cord. Zeynep momentarily came out of her frenzied screaming and also climbed up onto the bed. This action upset the stability of the man on the mattress and made it more difficult for him to free the boy. She fussed about her son, stroking him tenderly like a precious sleeping thing.

Eventually he freed the boy and they set him upon the bed. He thought of artificial respiration but felt that the boy was long dead. The mother's tenderness was replaced by a need to consume him with passionate hugs and kisses. The neighbour went past Ali, who was still at the door, and telephoned the emergency services. Then he returned and after prying the dead boy from the woman he attempted to revive him.

Friday
01:24

Despite the hour the neighbourhood was a hive of activity. A wealth of people had left their beds. They jostled with the media people for a decent place at the cordoned off area with its powerful spotlights and uniformed officers.

Dannaks showed his identification card and dipped under the cordon a uniform obligingly lifted. An ache made him grimace.

At the entrance to the house he gave his particulars to a uniform with a clipboard. He signed in. "When you go in," said the officer, "keep your hands at your sides. Don't touch the walls or the banister. Don't touch anything." The man pointed to boxes of throwaway plastic overshoes and latex gloves. Light spilled on the street from the open doorway. Dannaks could see a technician clad in white.

"Don't I get an overall?"

The officer smiled wearily. "Not here. Upstairs. I've been told there's too much garbage on the stairs to get anything useful. The place was like a Turkish bazaar before it was sealed off."

Dannaks climbed the stairs. On the landing outside Suleyman's flat a technician was dusting the door-frame for prints. The door was ajar and Dannaks could see further technicians, one on all fours. The place was a nightmare for them. The clutter of a family flat could only swamp any evidence. The trick was to know what to look for. Perhaps Suleyman had been asked to scan the room for irregularities. "Dannaks?" said an officer at a neighbour's flat door. He lowered his voice when Dannaks approached him. "Have you any influence here?"

"I don't really know."

"It's a minor victory getting them out of their flat. But I'd like them all down at the station. The neighbour is already there. We taped interviews in one of the bedrooms. Not the most ideal of circumstances." Isolating witnesses was standard procedure. "Fingerprinting was done in the kitchen. For elimination purposes." Dannaks nodded. "We'd like to get the mother in hospital. She's in shock. If you can do anything... The doctor has given her a sedative, but she's resisting." He hadn't seen an ambulance outside and assumed they had been and waited and eventually left. Dannaks sympathised with the officer. Manoeuvring a grief-stricken family for interviewing would have been a task. Yet, it was she who had asked for Dannaks. She had shown the officer the card Dannaks had left when he had interviewed Faruk.

They entered the flat, passing two uniforms in the hallway.

Zeynep, Leila and Ali were seated on a sofa in the lounge. Zeynep was conscious, whimpering now and then, but appeared too drowsy to be aware of what was going on. Ali was having a disturbed and fitful sleep on Leila's lap. He stirred and flinched, trying to shake off some harassment. Leila's eyes were soft from weeping. She sat dumbstruck and effaced and didn't acknowledge Dannaks's sympathetic nod. All three on the sofa were devastated but tranquil. On the coffee table in front of them stood once hot beverages untouched. A policewoman sat in an easy chair next to the sofa. Suleyman was standing at the window. He was wearing a knitted blue hat. A man Dannaks assumed to be a social worker or doctor stood nearby.

Dannaks tried to talk to Zeynep, but she just mumbled incoherently.

He went and stood next to Suleyman. "Hallo." Suleyman didn't acknowledge him and continued to stare out of the window. His eyes were charcoal: dull and hard. His jaw set. The once leathery face had become worn suede, as if it had frayed overnight. Dannaks looked out at the floodlit street.

Since no one was talking, separating them was not an issue.

A technician came in and quietly spoke to the officer in charge. Dannaks caught something about body but Suleyman heard more. He wasn't as detached as he appeared. The officer followed the technician out of the room.

Suleyman strode to the empty sofa at the wall parallel to the windows and sat down. He leaned forward, his head in his hands. A huge flat screen television stood in the far corner, angled into the room and the two sofas that lined the walls. The room was a home cinema: a speaker mounted high in each corner. But the flat was shabby. It was a bachelor's pad: complete with stained carpets and the smell of beer and cheap cigarettes. Dannaks remained alone at the windows, looking into the room and the devastated family. The situation gagged him and he felt helpless.

A moment later Dannaks heard movement and talk from the landing beyond the flat. Suleyman casually looked over before returning to a spot on the carpet. There was the sound of more movement. Dannaks surmised that they were bringing the boy out.

Then Suleyman was up. He was out of the room before anyone could react. The uniform at the entrance was caught off guard too. He cursed and darted after him. There was a crash and shouts. Dannaks followed.

He was stopped at the flat door due to the sheer lack of space. Suleyman was on the landing. Two uniforms were manhandling him. The grey fibreglass coffin was on the floor, the lid askew, the black plastic peeking out. An orderly at the top of the stairs was holding his wrist. Another was kneeling next to the officer in charge.

"I want to see my boy," he said swinging round to the officer.

"I'm sorry," he said, glancing at the two uniforms. Suleyman struggled. "You want to get his killer, don't you?"

"Don't take him!" shouted Suleyman, wrestling with the men. "He's not dead. You're making a mistake." He was crying now. Almost calmly he turned to the officer. "Let me see him. Please."

"I–"

"Please. He's my son."

A technician appeared at the flat door behind the officer in charge.

"What the devil's going on?"

"Let me see my boy."

The officer exchanged looks with the technician. "Okay," he said. "Okay," he repeated angrily. "But you stay there." He gave the uniforms another glance. "You can't touch him." The kneeling orderly got up with the aid of a hand upon the wall and shook his head in disgust. "With every minute you waste here the killer gets further away." The technician passed between the officer and the orderly and pushed the lid further aside without removing it completely. He reached in and unzipped the bag as far as the boy's shoulders.

Even Dannaks was unprepared for what he saw. He recognised the face to be that of the boy, but its strange colour and lack of animation, its expression petrified, said that the boy was no longer present. The essence of him had fled. Although the muscles had relaxed there was still something akin to shock in the sleepy eyes. Nonetheless, the boy was gone. Farrie no longer existed. Just a husk remained.

The stricken father flinched and the officer put out his hand to stop him nearing the coffin. Suleyman mumbled and Dannaks strained to hear him. "That's not my boy." For a moment the officer was confused and stared at Suleyman. He looked at Dannaks and

Dannaks nodded. The officer waited and then again nodded to the orderlies.

They lifted the lid to cover the coffin and Suleyman sprang forward. The officer blocked his approach and the uniforms assisted him. Suleyman wrestled. "Don't take him. You have no right. He's my boy." Then he was spent and became limp. "My boy." The uniforms adjusted their grip.

Faruk's head had lolled in the coffin and Dannaks noticed a piece of tape peeled back from his mouth and hanging from his cheek.

Suleyman looked past Dannaks into the flat. His eyes widened. He was already blanched at the sight of Faruk. Dannaks looked over his shoulder and saw a shattered Zeynep, Leila a step behind her, tilted by the weight of Ali on her arm. The doctor was behind her. The commotion must have pulled Zeynep from her slumber.

The orderlies lifted the now closed coffin.

Dannaks saw the confrontation in Zeynep's eyes. He sensed a role-reversal. Suleyman was defiant, yet subservient, weakened. And Zeynep was suddenly hard and cold, domineering. The stare continued and the officer saw it too.

The orderlies clambered down the stairs with the coffin.

"Zeynep." Suleyman's whisper broke the confrontation.

"Stay away," she said in German. Her voice was also a whisper, but hers was vicious, leaving no room for argument. She moved forward.

"She'll come with me," said the doctor.

"Okay," said the officer, moving aside.

"Zeynep," said Suleyman, but she ignored him and led the way down the stairs. Leila followed. The officer spoke as the doctor passed. "Keep them away from the body." He sent one of the uniforms with him. Then he spoke to Suleyman. "Let's sit down."

The three men returned to the lounge, the uniform remaining at the door. Suleyman went to the sofa.

"Can you explain what that was about?" said the officer. Suleyman did not reply. "Why does your wife want you to stay away from her? Suleyman?"

But he did not reply.

Carina had called him to the regional midnight news. Three quarters of an hour later Craig was at the scene. He'd had trouble finding a parking space for Carina's little red Renault. Amongst the multitude he recognised a cameraman from his interview on Tuesday. Snippets of information buzzed along the lines. There was talk that the *Henker* had struck again. Someone said a swastika had been painted on the wall. Someone else who lived in the house became the heart of a media rugby scrum, but he knew nothing. Nevertheless he knew Faruk and his family and he was interrogated for any anecdote regardless of triviality or relevance. Essentially it was all waiting.

He'd seen the removal of the fibre-glass coffin and then the family, apart from Suleyman, leave the building.

He was contemplating leaving for the umpteenth time when Suleyman and two uniforms emerged. Cameras clicked and reporters tussled with each other to get at Suleyman. His formidable mood was such that he pushed his way through the throng, neighbours and friends began to hold back the reporters and cameras. Caught up in the surge Craig was able to slip his card in Suleyman's jacket pocket as he ducked under the red and white striped tape. "Give me a call!" he shouted in his face. "I'll pick you up from the police station."

08:00

When Suleyman left for the police station Dannaks returned to his flat. He was too wired to sleep. But decided to make tea rather than coffee. There was a slim chance he could doze off in the two hours before he would have to go to work.

The kettle had just boiled when the phone rang. It was Frank.

"Sorry to wake you."

"You didn't." Dannaks told him about being at the crime scene.

"The *Sokos* want our assistance. But I can say you're too tired."

"No. I can't sleep."

"There's a meeting at the presidium at eight."

"And they're treating Faruk's murder as a Henker case?"

"I don't know."

After hanging up he made a cup of strong coffee.

When Dannaks arrived he found the media had the *Polizeistern* under siege. A press conference had been promised. For the moment all the media could do was excitedly hover about the building craving titbits of information. Some television stations ran small pieces with the building as a backdrop.

He entered the large conference hall and was lucky to find a seat; it was as if the entire force was in attendance. A number in the audience were already on the case and looked as if they hadn't slept. He recognised members of at least three *Homicide* squads and *Soko* Doermer. There were ranking officers of the *Schupo* too and at least two suits from the state prosecutor's office. Willy Fischer, the police president's number two, was also present. All the seats near Reinhart were taken.

A covered incident board stood in the space between the front and the first row of seats.

The presence of the police president confirmed the importance of the case. He was the first to speak. His was a pep talk, encompassing recent events centring on the riot, touching on the hanging of S-Bahn Stefan, before speaking of the murder itself. He did not talk of what was known of the case; he spoke of the importance of it and the implications of not bringing about a quick and satisfactory conclusion. Expedience but a thorough textbook investigation was imperative. Waves had been sent down the length and breadth of the country and ripples were beginning to seep out at an international level. The event was not merely a matter of the reputation of the police; it was turning into a matter of international stature. Germany was at the heart of Europe. The world was watching and a lack of international confidence would be too damaging.

Dannaks knew the mounting pressure was like stacked fallen dominoes starting at government level, leaning on the mayor, who leant on the president of the Hamburg force, who in turn pressed the head of the new *Soko* Faruk. Added to this was the likelihood of repercussions. The organised fight remained unconfirmed. But there was a real fear of a repetition of last weekend's disruptions.

"Therefore," he concluded, "I hope you'll appreciate we are not merely investigating the murder of a Turkish schoolboy." He scanned the audience to make sure he had conveyed the gravity of the situation. "Enough waffle. I'll hand you over to the head of *Soko* Faruk." He gave them a tired smile. "I have to feed the media hounds." He folded up the sheet of paper in front of him and scanned the audience as if he would take questions, but his expression said: don't you dare. He turned to one of the men from the state prosecution who shook his head. Apparently he had nothing to add.

"I'll see you later." He popped the paper in his jacket and left. The state prosecutor who had nodded followed him.

The next speaker to step up to the podium was the head of *Soko* Faruk. "I'll briefly tell you what we know of the murder, but I'll leave the details of the death to the pathologist." He nodded to a prim looking woman behind him. "You'll get further information, technicians' reports, house-to-house statements and so on from your group leaders." He took a breath. "Before I begin I want to say that the most puzzling aspect of the murder is the motive. Why murder a thirteen-year-old schoolboy? Find the motive and I believe we'll be an important step closer to the killer or killers.

"Now to the murder itself. It would be better described as an execution. The evidence suggests that the boy willingly allowed them into the flat. This suggests he knew his killers. I'll speak of killers although it could feasibly have been one killer. We have no sightings of anyone entering the house at this time. The front door was locked. But it's possible to enter the neighbouring building through the cellar get onto the roof and walk across a plank to the victim's house." He consulted his notes. "There was some spilt cement powder in the cellar and we've got a shoe print in it." He paused. "We believe that the victim was attacked immediately after opening the door. The general order within the flat suggests that there was not a prolonged fight. He had lots of bruising. But a hefty blow to the boy's left temple with scuff markings point to him being hit with a rubber truncheon or kicked. This blow would have severely dazed or knocked him unconscious. Other bruising on his arms and legs show that he was manhandled. As I said, the pathologist will give you the details in a moment. I can tell you that he was not sexually abused." He looked down at his notes again. "The cord with which the boy's thumbs were tied behind his back and the tape that covered his mouth were common materials and tell us little. We have a good shoe print on a piece of carpet in the bedroom. The family did not wear shoes in the flat. All I can tell you at the moment is that it's from a size forty-four shoe. Finally, there was a swastika and the words "*Türken raus*" written in black marker pen on one wall. You'll read the available reports so I won't linger on the details here. What have we got? We—"

A high-ranking uniformed officer approached him. The speaker covered the microphone with a muffled thud. They talked quietly. Then the uniform left and the speaker lifted his hand from the microphone. "It appears we have a break-through. A few minutes before this briefing the victim's school friend, the one who was with him at the time of the beating two weeks ago, said that the victim had told him that he was expecting a visit from a Turkish television team. This boy seems to be the only one to have been privy to this information. So our victim was expecting visitors, but not necessarily someone he knew. I think we can assume that this television crew was bogus, but we'll have to contact all the television and radio companies." He paused for thought. "What have we got? A lot. The swastika implies that this was the work of a skinhead or right-wing gang. However, something is not quite right. The execution, for that is what it was, was carried out with premeditated efficiency. And there are similarities to the *Henker's* MO. Our biggest problem is motive. If it's organised crime the most likely connection is drugs. There has been talk of scars. I can tell you that the boy has welts at the tops of his thighs and on his buttocks. I have been told that these are burn marks. Some are maybe a year old, others two. They were half-moon shaped and three to four centimetres long. Was the boy in a sect? A gang? Or what? Because of the boy's prominence the killers could be members of an extremist group wanting recognition.

"The press have the basic story. However, the story circulating is not complete. They believe the killing to be the work of a right-wing group. As I speak the president is holding the press conference. Until now we have suppressed the fact that the boy was hung, but the Turkish community know it and in the conference we will give the press permission to officially release it. Normally we could get away with saying as little as possible, but this is not normal. We want to emphasise that this was a professional execution. The swastika and "Turks out" will not be mentioned. By being selective with our information we want to sow seeds of doubt in any theory that it was the work of a right-wing group. We're going to emphasise a drugs connection. I hope the reason is obvious. But I'll spell it out anyway. Turkish gangs are going to seek revenge and we have to avert an all-out war. The father of the boy has already been told that the execution was carried out by professionals and hopefully word will get round. This story compounds our problem and lumps that extra bit of pressure on us." He looked down at his notes. "Finally, let me talk about the similarities – and differences – with the so-called *Henker* killings. *S-Bahn* Stefan joins Doermer and Jensen. The *Henker* killed him. But there are similarities between this killing and that of Stefan. Both boys were executed. Both appeared to have arranged to meet their killer. Stefan thought he was going to be interviewed, Faruk too. Like all the others Faruk's thumbs were tied behind his back. A blow to the head incapacitated him. But with Faruk there is no fruit. It could be that the fruit symbolises something for the killer that didn't fit here. And there is this swastika. No fruit and the swastika could mean a copycat killing. That's why we can't, with any certainty, put this on the *Henker's* account." He scanned his notes again. "Questions?" There were none. He was silent for a moment longer. "I don't think we need a profiler to tell us that we are dealing with a cold-blooded killer. There is no evidence to suggest that the killer covered their eyes. So he's a cold sociopath, indifferent to the plea in his victim's eyes. Maybe he gets a kick out of watching their light go out. You know, I am the last thing you see." Then he straightened and cleared his throat of his obvious digression. "It goes unsaid that your full co-operation is requested." In other words overtime was not compulsory but expected. "I'll hand you over to the pathologist after which your group leaders will tell you about your assignments. Langman, can you and your team also take on the television crew aspect? Good."

The pathologist unveiled a moveable pin-board carrying photographs of the dead boy. She supported her discourse with projections of some of these pictures. A running noose had been fashioned and the victim had died within minutes. She did not dwell on details such as the V-shaped rope burn, the state of the victim's steno-mastoid muscles, thyroid or hyoid bone or the engorgement of his penis and emptying of his bowels. She said it was reasonable to assume that the victim had not allowed himself to be tied up. One person could have held him and adjusted the noose. There was powder residue on the tape that covered the victim's mouth. This powder was commonly found on latex gloves. She concluded by asking them to file past the board and examine the pictures before leaving.

The head of *Soko* Faruk returned to the microphone and told them to find their group leaders and get to work. They were to reconvene at four o'clock that afternoon.

The entire briefing had lasted fifty minutes.

There was a lot of milling about and Dannaks made his way to Reinhart.

"This is Reupke," he said, gesturing to the youthful-looking man next to him.

"Dannaks," he said extending his hand.

"Welcome aboard." Somebody tapped Reupke's shoulder, but before turning he said: "Look at the boards."

Dannaks saw photographs of the boy's poster-covered bedroom. The swastika and words were highlighted in a separate photograph. Two pieces of fairly nondescript cord had been photographed. He saw it about the boy's thumbs and the bruising that had been inflicted as he had struggled. Dannaks could almost envisage his appalling death throes. He saw the piece about the boy's neck and noted the complicated knot. Bruising on the boy's biceps suggested that he had been lifted into the noose. The tape used to cover his mouth had been common packing tape. Closer inspection revealed why his face looked unreal. Like Doermer his face was covered by a minutia of haemorrhages. His hooded eyes were bloodshot. Without the plaster his lips had the same bluish hue as his ears. Finally there were some shots of the mysterious scars on his thighs and buttocks.

Reupke stood next to Dannaks. Reinhart had moved on to the next board.

Dannaks waved at the board. "You think this was the *Henker*?"

"It's possible. But it doesn't really fit. Until now all the other victims have been right-wingers."

"Maybe the *Henker* is a right-winger?"

"Maybe," said Reupke. "But why the swastika? And there was no fruit."

"Hanging and the tell-tale blow to the head."

"There's that. But the boy was beaten."

"Staging?"

"To disguise the blow to the head. The strongest argument that it was the *Henker* is the hanging itself. But it's also the weakest, because it's public. And our killer likes to exhibit his work. So it could be a copycat killing. But the fruit is common knowledge. And there is none. Another telling thing is the absence of the letters SF."

They were silent for a moment.

"If it is him, he wanted to make us think it wasn't." Dannaks sighed wearily. "Find the motive, eh?"

"Yes. Look, what I've got for you is the scars. Find out how he got them. Was it some gang initiation thing? Bullying at school? Get a copy of the autopsy report. You'll have to contact his family and friends, teachers, doctors, social workers. Get back to me as soon as you have something."

11:12

Craig had not properly slept. He had dozed on the sofa until Carina had got up for work. She wasn't impressed when he said that he needed her car should Suleyman call.

He drove her to work and was on his way back to the flat when Suleyman called. Craig raced to the presidium and managed to get Suleyman through the media throng to Carina's car.

"Home?" asked Craig.

Suleyman merely nodded.

"You want to talk?"

Suleyman shook his head.

During the drive Craig silently scoured his mind for a new approach.

Parking was easier due to people having driven to work. Craig locked up and hastened after Suleyman, who had stopped in front of his house. He was looking at flowers: bouquets, posies and even wreaths propped up against the building. There were candles too, and someone unaware of Faruk's religion or perhaps wanting a Christian presence, had left a small wooden cross.

Then, taking Craig completely by surprise, Suleyman swiftly walked away.

Craig followed.

"Where are you going?" Craig asked.

His question went unanswered.

Suleyman's pace was brisk and twelve minutes later he was at another tall house. He pressed the bell and the main door buzzed. Suleyman pushed it open. Craig slipped in behind him and Suleyman looked round, as if noticing him for the first time.

A door on the ground floor at the far end of a corridor near the stairs opened.

The smaller man at the flat door made to embrace and greet Suleyman. The latter's expression stopped him.

"Suleyman."

"Mustafa," he returned, moving past him into the flat.

Craig smiled and followed. "I'm a friend."

Mustafa stepped aside and Craig removed his shoes. Suleyman had already slipped his off.

They went into the lounge.

361

"You are leaving," said Suleyman, having sat in the proffered armchair and declining further hospitality. Craig saw him note the sound from the bedroom: a drawer being slid open or closed.

Surprisingly, Suleyman had chosen to speak German to his younger countryman. Craig didn't think it was because he was present.

"Yes," said Mustafa.

Craig followed every gesture, for it seemed to him that there was more here than what was being said.

Suleyman looked directly at him when he asked a direct question; otherwise he chose to cast his eyes elsewhere – though never downwards. He could hear Mustafa's compassion, but Suleyman wanted straight answers, not congeniality. More than this Craig felt Suleyman wanted Mustafa to sense the threat in his flimsy composure.

"Why?"

A tangible tension began to make its presence felt.

Mustafa looked away from the piercing wild eyes. The expression was so determined it was comical. Had it not been for the gravity of the situation Craig thought Mustafa would have laughed it off, slapped him on the shoulder and, because they were Sunni-Muslims, broken out the liquor.

Mustafa's gaze returned briefly to the eyes.

"I think you know why, my friend." The eyes were still drilling into him. "Ahmed is our only child." Did the intensity of the stare melt? "Fa– your son and mine were friends. We fear for our son's life. He fears for his life." Suleyman closed his eyes. When he re-opened them, he was looking in the direction of the sound of the bedroom. "We will return later."

"I understand," he said quietly.

There was a moment's silence. Even the person packing – presumably Mustafa's wife – seemed to be holding their breath.

"Can I speak Ahmed?" The eyes and tension again.

"He's too upset to speak to any–"

"And me?" Suleyman asked in a pleading voice that was ripe for a theatre stage.

Despite his size, Mustafa was a feisty little man, bolstered no doubt by the presence of his own family.

"Suleyman, you can't take it out on my son," he retorted.

"I don't take anything out on him. I want to find who murdered my son."

"He doesn't know."

"Let me ask him."

Under the drilling eyes of the enraged man, Craig felt Mustafa weighing up the request. The man rubbed his chin and the glittery grey stubble rasped. His family and he had probably had as much sleep as Suleyman.

"My son," Suleyman began slowly, "blood of my blood, flesh of my flesh has been murdered."

Mustafa held up his hand, as much to arrest the man's anger as to stop him speaking. He nodded slowly, put his arms upon the rests of the chair, and spread his fingers in readiness to rise. Then he changed his mind and the tension left his body.

"Ahmed," he called.

The boy appeared at the door. He too looked as if he had not slept. His eyes were bloodshot and his face moist and bloated. Fear was also present in his expression. He entered the room, but did not take a seat, preferring to stand some distance from Suleyman.

Mustafa glared at him. Before he could verbally scold his son, Ahmed moved forward and formally greeted Suleyman. Suleyman remained impassive and seated throughout. When the boy made to pull away he grabbed him by the wrist.

Mustafa froze, his fingers beginning to dig into the armrests of the chair. Ahmed held his breath and tears welled up in his eyes.

Craig was spellbound.

Suleyman looked into the boy's face and spoke in a voice charged with spite.

"Who killed my son?"

Ahmed shook his head and closed his eyes to keep back the tears. "I don't know."

"You know something, that's why you run."

"Suleyman," protested Mustafa, springing out of his chair.

"I swear," said Ahmed, looking at the wild man squeezing the life out of his wrist. "I don't know."

"Why you running?"

"That's—"

Ahmed cut off his father. "Because I'm scared. I don't know." The pain in his wrist was obviously becoming too great and he began to struggle. "I don't—"

"Is it same Nazis who attacked him?"

Ahmed's eyes widened. In them was not fear, but horror. He glanced at his father, who had an incredulous expression on his face. In this lax moment the boy tore himself free.

Ahmed stepped out of reach, rubbing his wrist and fighting back tears.

Suleyman looked at him and then at his father. Both seemed appalled by the question. Neither appeared to want to speak.

"What is it?" he demanded.

Still they did not answer. The boy seemed to want his father to speak and the father seemed too afraid of the consequences.

Suleyman got up and for fear that he would lunge at Ahmed, Mustafa came between them. The two men faced each other, expressions in turmoil.

Suleyman's face then lit with realisation.

"You know gang that attack Farrie," he said to Mustafa. "You know who. You—"

There was a wail and Suleyman looked away from Mustafa to Ahmed, who had issued the cry. Tears were streaming down his face and he was having trouble breathing.

"You stupid man," Ahmed screamed. "You must be the only one who doesn't know. Farrie tried—"

"Ahmed," snapped Mustafa. "Go to your room."

There was a long moment of suspension before the boy fled. Suleyman made to go after him, but Mustafa barred his way.

"I'll explain," said the smaller man quickly.

"Explain?"

"Listen, Suleyman. Please." He gestured for him to sit, but Suleyman refused. "Okay. When my son spoke of everyone knowing, he did not mean everyone. He meant some of your son's friends. The rest is just rumour. He—"

"Knowing?" he hissed.

There was a pause in which Mustafa braced himself.

"Knowing that there was no gang that Friday."

All the while Suleyman had only been half-listening to Mustafa. He had been determined to go after Ahmed, to find out what he knew. But this perplexing statement was a slap in the face and he stared at Mustafa.

"Wh—" was as far as he got.

"Sit down." Suleyman was so devastated he simply obeyed.

"Our sons were not attacked by skinheads that night. There was no gang. The two boys made it up. Ahmed beat Faruk." Before the flash of anger in Suleyman's face could take proper hold, he quickly went on. "Your son asked him to do it. He couldn't take the tests at school. He wasn't ready and needed more time. He—"

"This is lie."

"No. My son has no reason to lie. He told me that Faruk was so worried he thought of injuring himself during the tests. He talked of falling on his pen at the desk. Yes, in his eye. He—"

"I not believe you. It not true. My son—"

"It is true. We have no idea who killed him, but my son is involved and I'm taking him away from here."

Suleyman shook his head, his face blanched and contorted with disbelief and sickness.

"My son never do such thing. This is lies, lies, all lies."

"Why?" asked Craig in a small voice. It simply didn't make sense.

Mustafa merely looked at him.

12:09

His mother had just gone shopping and his father was still asleep. His father had come in at seven and was in bed by eight. He wouldn't be up for hours.

Cenk paid more attention to his ritual than was normal for him. He was in the bathroom, his foot awkwardly crooked into the sink. The prayer mat was out and aligned towards Mecca.

As he washed his feet, forcing a finger between his toes, he tried not to think about the situation. Would it have made a difference if they'd patrolled? Could they have saved Faruk?

He had spoken to Hasan.

"I've just talked to Murat. I'm helping."

"Because of Faruk?"

"Yes. And the swastika—"

"So it's true." Cenk wanted confirmation.

"It's what I heard."

"I heard that they'd written: 'Turks out'."

"Maybe." There was nothing in the media about it. "Cenk, I want you with me. You and Nazim. You'll be safe."

"What do you mean?"

"I can't tell you unless you're with me."

"What did Murat say?" It sounded funny calling Basha by his real name.

"I haven't asked him."

Silence.

"Join me. With Murat you could get hurt. This won't be like Saturday."

"I can't. They need all the help they can get."

"Cenk, the language of violence is violence. Don't be part of that."

"I can't. Murat wants me at his side."

"What I'm doing is important."

"I can't. Ask Nazim."

12:34

Carina and Craig had their lunch outside at a table on the pavement. There was no wind and the warmth from the climbing sun pleasant. Summer was coming.

Craig had left Mustafa's flat with Suleyman.

"Do you–" was as far as he got outside.

"No," said Suleyman, striding away.

Whether on television or in the papers everyone had something to say about the boy's murder.

The right wing politician, Volker Herbst, got his inflammatory two-penny worth in: "*Die Stadt ist Farukt geworden.* (The city's gone crazy. He'd incorporated the boy's name replacing the German word crazy: *verrückt.*) Naturally, it's a tragedy, but the good German youth I represent are the real scapegoats of liberal Hamburg. Stefan didn't receive as much publicity. And don't tell me he wasn't a celebrity. I'm told all the stops are being pulled to solve this Turkish boy's murder. Have the police got any closer to finding Stefan's killers?"

The Turks and Leftists complained that the police were spending too much effort investigating their community and the possibility that Faruk had been a street thug, whereas they should be examining the leads pointing in the right-wing direction.

A police press officer defended their position by saying that they were treating all leads seriously. In addition, there was increased police presence in some quarters because the probability of retaliation was high. Unfortunately there was no localised right-wing community to patrol. So it appeared as if they were concentrating their efforts on the Turkish community.

Reporters were trying to ascertain how much support there was for a planned 'Day of Action'. The left-wing group leader, Klaus, who was under threat of prosecution by the authorities for allegedly initiating Saturday's rioting, was asked for his opinion. The lanky figure uncannily echoed Stefan's words: "It's time the government sat up and listened to what the people are saying." Speakers were trying to recruit the support of the entire country; they wanted a 'National Day of Action'. When confronted with the proposal the politicians could only warn that this was not the way to protest, the country would be brought to its knees.

The city seemed to be holding its breath.

Almost in defiance Carina had insisted that they ignore the situation and eat out. People were canoeing, rowing or pedalling in the water. There was a true sense of time standing still.

Carina had no problem relaxing. Craig struggled to forget the situation and she helped him until her patience ran out.

"It makes a mockery of my article."

"I did not want to say it, but nobody could tell you anything. Your article was written before you arrived in Germany. You decided everything and now it turns out to be completely different. If it had stared you in the face you probably would have ignored it because it did not fit in with your ideas."

"Don't forget one thing. It was the system that warped Suleyman. He wanted his son to be as good as – if not better than – the Germans. And this is a result."

Silence.

"I feel so stupid," he said.

She was not ready for reconciliation and blazed on, pleased with the aptness of the phrase he had explained to her two weeks ago. "I guess you are up the shit creek."

13:13

Karsten was in the cellar. He needed time alone. Time to distance him from the fight. Woodwork was meditative. He was on the mortise and tenon joint of the neck of the rocking horse. He'd made a fine job of sculpturing the head. Smooth and hard as his biceps. But the tenon was worrying. There was a knot in the wood he hadn't seen. How could he have missed it?

He had been questioned about the killing of the Turkish boy around midday. Although he'd been out on his bike at the time, Jutta had said that he'd not left the flat. After they'd gone, he made a few

367

calls. His friends had been swooped upon too. Nobody had been arrested.

As a precaution Karsten cancelled the hand-to-hand training session scheduled for that afternoon. This was not such a tragedy. Many had gone through National Service. Indeed, two members of tonight's force would be professional soldiers. A briefing a few minutes prior to the fight would suffice.

His gang was a pseudo army. He had a communications man and a nerve centre that controlled operations. They were equipped with handies and had their own military jargon. He had his lieutenants with age predominantly depicting rank. Apart from those with specific responsibilities the ranking was ill-defined. His group were a motley bunch. The youngest was thirteen and the eldest around the same age as himself, twenty-seven, but the average age was twenty-two. Tonight, however, the numbers would be swollen.

Jutta knew something was happening, but she was too afraid to ask. References to herself and their daughter were her way of telling him to be careful: that a young family relied upon him. At some point she'd been to his bedside drawer. He'd noticed that the fold of cloth upon the revolver was not right. It surprised him that after all this time together she had not come to appreciate his fastidiousness.

The boy's death had enraged the Turks and they would fight tooth and nail. His edge was blunted. On Tuesday he had given them the impression that it would be a fair, even honourable, fight. Nothing could be further from the truth.

Then it happened. He'd pushed too hard and the knot had fallen out, the wood splintered. He stared at the flaw. Looked at the pieces that made up the rest of the horse. More work. Could he shorten the neck? His Esmeralda would be a Quasimodo. Start again? A new head? He couldn't face it. There was no point in continuing. The thought of smashing the thing shot through his head. But he was too controlled for such fits of rage. Rage could seethe through him, but he could channel it. That's what set him above the others. His emotion never fully got the better of him.

16:00

This meeting was substantially smaller than the morning one. About thirty officers were present. Although Dannaks had told Reupke what they had discovered he had asked him to come to the meeting. Frank had consented. He could have decided to come instead.

Reupke seemed excited but harassed. Dannaks didn't press him.

The head of *Soko* Faruk opened the meeting by asking all the group leaders to report. Dannaks was at first shocked to hear that the victim had fabricated the story about being beaten by skinheads two weeks earlier. But then everything fell into place.

Frank had given Dannaks a free hand at REX. He had Reinhart on the phone for the entire morning. He even pulled in Schuppenhauer and Wulff for a while. He used the phone in the storeroom. Nobody wanted to lose the weekend and they toiled fervently through their lunch break. Frank ordered pizzas. Reinhart made the break-through just after one o'clock. There was a social services file. Reinhart found and spoke to the social worker. Dannaks listened to Reinhart.

"There's no proof, the boy won't – wouldn't – speak, but I think his father was responsible," said Reinhart.

"He tortured the boy?" said Dannaks.

"I'd say so."

"Why?"

"To make him do better at school."

"That's ridiculous."

Reinhart raised his eyebrows.

But it did explain Zeynep's attitude. She probably blamed Suleyman for their son's death.

The head of *Soko* Faruk asked for brief reports. Reupke's boss spoke for REX. He said after hearing of the torture, they'd interviewed the family again. The daughter, Leila, had talked.

Other group leaders reported. No new witnesses had come forward. No television crew had interviewed or planned to interview Faruk. The motive was proving elusive and most avenues of investigation were ending in cul-de-sacs.

Yet, the head of *Soko* Faruk appeared strangely unperturbed by lack of progress. He impassively listened to the reports. The head of *Soko* Doermer, which covered Jensen, was also present; as was the leading officer from *S-Bahn* Stefan's murder investigation.

The reports ended with an officer forgetting himself and running on. "Our interviews, particularly with the Turks confirm that a form of retaliation is brewing. Our informants have corroborated this too. Nobody seems to know what, where or when. It's all rumours, but everyone's talking about the worst. I–"

"Okay, Norbert," said the head of *Soko* Faruk. "Sorry to interrupt. But that really is another problem. We're after Faruk's killer." Norbert nodded. "And I think we're going to get him." He paused for dramatic effect. Moments ago it'd looked hopeless. Reupke gave Dannaks a ghost of a smile. "I still haven't found a plausible motive, but I think this killing was the handiwork of the *Henker*. Even if it's not, the killer is near to Faruk. Faruk may not have known his killer, but his killer knew him. I say this because the killer hung him from the light fitting. The boy was nicknamed Monkey when his father caught him swinging from the light fitting. Only somebody with this knowledge would have known the light fitting could carry the boy's weight. Inside information. This is the killer's mistake. Why did he use it? I think it's arrogance. And arrogance is the *Henker's* hallmark. The knockout blow fits too. I won't bore you with MO, signature and staging. But VICAP corroborates our suspicions." He allowed them a moment's digestion. "Of course, we've nothing. But I want to do DNA tests on everybody who knew the victim." He turned to the state-prosecutor. "Do you want to say something?" The man shook his head, his glasses glinting in the light. "I hope we can smoke him out. Any questions? Remarks?"

"I can suggest a link," Dannaks began, "between Faruk's killing and two of the three right-wingers."

"We're all ears."

"Publicity." He paused. "Jensen and Stefan were highly-publicised before their deaths. Faruk too."

"Good." He pondered. "When one talks of a learning curve, the first murder, Kai Doermer's in the city park, can certainly be ruled out." He paused again. "It's a good point. You are?"

"*Oberkommissar* Dannaks. *Soko* REX."

The head of *Soko* Faruk nodded. Then he looked around the room. "I want volunteers for the DNA tests. We'll start with the members of this terrorist cell *Schwarzer Freitag*. We've had them under a magnifying glass." He slid a wad of papers to his left. "This is a list of suspects. The names with an asterisk are known members of the *Schwarzer Freitag*." The wad was passed about the room until everyone had a sheet. "I want to hit everyone on this list at the same time. But especially the known gang members. And I want to do it soon. As you can see there're thirty-seven names on the list. I want three men on each name and five on those with an asterisk. We saw some of them in action on Saturday. That's a lot of manpower, I know." He cleared his throat. "I want this set up as soon as possible. We may be able to hamper this retaliation. In any case we have to show presence."

"All *MEK* units are on standby," said the high-ranking uniform to his right. "We have reinforcements from the neighbouring *Länder* (states) too."

"Now to the cherry," the head announced. "We have a prime suspect. He's already under surveillance. As you can see we've tagged key figures on the list with an asterisk. Our main man's name is one of these." He picked up the top sheet from the remaining pile. "He's seventh from the bottom. I won't attempt to pronounce his surname." He opened the paper file on the desk in front of him and took out a large photograph. He looked at it before passing it to the man on his right. "He's the one in black, far left." He stopped as if wondering whether to go on. He followed the photograph as it was passed around and then he looked at his watch. "Okay, settle down. Let's not split the bear's fur before it's bagged." Dannaks smiled at the choice of saying. "Let's get this right. I want you and your volunteers in the large conference room at five thirty. I know it's tight, but we have to move fast."

There was a lot of chair scraping and murmuring as the gathering broke up.

18:15

Karsten spotted the plain clothes man the moment he set foot on the pavement. His father had inadvertently taught him how to pick them out.

He was crouched behind his bike on the opposite side of the road. A toolkit lay nearby. The bulls were capable of learning. The last time they had tried to tail him they'd used cars. He took them down cul-de-sacs, swung round and left them to practise their three-point-turn. Simpletons.

"Trouble?" asked Karsten, playing the bikers' brotherhood card. He had his own helmet in his hand.

"Nothing I can't handle." The man could only be a couple of years older than him. He was clearly unsettled by Karsten's boldness. Young and inexperienced: easy meat.

"Nice bike."

"Thanks."

"Do you mind?" He handed the man his helmet. Then he straddled the bike. Karsten's boldness kept the man totally off balance and Karsten wanted to keep him that way. The keys were in the ignition ready for a quick take-off. "Nice toolkit. Did it come with it?" They looked at the box on the pavement next to the man's own helmet.

"Er, yes."

"Oh well, must get on." Karsten took his helmet and was away. "See you around."

"Yes."

He got on his bike that was standing in the parking area. The man remained crouched. He was probably talking into his collar. Did they have others around? Karsten fired up his bike and the man stood wiping his hands on a rag. He revved and was off. He nodded as he passed the man. In the rear-view mirror he saw the man packing away his toolbox.

Karsten stopped at the top of the road, some one hundred metres from the man. He waited for him to put his toolbox in a pannier. Then he turned left and shot away, turned sharply and returned to the top of the road. The man was sitting on his bike. Unfortunately he had his helmet on and Karsten couldn't see his expression.

Karsten dangled the ignition keys high in the air. He had nabbed them when they looked at his stupid toolbox. He thought about tossing them down the drain. But there was no fun in that and he simply dropped them. He then turned and roared off.

18:21

Dannaks waited in the back of the double-parked *Peterwagen*. He was grateful for the silence. In front of him sat two *Schupomen*: an archetypal partnership of sweet youth and bitter age. It was thought that the presence of a marked police car could act as a deterrent. Further down the road an unmarked van containing a *MEK* unit had found a parking space. The target for both vehicles lived across the road: a youth called Nazim. He lived with his parents and two sisters in the first floor flat of a house almost opposite them. No one had left or entered the house since they'd taken up position. But there had been a lot of movement at the windows of this house and its neighbours.

The streets were unusually barren. As if a curfew had been declared. A car eased past them.

Dannaks checked his watch. Another couple of minutes to the planned six-thirty go-ahead.

The younger *Schupoman* checked his gun for the umpteenth time and the older man grumbled something Dannaks didn't catch.

At six-thirty some kids came onto the street. Nobody came from Nazim's house. They met up and moved off. At the top of the road they met other youths or kids and then they were gone.

"What was all that?" said the younger uniform.

"Something's going down," said the older man. "What do you think?"

Dannaks met the man's stare. "I don't know. We'll just have to wait."

"It could be a diversion to protect what's-his-name–" suggested the younger man.

"Nazim," said Dannaks, feeling he'd disappointed them with his lack of contribution.

"We should get the signal to go."

"We'll get it," said the older man.

They slumped back into silence.

At twenty to seven, just as they began to get fidgety, the radio crackled that they should get ready.

One minute later they were racing across the road, the *MEK* men moving ahead of them. The front doorbell was answered almost immediately and they were in the hall knocking on the flat door. The man who opened it was yanked out onto the hallway floor, the barrel of a machine pistol arresting any protest. Three further *MEK* men burst into the flat, covering angles and shouting at the woman and her two clinging daughters.

Dannaks and the *Schupomen* were not far behind, P 2000s in hand. His weapon's safety was off and he rested his finger on the trigger guard.

"Where's Nazim?" he asked the mother.

She was speechless and could only shake her head. He was about to repeat the question when the elder daughter, who looked to be about twelve, said that he had left almost an hour ago.

18:32

Peter 15/2 was the first to radio in to say that a lot of activity had begun in a section of the Turkish community. The patrolman reported that numerous youths were leaving their homes. Many were masked with scarves or jogging-top capuches – hoodies. About fifty made up the main group but more were joining from the side streets.

Then the *Einsatzleiter* (co-ordinating officer) sitting in a command van heard that youths were gathering on the street outside one of the *Schwarzer Freitag* leaders they had under surveillance. The officers wanted instructions. There were too many to tackle. Most of them had their faces covered and it would be easy for their target to slip amongst them. He heard that more were taking to the streets. He dispatched a helicopter and told everyone to sit tight.

He needed more manpower before he could give the go-ahead.

At six forty-five it was reported that the group was on the move and that their target could be among them. Smaller groups were joining this group, swelling its numbers. The helicopter estimated between one hundred and one hundred and fifty youths heading eastward across the city. Traffic was being brought to a halt. They would hit the ring road 2 where it met Königstrasse in five minutes. This disruption in itself was enough to allow him to break them up. But although he had a lot of manpower at his disposal it was dispersed.

Reports of further groups started coming in.

He mobilised as many units as possible. Their vehicles flanked the main Turkish gang and moved parallel to it. Units of *MEK* were travelling to cut the horde off.

After checking the map and a short consultation, he decided to move his operation to the front line. He'd had enough second hand information. At times it had sounded as if half the population of Hamburg was on the move.

19:01

Elsewhere two groups approached each other. Each group had parked their vehicles and gathered some half a kilometre from the site. They entered from different sides by bending back or tearing down the wire mesh and assembled at approximately the same time.

During the walk to the site, after Basha had decided that all were present and given the command to get going, they were silent. Nazim and Cenk, each with thoughts stunted by anticipation, walked side by side.

They had left at five to meet at six-thirty.

For Cenk the situation was unreal. Although he looked straight ahead and felt the militancy of the gang – clung to it in his mind, using it to smother panic – he was aware that people were watching from their homes. There were few pedestrians and those that were present took to the other side of the road. There were conflicting thoughts going through his mind. He spotted one woman looking from her window and hoped that she would call the police and halt this madness. A part of him wanted the walk to the site to go on forever and another part wanted to hit out at Farrie's murderers. He inflated himself on the aggression of his colleagues. They were a formidable bunch, many of whom he had never seen. Two or three were wearing gaudily patterned and brightly coloured handkerchiefs or bandannas that almost completely encased their hair. Most were in black or dark colours.

There was a group on motorbikes and he wondered about Ponytail who was nowhere to be seen. Perhaps he was planning a spectacular entrance.

Despite his fear, being part of this group made him feel invincible. There was safety in numbers and they were a large body of men. He kept thinking of gladiators making their way to an arena. They must have felt this same mixture of dread and exhilaration.

But it was all unreal. Even when he followed the others through the boundary wire mesh there was a feeling that this was not happening.

His heart was thudding so hard he looked down to see if it was visible.

Again Basha was the spokesman for the Turks and Karsten represented the right-wingers. Because the groups had gathered at opposite ends waiting for seven o'clock there was a strange procrastination. Although it had not been planned, as the two groups approached one another, the leaders emerged slightly ahead of the main body. It seemed natural that they speak to each other.

Raw hostility brutalised the building site. To Cenk it was like being a figure in an enclosure full of lions. The earlier feeling of invincibility and belonging had suddenly flown. He felt unbearably alone.

Basha had wanted him close. But he only caught some of what was said. He was distracted and scared that the pounding of his heart was doing irreparable internal damage. Nonetheless he caught the clichés and empty words that normally would have been termed cool. What was about to happen exceeded words. There was talk of respect and for a moment Cenk hoped that the entire thing would be called off. Karsten repeated what he had said on Tuesday adding that none of his lot had anything to do with Faruk's death. Basha returned that they had nothing to do with Stefan's death. At this exchange Cenk hoped they could shake hands and go home. The sentences had come in fits and starts with the entire dialogue lasting no more than two minutes. Then there was a void.

The enclosure became an arid savannah. Predators were growing restless. Aggression was becoming tangible. They were beginning to stalk their prey. Unbelievably a higher degree of dread was being reached. Would his heart explode?

It was growing dark fast, but this too promised no sanctuary.

Cenk wondered whether his face showed his fear. Nazim looked pale. Others, the strangers, had hard, set features. Their faces were livid. No thoughts were betrayed. Perhaps they were not thinking?

He tried to concentrate on the fight and form a vague plan. All the right-wingers looked competent. The smaller ones looked vicious.

Many had their trousers tucked into high-laced paratrooper boots. There were steel toe-capped boots too and white laces were prominent. Combat green was the colour. There was an occasional arm insignia depicting a right-wing group or simply "*Ich bin stolz ein Deutscher zu sein.*" Cenk spotted a lightning SS on a belt buckle and one lad was wearing a *Reichskrieg* flag as a cloak.

Their dress alone did not set them apart. Not all were skinheads. One had a shiny, bald head except for a strip of suede in the middle. Another was bald except for a tuft hanging at the front of his head. These were the traits of punks not skinheads.

Who were these aliens? Where had they come from? They were frighteningly different. Yet, though Cenk was filled with trepidation, a duality ran in his mind. He knew that he had to destroy something in his head. He had to annihilate the invincibility of the skinheads, the invincibility of the Nazis. Therefore hate caused him to clench his teeth and firm his cheeks until they hurt.

His arms hung at his sides. His hands near the deep pockets of his trousers. He allowed the fingers of his right hand to touch the hard blade of the carving knife concealed in his pocket. He pressed it to reassure himself of its presence. However, the level of reassurance disappointed him. Even the sawn-off broom handle up his sleeve offered him little comfort.

Basha and the right wing leader, Cenk knew to be Karsten Krohn, smiled at each other. The smiles were supposed to be relaxed and hard, but the necessary confidence was absent. Instead they were fixed and sinister and a glaze of apprehension glinted in their eyes.

Cenk wanted to say something. Or he wanted someone to speak. He wanted someone to bring reason into the situation. Someone should suggest forgetting the fight. Someone should say it was fruitless. But he knew that words were useless. The language that was being spoken here had no sentences. Its words were too primitive. Such utterances could not be strung together to make sense. Reason was unattainable.

Karsten stepped back and Basha retreated. The huddles thinned out and the two sides spread out and braced themselves.

The hostility between the two groups was reaching an unbearable pitch.

"We didn't come unarmed," Karsten announced. "I hope you brought some metal."

The right-wingers pulled out knives and sticks. Some of the latter bristled with cruel bits of metal. Cenk noticed someone at the back distributing larger weapons from a chest: baseball bats and metal bars. There was even a sword. Most were large weapons that could not have been easily concealed or carried. This was going to be a massacre. Was no one else seeing this distribution of weapons? Why didn't someone cry out that this was unfair? Why couldn't they run away?

For a second he anxiously skimmed over his comrades faces in the hope of securing support. No one met his eyes.

He should have listened to Hasan. He should have gone with him. Or he should have stayed away. The civilised sanctuary of the restaurant, which had closed to protest Faruk's death, seemed of another time: deep in his past or something that he had not directly experienced but perhaps observed. Civilisation was not present at this building site. This was not a place for someone who felt fear. This was not a place for someone with feelings. There was no sensitivity here. Here was only raw aggression. They were going to smash and cut and hurt. And they were going to do this for the sake of smashing and cutting and hurting.

Then some of Cemal's words came to mind. "The minute we take up arms on the street, we become no better than the people we fight."

The intensity of the aggression was so great it was palpable.

"Don't worry about us," Basha sneered.

Why the fuck was he here? Cenk kept hearing this question. The only answer he could offer was because the others were here. This reminded him of the mountaineers' classic answer to why they climbed mountains. "Because they're there." Yet, his current situation presented no parallels. There was no glory in what he was doing. He could derive no satisfaction from breaking a nose or causing another pain. Mountaineers could choose not to climb. He was here not because he wanted to be. He had been manoeuvred here.

Cenk again looked about himself. No one moved. Nazim was looking at him uncertainly and carefully wiped his palms against his trouser legs.

Then Basha extracted a *nunchaku* from the side of his black trousers. He held the handles theatrically above his head and Cenk felt like crying out. It was like something from a film. Bruce Lee. A sacrifice was about to be carried out and the high priest was holding up the slaughtering implement. In any case, this symbolic act, which was at the same time comical and frightening and testified to the demented thinking or unthinking that was behind what was about to take place, signalled them to disclose their weapons.

The fighting did not begin. It was more a case of all hell breaking loose. Mayhem would best describe what transpired. Only one event would break the tumult and this would herald the end of the clash.

19:05

The punch hurt. It was full in the stomach and it was hard. Winded, Cenk fell to a kneeling position. He then lost the precarious balance on his knees and tumbled backwards. With both hands pressed into his pained stomach, he did not attempt to break his fall. His back hit the tarpaulin that covered the hillock of sand and he came to rest in a slumped sitting position.

His stomach was afire and he guessed that the skinhead, his assailant, had been wearing a knuckle-duster.

Fear widened his eyes for he wanted to get up and avoid the imminent hail of follow-up blows. But when he looked up the skinhead had left him. Naturally he was thankful, but he was also confused.

He watched the man charge a Turkish friend. He saw the glint of metal. Yes, he was wearing a knuckle-duster. No, wait; it was a knife.

In horror Cenk looked down. Dizziness engulfed him when he saw the dark growing stain on his shirt and felt the wetness on his hands. The pain suddenly became excruciating and sweat instantly blurred his vision. Or was it tears? Seeing his glistening bright red palms his eyes rolled to the sky.

19:21

At the *Polizeistern* Dannaks learned very little. Nearly all the members of the *Schwarzer Freitag* had escaped. Rumours abounded, but the prime *Henker* suspect had not escaped arrest. Or he was shot when they stormed his flat. Or he was killed in a struggle. Or he'd barricaded himself in his flat and committed suicide. Nobody could say. Dannaks gathered that whatever happened, the police would appear to have botched it.

He hung around for as long as he could stand the gossip and rumours; then he went home.

19:23

The Einsatzleiter was confident. As long as the youths didn't deviate from their course he'd have them surrounded within five minutes. He still hadn't figured out where they were going. There was no sign of any other movement. But then they had concentrated their manpower on the Turks. They had only tagged key right-wingers. They simply didn't have the manpower to spread. Keeping tags on one force was simpler and made sense. It would lead them to the other. There was nothing racist in their choice. No doubt someone in the media would later claim the opposite. The logical choice was to watch the Turks, if only because of the Schwarzer Freitag.

He was outside his command van at the roadblock at the St. Pauli U-Bahn end of the Reeperbahn. He would meet them head-on. *MEK* men stood in front of the vehicles stiff like soldiers on parade.

Car horns hooted. Not all traffic had been successfully diverted. The roads were choked with vehicles fuming exhausts and fuming drivers. He viewed the dark congestion of Turks through binoculars and ordered the flanking units to plug the side streets and move in. The men in riot gear first.

The sound of a helicopter decimated further commands. He looked up but the sound bounced off the buildings and confounded its approach. It was impossible to say where it was. When it appeared he shook his head in disgust. It wasn't the Libelle he'd dispatched but a television station.

The youths were drawing closer. They were slowing too. They'd probably looked left and right and seen that turning round was the only option. But maybe they knew that they were also being followed.

An officer passed him a loudhailer when the youths had almost come to a standstill about fifty metres away. Before he could speak another interrupted him. There were reports of violence at a building site in Lurup. Irked he told the officer he would have to sort out what was in front of him first.

19:24

There was a volcano in place of his stomach, with molten blood for lava.

All about him was madness: men viciously tearing at each other.

At the beginning, before the short talk between Basha and the right-wing leader, Cenk had positioned himself near a big Turk. The talk froze their positions and like a football team awaiting kick-off they could not move. This Turk came under attack and Cenk had lunged forward with surprising cruelty and struck the assailant hard on the shoulder with his broom handle. Together with the big Turk he had kicked the fallen attacker. Then there was a time when it appeared he had to wildly search for an opponent. He struck out at engaged adversaries, until he was distracted by a charging right-winger who was kicked down by one of Basha's friends. He searched again and caught another charging at him and he made ready to dodge him. At the last minute the assailant kicked out his knife and punched him in the stomach.

Cenk watched the clouds. The deepening blue of the sky gave them a strange luminous quality. They drifted in peaceful ignorant bliss. He thought them beautiful. Holding on to them he tried to block out the bedlam. He tried to silence the shouts, grunts, curses and screams. He also tried to ignore the inferno that was his stomach. But he could not attain the level of solace he sought in the clouds. Oh, he was sure the solace was there: hidden in the mystery of the silent leviathans. And there too dwelt the enigma of being. He felt near to the key of life, a hair's breadth away from unlocking the secret, of attaining a coherence of self. If only he could block out the distractions: this absurdity of Man.

He was constantly wrenched back to the fighting about him. Wrenched back to the cruelty of life. Was life disrupting the strange uplifting peace of dying?

He saw the stabbing, the kicking and wrestling. Everywhere dust was being kicked up. He watched the wielding of baseball bats; heard the soft thuds and nauseating cracks. Projectiles flew through the air: bricks and stone. It was insufferable. Nobody noticed him. One part of him wanted to scream at them. Then again, he was not alone, others were down: groaning, squirming or lying ominously still. There were fallen right-wingers too and he realised that it had been absurd of him to think of them as invincible.

Time adopted a beguiling elasticity. Some things were *blitzschnell*: literally a flurry of activity. Others seemed to take place painfully slowly. Excruciating seconds went by as a fist broke a nose or a boot kicked a head. Blood and saliva arcing through the air. Yet, none of it was sensational or spectacular. It conjured words like horrible, atrocious, dire, abysmal. But even these weren't enough. If any one word came to Cenk's mind then it was the word stupid. Stupid. Stupid. Stupid.

People were running this way and that. On a farm in Turkey he had seen a chicken without a head frenziedly running about... And this image came to mind. He realised then that there could be no winners. Only those who came out of this madness unscathed could claim some victory. But these would be few. There would probably be equal numbers from either side. For despite their karate training Basha and his friends were taking a good beating. The chaos of people rendered everything unpredictable.

The clouds were unblemished.

A flare shot horizontally across his field of vision. He did not see where it went for the sight of a Turk staggering and holding his bleeding head seized him.

Nearby were large drops of blood. Fully rounded plops with crenellated edges planted in the dust. A nosebleed perhaps?

Somebody was beside him, speaking to him.

He looked at the person crouched over him and realised that this person was blocking his view of the clouds. He weakly tried to push the person aside, but his attempt was little more than a flutter of his hand.

Whoever it was ignored him and Cenk opened his mouth to speak but words did not come.

The person was not talking to him, he was shouting at him.

Cenk tried to look to another part of the sky but the person persisted. The face kept moving to take up the centre of his field of vision. He tried to move his head, but he could not. Was the person holding him by the chin?

Why was he shouting? What was he shouting?

The face was pale, shocked. The talk frantic.

Then he was saying the same word over and over again. It was his name. "Cenk. Cenk." Yes, what do you want? But the person carried on with repeating his name. Yes. Yes. What?

Cenk realised that he was not speaking and nodded his head. The person seemed to understand and changed his words.

"It's me. Nazim. You're going to be okay. Hold on. Do you understand?"

In answer he smiled weakly and looked away to the battle.

The fighting would never end. It was a nightmare from which he would never wake.

19:33

The group was stationary and obviously surrounded. They remained closely-knit and chanted in Turkish punching the air in unison. The playback later would reveal that their chant was: "Justice for Faruk"

The *Einsatzleiter* was all too aware of the ugliness of the situation. His own men were unnerved. Their effaced expressions spoke volumes. They could become heavy-handed. Then there was that damned television crew in the air. He could only use the loud-hailer intermittently. His repetitiveness bordered on a chant too. He poured his irritation into his commands. This was an illegal gathering. They were disturbing the peace and would have to disperse. He wanted them to come forward in small groups of five or ten.

He said every one of them would be arrested, if they had to come and get them.

Ground television crews were arriving. They never ceased to baffle him. How had they got through the traffic jam?

"Okay, let's get them. Go easy. We're on film." He sent a dozen *MEK* men in to bring out some of the youths.

He didn't have enough vehicles. They'd have to be held and ferried.

As they moved in the chanting died. The youths moved closer together. There was still some stifled singing in defeated and uncertain tones.

Were they armed?

When the *MEK* men were ten metres from the group Hasan slipped off his hood and called out a command in Turkish.

The entire group took off their hoods and masks and sat down in the road. Apart from Hasan they were predominantly kids of between ten and fourteen years old. Protocol would later record the youngest as eight years old.

19:36

He had tried to ignore his predicament by looking at the clouds. But Nazim had persisted in obstructing his view and he was forced to watch the violence with Nazim. At some incidents he winced, but for the most he watched impassively as blows were dealt and he heard from afar the sickening sounds of hurt. The incidents presented themselves in varying degrees of lucidity. He could not concentrate on any one particular thing. He did not have the will. And he was delirious. So some moments burned with razor sharp clarity whilst others were a blunted and smoky.

One such clear incident was when Basha kicked someone in the face. As the victim went down, Basha with his leg still poised in the air after the first impact, flicked his leg out again and hit the man a second time. However, it was the expression on Basha's face that was branded in Cenk's mind. His eyes glittered. They seemed to be drugged. There was elation in them. As he delivered the double kick there was a ghost of a smile on his face. What clinched it for Cenk was the cry. Basha gave a primitive, guttural, war cry. The triumphant cry of the victor.

Cenk closed his eyes in despair.

When he reopened them – he had no idea how long he had them closed – the mayhem about him had taken a turn.

An explosion, like a firecracker, had jolted him.

Basha was still before him, about twenty metres away, perhaps a little closer. Nazim too had turned to look at the changed scene. His friend remained crouched at his side. Was there a purple mark on the left side of his face?

He looked at Basha. What was wrong? Then he looked beyond him and saw others. And it was upon seeing them that it dawned on him what was peculiar about the scene. Everyone had stopped. Bizarrely the combatants had stopped in the middle of fighting. Some were on the ground, mid-struggle. Others were standing, hunched over and wary of each other. Yet others were at a stage where one stood over the other. All were looking in the direction of Basha, but not at him. They seemed to be looking somewhere off to Cenk's right, beyond where Nazim was crouched. Were they disentangling one another? Edging away? It seemed important that he should see what it was they were watching and he lifted his head.

About ten metres from them stood the leader of the right-wingers: the big blond man who had spoken to Basha before the pandemonium broke out. He was at an angle to Cenk, a little beyond a profiled stance. Cenk could see most of his back, his side and rear of his head. He seemed to be pointing at Basha. Yet, despite the angle and the fact that most of his pointing arm was hidden from Cenk, the arm seemed too long.

Cenk grew aware of two noises. One was distant and repetitious and he dismissed it. The other was a voice spitting out two words. "*Mach schon.*" (Do it!) Another voice joined this first and added the word "*Los.*" (Go ahead!) This single word then became a shouted chant for at least three voices.

Basha was still. They were all still. Again Cenk saw Basha's expression. Was there the faintest hint of a smile? Like before, his eyes were glittery. They sparkled with the same drug. But the drug was fading. The feral glow was leaving his eyes and the joy was dying and being replaced by what? Arrogance? Fear? Cenk could not tell. His eyes betrayed the faint smile and the smile lacked confidence. This complex expression was what remained with Cenk.

The chanting went on.

What took place was strange and dream-like. Cenk's eyes were locked on Basha's expression when the change took place. The expression was unchanged but there was only half a face. Cenk was perplexed and horrified. The expression was rendered comical, a caricature, by the fact that it was incomplete. The left side was gone. The eye, the cheek, the face were torn off. It was unreal. Then there was an explosion that caused Cenk to flinch. In spite of the proximity of victim and killer he saw the effects of the projectile before he heard the weapon. In reality everything occurred in a split second, but in Cenk's altered state of consciousness Basha's head was torn asunder ages before the explosion and he seemed to stand for quite a while, with the same idiotic expression. An awesome silence descended upon the site. The chanting was snapped out by the explosion. The other noise, which was in fact the sound of a number of sirens, was increasing in volume. After Basha fell to the ground with a dreadful abandon, the expression was gone. Without substance behind the face there was no face. Skin and muscle and tissue, something that had the appearance of part of a face was on the ground. It was wrong. The stuff of the broken head allowed the ground to deform the face so that it was strangely flat and lifeless: no longer human.

Nazim was again shouting at him. People were fleeing.

Cenk's head fell back. Was he crying? The energy required to hold himself up had sapped him.

The sky he could see was clear: icy blue. Not a cloud to be seen.

His eyes closed and his body went limp.

Saturday
07:18

Karsten could not get it out of his mind. He kept seeing the *Kanake* standing there with the side of his head missing. With a loud clap of his hands half the head burst in a spectacular gush of colour; the red and flesh of an exploding tomato. The man spun round in a ragged pirouette, arms flailing wildly. Astonishingly he remained on his feet. His 360-degree motion returned him to his starting position, his legs not quite accomplishing the full circle, and for an instant the half-face stared at Karsten.

"You should go to hospital and get it stitched up," Jutta said, when she returned to the bed with Eva. He didn't move and barely glanced at the baby as she found Jutta's breast.

What had made him pull the trigger? Part of him had wanted to see what would happen: how would it be? Another part of him was consumed with anger. This Turk had thrown the metal star that had caught his shoulder at the very start of the fight. He had flicked it back but missed and the projectile had embedded itself in some bags of cement. The Turk had then brought him down with a complex sequence of blows from his *nunchaku*. As senses returned he spotted the man cutting down his friends with his fancy martial arts stuff. Karsten could see that his men were taking a pasting. He thought that by taking out the leader, tearing down the enemy's flag, he could splinter the Turks' unity. But more than anything it was the bright satisfaction in the Turk's eyes that enraged him. He'd taken out his gun and fired in the air. And then, he was standing there with the gun pointed at the arrested man. He had barely heard his companions shouting for him to shoot. What made him squeeze the trigger was the Turk's foolish smile.

Impressed by the sheer potency of what he had done Karsten had hissed: "Shit."

Then everyone was running and someone brushed past him. He still had his arm outstretched, the gun pointing at where the Turk had stood. Something was said. The activity and the intensifying sound of sirens brought him out of himself and he left.

He had arrived home at nine-thirty. Jutta had been waiting for him. He'd stripped off in the bathroom and inspected the gash at his left shoulder. She found bandages in the medicine cabinet and left him alone. The Turk stared at him with one eye, the side of his head gouged away, grey, white and red as if a tyrannosaurus had taken a bite out of him. Jutta had returned. "I can't find my big safety pins."

He lay there thinking about his next move, but she kept interrupting him, trying to goad him out of his abstraction, becoming ever more daring with each remark. "You used the gun, didn't you?"

He had his next move sorted out. The bulls would be calling soon enough. Eva slurped and the Turk's head broke up again.

"Karsten?"

"Yes," he said wearily. "I used the gun." He stretched the silence. "I blew away a *Kanake*."

"Dead?"

"That's what blowing away means."

Long minutes passed before she spoke in a fragile voice.

"What are you going to do?"

"That's what I've been thinking about all this time, you dumb nut."

"The police will come," she said.

Her statement didn't deserve comment.

He could feel her staring at him, but he watched the ceiling, letting the silence divide them. He grew annoyed at the thought of her racing mind formulating yet another question. He waited and then got up, snarling at the hurt of his shoulder, jaw set against any words from her. He went to the lounge and sat beside the telephone. She could see him. Eventually he dialled. He wanted to explain briefly, but the gravity of what he said posed too many questions. He knew Jutta would be clinging to his every word.

08:26

"Dannaks," he answered curtly. The phone had shocked him out of deep sleep.

"Krohn."

The name was a slap of cold water.

After leaving the *Polizeistern* Dannaks had made his way home. The television news had sent his mind spinning. The face had been exposed and then over-exposed; the features washed out by the brightness. Unsteady footing had rendered the cameraman drunken and Dannaks had been distracted by what the commentator was saying and then by the buzz of activity: the media, the ambulance personnel, the police and *MEK*. Yet, the man on the stretcher, his face coming out of half-shadow into the glare of camera lights was the man who had followed him on Wednesday. He felt sure it was him, but he wanted to be absolutely certain.

The police had the man, so there was no reason to panic, but Dannaks was excited. This was the link he wanted. The man was a right-winger and if not one of Karsten's gang, then he was at least connected to it. So Rüdiger had access to right wing manpower.

He had made a number of calls and discovered that the man was in St. Georg hospital. Walking distance.

The place was on full alert. The staff acting with controlled urgency. In house C the less severely injured were being patched up behind curtained cubicles. A skinhead in one, Turk in another. A gulf of empty chairs divided those seated in the waiting area. Five uniforms stood about talking. His man was not there and a nurse gave him directions to where he would have been taken. He took the stairs; every floor looked bewilderingly the same. On the other side of a glass door stood two uniforms. One checked his ID. "Turks in the rooms on the right; Nazis on the left."

"There's irony there," said Dannaks. The men smiled and went back to their conversation. Each room held one, two or three beds. Dannaks found his man in the fourth room: a single. He was unconscious, but he got his particulars from the clipboard and afterwards from one of the uniforms. In the man's bedside cabinet he found a pair of training shoes with a zigzag pattern and he smiled to himself.

During his conversation with the uniforms he heard of the terrible injuries and that a Turk had died.

Back in the flat that night he watched television, primarily for the news, but got into some film and half a bottle of Merlot. By the time he slumped into bed it was after two in the morning.

So this phonecall was a rude awakening.

"I'm Rüdiger's son."

"Yes," was all he could say, easing back onto the edge of sofa bed.

"You know who I am?"

"Yes." His brow furrowed as he tried to concentrate.

"Okay. If I say I can give you the connection you're looking for, you'll know what I mean?"

"Yes."

"We'd better meet, then."

Dannaks was silent.

"Do you want to?"

"Yes. But why can't you tell me over the phone?"

"There's too much to say."

"Why are you doing this?"

"I want to make a deal."

"Go on."

"I killed that Turk. I want to come in. But I want to make a deal first."

"I'm not a lawyer."

"You can protect me though?"

"Yes. But why not just turn yourself in? You don't need me."

"I need somebody I can trust."

Again Dannaks was silent.

"What's it going to be?"

"Where and when?"

He told him the razed farm they had staked out two weeks ago.

"In an hour. Leave your gun at home. Come alone."

"I'll have to take the *U-Bahn* and a taxi."

"You can come by skateboard for all I care. Just be there. Alone."

Dannaks telephoned Uwe. He got no answer. He then called Reinhart.

"Yes. What? Oh, Dannaks. What time is it?" He sounded groggy.

"Eight-thirty."

"Jeez Dannaks, it was opening night last night. There's an axe splitting my head. What—"

"Listen, just listen. I wouldn't have called unless it was urgent. I need back up."

"Back up?" He was coming round.

Dannaks explained the call and when he finished Reinhart's exclamation told him that his message had been received. "Shit on toast."

09:27

The taxi dropped him off where the track met the main road. He watched it disappear. He felt like Cary Grant in North by Northwest: alone and in the middle of nowhere, with danger lurking in his abandonment. The day was young. The sun was weak. Leaves and shrubbery were still wet with dew. The cold of the night still lurked in the shadows of the trees.

He waited for the taxi to disappear before moving off in a

running crouch, his gun in hand.

There were four buildings in all. The walls were of half-brick half-wood structure. A brick wall enclosed what would have constituted the ground floor and wooden walls encased what would have been the first floor. Little of the latter had survived the fire. Only some stubborn blackened beams testified to a further floor or loft. Mostly only the scorched red brickwork remained; it too was blackened in places with stains that reached for the heavens.

The scene had an eerie cemetery hush accentuated by the absence of wind.

He moved stealthily using the foliage for cover, all the while scrutinising the buildings.

At first he did not see the youth, then he spotted him sitting on his haunches against the inside wall of a large building. Indeed all that remained of this building were two parallel walls; the ends were missing. He appeared to be alone. But Dannaks recalled that over two weeks ago some forty officers had successfully hidden themselves in and around the buildings. He waited and listened for movement.

He edged closer to the big lad. He had Rüdiger's height, but not his girth.

With his service weapon trained on him Dannaks calmly rose. When he did not react Dannaks wondered whether he was asleep. He moved closer and something crunched under his feet and startled the youth.

Karsten shot up, a gun in his hand.

For a moment they stood in silence, guns levelled.

Some thirty metres separated them. Should it come to a shoot-out Karsten had the advantage of slightly better cover.

"I told you to come unarmed," said Karsten.

"That would have been foolish."

A skewed smile twisted the blond youth's face.

"I'm not talking to the barrel of a gun," said Karsten.

"Listening with that pointing at me won't be easy, either. I've shown trust in turning up alone. You put yours away first."

Karsten's cock-eyed smile returned and he pocketed his gun.

Dannaks pushed his weapon into the holster behind his hip, but he didn't clip it down.

"I don't want to shout," said Karsten.

Dannaks picked his way through the bric-a-brac towards the building, which must have once been a barn. Within the walls was a clutter of burnt objects: remnants of the furniture collected for the refugees. Many were metal skeletons, a twisting of bed-frames and settees. Others were stained and buckled sink-units, stripped and blistered ovens and refrigerators. Parts of the building itself, wood and masonry, lay beside broken wardrobes and tables.

Dannaks had to watch his footing and only heard Karsten's movement. He looked up.

"Keep coming," ordered Karsten, his gun aimed at Dannaks's stomach. "Shut up," he snapped, as Dannaks made to speak. The new proximity of the youth greatly reduced the likelihood of missing.

The man was in his late twenties. He wore jeans and a loose fitting sweatshirt. His hair was close-cropped, but he could not be called a skinhead. In a hungry way he was good-looking. But his glazed eyes unnerved Dannaks. They were wild with the look of a profoundly distressed person: someone on the edge.

Five metres separated them when Karsten told him to stop.

"Very slowly open your jacket with your right hand so I can see your gun. Turn this way so I can see it." The holster was located behind his right hip. "Now with a finger and a thumb of your left hand pull it out. Nice and slowly. This baby's already exploded one man's head." The left-over-right action was necessarily awkward. "Throw it this way," he said, when Dannaks held it up like a distasteful object. He made sure it fell short of the youth.

09:33

Talking to Robert had solved the puzzle of a group claiming to have come to Faruk's aid when there was no attack. Craig had thought Faruk had spoken to his bogus rescuers to share the prize money. He was wrong.

"Do you remember Siggy?" said Robert. "He burst in on us when we were with Diana."

"The newbie?"

"Yes. Diana fired him. I never liked him. He thought himself something special. Better than everyone else. I think he saw the *Tagespost* as a stepping stone to greater things. I don't know who's going to employ him now."

"What are you going to do?"

"Good question. It's embarrassing for the paper. Ideally we'd like to keep a lid on it." Craig knew that if Robert's paper didn't clean up, rival papers would clean them up. "If we can, we'll settle out of court. If not, I know Diana will chew them up and spit them out."

391

They were silent for a moment.

"What about you and your article?" said Robert.

"I don't know. Maybe I can get away with burying it under a list of similar recorded incidents. And make it academic. Or I'll highlight it a symptomatic of the state of this society. How far a boy will go to impress his father. And how far a father will go to get son accepted."

They then exchanged a few words about the girls before hanging up.

09:38

"You wanted to talk to me?" asked Dannaks, grasping at straws in his effort to distract Karsten. "Okay, you're going to kill me, but you can at least tell me the set up."

The askew smile again. "That's the stuff of movies."

The achievement of having broken the youth's silence sent Dannaks cautiously on. "Maybe. But it's courteous." Even he thought the word inappropriate. "A sentenced man's last wish?"

Way off a bi-plane flew. It sounded like a lawn mower. Dannaks couldn't look and he had no time to muse about crop sprayers.

"There's nothing to tell."

"Why do you want to shoot me? How am I a threat to you?"

"You're no threat to me."

"So you're doing this for someone else. Who? Your father?" Dannaks thought he sensed that Karsten also wanted to put off the execution. Nonetheless he scolded himself for his eagerness. "You can't get away with this." He went on weakly knowing he was losing the man. "Where's your father? Why isn't he here to do his own dirty work? Why do *you* have to kill me?" The wild eyes were losing their emotion, becoming dead as the mind abandoned thought, shutting it out and giving itself up to the physical act of squeezing the trigger. "You're probably being set up." He sensed he'd got him thinking when a flicker of life returned to the eyes. "That's why he's not here."

The moment was pivotal and Dannaks hesitated before speaking. "If you come with me there's at least a chance of a lighter sentence. Killing me works against you."

The man chewed his lip.

"You—"

"Shut up." Emotion had returned; tremors from a hot spluttering pan of water.

392

"Take it easy."

"Shut up!" screamed the man, suddenly looking about himself. "You'll be the one taking it easy. You'll be taking it easy for the rest of your fucking life."

Dannaks froze.

"Move that way," Karsten ordered waving the barrel of the gun.

Dannaks again had to watch his footing as he moved, for although his arms were wide and therefore aided his sense of balance, he could not afford any sudden movement. He almost tripped on a large rusted girder.

Karsten took a parallel course through the debris.

"Stop."

Dannaks froze again. He saw the hatch in the ground. The entrance to a cellar.

"Open it."

He went down on his knees and lifted the ring-pull catch. He tugged the door open. Hurt stabbing his side. His chest pained. Stones skittered to the ground and dust fogged the area.

When the dust had almost settled Karsten lifted himself onto his tiptoes to peer in. Stone steps disappeared into the darkness.

"Go on down."

Dannaks looked at him as if his hesitation might change the man's mind. Then he cautiously stepped down. He stared into the depths hoping to make out what was in the cellar. But it was impossible to see. When he was below ground, out of sight of Karsten, he crouched and pulled his .38 "Chiefs Special" from his ankle. He took another step and turned, hunched with his knees on one the steps. He would have liked to cock the revolver, but the noise could give him away. As soon as the boy appeared he would shoot. He saw a shadow and tensed. Then the hatch slammed shut and he was in darkness.

"Shit," he cursed under his breath.

He heard movement. The youth was putting something on top of the hatch.

Dannaks's thoughts raced. He was still alive: not executed. Karsten was going to get someone or he was waiting for someone to arrive.

Where the hell was Reinhart?

The darkness was absolute and Dannaks remained still. His knees began to hurt and he carefully stood. He had heard nothing. He pulled back the hammer of his revolver and took a cautious step towards the hatch.

09:51

He listened at the hatch. Should he risk speaking? Perhaps he could reason with Karsten?

The air was musty. His skin had begun to tingle and his palms grew clammy. Was someone moving? Was that the sound of crunching grit or the wind rustling leaves? He held his breath and strained to hear.

Dannaks stifled a coughing fit, the spasms reminding him that his body was still healing.

He moved to one side of the steps and touched the rusted metal handrail. He decided against testing its strength. Just as he was about to speak, his words carefully chosen, he heard movement. Yes, definite movement. The clunk of a car door slamming. Silence. Now grit crunching underfoot. Now muffled voices. A voice was raised. He couldn't make out what was said, but he didn't think the voice belonged to Karsten. Or Reinhart. But familiar. Then silence. Voices again.

His breathing became raspy and he felt his heart began to pound. Hammering his sore ribs.

Dannaks holstered his revolver again and placed both hands on the overhead hatch. He pushed, slowly increasing the pressure. It creaked and then a split of light made him squint. He stopped pushing and tilting his head he tried to look out. He located the voices, but he need to raise the hatch higher. With his head pressed against it he pushed again. Something shifted on top of the hatch and the two men looked at him.

He let it drop and went for his revolver in the darkness. He made a conscious effort to get his breathing and heart under control.

Willy Fischer was with Karsten.

He descended the steps as quickly as he dared. They could shoot through the wood. He waited, his Smith and Wesson out and trained on the hatch.

Then he heard an indiscernible shout. He waited. Voices once more. Had a third person arrived? Reinhart? He crept up the steps again. He strained to hear what was being said. Reinhart's voice? No. But a strong voice he also recognised.

He cocked the hammer of his Smith & Wesson. He wasn't going to stay below ground waiting for them to execute him. They were still talking. What was there to say? Perhaps they couldn't decide who should kill him. He began to take long deep breaths, shortening them to blowing, as he made ready to burst out.

One. Two. Three. He pushed upward using his shoulders more than his arms. Something slid and the hatch flew up. He stumbled into the daylight. Then he hesitated. They all looked at him for a split second. Rüdiger Krohn had his gun trained on his son and Willy. They were standing together. Karsten had a gun in his hand, but his arm hung at his side.

In that instant of distraction, the three of them looking at him, Dannaks trained his revolver on Rüdiger.

Karsten's arm was coming up. Rüdiger stiffened. He was taking aim. Willy was leaning away. Dannaks's finger was adding pressure to the trigger. Karsten was twisting. Willy diving towards bricks and wood. Did Rüdiger speak? Did Dannaks speak? Rüdiger fired. Two explosions fractured the air. Flocks of birds from the surrounding woodland took to the air. Dannaks fired. He felt the sharp brush of air of the bullet from Karsten's gun fly past his ear. A spasm of pain stabbed his right side. Rüdiger went down. Karsten was falling too. Dannaks dived behind a blistered deep freeze, rust bursting like pestilent boils. He checked his side. Nothing. Just a wound from last weekend's beating screaming at the sudden exertion.

Karsten wasn't moving. He was lying flat on his back, his chest rising and falling. Rüdiger was scampering away, out of Dannaks's field of vision. Willy had a gun out. He fired in Rüdiger's direction. Did he hit him? Then he was pointing it at Dannaks, who instantly swung out of sight. A bullet whistled past. Dannaks was at the other end of the appliance. Where was Rüdiger? He couldn't see him. A bullet ripped through the freezer. There was movement from Willy's position and Dannaks dared to edge out further. Still no sign of Rüdiger. But from this vantage point he had a clear view of Willy. He was moving away, making for a large clump of masonry. Where was Rüdiger?

Dannaks took aim and shouted for Willy to stop. Willy spun round, aiming wildly and fired. Dannaks got him in the leg. His gun flew from his hand and clattered to the ground. Rüdiger appeared and Dannaks took aim. But Rüdiger ignored him and went straight to

Willy, stones and grit crunching underfoot. He picked up Willy's gun and with his own trained on Willy returned to his son. Dannaks climbed onto the ground, located and picked up his service weapon and the one Karsten had used.

Willy moaned. If he said something it was incoherent.

"Phone," said Rüdiger, giving Dannaks a handy.

10:11

Rüdiger was kneeling at his son's side. The youth looked at him blankly. Dannaks got Willy's belt off and tied it about his bleeding leg. Then he called the emergency services. Rüdiger pulled up his son's sweatshirt.

The birds would return, but for now the silence was eerie. The debris of broken stone and masonry lent to a sense of aftermath.

After the call Dannaks watched Rüdiger pressing on his son's wound. Nothing was said between them. Karsten appeared emotionless. Dannaks watched life leave his body and set his eyes in a hard glaze. Rüdiger became distressed, maybe angry, but he didn't cry.

10:17

Karsten felt nothing. He sought memories, positive or negative, it didn't matter. He wanted his father way off, behind the cripple with the bright banana grin. And he wanted his mother coming to offer him a warm quiche. But he could conjure none of this.

Karsten felt nothing. He felt no pain or aggression. He had no feelings in himself. His being had stopped feeling. He had hoped the pain would be exquisite. This should be the ultimate experience, crowning all his excruciating sex with Jutta. Oh, but his sex with Jutta paled to insignificant water-colour by comparison. This absence of pain was a heavy blue-black masterpiece: a chasm of darkness setting his life forever in meaningless relief.

Karsten knew he would become nothing.

Rest of the Year
Wednesday (June)
10:15

"I get out tomorrow," said Cenk. He was sitting up in bed, a hand resting on his bandaged stomach. The thought that he could have bled to death still caused him to shudder.

"Shall we pick you up?" asked Nazim, seated at his bedside.

"No, thanks. My father's coming."

A nurse came in and went to one of the other patients. Nazim followed her with his eyes. "Forget it," said Cenk, quietly.

"Why?"

"They think I'm a thug, so you're a punk at best."

"I hate hospitals, anyway."

"It'll take a while for that image to rub off," said Hasan, seated next to Nazim, furthest from Cenk.

"I'm out," said Cenk. As far as he was concerned the gang had died with Murat.

"Me too," said Nazim.

"Maybe," began Hasan, lowering his voice so that the neighbouring patients and their visitors could not hear him. "For some SF is associated with shame, but there are enough out there who think we're all heroes. Even if they ban SF somebody will want to start a new gang and they'll want you."

"Like I said, I'm out."

Cenk thought Hasan's calling them heroes might have effected Nazim for his "me too" was not entirely convincing.

Hasan evidently registered the hint of doubt. "It was all rubbish. I see that now. We wandered the streets looking for trouble and if we didn't find it – we made it. There's no getting round it. That's what gangs do. Full stop."

They were crowded in the small storeroom. On the desk the computer had been usurped by a television and an ancient video player borrowed from the *Schupo* below. Reupke sat on a chair next to the desk facing them like a lecturer. Frank, Schuppenhauer, Wulff, Reinhart and Dannaks sat in roughly two rows. The police chief from downstairs was there too. The loan of the television and video secured his place.

"I can see you're impatient," Reupke began. REX had waited a while to see the video. "But just to set the record straight – you've all read the papers, seen the news – I'll briefly go through what happened." He had their undivided attention. "On the Friday in question we singled out the key members of the Schwarzer Freitag gang." He looked at Dannaks. "The plan was to arrest them before any retaliatory action because of Faruk's death. Although we now know that a fight was planned before his death. Unfortunately we were too late. All our targets had gone. All but one. And he was our main target. As you know one of these gang members was thought to be our serial killer, the Henker. His name was Sinan. We had him under observation long before the others. He hadn't left with the others. Probably because he was going by motorbike and could afford to leave later."

"Let's get on," said Frank.

"Okay, our team monitoring Sinan's flat still hadn't been given the go ahead, when he came out and headed for his bike. Before a decision was made he ran back into the house. A marksman said he looked straight at him. Either way something spooked him. The house door was broken down, but by then Sinan had barricaded himself in his flat. The house and neighbouring houses were evacuated and the area sealed off. Of course he wouldn't come to the window and he wouldn't answer the phone. We tried to talk him out." Reupke picked up his beaker of coffee. "About an hour later his flat was stormed. You already know what we found. But I'll let you watch for yourself." Although he was sitting beside the television and video machine he picked up the two remote control devices. "As I said they went to town documenting this one. It's not often you have a serial killer in Hamburg." He got up and moved away from the desk and half turned casually aiming the controls. "Aside from this video I think there're about a thousand stills, six boxes of documentation and that's just of his flat." They knew the video had been taken from digital copy. There would be a few discs too. "There's all the stuff from Kai Doermer, Martin Jensen, S-Bahn Stefan and Faruk –"

"Yes, about Faruk," interrupted Frank. "I can understand the right-wing murders, but he was a Turkish schoolboy. One of his own."

"Who knows how a twisted mind works," Reupke began, turning to Frank. "I think Sinan wanted to change a private war with the Right into something bigger. His opportunity came with the formation of the Schwarzer Freitag gang. And they were founded on Faruk's beating. When he heard that there was no beating he believed that the confrontation with the right-wingers was jeopardised. Or maybe he wanted to bump up the numbers of those taking part. So he murdered Faruk." He switched on the television. "But that was his mistake. He decided to make it resemble a Henker murder. We can only speculate as to why, but my bet is that he wanted to throw us. Killing Faruk would put the Henker's motives in question and baffle the profilers. But he was getting too cocky. The media didn't help. I think he was beginning to play to them too."

"There's talk of a book," said Reinhart.

"There'll be a film too," said Schuppenhauer. The Henker cases were rolled out in specials in the dailies and magazines. Media hysteria was only just beginning to ebb.

Reupke pressed play and the group became still.

Dannaks felt as if he was entering the flat in a deep-sea diver's helmet. The limits of the video screen were frustratingly small and the sounds were distorted, somehow hollow and raw. Shadows, others in the flat, were distracting. There was a strange crying and the light continually swung from dull to over-exposed before settling. There were muffled noises, subdued voices, clothing and the distant sound of vehicles: a window was open. Just inside the door was a car mat with a line of three pairs of shoes. They went down a corridor, tilting to the left to make a cold reconnaissance of the bathroom and toilet. Each banal item became an object of scrutiny: his shaving implements, toothbrush, shampoo, soap, a good selection of colognes and fragrances for men. Then they went on towards the lounge cantering right into a kitchenette, tantalisingly sweeping over the suspended body. The strange crying was music. It was painful, the words indiscernible.

"What's playing?" asked Dannaks.

"Billie Holiday," said Reupke, unable to suppress a smile. "The stereo was set to play the same track over and over. He set it and hung himself. It's called—"

"Strange Fruit," said Schuppenhauer. "It's about Deep South lynchings."

"SF," said Reinhart.

Reupke put the machine on pause and the picture shuddered under the strain. "Nothing to do with the Schwarzer Freitag." He spoke to Schuppenhauer. "You know your Blues?"

"Yes," he answered. "It was Billie Holiday's signature tune. She first performed it in 1939." He paused, deciding whether to elaborate. "Sorry, I didn't make the connection"

"I don't think anyone could have guessed."

"So the initials were just coincidence?" asked Frank.

"It looks like it. Just one of those things. Unless, of course, he proposed the name of the gang. We think it's a coincidence." He waited for more questions before pressing play.

The camera took them along the satin black work-surface cum eating area that separated the kitchenette from the lounge, pausing at a bowl. "Sunflower seeds," said Reupke. "From the looks of him, I'd say that's all he ate." They panned over the kitchen appliances and the black units with their long brushed steel handles, before taking on the wall, window, black shelving, black stereo, Japanese wall pictures and solid black coffee table; the grain of the wood giving it texture. The table was askew and one of the tubular chrome legs bunched an oval black and red rug. On the table was a biker's crash helmet with opaque visor. They turned to the corridor whence they came, the bathroom and toilet now an opening on their right. The music was irritating.

"This is not music," said Reinhart. "It's a form of torture. Can't we turn the sound off?"

He was all but ignored. The camera again avoided the body, swiftly moving along the kitchenette work-surface to the door at the end. Reupke felt their frustration. "Don't worry we get to see the body." They were plunged into the bedroom. The curtains were pulled back but the windows were so dirty that the light was on. A double futon dominated the floor space. There was a cheap and modern wardrobe that was out of place in the flat. All the furniture they'd seen so far had also been modern, but highly stylised. This thing was tasteless. Surely appearances didn't stop at the bedroom door? They moved around the room until they reached a dressing table and with a three-piece mirror. This was old and equally incongruous in the flat. The surface was a shrine. It hit Dannaks that he'd not seen any ornaments, nothing personal. The entire flat had been cold and utilitarian. But here were photographs and what looked to be a jewellery box. There was a framed picture of a woman Dannaks took to be Sinan's mother and there was one with him, as a youth sitting on a fat motorbike next to an older youth also astride a bike. "His brother." There was no photograph of his father. In a half moon ribbed shell was a silver link chain necklace. They saw the cameraman as he went up the edge of the mirror, coming to focus on another necklace that hung from wooden spires that framed the main mirror and supported the two, hinged mirrors. And Dannaks knew that these pieces of furniture were heirlooms. The camera found a newspaper cutting wedged in the edge of one mirror. It lingered on the text, but the cameraman's hand was not steady enough for them to read it. "I've got a copy of the cutting here." They left the room. "There was a box of surgical gloves in one of the drawers." They were suddenly moving up the legs of bare feet that didn't touch the ground. Reupke again paused the video and the top of the picture stretched and quivered.

"You're doing this on purpose," said Reinhart. "Talk about suspense." The flat wasn't big, yet the cameraman had successfully avoided showing the body.

Reupke smiled, but ignored him. "We found a couple of pairs of size 46 training shoes in his wardrobe. One sole pattern matched the partial on Kai Doermer's scarf." He picked up his briefcase and pulled out a paper file.

"Not really conclusive," said Frank.

"No," Reupke agreed. He considered before speaking. "But the profile fits. He didn't take trophies and with the exception of the fruit and rope he only used what was to hand. The clinching thing for us is a roll of packaging tape we found under the kitchen sink. The shape of the end is a perfect match for the end taped over Faruk's mouth. And there is the music."

"And his method of suicide," said Dannaks.

"Yes," said Reupke. He queried their faces before opening the file and removing a piece of paper in clear plastic envelope. He handed it to Frank and looked up for more questions before pressing play.

They steadily climbed up the naked body. His arms hung limply at his sides. The camera halted at his face. The expression was bitter. His sleepy eyes were black and hard, yet somehow determined and manic. Dannaks could see two rings bunched under his neck. They were attached to leather cords tied about a chrome bar, itself secured to the ceiling like a strip light. Then the camera backed away to the corridor to try to take in the entire body. But the confines of the flat meant that his head or feet were cut off. Retreating further allowed the wall of the kitchenette to encroach the side of the body.

"He was an ectomorph. There's not an ounce of fat on him." The textured strands of his muscles showed through his skin.

"Was he a trapeze artist?" asked Frank, as the camera held the shot.

"No, we didn't find anything to link him to any athletic club or training. He was just a sports fanatic."

"Yeah, a fanatic," said the chief of the *Schupo*. "All he had to do was reach up to save himself. What a thing to do."

"He pushed himself off the coffee table," said Reupke, as the camera closed in on the chrome bar. "Looped the rings through the bar and slipped his head in." He looked at the chief of police. "And yes, before losing consciousness he could have saved himself." The camera now descended the body.

The newspaper clipping in transparent plastic reached Dannaks. He glanced at it. The end was torn, making it a fragment. He read, looking up now and then to check the film.

"Turkish youth beaten to death by skinheads.

In the early hours of Sunday morning 22-year-old Mürtüz Tasköprülüzâde died after being attacked by youths of the Bremen skinhead scene. His younger brother, Sinan, who was also attacked, lies in intensive care and is said to be in a critical but stable state. Police are waiting to interview him.

Apparently it all started by chance, when a group of about twenty right-wing extremists underway in convoy, spotted the two brothers in the street.

After a verbal exchange a chase ensued and the boys were beaten unconscious. When the police arrived they were able to apprehend five of the skinheads who had not been able to get away due to the injuries they sustained. Witnesses say that the brothers, who both belong to a local martial arts club, gave as good as they got. There has even been speculation that the brothers provoked the attack."

Jutta treated Eva casually in front of Wolfram. She wanted him to believe that the baby was no trouble. More than this, she wanted him to notice her. He was on the floor bent over Karsten's CD collection.

"You want another beer?"

"Naw." He didn't look up.

Jutta was also on the floor, sitting beside the blanket, upon which Eva gurgled under the standing mobile. The baby was like a fat upturned beetle, all legs and arms, joy sparkling in her eyes. She was hitting the hanging mirror and rattle with her hands and feet.

"I can't remember what I lent him and what's his."

She knew he was lying, but reacted generously. "Take what you want." Then his selfishness registered. "But some are mine." That would hamper him.

She knew she intimidated him. She intimidated a lot of Karsten's gang. Not because of herself, after all she was just another Renée, but because she had been Karsten's girlfriend. She was not sure what had happened, but cultivated the belief that Karsten had walked into a police trap, so consummating the legend of him. He had been a Ghengis Khan among them and large as he was in life, she succeeded in making him even larger in death. She now saw that sitting in his shadow had a downside.

Jutta could cope with being alone. But she didn't want to be alone. She'd been alone for far too long, maybe even when Karsten had been alive.

She got up and sat in the soft chair: Karsten's throne.

"I'll be sorting out a lot of Karsten's stuff. You're about his size..."

She caught his smile before he could suppress it. He had to be told that there was a bill to pay.

"I'll have a look," he said casually.

"You'll have to come back again." She could deposit her daughter with one of her girlfriends for a few hours. "I need to sort it all out."

He nodded.

Damn those CDs, why didn't he look at her? Yet, she felt superior to him, sitting over him as if in judgement.

Karsten's death had weakened her. Or perhaps it had made her realise her softness since Eva's birth. Yet, she had an image to maintain.

"The gang is falling apart, you know." He looked over at her. Even Eva was quiet.

"And?" he asked, casually.

It was true. The gang was headless and had deteriorated into splinter groups. Many had taken a renewed interest in one of the established right-wing organisations, the very thing Karsten had held out against.

"They need a new leader."

"And?"

"You're not twenty-two any more." He frowned, but she persevered. "You've got a good head on your shoulders. A good-looking head." That flattered him. "You ought to think about where you're going." His brow grew heavy. "Don't tell me you haven't been thinking about it?"

"I have—"

"Then go for it."

His concentration hardened his features. Then he saw her and his expression relaxed. "These are mine." He got up holding a stack of CDs in one hand. Eva lay between them.

He was going to go through them with her, but the child suddenly screeched and Jutta said: "I believe you." She stood as he turned to the door.

"You want a bag?" she asked, walking round her child.

"No."

"I'll call you when I've sorted out Karsten's stuff."

He grunted and opened the flat door. She stood behind him, holding the jamb as he went into the corridor. He stopped at the top of the steps as if he'd forgotten something. "I'll come next Friday evening. You can cook."

"Okay," she said, her smile skewed by his cheekiness.

14:06

Dannaks was surprised by the back garden. He'd seen Detlef's house from the road after his R&R visit, albeit in the dark. On this bright summer's day, it still looked modest. A small detached house fronted by a patch of green and a strip of crazy paving to the door. The back garden it shielded was a pearl. It was a long grassy rectangle, wide enough to comfortably contain the pond. Flowers and bushes were bedded in a border of earth, which obscured the wire-mesh fences that came midway between hip and chest height.

Detlef's wife had met him at the door. She introduced herself as Gudrun and led him through the house to where Detlef was lying on a green plastic lounger. He got up when he heard them coming.

They greeted each other. Dannaks suppressed his awkwardness, something he found easier in the personal surroundings. Or perhaps it was the presence of Gudrun.

"Can I get you something, *Herr* Dannaks?" Gudrun was a slight woman, more a pixie than a human. She had white, close-cropped hair, short like a boy. She was dainty and sprightly. Dannaks was ashamed that he'd come empty-handed. He had only thought of Detlef.

"We've got a pitcher of orange juice here," said Detlef, gesturing to the matching green plastic garden table.

"That'll be fine," he said.

"Biscuits?" she asked.

"Not for the moment."

"I'll have some," said Detlef. "Those shortbreads."

Her answer was a pout full of humour and Detlef smiled guiltily.

"Relax, Dannaks," Detlef said when his wife turned back to the house. He looked fatter in his shorts and short-sleeved shirt. Yet he looked well, his strained wrinkles had relaxed, or his crab-apple face was simply flattening out with fat. The poison dwarf was becoming a benign elf. "Take your shoes off, if you like." He was barefoot. This accentuated his dumpiness. Detlef climbed on to his lounger and Dannaks sat on the one next to it, slipping off his shoes and contemplating leaving his socks on. Did his toenails need cutting? He knew he would look foolish leaving his socks on and he wasn't sure whether they had holes. So he pulled them off and stuffed them in his shoes.

"You want a drink now?" Detlef lay nearest the table, but he too would have to get up.

"Later," said Dannaks, feeling the sun beginning to caress his body. For the moment it was a pleasant sensation.

They were silent for a while, staring at the pond. Yellow bulrushes stood at the fence, swaying easily. Two sunflowers were also present, their heads straining on their stems. Sprays of creamy white meadowsweet separated much of the grass from the water. In the pond were lily pads sprouting large white flowers with many petals.

Beyond it was more grass and then something of a rockery rising to a wooden fence crawling with pink bindweed. Two fir trees stood guard over the rockery which was ablaze with flowers: blue forget-me-nots, white roses and more.

"Nice place," said Dannaks.

"The fruits of Gudrun's labours." Then he may have felt a need to explain his wealth. "It was Gudrun's parents' place. Her father died a while back. We lived with her mother. She passed away last year." Dannaks felt guilty that he knew so little. It depressed him to think that he was just a workhorse. What had Reinhart said? "I thought you were a robot." It shamed him that he took so little interest in others. Unless, of course, they were criminals. Or was it that he felt he was generally missing out? Was he passing up the finer things in life? Was there more to be had than justice?

"You look well."

"You mean I look fat."

"Maybe you should cut out those chocolate eggs." He wished he hadn't said it. Did he still hold little respect for Detlef? Or could it be that he was envious of him?

"I have. I only ate them at work, anyway. Gudrun doesn't know. I've got high cholesterol, you see."

"What did you do with all those little toys?"

"She never saw them. I gave them to an orphanage."

Dannaks nodded. He felt rotten.

"You're not here to hear about me," Detlef went on after a moment. He was at ease and confident; enjoying retirement. Dannaks forced himself to relax. "You know Rüdiger–" he corrected himself – "Krohn is on bereavement leave."

"He wouldn't have wanted to speak to me."

Detlef considered, but did not answer. "He needs to get over his son's death. He's got no one now, you know."

Dannaks stared at the bird he took to be a kingfisher. Surprisingly he hadn't noticed it before. It was large and stood rigid at the pond. Perhaps its stillness had camouflaged it.

Detlef sighed. Was it because of Dannaks's lack of compassion? "I'll start from the beginning. Rüdiger, erm, Krohn and—"

"If it's easier for you, call him Rüdiger." Dannaks was annoyed by the harsh tone in his own voice.

"Rüdiger and I go back a long way. We weren't great pals, but we came together on a couple of courses. He—"

Gudrun returned with a plate of assorted biscuits. She lowered it to Dannaks and he took a plain wafer. Then she went to her husband and he picked out a shortbread. She put the plate on the table. "I'll leave you boys alone now." Had she read some tension in their silence? "I've got some weeding to do." They watched her go to the end of the garden. There she put on gardening gloves that looked too big for her. She picked up a trowel, went down onto a knee bench, and began prodding the earth.

Dannaks waited. The sky was virtually cloudless, those that were present were whipped down to smudges of cuckoo spit. The kingfisher was stock-still.

"I owed Rüdiger a favour. He wanted you to finish the job."

"And if I'd said no?"

"He knows you. He said the job was more unfinished for you than it was for him. You felt you'd sold yourself out."

Dannaks felt his anger rising. "Why didn't he get it officially investigated?"

"He didn't want his name near the investigation. And you know how strapped for cash we are. Those above him wouldn't have sanctioned something that was considered closed. And you said that it was DIE's patch. And they'd closed it. But ultimately he suspected Willy and there was no way he would not hear about the investigation."

"What about all the money wasted through leaked information?"

"Good point, but not within the parameters of the budget."

"And I'd put in unpaid overtime." Dannaks shook his head. The anger had almost consumed him. "I almost got killed."

"Yes."

"Yes?"

"I think Rüdiger was surprised how quickly things escalated."

"Great."

"Oh come on Dannaks; he cares about you as much as you care about him."

Dannaks smiled bitterly and shook his head. "He sent me his R&R membership invitation, to make sure I hadn't given up after the good beating."

Silence.

Although they hadn't raised their voices Gudrun looked over. She was on her hands and knees, a trowel lost in oversized gloves. Detlef waved and smiled.

The exchange defused their rising temperaments. Dannaks knew that if he should be angry with anyone, then that person should be Rüdiger Kohn.

"Drink?" Detlef asked.

"Please."

Detlef rose and Dannaks sat up, swinging his feet onto the grass. His soles twitched and he moved his toes. Aware of his allergy he wondered whether he imagined the itchy sensation. "I can offer you orange juice, if you like."

"Water's fine." Detlef poured two glasses of water, clumps of ice tumbling into each glass so that he had to wipe his wet hands on a paper serviette.

Dannaks accepted a glass with thanks.

"I'm going to the shopping centre." It was Gudrun. Dannaks hadn't heard her approach and was shocked by her sudden proximity. "Do you want anything?" she asked her husband, pulling off her gloves.

"No," he said sitting down.

She smiled at Dannaks. "Maybe I'll see you later?"

"Yes."

The two men settled and sipped their drinks in silence.

A pair of ducks circled and then flew in and landed in the water, fluttering and splashing before settling.

"I thought that kingfisher was there to frighten them off," said Dannaks, realising that the bird was not real.

"It's a blue heron," said Detlef. "It's there to keep other blue herons off the fish." He fell silent again. "It doesn't work." He reflected before continuing. "I saw one the other day. He stood right beside our one. Kept looking at him, but still went for the fish."

"It certainly looks real."

"Yes. But apparently only to us."

They fell silent again.

"What's the new president like?" asked Detlef.

"It's too early to say." Without Willy there had been no obvious candidate for the outgoing president's position. The new man was an outsider, a man called Wischnewski, from the BKA.

"Other than Rüdiger Krohn," said Dannaks, unable to use his first name alone, "nobody knew what I was doing."

"No." There was no committee. No official approval. "Rüdiger wanted to exonerate himself completely. He was willing to support you. But in no way guide you." Dannaks thought of the R&R invitation again. "Now he's broken." The ducks waddled out of the pond, shaking off drops of water. "He said that after shooting his son he wondered whether Karsten was trying to save him."

"I don't understand."

"You aimed at Rüdiger and Karsten aimed at you, right? So maybe Karsten was trying to save his father?"

"It's possible, but I'd say unlikely. Everything happened too fast. Even Rüdiger probably acted on instinct." He was uncomfortable referring to him by his first name.

"The tragedy is that there was no reconciliation between father and son. I think Rüdiger hoped it would happen one day."

"I'm just glad he was there." Krohn's presence had saved him. Reinhart had got lost and turned up with the ambulance and police. Dannaks knew that Karsten's girlfriend had called Krohn asking for help. All she knew was that Karsten had spoken to his uncle. Since childhood Willy was known to Karsten as uncle. Krohn drove to Willy's place and caught him in time to follow him to the farmhouse. He had suspected Willy, a friend and past colleague, was corrupt. He was not only in a superior position, but also personally too close for him to investigate.

Dannaks knew Willy and Krohn had worked together. He had never entertained the idea that Willy and not Krohn could have been corrupt.

Detlef nodded, again disappointed by Dannaks's lack of compassion.

The silence had grown awkward.

"I don't often get the opportunity to catch up. Do you know what's happening with the old team?"

Dannaks spoke of Uwe and what he knew of other team members. Detlef was really only mildly interested. He was out of it. "You heard about the big Narcotics bust last week? I'd say that goes back to Raul's death. You know he was killed in some domestic feud in Columbia. Cali, I think. Everything unravelled after that. The bust bagged a lot of his old gang. At least one is giving state evidence. He named Freddy's killer." Dannaks looked into the distance. "He didn't know for sure, but he thought Raul had been on to him for a while. Feeding him false information. Giving us the successes Raul wanted us to have."

"Sounds like a gem of turncoat."

"Yes. But he didn't know about Willy Fischer. Nobody did. We found his name in a ledger Raul left. People always have insurance. There were some other big names in it." Willy had been held in custody since the encounter at the farm. Nothing incriminating had been found. It was believed that through Raul's departure he hoped to make a clean break and appear legitimate. An offshore account had already been found. "Being on the gang's payroll he should get about ten years." Dannaks knew that the youth with the zigzag training shoes had worked for him. Whether this arrangement was with Karsten's knowledge was now academic. There was no hard proof, but a lot of circumstantial evidence that he had also supplied Karsten with inside information he passed on to Raul. Karsten had sometimes acted on this information, pulling off daringly big operations.

Bagging Willy Fischer was a success. But Dannaks was not satisfied. "You'll never be satisfied," Uwe had said. He felt he'd only scratched the surface of something. He'd smelt that something in the R&R club. Willy Fischer was small fry. He'd gone down quietly. So quietly he didn't even say why he wanted Karsten to kill him. Dannaks surmised that he would have killed Karsten afterwards and come away the hero. Ultimately his silence meant powerful people were at play: people who could reach him wherever he was.

It bothered Dannaks that things didn't work out like in novels: the protagonist relentlessly driving the story towards a satisfying conclusion. In reality there were loose ends, unfinished business, neglected leads, unsolved cases.

He had spent half a day with a DIE officer named Möller. But so far they had not launched an investigation. If Willy talked they would act. The likelihood of that happening was close to zilch.

Now it was Detlef's turn to adopt a faraway look. "How about you? You had your reservations about REX. Was it a good move?"

"I think so."

Sievekingplatz, where the courts of Hamburg were situated, was alive with reporters and cameras. Cenk and Nazim managed to slip the swarm, with only the odd reporter chasing and pestering them. Hasan was penned in, surrounded by the media, microphones pushed into his face. His lawyer shouted answers to their questions and tried to shield him.

The state wanted to pin a charge of terrorism on Hasan, but the deeper they dug the more evident it became that they were dealing with little more than a street gang. Nevertheless justice required someone take responsibility for what had happened and the obvious choice was Hasan. Charges, trumped up or otherwise, of grievous bodily harm, trespassing, disturbing the peace, illegal gathering, causing an affray, property damage, etc. were brought to bear. But as the months went by, the legal wrangles grew exceedingly complicated and it became apparent that nothing of worth could be successfully pinned upon him. He could be fined for causing a disturbance and inciting violence, but it emerged that he had not been the leader. Murat's martyrdom was further consolidated when he slipped into the role of scapegoat. The wheels of justice ground on for a further year and Hasan received a one-year suspended sentence.

As soon as Nazim's arm had healed he resumed the karate course, the number of members of which had peeked shortly after Murat's death and now settled. Officially Schwarzer Freitag was redefined. It was not a terrorist cell, but a gang. In unofficial circles it was a vigilante group and a legend.

Cenk was well enough to attend Hasan's marriage later that year; a move that returned Hasan into the Turkish fold. Cenk did not join Nazim at the karate club and although he carried a flick-knife, he stayed well clear of street life. Like Nazim he received a three-month suspended sentence.

Friday
11:03

Craig waited at the carousel. Three of his four pieces of luggage were stacked on his trolley. He'd only left a few weeks ago, but it seemed a lifetime away. Perhaps this was because he'd accomplished a lot since then. He'd rented his London flat: ferrying everything of worth to his parents. He'd written umpteen official letters and had as many farewell bashes, be it a quiet meal or a rowdy booze-up. But then it seemed like only yesterday that Robert was meeting him. It had been a Friday then too.

Returning to Hamburg he would have no excuse for avoiding Suleyman should he want to contact him. He'd heard that Zeynep was returning to Turkey and he gathered that Suleyman was planning to do the same. Whether they were going together was unclear. After what the man had done, Craig felt he couldn't face him. Suleyman's remaining children had been examined for signs of torture. "My son is have better chance than me. With education we beat them at their game. We be part of system. I push him a little..." Oh, he'd pushed him along, all right, but certainly not a little. He'd heated up the back of a dessert spoon over a candle and burnt him when his school results were bad. Craig wasn't sure whether the authorities would be pursuing him for child abuse.

Strangely Craig had come to Suleyman's defence when Carina criticised him. In anger he had said that Germany had warped him. The system had given him little choice. Of course his anger had been directed at himself rather than Carina. Moments later he'd apologised and tried to explain.

He heaved his last case onto his trolley.

He'd read that Herbst's political career had been damaged but he was still active. The charges of inciting a riot at Saturday's march were eventually dropped. He'd used the identity of the Henker to his political advantage. Then he made an ill-advised remark about an abused kid turning Hamburg on its head. Too many people were hurt or embarrassed by the entire affair. The last thing they wanted was someone prodding their wounds. His ravings, that the parents of the kids who'd decoyed the police that Friday should be held responsible, was lost in the tumult. He had dropped his party and joined the National Socialist Offensive (NSO).

Clear of customs, Craig pushed his trolley through the parting doors. Behind the barrier was a sea of faces jockeying for a view of the arrivals. One face stood out from the rest. He barely had time to park his trolley out of the arrivals' path before Carina placed a long stemmed red rose on his luggage and embraced him in an overwhelmingly passionate kiss.

"*Moin, moin,*" said Reinhart, entering the office behind a crinkly paper cone the shape of which resembled a leg of lamb. "You're early." He rested the leg carefully on his desk.

Dannaks looked up from the newspaper. He'd just finished reading about the banning of the *Schwarzer Freitag*. The act didn't quite close a chapter for him. He'd never discovered who painted the swastika on his flat door. And he hadn't delved deeper into the air of secrecy that surrounded the private members' club R&R. Such things came out much later – in the wash – as Reinhart would say in English.

"You don't look too happy," said Reinhart, hanging up his coat.

"I was just remembering all that business in May, when I first came to REX."

"There was a lot," said Reinhart, retrieving a notebook and banana from his coat pocket. "Which business?"

"I suppose the business with Krohn." He sighed. "I was so certain of his guilt. I guess I was a bad detective."

"I wouldn't say that." The thing attached to his desk diverted his attention. "You doggedly pursued your suspicions, like any good detective."

"I blindly pursued my suspicions."

The emphasis caught Reinhart's attention. "Ah yes." He nodded and then frowned as he began to drift away. "Überzeugung fördert Intoleranz." (Conviction/certainty promotes intolerance.)

Dannaks was stunned by Reinhart's words, but Reinhart was too absorbed to notice. It was even possible Reinhart wasn't even aware of what he had said. He was unwrapping the leg and lifting out the bunch of white, pink and red flowers. Dannaks was too embarrassed to admit he would have to guess their identity. Reinhart had taken to remarking on the flowers he brought. "Don't you think this bouquet of carnations and chrysanthemums is a work of art?" And: "There's nothing more cheery than sunflowers. Wouldn't you agree?" Dannaks suspected he did this for his benefit. He made some such remark now but Dannaks was too preoccupied and caught only that they were winter lilies. Reinhart too was distracted. He had seen the new office appliance.

Dannaks's thoughts were reeling. Certainty promotes intolerance. Embedded in the national psyche was the idea that doubt was frequently interpreted as weakness. Conversely, certainty was strength. Of course such forthrightness could be mistaken for arrogance. But should anyone be so certain, of such conviction, that they willingly inflict pain on others? Truly, conviction blinds. Certainty nurtures intolerance. Wasn't this what they were supposed to be fighting?

Dannaks was also annoyed by his own arrogance. A few months ago he would have said he could learn nothing from his colleague.

"I hope this monstrosity is not what I think it is." Reinhart nodded at the squat machine clamped like a perched owl on the end of his desk.

"I'm afraid it is." Dannaks smiled. "The office Christmas present. Electric. Takes seconds. Look at these," he said, holding up four beautifully sharpened pencils.

Epilogue

Since completing this book there have been a number of relevant developments:

- Numerous clashes between Left and Right have occurred in Hamburg.
- Stefan's form of *Bahnsurfing* is no longer possible. The rising number of deaths caused by this dangerous hobby necessitated the removal of the emergency red button that unlocked the doors whilst the train was in motion.
- In 2007 the BKA, under pressure to expose its brown roots, opened its historical files. Founded in 1951 it was discovered that in 1959 only two of the forty-seven commanding positions were held by those without a National Socialist past. Thirty-three of the positions were held by former ranking SS officers.
- There is no evidence to suggest a secret society. Just the manoeuvrings and influence of privileged closed circles that exist in all countries.
- From 2000 to 2007 the so-called "Zwickau Trio", members of the *Nationalsozialistischen Untergrund* (National Socialistic Underground), murdered ten foreign nationals. The murder weapon, a Ceska Type 83, linked the killings in different states across the country. Robberies and bombings have since been put down to the NSU. Clues to a right-wing connection were neglected by the various authorities in each state and the group acted with virtual impunity. Contract killings, familial feuds and criminal connections were sought. Also interstate jealousies and bureaucracy hampered, if not blocked, progress. The victims' families have since received official apologies. Institutions have been shocked; shamed, accused of cover-ups, destroying documents and incompetence. The investigations are

ongoing and well-documented. The fact that the killings were known as the *Döner-Mordserie* (doner kebab murder series), somehow playing down their gravity, but most importantly betraying a latent racism in Germany, has also been acknowledged. "*Döner-Morde*" was voted the non-word of 2011.

Acknowledgements

An author alone rarely writes such a book. Here I wish to extend my thanks to those who assisted me: Holger Vehren of the *Polizeipressestelle* Hamburg, Ali Atasoy for advice on Turkish matters, my daughter Mariana who, after reading *Deutschisch*, drove me to go back and finish this book, Bernie Morris for her editorial skills, and Mariana again, for her fine-point advice on the final draft.

If you enjoyed *Ausländer* you might be interested a second *Oberkommissar* Dannaks novel.

Here are the first few pages.

Deutschisch

June
Sunday
18:23

By the time *Hauptkommissar* Hofmann reached the second floor he was out of breath.

Rising after dipping under the tape outside had given him a moment of dizziness. He didn't show his infirmity to the media behind him and soldiered on. On such occasions he was grateful for his no-nonsense mask. His face was an ancient motorway pile-up, more crumpled than wrinkled, his skin rusting, almost flaking, brittle metal. It suited his fixed bulldog demeanour. More than the media he relished his ironclad authority over the uniforms. The lad with the clipboard on door duty almost cowered as he signed in. And the offer of paper overshoes and latex gloves could best be described as meek.

Hofmann would have liked to use the metal banister to pull himself up the concrete steps, but at least one technician was strategically dusting it for prints. A numbered plastic card on one of the steps marked a drop of blood.

On the second floor he had no option but to take a pause. Bent over, his hands upon his thighs, he coughed and rattled. In this position he noticed the small puddle of water and remainder of drops on the spacious landing. The flat door was open and he felt the others watching him, hearing their unspoken thoughts about soiling the crime scene.

His spirits lifted somewhat as he remembered an old joke about a student doctor who smoked. His dormitory friends continually said: "One of these days you're going to cough your guts up." He ignored their jibes and as a gag some of them got together and laid out all manner of internal organs on his chest whilst he slept.

In the morning he was pale when he came down to breakfast and they asked him what was wrong. "Guys, you were right," he gasped. "Last night I coughed my guts up."

"That's awful," said one.

"Yeah, but not half as bad as putting them back in again."

Hofmann regained himself. His breathing was down to a laboured wheeze.

Thiel, his partner, was at his side. "*Alles klar* (everything okay), boss?"

"Yeah, I don't normally put my guts in on a Sunday." He ignored Thiel's querulous look. "What have we got?"

"A double," said Thiel, leading the way to the flat. "A Turk and what looks like a national. It's hard to tell. His face is pulped."

Before entering the flat Hofmann stopped. Thiel had stepped over the small puddle. "What's with the water?"

"Don't know," said Thiel. "The first officer said it was already there when he arrived."

"Was it dirty?" Parts of it were blackened.

"I asked the same question," said Thiel, proudly.

"And?" said Hofmann, letting his lack of breath underpin his impatience. He knew Thiel was in awe of him. This was how a detective should be: thick skinned, larger than life and exceedingly bitter. Poor Thiel, to give his voice the right timbre he would have to increase his tobacco consumption five-fold and maintain it for at least a decade.

Many years ago Hofmann had tried to give up. The days counted as some of the worst of his life. He had felt sick and depressed.

"He thought not. You can talk to him."

"I will," he said gruffly. The water could have been dirtied by any number of people: the uniform first on the scene, a witness, emergency personnel, the killer or one of the victims.

"Identities?" he asked stepping into the flat.

"Unconfirmed," said Thiel. "But I think they were the occupants." He fell silent and Hofmann purposefully avoided inspecting at the bodies. Lorenz, the *Rechtsmediziner* (forensic medical expert), was crouched over the male victim and Hofmann could see neither of their faces. The girl looked asleep. Instead the *Hauptkommissar* surveyed the lounge and dining room. This was his way. Doors further in led to a kitchen, which appeared undisturbed, the bathroom that was in the throes of being tiled and the bedroom. Here the cupboards and drawers were all open as if someone had been searching for something. Was robbery the motive?

Thiel followed him about the flat like an obedient dog.

Hofmann returned to the lounge and turned his attention to the bodies. Lorenz was now standing looking down at the victims. The girl was in casual attire and the lad in an overall. Contrasting the peacefulness of the female victim, the boy had taken a severe battering.

"He took a pasting," said Thiel, unnecessarily.

"First impressions?" He knew better than to ask Lorenz for the cause of death.

Without looking up Lorenz said: "I thought we were about to have a third body at the door of the flat." For a moment Hofmann didn't know what he was talking about. Then he realised he was referring to his coughing fit. Hofmann gave a huff. "Rigor hasn't begun, so we're talking of a tee-oh-dee of two maximum three hours ago." This time of death margin concurred with the initial call to the police. "The girl's neck is broken. She died instantly. You can see the bruising to her jaw. It's ante mortem and probably knocked her out. The lad is another story altogether." His head glistened with blood, his mouth and lips were split, the jaw looked smashed. "He took a pummelling. The back of his head is cracked open too. That could be a result of trying to lift himself off the floor and being bashed down again. Or the person straddled him and lifted and banged his head a number of times and then laid into him. I can't see the marks of any weapon. But you can see from his neck that the cause of death may be strangulation. I'll know—"

"— more when you get him back to your lair," Hofmann said. Yes, he thought. The beating meant passion. Hatred. And he hoped that made it a *zwölf* (twelve).

Unlike other police forces that used code numbers to relate incidents the Hamburg police force communicated clearly. However, ever since a woman had killed her husband, stabbing him with a carving knife, because he hadn't cleaned the bath after taking a shower, the number *zwölf* had become synonymous with a domestic. During her confession she admitted that the trigger for her rage that led to the killing had been counting twelve of her husband's hairs in the bath.

The likelihood of this double being a *zwölf* raised Hofmann's hopes of clearing it. It would be nice to retire on a closed case. "What I—"

"Sir," said a technician behind them. Whether he was addressing Brauer, the chief technician who stood nearby or Hofmann was unclear. "You might want to see this."

He was pointing a torch under the sofa. Like all the technicians he too was clad in a hooded white overall.

"Anna," called Brauer, to the technician with the camcorder. "Have you done there?" He nodded at the sofa.

"Yes," she said.

"Then we may need some stills of what's underneath."

"Simon?" He was talking to the technician with the torch.

"There's nothing to dust. But I haven't done trace."

"Let's leave it in position and tip it on its back," Hofmann suggested.

Thiel went to one end, Simon to the other and tipped the sofa to reveal the floor underneath.

They all found themselves staring at a single dining fork. The prongs were stained red.

Book One

July
Tuesday 20:45
(25 months later)

Pride and fear sat uneasily on the hotel manager's face. Like an ill fitting photo-fit the top of his expression didn't match the bottom. Dannaks could see it in his smile and his eyes. The smile was fixed and nervous and prolonged well beyond sincerity. It was the sickly grimace of a schoolboy caught red-handed: a liar's smile. And the mania glistening in his eyes said that even he knew he was deceiving no one.

Anyone would think heads of state were visiting. Then, in a way, this was something of a state visit. Hadn't they just arrived in a mini motorcade?

"Someone will come tomorrow," said the young officer, who had not introduced himself and couldn't be more than twenty years old. A boy dressed like a soldier, fresh-faced and aghast with the burden of responsibility.

"When?" asked Dannaks's colleague, Reupke.

The hotel manager, following the conversation intently, seemed strangely unaware of what was being said; his face a set grinning mask.

As far as Dannaks could tell there were no women present. He was part of the loose inner circle of five men. Beyond them, distance diminishing their importance, was a cluster of ranking officers. Further still were a line of hotel staff and two waiters at the display table of colourful cocktails. Finally there were the uniforms standing like sentries at the entrances.

The boy officer spoke to his superior, a much older man in the full parade regalia of the Turkish National police with colours and medals, highlighting the lack of adornment on the younger man's uniform.

The superior's answer, like all his answers since meeting, was measured and clipped.

"Ten o'clock," the boy translated.

Reupke nodded and the hotel manager did too. But Dannaks stopped the officers leaving. "To show us the body and photographs."

Being shown the body was the reason for picking them up tomorrow. In the car on the way to the hotel Reupke had asked about seeing the crime scene photographs. The young officer had said he was not authorised to answer such a question. His superior had ridden in the limousine in front of them.

Irritation flashed across the youth's face before he spoke to his brass superior. For that is how he appeared to Dannaks. He was too old to be called bronzed. He was tanned and hard. The orange tinge to his skin, remnants of freckles, the gold bracelet of his expensive looking timepiece, the fair close-cropped hair and his overall stockiness reminded him of Gert Fröbe, the actor who had played the villain *Goldfinger* in the James Bond film of the same name. Dannaks watched him. His expression remained impassive, but this time his reply was not immediately forthcoming.

Even the hotel manager had suppressed his fake smile in favour of mimicking Goldfinger's expression.

Dannaks didn't need his smattering of Turkish to register the annoyance in the man's words. When Goldfinger finished speaking the young man said: "Yes." He then chose his words carefully. "Deputy Director General Özüdogru wants me to repeat that you are here as our guests." The tone implicitly conveyed that they were not here as investigators.

Goldfinger smiled. It was the first show of feeling since introductions at Antalya airport. But it wasn't a pleasant smile; it was a triumphant smile, a predator's smile.

Oh, he'd smiled for the photographers at the airport and in front of the hotel. But those formal smiles had been for the camera. Emotion hadn't been part of them.

Now there were no cameras. Security had kept all but the hotel photographer out of the building and even he'd been ordered away.

Hands were shaken. The Turks exchanged farewells. One of the half a dozen ranking officers behind Goldfinger issued a command and the uniforms left their positions at the entrances. Then *Oberkommissars* Reupke and Dannaks were left standing in the lobby with the hotel manager Erdal Tasköprü and a deputy of sorts. There was also a bellboy, loading their bags onto a trolley and an older man behind the front desk. The deputy's little golden name-shield pinned to the left lapel of his sombre jacket shone and Dannaks couldn't read it. Whoever he was, he was suffering in his suit. The sheen of sweat made him glow. And the strands of hair that spanned his glistening bald head clumped together like liquorice strings.

"Welcome to our hotel," said the manager, who was contrastingly comfortable in his suit. Even under pressure he had not appeared to sweat. His earlier nervousness along with his inane grin had vanished.

Of course he had already welcomed them. Yes, in the presence of the officials it had been a formal welcome. Even the refreshments had done little to ease the atmosphere.

The detectives could only nod and smile weakly.

With the departure of Turkish police the lobby took on a semblance of life. But apart from one person there were no guests. The staff went about their mundane business, still hushed by some vestiges of the formality that had forced them into hiding. Two waiters wheeled in a trolley and began removing the welcome drinks.

Dannaks had expected to meet a tourist representative or someone from guest relations. The German consulate minion had made his excuses on behalf of his office at the airport. Only the Turkish authorities had put on a show of importance. Even then, there were no government officials, only members of the national police and gendarmerie.

A frail old lady was sitting alone at one of the many sofa and easy chair arrangements around glass-topped coffee tables on the carpeted area. If it were not for the fact that all the furniture was the same the area could have been mistaken for a furniture showroom.

Dannaks assumed the area had been closed off to guests, but for some reason she had been given special dispensation.

"But of course you are weary after your journey." Jaded would have been a better word. Behind them was a three and a half hour flight from Hamburg to Antalya and a 40-minute journey to Side (pronounced See-dah).

Dannaks suspected the manager was eager to get rid of them. His day undoubtedly finished at five o'clock.

"Actually I could do with a bite to eat." They'd eaten nothing since the in-flight meal. And because Germany was an hour behind Turkey it was only eight o'clock for them.

Tasköprü was momentarily taken aback. He recovered quickly. "But of course, of course." He glanced at his gold watch.

"The kitchen is closed, but I am sure we can get sandwiches, okay?" Then as an afterthought: "And fruit."

"Great," said Reupke.

Dannaks nodded. He was wondering whether Tasköprü thought every German sentence began with the word but.

The manager said something to the man behind the front desk. "But you will eat in your room, okay?"

"Fine," said Reupke.

Dannaks nodded.

Despite the fact that the man behind the front desk was talking on the phone the manager spoke to him. He turned to the detectives again. "But first we have some formalities," he said ushering them to the reception desk. Then he seemed to notice his colleague. "But of course I will now leave you in the capable hands of our front office manager, Mr. Turgut. Okay?"

He looked to each of them and when no questions came he again welcomed them to the hotel. When he was gone Turgut took off his jacket and laid it on the counter. His wine coloured waistcoat – part of the hotel uniform – remained buttoned over his white shirt like a straitjacket.

"Please, you do not mind."

"Not at all," said Reupke, loosening his tie and opening the top button of his shirt. Dannaks followed suit. His neck was sore. He wasn't used to collared shirts and certainly not ties, of which he possessed only two. Reupke had donned his tie just before landing; Dannaks had made the mistake of wearing it throughout the journey.

A casually dressed man – a guest – wandered in from somewhere. He sat on an easy chair not far from the old woman, placed the drink he carried on the coffee table and opened a paperback he'd also been carrying.

Turgut leant over the counter to look at the monitor the man behind the desk was operating. They spoke and the man sitting behind the counter – his name-shield fastened to his waistcoat was beyond reading distance – called out. The bellboy, who'd been standing by the loaded trolley, stiffened. He then pushed the trolley out the front entrance.

Although the bellboy was probably called a porter, his spotty youth made Dannaks feel the label bellboy more appropriate.

Dannaks watched him until he was gone. He was a little disconcerted. His holdall was all he had. Reupke had turned up with hand luggage and a small hard turquoise case. The colour suggested it belonged to a woman. His wife's? Was he married? He didn't wear a ring.

Turgut took a form from the man in the waistcoat and placed it on the counter in front of them. He plucked a pen from his shirt pocket and placed it on the form. "Only one needs to fill it out. It is for the room."

"Room?" said Reupke looking at him and then at Dannaks.

"Yes, we have only one room. We are fully booked. All the hotels here are fully booked. This is the high-season."

"Twin beds, I hope," said Dannaks, jokingly.

Turgut looked at him severely. Reupke's face dropped. Dannaks blanched.

"Naturally," said Turgut, relishing the relief on the detectives' faces. He said something to Waistcoat behind the counter. Waistcoat smiled and shook his head.

Reupke laughed nervously. Dannaks smiled. He realised that apart from Reupke Turgut was the first person they had met since arriving who wasn't nervous or profoundly bored.

"I'll do this," said Reupke picking up the pen. "Do we get a safe?"

"Naturally." Turgut spoke to Waistcoat again who put another form on the counter. Since Reupke was occupied Turgut spoke to Dannaks. "You will have to sign for the safe. Three nights?"

"We leave on Friday," said Dannaks. "Yes, three nights."

Turgut wrote on the form and showed Dannaks where to sign. He then handed Dannaks something akin to a fountain pen refill but solid and made of a heavy metal. Dannaks dropped it in his trouser pocket hoping Reupke knew what to do with it.

"Passport," said Reupke. Dannaks handed his to him, noting that the procedure meant that all guests were traceable.

Turgut then held a strip of green plastic to him. Dannaks lifted his left arm. Seeing his watch he switched to his right arm. Turgut clipped it about his wrist, pressing it home with the end of a pair of scissors and using them to snip off an extraneous piece. Dannaks looked at him questioningly, but Turgut didn't answer until he was clipping one about Reupke's wrist. "This allows you access to all the facilities in the resort. All-inclusive, you know?"

"When it begins to pinch, you're over-eating," said Reupke to the form he was completing, then pushing away Dannaks's passport.

429

Dannaks retrieved it.

He got the impression that Reupke was treating the trip as a kind of holiday. Neither outranked the other, and Dannaks was dismayed that neither of them had been appointed to lead. It was an oversight.

Was it only yesterday afternoon that they were shaking hands with the police president in his fifth floor office? Dannaks had never met him personally. Oh, he'd seen him on numerous occasions, holding speeches in the large conference room. They were either for award ceremonies or they were pep talks to emphasise the importance of a crime before the case officer took over. Here the word importance was synonymous with media and therefore public interest.

Even when Dannaks had worked in the building he had never been to the upper floor. They housed the big birds. Like many establishments the air was rarefied, the tone old school.

The office of Hamburg's police president was not presidential. But by comparison it was plush, only because it was bereft of clutter. The carpeting was hardwearing and functional. The furniture was equally utilitarian, if not better kept than that in the rest of the building. This was a man who wanted to be on the same level as his officers. His office window offered a breathtaking view over the city park. Dannaks could picture him spending time pondering some strategy whilst staring at the view. His predecessor had been a train lover and had chosen an office on the other side of the building overlooking the U-Bahn station Alsterdorf.

When Dannaks and Reupke were ushered in, Wischnewski, or Iceman as he was known outside the office, the police president was not sitting behind this desk or looking out of the window. He was sitting with two officers at the small conference table near the door. He was the first to rise. Although he didn't introduce himself, he did his companions. They were the officers from *Zeugenschutz* (witness protection) who had liaised with the Turkish authorities until now.

Iceman's close-cropped shock of white hair seemed whiter than Dannaks remembered. And his ice-grey eyes were more piercing than ever. Although he had a suety complexion, his features were cast in mottled stone, as if the muscles of his face were set in such.

Many of the ranking officers had nicknames and the police president was no exception. For a while he had been known as "New skis" or just "the skis". If you were to meet him you were going skiing. And if he was dishing you a tough or bad assignment, then he was sending you down the piste. The story went that one of the computer whizzes had been working on their website and sent the text through an automatic translator for the English version of the page. Wischnewski's name had been translated into "wiping new ski".

Eventually he became Iceman because of his white hair, his renowned glacial silences and cold laser stare. So that when you were summoned he was either going to hand you an ice cream or send you out into the cold.

When Iceman re-seated himself in the chair at the head of the table, he regarded the two newcomers for a moment before speaking. Dannaks wondered if he was assessing their competence by the way they were dressed. Reupke was in blue designer jeans, but he wore a dark blue shirt with a blue and yellow tie. Whereas Dannaks himself could only offer his black jeans that had lost some of their blackness and his best sweatshirt with the Japanese water-like emblem of the band *The Waterboys*. Iceman and the two liaison officers were in pressed slacks, shirts and ties and it looked as if they shopped at the same outlet.

"Gentlemen, I don't want to keep you from your briefing, so I'll come straight to the point." He paused for a moment. His cold eyes that were at once piercing and vacant, as if he was disinterested or everything was bagatelle and didn't deserve his full attention. "I have to say that I would have liked to have sent at least one of our Turkish officers." As far as Dannaks knew there were only six of them in the entire police force and five were *Schupos* (of the *Schutzpolizei* – the uniforms that mainly did the soldiering). The detectives were *Kripos* (of the *Kriminalpolizei*). "I believe you speak some Turkish." He directed his terrible gaze at Dannaks, who thought a nod was appropriate. He would have liked to say that his knowledge was weak, but he sensed the man didn't approve of what he saw and didn't want to aggravate him. He obviously wasn't a *Waterboys* fan. "Firstly, your job is to collect the body. You are not there to investigate. If you're asked to assist, then fine. From what's happened so far I think that's unlikely." He glanced at the more senior of the two liaison officers, before returning to the detectives. "However, by all means gather as much information as you can. Asking to view the available evidence won't hurt, just don't push it. And there is no reason why they shouldn't let you see the body." He then leaned forward. "Now, I want you to bear one thing in mind when you're down there. Because I don't care what Matthias Kerner did. To me – and by default you – I care about who he was. And understand me correctly, I don't mean who he was on an individual level. I mean that he was a German citizen. That's all. So I want both of you–" he took a moment to stare at each of them "to know, that when you are there, that you are not only representing the Hamburg police force, you are also representing Germany. You are to all intents and purposes our ambassadors visiting their country." Ambassadors. Dannaks almost snorted and struggled to neutralise his expression.

Later Dannaks realised that Iceman was depending upon them more than was healthy. By snatching the task from under their noses Iceman had pulled something of a coup over the BKA (*Bundeskriminalamt* – equivalent to America's Federal Bureau of Investigation). Perhaps he was settling an old score. Or maybe he was calling in an owed favour. Whatever, he had left the BKA to head the Hamburg force. It wasn't a step upwards. At best it was a sideways career move. There had been much speculation about the move, not least by the media. There was talk of internal wrangling within the BKA and gossip about his health. Then, there was talk of his wife's job having an influence over their location. In any case the spotlight was on him and his men. And, as he would say: "by default", on Dannaks and Reupke.

And that was basically it.

The two liaison officers took the two ambassadors into the adjoining conference room. There they huddled at one end of the long table with sixteen vacant chairs extending away from them.

Other novels by D.M. Samson

Silent Violence (ISBN 978-0-9556796-0-5)

In 1984 Dawn Marie travelled with her husband to Saudi Arabia. He had secured a job replacing the outgoing foreman of a secluded farm near Riyadh. Almost two years later she would return home. Alone. Broken.

In *Silent Violence* she tells us of her journey: a long downward spiral. From the first inklings of things not being right, a pet killer in the expatriate compound, clandestine excursions by the farm crew, through to the rising hysteria within the expatriate community, then the killings at the farm, the ensuing imprisonment, moral deterioration, government procrastination and eventual deliverance.

Without question her story is harrowing. Yet it contains a great deal of humour too. For humour was the life jacket that kept the displaced person buoyant in a strange culture.

After years of psychiatric treatment she was persuaded to write her story. The road to publication is a story in itself. Ultimately the book was suppressed in the interests of international relations.

Silent Violence should be a warning to prospective expatriates. Its portrayal of Arab mentality could help policy makers too.

Nails (ISBN 978-0-9556796-1-2)

There is little one can say about the plot. Succinctly put, it is the story of one day in the life of a car mechanic. Admittedly, not much in itself. But it's hard, raw, violent, sexy, sensitive, funny, poetic and philosophical to boot. It's a page-turner that grabs you by the short and curlies.

Bottle (ISBN 978-0-9556796-2-9)

In *Nails* Kevin was a prisoner of frustration, middling, but waiting for who knows what. In *Bottle* he's liberated with the proverbial "kick up the arse" he needs.

This book has got everything. Even the kitchen sink! It's teeming with life and death, tears and laughter, sex and violence, parents and children, brutality and tenderness, anger and contentment... But why should I go on? Look up further antonyms yourself. Or save yourself the trouble and simply read the book.

Although *Bottle* is the sequel to *Nails* it can be read in its own right.

Deutschisch (ISBN 978-0-9556796-3-6)

What starts out as a routine task of collecting the body of a German national murdered at a Turkish resort becomes an emotional odyssey for *Oberkommissar* Dannaks (of REX: Racism and Extremism).

Intent on contributing to the investigation he is confronted by a wall of silence from the hotel staff. The Turkish police aren't giving anything away. And if that wasn't enough even his companion Reupke (from Homicide) is happy to treat the trip as a holiday. Finally, the resort begins to seduce Dannaks, culminating with the distraction of a fledgling romance.

Then when a girl, missing since the murder, gives herself up and confesses to the killing, Dannaks appears to be the only one to believe she is lying.

Back in Hamburg he unexpectedly finds himself suspended from duty. Using the time to investigate the girl's past he uncovers not only her terrible secret, but also a mistake by Reupke's Homicide colleagues. His emotional odyssey turns into a quest for truth and justice that takes him to Berlin and Central Anatolia.

...and the man who loved cats (ISBN 978-0-9556796-4-3)

A collection of nine haunting stories:
a woman is stalked by a caller;
a young couple move into a house besieged by cats;
a commuter is uplifted;
a family man with dubious motivation aids an attractive neighbour;
a backpacker vets prisoners' letters;
a jilted man becomes suicidal;
a woman kills her husband and uses acid to dispose his body;
a man worries about his wife's fidelity;
a blinded neo-Nazi discovers a new life.

www.davidmsamson.com

www.ingramcontent.com/pod-product-compliance
Lightning Source LLC
Chambersburg PA
CBHW030348030726
47497CB00002B/234